"*While Mortals Sleep* is extraordinary historical fiction. With every turn of the page, I was drawn deeper into the life of Pastor Josef Schumacher. I held my breath in suspense, shed some tears in sorrow, and stayed up reading into the wee hours of the night because I simply couldn't put the book down. I can't wait for the next installment of this fascinating series. Bravo, Jack Cavanaugh!"

—Robin Lee Hatcher
Author, *Ribbon of Years*

"No one writes historical fiction like Jack Cavanaugh, and *While Mortals Sleep* is a masterpiece. Cavanaugh tells a gripping story while also addressing the need for those who possess Truth to take a courageous stand during dark and duplicitous times. I found myself alternately chilled and thrilled as Josef and Mady struggled to survive Hitler's manipulation. I highly recommend!"

—Angela E. Hunt
Author, *The Note* and *The Truth Teller*

"Jack Cavanaugh has always been a master of the historical detail mixed with vivid drama. But in *While Mortals Sleep* he reaches the height of the storyteller's craft. In this stirring account of courage and faith during mankind's darkest hour, Cavanaugh illuminates what our merciful God can do even when the smallest hope seems lost and evil appears triumphant. You will not soon forget this book."

—James Scott Bell
Co-author, *City of Angels* and *Angels Flight*

"I've always wondered where the Christians were, why they didn't stand up to be counted in the early years of the Third Reich. Enter into Cavanaugh's well drawn world of Germany, circa 1940, and discover why many did not. Witness the swell of national pride after years of soul-killing depression, the hypnotic power of the Führer's rallies, the terror of the Gestapo's visits. And ask yourself if you'd have the guts that Jack's hero, Josef, exhibits. Powerful, moving, an excellent read!"

—Lisa Tawn Bergren
Author, *The Bridge* and *Midnight Sun*

"More than accurate history and high entertainment, Jack Cavanaugh delivers important spiritual truths that remain eternal for any age."

—Bill Myers
Author, FIRE OF HEAVEN TRILOGY and *Eli*

BOOKS BY JACK CAVANAUGH

An American Family Portrait series

The Puritans
The Colonists
The Patriots
The Adversaries
The Pioneers
The Allies
The Victors
The Peacemakers

African Covenant series

The Pride and The Passion
Quest for the Promised Land

Book of Books series

Glimpses of Truth

Songs in the Night series

While Mortals Sleep

While Mortals Sleep

Jack
Cavanaugh

BETHANYHOUSE
PUBLISHERS
MINNEAPOLIS, MINNESOTA

While Mortals Sleep
Copyright © 2001
Jack Cavanaugh

Cover by Dan Thornberg
Photo credit from cover montage: Hitler's Children by Heinrich Hoffmann.
Bavarian State Library, Munich.

Published by Bethany House Publishers
A Ministry of Bethany Fellowship International
11400 Hampshire Avenue South
Bloomington, Minnesota 55438
www.bethanyhouse.com

Printed in the United States of America by
Bethany Press International, Bloomington, Minnesota 55438

Library of Congress Cataloging-in-Publication Data

Cavanaugh, Jack.
While mortals sleep / by Jack Cavanaugh.
    p. cm. — (Songs in the night ; 1)
  ISBN 0-7642-2307-0
    1. Germany—History—1933–1945—Fiction. 2. Anti-Nazi movement—
Fiction. 3. Clergy—Fiction. I. Title.
PS3553.A965 W48 2001
813'.54—dc21

                                        2001002673

Dedication

To those believers who,
since the earliest days of Christianity,
did not fear the high price of living one's faith;
may we be as faithful in our generation
as they were in theirs.

JACK CAVANAUGH is the author of twelve novels, including the award-winning AN AMERICAN FAMILY PORTRAIT series of which *The Puritans* won a Silver Medallion Award. His novel *Glimpses of Truth* was a Christy Award finalist for excellence in Christian fiction. An inspirational speaker, Jack and his wife, Marni, live in southern California.

Prologue

Sunday, November 12, 1989

The night wind sliced through the folds of Elyse Scott's woolen coat. She shivered. Not from the cold, but from anticipation. The electric feeling connected her to the crowd.

As far as she could see in any direction pockets of people babbled excitedly in French and German and Italian and English and Dutch. Like her, they had abandoned their cars and were continuing on foot, flowing around the darkened vehicles like water around rocks in a river. Like her, they were drawn to the white haze in the distance. Like her, they had come to see for themselves. To see if the reports were true.

Everyone had radios. Music, special reports, and deodorant ads blared from tinny speakers. People climbed in trees, hung on signs, or stood on car tops to get a better view, or to wave and shout.

There was an incredible joy on everyone's faces.

Elyse remained guarded. Forty-nine years of propaganda and lies had hardened her. Her earliest memories were stories of grand celebrations—Hitler rallies and parades with their banners and songs and speeches—of a time when people's hearts swelled with patriotism, cutting off the flow of blood to their brains so they couldn't think straight.

The price of their shortsightedness? Everything was taken from them: their houses, their land, their dignity, their livelihoods, their sons, their heritage, their very identity. They became beggars in their own cities and objects of ridicule and scorn to the rest of the world.

The German people fared no better under the Communists, who fed them one lie after another. False promises were their daily bread, washed down with cynicism. So hardened was Elyse against official reports that if one promised the sun would rise the next morning she wouldn't believe it even as the eastern sky grew bright.

Tonight was more of the same. A communist spokesman had made an announcement. So what? She would believe it when she saw her mother walk freely across the border.

"A Trabi!"

Elyse looked in the direction Park pointed.

Sure enough, a small car moved toward them, sputtering along, making its way upstream through the crowd. Its characteristic fins wore a prominent display of rust. The two-stroke engine sounded more like that of a lawn mower than a car.

All around the Trabant, people cheered and clapped. The car's occupants—a middle-aged-looking man and woman—wore dazed expressions. They grinned and waved, awash in hundreds of camera flashes.

"It'll take more than an East German car to convince me," Elyse said to the man standing next to her. Her speech was labored, her words formed with practiced enunciation.

Blue eyes smiled back at her. Compassion resided in those eyes. The elderly man gave no reply. None was needed. The two of them understood each other. Hope may have driven them here, but doubt was their traveling companion.

Together Elyse and Park pressed forward toward the hazy light.

From the side of the road a woman standing behind a folding

table offered them a cup of steaming coffee. Elyse took the offering and handed it to Park, who smiled his thanks. A second cup was handed to Elyse.

"Amerikan?" the woman asked.

Elyse cocked her left ear toward the woman.

"Amerikan?" the woman repeated.

"I was born in Germany."

"*East* Germany?"

Elyse's impulse was to explain that it was simply Germany when she was born. Instead, she nodded.

The woman behind the coffee table grew animated. Suddenly she was drunk with joy, and a flood of German words gushed from her lips. "What a special day for you! Who would have thought we'd live to see this day! Do you have family on the East side? My husband and son went to see his brother . . . twenty-three years it's been . . . two days now they've been gone. Oh, but they've phoned, and Papa sounded so happy! So many people it's a wonder anyone finds anybody . . . and reporters . . . oh! Rude! I don't care who they are, there's no excuse—"

"Thank you for the coffee," Elyse interrupted, "but we really must . . ." Her voice trailed off, and, with the woman still talking, she turned and merged into the flow of pilgrims.

It was all she could do to keep the coffee from sloshing over the sides of the cup and burning her hands as she hurried away. It bothered her that she'd acted rude to the woman who would probably categorize her with the journalists now, but they were late already. Out of guilt, Elyse glanced over her shoulder. If the coffee woman had been offended, she didn't show it. Already she was jabbering in exuberant fashion to someone else.

Beside her, Park was grinning.

"What?" Elyse demanded.

He shrugged, with the grin remaining in place. "I didn't say anything," he shouted over the noise.

The crowd thickened. Several times Elyse felt Park grab her arm to keep them from being separated.

"More Trabi," he said.

The toylike cars ran bumper to bumper now. As with the earlier one, the occupants basked in flashes and the bright lights of movie cameras. On one side of the road a group of musicians played violins and accordions while men and women danced in circles. Elyse recognized the tune. Beethoven's Ninth.

The air grew dense with a mixture of exhaust from the Trabants and the distinct odor of burning coal. It was a heavy, acrid smell. Elyse associated it with downtown Berlin. They were getting close.

To their right a village of television trucks boasted giant satellite dishes, fed by emergency generators through coil upon coil of cable. The cables linked the trucks to a long line of camera operators, who pointed their lenses at an equally long line of television reporters. Lights blazed as the reporters spoke out in a dozen languages. The eyes of the world were focused on Germany.

Elyse pressed past a reunion of sorts. Men and women and children, all bearing a family resemblance, were laughing. Kissing. Drinking. Chattering. Jumping up and down. And embracing each other with grips that didn't want to let go. Elyse emerged from the other side of the reunion after having been hugged twice and kissed once. She didn't look back to see how Park had fared. She couldn't. The sight of the reunion made her hopes rise. And she was determined not to let that happen.

Just then she saw it. The crowd parted and there it was, beyond the cameras and television reporters. Dark in places. Brilliant with graffiti in other places, where the cameras were packed the tightest.

The Berlin Wall.

A pang jabbed her heart. Fear? Dread? Both. To Elyse the wall meant separation and death. No amount of cheering and drinking and bright lights was ever going to change that.

The wall came as an odd sight given its history. People stood fearlessly atop it, singing and dancing. Along the base of the wall, lines of people struck away at it like woodpeckers with all manner of tools. Concrete chips flew this way and that, leaving the wall heavily pockmarked.

"Do you believe the reports now?" Park asked her.

Elyse said nothing. Not until she saw her mother's face would she believe.

A short distance in front of them stood a shingled guardhouse. The gateway between two countries. Checkpoint Charlie. An American flag flew over it. A line of guards watched as a torrent of Trabants and pedestrians passed in front of them on their way into West Germany.

On the east side of the wall the guard towers were empty. Barbed wire had been shoved aside in great piles. The counterparts to the American guards watched the parade with bewildered expressions. Two days earlier, had anyone attempted to get by them, the soldiers would have shot them.

Elyse and Park found a good vantage point from which they could see the flow of immigrants.

"What time do you have?" Elyse asked.

Park pulled back his coat sleeve. "Nearly midnight."

"We're two hours late."

"Couldn't be helped."

"What if we've missed them?"

"Chances are good they're late, too."

"Do you think?"

Park didn't answer.

Elyse scanned the crowd of faces passing through the gate. The nonstop music and laughter and shouts and lights and reunion scenes began to have an effect on her. She couldn't stop herself. Her hopes were rising.

"Maybe we should go in," Park suggested.

"No!"

The answer was curt. Emphatic.

Park knew better than to try to convince her. Their watching continued in silence.

11

After a while, Park said, "It's 1:15 A.M."

"Give them a chance," Elyse replied.

Her eyes hurt from focusing on one stranger's face after another. She blinked back the pain and forced them to focus again. Hundreds of people rushed by in front of them.

A little later. "It's 2:00 A.M., Elyse."

"People are still coming through the gate."

"We have no confirmation. For all we know they never got our message."

"They got it."

It wasn't hope that kept her looking, but desperation. As far as she knew, their last line of communication hadn't been compromised. If her mother wasn't coming, it meant she was unable to come. And this thought was unacceptable.

Elyse felt a hand on her shoulder. She heard her name spoken. She turned.

"Lisette!"

The kindly face in the shadow of the hat's brim bore more wrinkles than Elyse remembered, but there was no mistaking the person's identity.

Elyse buried her face against the woman's neck and, closing her eyes, lost herself in the embrace. Lisette's coat smelled of heating coal and lilac perfume.

"Let me get a look at you!" Lisette said loudly, aiming her words at the left side of Elyse's face. Gloved hands stroked Elyse's cheeks and wiped away the tears. Gentle blue eyes met hers and silently spoke of a love between the two women that had been forged over decades. "God has been good to you," Lisette said. She turned toward Park.

Reluctantly, Elyse let her go.

"Park, you're as handsome as ever."

"After all these years you'd think your taste in men would have improved," Park replied.

Lisette laid her head against his chest as the two hugged.

"Sorry we're so late," Park said. "Have you been looking for us long?"

"I crossed a few minutes ago."

"But how . . . we've been watching for you," Elyse said.

Scanning the hubbub, Lisette said, "It's a wonder we found each other at all."

"Are the others with you?" Park asked.

The smile faded from Lisette's face. The change of expression sent Elyse's heart plummeting. "Mother?" she cried.

"I'm sorry, dear. I lost contact with her two weeks ago. I was hoping she'd be here."

"The Dittmer mission," Park said.

Lisette nodded.

"That was the last we heard from her, too," Park said.

There was more. Elyse could tell by the way Lisette's eyes avoided hers. "Tell me what else you know," Elyse urged.

The older woman took her by the hand. "We have no confirmation, so let's not jump to conclusions."

"Tell me!" Elyse demanded.

Lisette bit her lip. "She . . . may have been picked up."

It was too cruel to believe. For her mother to survive the war, and then years of communist oppression, only to be arrested a couple of weeks before the gates of Berlin swung open!

Lisette embraced Elyse and held her tight. "God has brought us safely this far," she whispered. "We'll just have to trust Him to complete what He has begun."

All around them the laughter and shouts and music and dancing continued.

"Oh! I have something for you," Lisette cried.

Reaching into her coat pocket, she pulled out a small medallion that dangled at the end of a purple ribbon. She handed it to Elyse. A gold wreath formed the border of the medallion. The center was a white field upon which rested a black swastika.

"What's this?" Elyse asked.

"It's the medallion Willi hung on your father's Christmas tree

13

in '39," Lisette said, "the same night your father gave all of us the Scripture coins, and the night we learned you were going to be born."

"The German people should once again examine what I and my comrades have done in the five years since the first Reichstag election in March 1933. They will have to agree that the results have been unique in all history."

—Adolf Hitler, 20 February 1938

Chapter 1

Saturday, December 23, 1939

The swastika medallion dangled from the limb of the Christmas tree.

Christmas and Hitler.

There was something unnatural about the pairing. Like oil and water. Or chocolate and grape juice.

What accord has Christ with Belial?

For seven years the evergreen and the swastika had shared the Christmas season in Josef's native Germany. And each year he grew increasingly more uncomfortable with the way the Third Reich had shouldered its way into areas where it didn't belong.

"Reverend Schumacher, is it all right if we turn on the radio?"

Lisette Janssen's youthful blue eyes looked up at him inquiringly. Behind her the parlor was alive with a half dozen young people hanging decorations and untangling a string of lights.

Safely to one side, Mady observed the activities from an upholstered chair. On her lap a nervous kitten cowered despite her reassuring strokes. A gray-and-white tomcat, it was Josef's early Christmas gift to his wife. She'd dubbed it The Kaiser.

"Try to find some Christmas music," Josef said.

"*Good* Christmas music!" Konrad yelled from behind the tree.

Lisette and Gael ran to the console and switched it on. They waited impatiently for the set to warm up.

"Who stored these things?" Ernst cried. The lanky youth and his friend Neff were hopelessly entangled in a mess of electrical Christmas tree lights.

All of a sudden the tree shuddered.

"Hey! Watch it, dummkopf!"

"I was here first!"

"Konrad . . . Willi . . ." Josef gave the boys one of his pastoral glances, warning them to settle down.

The purple-ribboned swastika medallion on the tip of the tree limb swung wildly. To Josef it was an irritant, a pebble in his shoe that grew increasingly uncomfortable.

It was Willi who had placed the medallion on the tree. Josef had watched as the twelve-year-old boy pulled it from his pocket—along with cigarette picture cards of German athletes, two wooden matches, and a piece of string—and hung it on the limb.

The boy didn't know any better. To him the Third Reich meant songs and games and outings and colorful flags and camping trips. Innocent enough for now. But what was to keep him from becoming another Norbert Brettschneider?

When the phone rang earlier that afternoon the call couldn't have come at a worse time.

"Pastor Schumacher . . . come quickly . . . they're taking Klaus away . . . please hurry . . . how will we live?"

Josef had been working in the attic. Though it was winter, his shirt was soaked with sweat, and his back complained from the constant stooping over. He'd been given until today to remove everything that was flammable and to position pails of water and sand according to civil defense standards, to prevent fire from spreading in the event the house was hit by an incendiary bomb.

Fräulein Baeck, a sixty-nine-year-old spinster and air-raid warden who lived three houses away with her identical twin sister, had warned him that this time the job had better be done to her satisfaction. The old biddy. Give her an armband and she acts like she's Gestapo.

The inspection was scheduled for four o'clock that afternoon. The church youth Christmas party was at five. Frau Brettschneider called at half past three.

When Josef told Mady he was leaving and that she'd have to face the fräulein storm trooper alone, she got angry. Then angrier still when he couldn't assure her he'd be home by the time the youth began arriving. He argued that, her being the daughter of a minister, she of all people should have known there would be days like this.

That didn't go over well.

Josef jostled back and forth as his motorcar rattled down the cobblestone streets of the Pankow district where the Brettschneiders owned a small clothing store. They lived in the rooms above the store. Josef's ten-year-old Opel shook as if it would fall apart any second. To say it had seen better days would be kind. The exterior was a dirty white with patches of rust that looked like liver spots. The engine coughed and wheezed like an old man, and the gearshift kept popping out of gear. The only way to keep the motorcar moving forward was to hold the gearshift in place with one hand while steering with the other.

Normally Josef would have taken his bike for such a short distance, given the fact that it had been a dry winter and the roads were clear. But there was something about motors and pastoral duties that seemed to go together. Telling Frau Brettschneider he would hop on his bicycle and pedal right over lacked a certain dignity, even though the bicycle would have probably gotten him there sooner.

He downshifted around a corner, and the store came into view. Overhead the sky was a flat gray slate. An icy wind served as a reminder of the winter season.

Standing in the middle of the street were a number of brown-shirts—Nazi bullies working for the Third Reich, who terrorized and spied on ordinary Germans, at times torturing them by making them swallow large quantities of castor oil or eat old socks. Stripped of much of their power by the surging SS, they compensated with sheer meanness.

They stood over a shivering man in shirt sleeves. The man was on his knees, facing the brownshirts. Klaus. Slumped in the doorway of the clothing store was his sobbing wife, a solid woman of medium stature. A few feet away stood their son, Norbert, who appeared trapped between two more brownshirts. Norbert was built solid like his mother but with a little extra around the middle. He was one of the church youth who had been invited to the Christmas party at Josef's house.

For Josef the scene was hauntingly familiar. He'd witnessed it before. A man on his knees in the middle of the street. That time it had been night. And the man was his father.

Three SS agents had pulled Wilhelm Schumacher from his bed. Josef was twenty-one at the time and on a break from his studies at Tübingen University, a school with a history of innovative thought, having produced such German notables as Philipp Melanchthon and Johannes Kepler.

Josef had been awakened by the sound of the front door splintering. Following a prearranged plan, he scrambled into the attic where his younger brother slept. Pressing his brother's face against his chest to keep the boy from seeing anything, Josef peered through a small, round attic window to the street below. The SS were taking turns kicking his father. Although he couldn't see her, Josef could hear his mother pleading for them to stop.

What happened next, happened quickly.

A Luger was drawn.

BLAM!

Josef jerked, as though the bullet had hit him. His mother's wails echoed up and down the street. His brother whimpered in his arms, frightened by the sound of the gunshot. Josef held him tight, biting his lower lip to hold back his own emotions.

Operation Hummingbird.

That's what they'd called it. Also, the Night of the Long Knives, the night Adolf Hitler secured power by murdering key leaders he'd deemed a threat. Among them, his good friend, Ernst Rohm.

But the killing of Josef's father had been a mistake. The SS had been dispatched to eliminate Dr. Wilhelm Schumann, not Nazi faithful Wilhelm Schumacher.

Josef's father died without ever understanding what was happening to him. His last words were "Heil Hitler! Heil Hitler! Heil Hitler!"

Three days later Hitler's deputy, Rudolf Hess, visited Josef's mother and ordered her to keep her mouth shut about the mistake. He then arranged for her to receive a pension. Only she didn't want a pension. She wanted her husband back.

Through the windshield of his Opel, Josef stared at Norbert Brettschneider. His heart ached for the boy. He knew exactly what Norbert must be feeling.

Josef climbed out of the motorcar. Actually, he unfolded out of the motorcar, the vehicle not being designed for someone with legs as long as his.

A blast of frigid air hit him. It was warm compared to the expressions on the faces of the brownshirts when they became aware of his approach.

Two of their number peeled themselves away from the others to intercept him. They looked Josef up and down, their eyes hard as flint. Their chins led the way as they swaggered toward him.

Just then Frau Brettschneider spotted him. "Thank God!" she cried. "Pastor Schumacher, do something! Please, don't let them take my Klaus!"

The taller of the two brownshirts wheeled around. "I told you to stay in the store!" he yelled. "Do you want me to shut it down? Is that it? Do you want me to shut your store down?"

Frau Brettschneider recoiled. Without another word, she retreated.

"What's going on here?" Josef asked.

Not until the tall brownshirt was satisfied that Frau Brett-schneider was back in her place did he turn his attention once again to Josef. Both men stepped to within a couple of feet of him.

"Heil Hitler!" they said in unison, their arms thrusting forward in salute. The two men were carbon copies of each other—black hair, hollow cheeks, unblinking eyes. Their uniforms matched down to the last insignia. The only differences Josef could detect were that the taller one had a crankier disposition and the shorter one had some kind of fascination with his nose. A nervous hand rubbed or tweaked it constantly.

"I asked you what's going on."

Tall Brownshirt scowled at him.

"What has Klaus done?"

"You will respond with the proper salute!" the tall brownshirt shouted.

"Who are you?" demanded the shorter one.

"I'm Reverend Josef Schumacher. Now it's your turn. What's all this about?" His arm remained limp at his side.

Largely social outcasts, the brownshirts were insecure men who sought to make up for their insecurities with uniforms and symbols and weapons. They were notorious bullies, ambassadors of intimi-dation.

"Shut up!" Tall Brownshirt screamed. His face flushed crimson more quickly than Josef had ever seen a face flush before. "Shut up! Shut up! Shut up! We ask the questions! Is that understood?"

The man's warm breath hit Josef in the face with the odor of rancid onions and garlic. Josef stood his ground. He said nothing.

The shorter of the two men wore a permanent smirk on his face. He stood with his weight on one foot, a thumb hooked in his belt, his other hand rubbing his nose.

"What business do you have here?" he asked.

"Frau Brettschneider called me."

"And so you came. Now go home."

"Not until you tell me what's going on."

Josef had dealt with these kinds of bullies before. He knew that if you stood up to them, they usually backed down. Those who didn't back down . . .

SLAP!

Josef's head snapped to the right from the blow. His jaw cracked as he stumbled backward a step.

"I'll say this only once," Short Brownshirt said. "Get back in your motorcar and drive away!"

Just then another brownshirt emerged from the store, carrying a tabletop radio. "Found this in the back room," he announced. "It's tuned to the BBC."

The sickening smirk on Short Brownshirt widened.

Klaus hung his head in guilt, and Josef knew he was fighting a losing battle. Still, he felt he had to try. For Norbert's sake.

"Look," Josef reasoned, "destroy the radio, but leave Klaus here. His family needs him."

"His family is better off without him," Short Brownshirt replied.

Frau Brettschneider began to wail.

"Be reasonable," Josef pleaded. "Times are difficult. Just this once could you—"

"Could we what?" the short man shouted. He stepped within inches of Josef's face. "Could we what? Ignore the law? Is that what you're advocating? Turn our heads while foreign countries fill our people's minds with seditious lies about Der Führer? Ignore the fact that they're promoting revolt and anarchy? Is that what you're suggesting?"

Despite this onslaught, Josef did his best not to flinch. Still, the aggression was having an effect on him, and he felt his fear rising. He swallowed it, determined not to give them the satisfaction. These men were brownshirts, not Gestapo.

When he spoke, he spoke softly. "I was going to suggest that just this once you might show a little compassion. Think of the boy. What will it do to him if you take his father away?"

Short Brownshirt stared at him incredulously. The corner of

his mouth twitched, his eyes wrinkled. Then he burst with laughter.

Turning to the other brownshirts, he shouted, "The good reverend is concerned how our arresting the father will affect the boy!"

To the man, the brownshirts laughed.

Turning back to Josef, the short man said, "You can be assured the boy is in good hands. The National Socialist Party is now his mother and father."

"But the boy needs—"

With an upraised hand, the short brownshirt stopped Josef midsentence. He said, "This boy you're so worried about is a hero to the Third Reich. Who do you think informed us that his father was listening to seditious radio?"

Josef was dumbfounded. He glanced over at Norbert standing between the two brownshirts, then at his mother. The look on Frau Brettschneider's face confirmed that it was true.

The brownshirts on both sides of Norbert patted him on the back.

Norbert stood there with the buttons of his Hitler Youth uniform straining to contain his belly and basked in the attention he was receiving.

With a flip of his hand, Short Brownshirt ordered, "Load the prisoner for transport."

"Where are you taking him?" Josef asked.

Short Brownshirt didn't answer him. To his taller counterpart, he said, "And bring the reverend along, too."

"What?" Josef cried.

"Just a few questions," Short Brownshirt said, his smirk firmly in place. "If you're a loyal German, you have nothing to fear, do you?"

Tall Brownshirt happily grabbed Josef by the arm. He was soon assisted by three of his friends.

At that moment Josef realized there was no one else on the street, only eyes peering through window curtains and doorways from the adjoining businesses and residences. Which was just as well. From that distance they couldn't see the shaking of his hands.

Mady looked at the kitchen clock for the hundredth time. Two minutes had passed since she looked at it last.

Where is he?

She checked the clock again out of sheer nervousness. The second hand eased its way past the number eight on its upward climb, in no particular hurry.

Josef had been gone for nearly three hours. It took less than ten minutes to drive to the Brettschneiders'. It was just like Josef to leave her in the lurch like this. She wanted to scream.

Instead, she pulled at a lock of hair and began chewing the ends. Her mother's voice sounded in her mind. *"Are you still chewing your hair? You're an adult now. And a pastor's wife! Is that the kind of example you want to set for the younger girls in your church?"*

Mady kept chewing.

She checked the clock again. The second hand had yet to make a complete round.

Try as she might, she couldn't abate her growing anxiety. Annoyance had given way to worry a good thirty minutes ago.

It was she who had initially taken Frau Brettschneider's call. The connection was poor, but not so poor that it masked the woman's fear. At the time Mady merely took note of the woman's feelings. Now she shared them.

What's keeping him?

She'd managed to appease Fräulein Baeck, who clucked and fussed and bristled over the fact that Josef himself wasn't present for the attic inspection. It was a toss-up as to whether the old spinster with the armband was more upset at Josef's absence or that she could find no reason not to approve the work he'd done.

Then, just as Fräulein Baeck was leaving and before Mady could take a breath, the youth began arriving for Josef's Christmas party.

"Leave it to me. I'll take care of everything."

Weren't those his exact words? Exactly what was she supposed to do with six bored youth sitting in her parlor? And how much longer could she hide from them in the kitchen?

Chapter 2

The whispering in the parlor unnerved her. When Mady could take it no longer, she directed the boys to the shed where Josef kept his ax and sent them into the woods to find a Christmas tree.

That had been nearly an hour ago.

Still chewing her hair, Mady pulled back the kitchen curtains. If the tracks in the dry winter grass were any indication, a whole herd of boys had migrated to the woods. While she couldn't see them, she could hear an occasional whoop or holler.

The girls—there were only two of them: Lisette, tall and blond, her hair wrapped in the traditional Gretchen wreath of braids; and Gael, short with brown hair, which she wore in plaits—were still in the parlor. The whispering continued.

Mady let the kitchen curtain fall back into place.

Josef . . . why are you doing this to me?

She heard the front door latch and ran to see if it was him.

Lisette and Gael were standing half in, half out of the doorway. They were pulling on coats and mittens.

Mady smoothed the wet ends of her hair nonchalantly.

"We thought we'd see what's taking the boys so long," Lisette said. "Is that all right, Frau Schumacher?"

Mady nodded her consent.

Then, just as the girls were closing the door, the clattering sound of the white Opel could be heard as it moved toward the house on the rutted dirt road.

Mady didn't bother putting on a coat. She opened the motorcar door before the engine gave its final gasp.

"What took you so long?" Her voice was low enough to keep the girls from hearing, yet intense enough to convey her anger.

With a groan Josef climbed out of the motorcar.

"I see they're already here," he said, looking at the backs of the girls as they ambled toward the woods.

"Yes, they're already here. And so was Fräulein Baeck."

"Did the attic pass inspection?"

"I have been going out of my mind! Where have you been?"

Josef moved slowly, more slowly than usual. His eyes were half-closed, and his mouth was little more than a thin line.

"SA Headquarters," he said.

"Berlin?"

Josef looked down at her. His face had grown much thinner and wasn't nearly as comely as when they courted. Waves of brown hair fell upon his brow. The only thing deeper than his brown eyes was his voice, which, at the moment, had a huskiness to it that appeared when he was tired.

"A couple of brownshirts didn't have enough playmates to occupy their day. So they enlisted me."

The implications were not lost on her.

"Did they . . ."

Hat in hand, he closed the motorcar door and started toward the house.

"They took offense at my presence during Klaus Brettschneider's arrest," he said matter-of-factly. "There was a lot of blustering . . . and posturing . . . that's all."

Mady examined his face and hands for marks. If they'd hurt him, would he tell her?

"What had Klaus done?" she asked.

"They caught him listening to the wrong radio station."

"How did they find out?"

"Norbert."

"Norbert informed on his own father?"

"That's the kind of Germany we're living in now, Mady."

Reaching the doorstep, Josef stopped. Something about her caught his attention. His fingers touched the wet ends of her hair. Mady felt her face flush.

———

With folded arms, Josef leaned against the doorway and watched as the boys decorated the tree. Lisette and Gael hovered over the yellow glow of the console dial, searching through the static for some Christmas music. He knew he should join them, mingle, get acquainted. This was, after all, the purpose of the party. And he *would* involve himself. As soon as his hands stopped shaking.

For over an hour he had endured the crimson faces, strained necks, expletives, and projected spittle of Sturmabteilung interrogators by focusing on the swastika medallions and pins and patches of their uniforms. If the ever-rising level of their voices was any indication, he'd somehow managed to fool the SA into thinking their barrage of threats had no effect on him. Likewise, he believed he'd kept it from Mady.

Now if only he could stop shaking.

"You don't fool me."

The voice, though intimately familiar, startled him. He turned to see Mady holding Kaiser.

"You didn't go to Berlin at all," she said with a coy smile. "If I know you, you hid in your office at church until you were certain Fräulein Baeck was gone."

Josef grinned. It had been a long time since she'd looked at him like that. "You found me out. However, I'm sure you handled Fräulein Baeck with tact and diplomacy."

"No, you're not getting off that easily! You owe me a favor."

He kept his tone light. "Frau Schumacher, I acknowledge I am in your debt."

"The stove needs to be lit."

Josef grimaced. She'd set him up. If there was anything he hated more than spittle-spewing Nazi interrogators, it was lighting the stove. Some days it seemed that was all he ever did. For him, life consisted of only two things: lighting the stove and everything else.

He started to protest.

A raised index finger stopped him. "You owe me!"

"Where are the matches?"

Resigned to his fate, Josef moped into the kitchen. He only hoped he could steady his hand long enough to complete the task.

Adolf Hitler was right about one thing. Germany's youth was the key to her future. The state's unprecedented investment in the Hitler Youth and German Girls League organizations was evidence that youth were a Third Reich priority. How better to ensure the success of Hitler's much vaunted thousand-year Reich?

The product of a Nazi household himself, Josef was well acquainted with the teachings of Hitler. He was also aware of the National Socialist tendency to paint everything black and white. Germany and everyone else. Those who aren't for Germany are against Germany. Taken to the extreme, Nazi ideology eclipsed everything. Even God.

Not in Josef's house. And, God willing, not with these six youths.

The boys were dressed alike in their Hitler Youth winter uniforms—navy blue shirts and pants, leather shoulder straps, and swastika belts—as they decorated the tree with candy and ribbons and ornaments. Empty ornament boxes and discarded coats and scarves were strewn about the room.

From the look on Mady's face, the boys' haphazard method of hanging things was not at all to her liking. Josef guessed that the youth would be out the door less than five minutes before she'd begin rearranging the decorations.

It amused Josef to think that only three years ago Mady was herself one of the youth of the church. Now, sitting leisurely in her chair, she looked so much more mature. Her legs folded under her, she wore a black skirt that discreetly covered her knees and a festive long-sleeved blouse with thin alternating red-and-green stripes on a black field. Her hair was fashionably wavy and short, but not so short that she couldn't pull the ends into her mouth when she was upset.

The orchestral strains of "Silent Night" issued forth from the radio's speakers. Lisette and Gael smiled at their success.

Konrad, the oldest and most athletic of the boys, scoffed, "Just because you found a radio station, you think you deserve a medal?"

Lisette wrinkled her nose at him. "At least it didn't take us an hour to chop down a little tree. What's the matter, Konrad, couldn't find one in the forest?"

Willi, Konrad's younger brother, found Lisette's remark amusing. He laughed.

"Shut your trap, runt!" Konrad snapped. He punctuated his remark with a shove.

Willi stumbled backward. His foot snagged a coat lying on the floor, causing him to reel and sprawl back against the Christmas tree.

"Hey! Watch out!" Neff yelled.

The tree tilted wildly.

Ernst, a tall, skinny, and bespectacled boy, lunged for it. He missed.

The tree toppled over with an unceremonious thump, narrowly missing the girls who had backed up against the radio console. The top of the tree fell inches shy of Mady's feet.

Startled, Kaiser scampered into the back bedroom. For a moment everyone fell silent.

Willi rolled off the branches and jumped to his feet. Although physically unhurt, his face became a portrait of adolescent guilt.

The next thing Josef knew, his presence loomed over the room like an uncertain sky. Six pair of young eyes turned to him and awaited judgment. Even Mady, rubbing a freshly scratched forearm from the cat's hasty exit, awaited his reaction.

Josef gazed solemnly at the fallen tree.

"O Tannenbaum" played softly in the background.

Josef looked at each of the youth. Konrad, Neff, and Ernst met his gaze. Lisette glanced at him, then lowered her eyes. Willi and Gael stared at the floor.

What Josef saw in them made his heart ache.

Fear.

Fear of reprisal. Fear of punishment. Fear of not measuring up.

Every day he saw the same look in the eyes of countless German people. Fear had become their national expression.

Willi was the most frightened. His lower lip trembled. A hand moved quickly to his face to wipe away tears.

Shaking his head, Josef said softly, "Poor Kaiser."

Puzzled looks scrunched the faces of the youth.

"Poor Kaiser. Just look what he did."

"But . . . Pastor Josef," Lisette said, "Kaiser didn't knock over the tree."

"I don't know. Did you see the way he ran out of here? Sure looked guilty to me."

"Kaiser didn't do it!" Lisette insisted. "Konrad and Willi—"

"What Kaiser doesn't know," Josef interrupted her, "is that it really doesn't matter who did what. Accidents happen. It's nobody's fault. There's really no one to blame. But poor Kaiser, he feels so guilty. He just doesn't know any better."

"Poor Kaiser," Mady chimed in.

The next few moments were quiet. Josef fought the urge to say something more, to press home his point. Thinking better of it, he let the silence do it for him.

Just then, he caught Lisette's eye. A grin passed between them.

"Poor Kaiser," she said.

Neff caught on next. He shook his head. "Poor Kaiser."

"Poor Kaiser," Ernst echoed.

Konrad: "Poor Kaiser."

Gael: "Oh! I get it! Poor Kaiser."

Willi stood silent, his lower lip quivering. Everyone looked at him expectantly.

"Come on, Willi, say it!" Neff urged him.

The others urged him, too.

Willi stared down at his feet.

"Say it, Willi! Say it!" they chanted.

Finally a crooked smile creased the boy's face. "Poor Kaiser," he said.

Everyone cheered. Then they all lent a hand righting the tree. Overall, it was no worse for wear. A few needles had shaken off along with several ornaments, but nothing was broken.

While Mady went to the back room to check on Kaiser, Josef helped pick up the ornaments that had fallen onto the floor.

That's when he spotted it.

The swastika medallion that Willi had placed on the tree.

Josef spied an opportunity. Dropping nonchalantly to one knee, he scooped up the offending medallion and pocketed it. As he stood, he glanced around to see if anyone had noticed.

Lisette was looking straight at him. She smiled, then turned away.

"The lights aren't working," someone said.

"Happens most every year." Josef studied the string of lights even though he didn't know what he was looking for. "Neff . . . do you know anything about Christmas lights?"

An odd expression crossed Neff's face. He glanced up at his taller friend, then back to Josef. "Ernst is the genius when it comes to these things," he said. "He knows everything about electricity and chemicals and all that stuff."

"A genius, you say?" Josef peered through the branches of the tree to Ernst. "Do you think you can get the lights to work?"

Ernst was already working on it. Without taking his eyes off the electrical plug in his hands, he replied, "Just give me a few minutes."

"Neff is good at photography."

"What was that, Gael?"

Gael looked perturbed at having to repeat herself. "Ernst is good at science. Neff is good at photography."

"Photographs!" Mady exclaimed. "We must take some photographs!"

Mady hurried to the next room and emerged a minute later with a camera bag. She thrust the bag at Neff. "This was my father's camera," she said. "To tell you the truth, I don't know how to use it. It's rather complicated."

Neff peered into the bag, appearing as comfortable sorting through the equipment as he would fumbling through his own sock drawer. He lifted the camera out.

"Do you know how to work it?" Mady asked.

"It's an Ikoflex 850, twin lens reflex. Not as good as a Rolleiflex, but it'll get the job done." He loaded the camera with experienced fingers.

By the time Neff had the camera ready, Ernst had the lights working. While Josef watched with an amused grin, Mady rounded up the two preening girls for a group picture. The boys were harder. She grappled, shoved, and coerced—whatever it took to get them to stand next to the girls and one another. Though they didn't show it, Josef could tell that the boys enjoyed all the cajoling as much as Mady enjoyed ordering them around.

"You, too!" Mady said, grabbing Josef by the arm.

Josef resisted. "I'll take the picture."

"*I'll* take the picture," Mady insisted.

The assembled youth snickered at the sight of Mady manhandling her husband into place just as she'd done to each of them.

Josef found himself standing behind Willi. He placed his hands on the boy's shoulders.

FLASH!

The moment was recorded. Then, like magnets of similar polarity, the youth spread apart until the distances between them were once again more to their comfort.

"How do you think it's going?" Josef whispered to his wife.

"With the tree incident behind us, pretty well, I'd say. In fact, that might even have been a good thing. It seems to have brought them together."

On the radio the final strains of Handel's "Hallelujah Chorus" rose to its dramatic conclusion. This was followed by the voice of the announcer.

The words that came from the radio's speakers were not German. The announcer's voice was very proper and very British.

While Josef didn't understand what the announcer was saying, he recognized three letters all too clearly, as did everyone else in the room.

"BBC."

Hitler's youth froze.

Chapter 3

"Turn it off! Turn it off! Turn it off!"

The sense of urgency escalated with every British syllable that came from the console.

"Please turn it off!" Gael sobbed, covering her ears.

The other youth stared at the offending radio, their mouths agape.

Calmly, Josef walked over to the radio and switched it off.

The resulting silence was as frightening as the broadcast. Fearful glances were exchanged.

Lisette was the first to speak. "I didn't know! Honestly! I didn't know!"

"Are we going to be arrested?" Willi asked.

"No one is going to be arrested," Josef assured him.

Konrad disagreed. "An entire family in Danzig went to prison for two and a half years for listening to seditious radio," he said. "People in Wurttemberg and the Rhineland were sentenced to fifteen months in prison."

With the image of Klaus Brettschneider on his knees and surrounded by the SA still fresh in his mind, Josef gestured with his hands in a way that looked like he was physically trying to hold down the rising level of fear. "We weren't listening to seditious radio. We were listening to Christmas music."

"On the BBC!" Gael cried.

"It was orchestral music," Josef replied. "You couldn't have known it was a British broadcast."

"What are you doing with a radio like that, anyway?" Konrad asked. "It can only get you into trouble. If you had a People's Receiver, this wouldn't have happened."

"That's true," Ernst added. "A People's Receiver is designed to prevent mistakes like this one. It's constructed so that only programs from German radio stations can be tuned in, that is unless you live in one of the border provinces, then—"

"Thank you, Ernst," Josef cut in. "I'm aware of the features of a People's Receiver."

"Then why don't you have one?" Konrad pressed.

"It's like having se-di-tious"—Willi had to sound out the word—"books in your house. Why do you have them, if you're not going to read them?" He was obviously parroting something he'd heard or had been told.

Josef could feel the back of his neck growing warm. He wasn't about to be cross-examined in his own house. Yet he knew all too well that a mere accusation could qualify him for a personal visit from the brownshirts, or worse, the Gestapo.

"I'll say this once," he said. "Frau Schumacher and I don't listen to foreign radio stations. We don't listen to them privately, and we certainly don't listen to them when we have guests in our home. What happened tonight, while regrettable, was simply an accident."

"I'll have to report this incident to my father," Konrad said.

Josef sighed. Rupert Reichmann was a fanatical Nazi. "Do what you must do," Josef said. "Now, let's continue with our party."

The evening continued, but devoid of its former spirit. With cinnamon cake in one hand and a cup of hot chocolate in the other, the youth stood around sullenly.

"Before you leave, I have something for each of you," Josef said.

"A Christmas present?" Willi cried.

"Don't be stupid," Konrad snapped. "Ministers don't make enough money to buy Christmas presents for everyone."

"They gave us hot chocolate!" Willi said.

"Thank you for noticing, Willi," Mady replied. "I saved ration cards for months for that treat."

Though the mood of the party had soured, Josef was determined to get through these next few minutes and hopefully redeem the evening. It was the reason he'd invited the youth to his house in the first place. He projected his voice enough to command their attention. "Everyone, please sit down!"

The youth scattered haphazardly around the room. Lisette and Gael sat next to each other. The gap between them and the boys was quite noticeable. Mady took her place in the upholstered chair as before, only this time she was alone. Kaiser had yet to forgive them for the tree incident.

Josef produced a shoe box.

"I take an eight and a half regular," Neff quipped, earning him a slap on the shoulder from Lisette.

Josef smiled. At least one of them was feeling comfortable enough to make jokes again. Good. "I'm going to hand each of you a small package," he said. "Don't open it until everyone has theirs."

Each youth was given a cardboard envelope that was sealed with a flap. It was small enough to fit in the palms of their hands. Josef had marked the envelopes with the initials of the recipient. He pocketed the one that was marked NB for Norbert Brettschneider.

"Now you can open them," Josef said.

Willi was the first to get his open. "Money!" he shouted.

As each person lifted the flap on their package, a coin slid out.

They turned the coins over in their hands, examining both sides.

"How much is it worth?" Willi asked his brother.

"It's not money, dummkopf. It's just a coin."

"Compare the coins," Josef said. "They're all alike on one side but all different on the other side."

"They all have a bear standing on his back legs," Lisette said.

"That's correct," Josef said. "The question is, why the bear?"

"Everyone knows that," Konrad scoffed. "The bear is the symbol of Germany."

"Correct. And the writing? Someone read it aloud."

Neff squinted at the coin and read the words across the top, "Rooted in the soil." He then moved his fingers to read the words at the bottom, "Reaching for the sky."

"Thank you, Neff. Now, the opposite side of each coin is unique to each of you," Josef said. "Turn your coins over. We're going to go from person to person, and I want you to read what your coin says."

"Why?" Konrad asked.

It was more a challenge than a question.

"Because the Scripture verse that's printed on each coin was selected specifically for each one of you."

Konrad held his gaze, but only for a moment.

"Lisette, you begin."

Seated on the floor closest to him, her back straight, Lisette lifted the coin to read it. Growing up within a troubled home, she attended church regularly with her mother, who often bore bruises from an alcoholic husband, Lisette's stepfather. Given the girl's circumstances, Josef was amazed at how well-adjusted and happy she had turned out to be.

Lisette brushed a few strands of blond hair out of her eyes and read the words on her coin, " 'Strength and honour are her clothing,' Proverbs 31:25."

"Very good. Gael, you're next. What does your coin say?"

Gael Wissing was a member of a solid German household. While she was the oldest of four children, all girls, she was the youngest person in the youth group, not counting Willi.

Her father, Herr Wissing, was a Berlin industrialist, which meant, given the new Reich, that the family was financially well-off. Gael always wore nice clothes to church, though she was the only one in her family to attend regularly. Her parents dropped her off at church every Sunday but rarely attended themselves. Mady had once suggested that they brought her because they hoped the church would instill enough religion in her to keep her chaste until marriage. Their plan didn't seem to be working. Gael had a tendency to be overly friendly with the boys.

Gael read her coin. " 'Receive her in the Lord, as becometh saints,' Romans 16:2."

"Those words are from the apostle Paul," Josef explained, "on behalf of a woman named Phoebe who served in the church at Cenchrea. High praise for a woman in those days. Neff, it's your turn."

Neff Kessel was the only son of a watchmaker and camera repairman. He had an uncle who died from mustard gas in the war. While his father hoped that Neff would someday take over the repair shop, Neff's interests tended toward the viewfinder side of the camera. He was of average height with a round face and black hair that he combed straight back. Friendly and good-natured, he was the kind of guy that girls sought out as a friend and source of information about the boys to whom they were romantically attracted.

Squinting slightly, Neff focused on his coin and read aloud, " 'For the things which are seen are temporal; but the things which are not seen are eternal,' Second Corinthians 4:18."

"Good. Ernst, you're next."

Tall, lanky, and bespectacled, Ernst Ehrenberg held up his coin, noticed he had the wrong side, and proceeded to drop it while trying to turn it over. Straw-haired and possessing a wry sense of humor, Ernst was the most intelligent of the group. Indeed, the boy was brilliant when it came to physics, chemistry, and mathematics. Like most of the others he was a half-year shy of graduation and already Hitler's Third Reich was making plans for him. He lived alone with his mother. His father—a former mathematics professor at the university—had been crippled in the war and then died, shortly after Ernst's birth, from pneumonia.

Ernst read, " 'The fear of the Lord is the beginning of wisdom,' Proverbs 9:10."

"And how about you, Konrad?" Josef said.

"Yeah?"

"You're next."

With thick fingers Konrad Reichmann rotated his coin to read it. In every way he was Hitler's dream youth. Broad-shouldered, athletic, strong. From the reports Josef received, the boy excelled in the Hitler Youth program, winning most of the games and earning the praise of his leaders. His jaw was boxlike, his hair thick, blond, and parted on the left side. He was the offspring of proud Prussian parents. His father was a highly decorated flying ace. Having crashed while on his final mission, the man now lived with constant pain in his right leg, which had been shattered on impact. But Konrad's father never spoke of the pain and did his best to conceal his limp. He raised both his boys with regimental discipline.

Clearing his throat a couple of times, Konrad read haltingly, " 'The Lord is my rock, and my for . . . my for . . .' "

Josef grimaced. Konrad wasn't challenging him earlier, he suddenly realized. The boy was afraid to read out loud because he couldn't read well.

"Fortress," Josef said.

" '. . . fortress,' " Konrad repeated. Then he cleared his throat again and continued, " '. . . my God and my strength,' Puhsss . . ."

"Psalm," Josef said.

"Psalm 18:2." After meeting the challenge, Konrad tossed the coin onto the rug.

"Willi," Josef prompted.

Physically, the twelve-year-old boy was everything his older brother was not—scrawny, short, and with stringy brown hair. Had he been a cat, Josef was almost certain the boy's Prussian father would have drowned him at birth. Willi was often rude and obnoxious, a constant source of irritation. The reason he was with the youth group was that his father insisted the boys do everything together. This was in keeping with Hitler's "Youth leads youth" ethos. To get Konrad to the meeting, Josef had to agree that Willi could come, too. He did so readily, for Josef liked Willi and saw potential in him.

Willi stared at the coin with a puzzled expression, as though he couldn't make out the first word. "Oh!" he cried, turning the coin right-side up. Grinning, he looked up, his eyes indicating he was expecting laughter.

There was none.

Undaunted, he proceeded to read from the coin. " 'Let no man despise thy youth; but be thou an example,' First Timothy 4:12." He looked up again. "Did everybody hear that? It said you're not supposed to despise me."

With a deadpan expression, Lisette replied, "It said, 'no man.' Gael and I aren't men. We can despise you all we want."

"Listen to me now," Josef said.

With the reading of the coins completed, they were beginning to fidget.

"I want you to carry these coins wherever you go. And every time you see them or feel them in your pocket, I want you to remember the words printed on them. On the one side, 'Rooted in the soil. Reaching for the sky.' This describes our life as German Christians. As Germans, our lives are rooted in our native land; as Christians, our goal is heaven. As Jesus put it in the prayer He taught us to pray, 'On earth, as it is in heaven.' "

"I like that," Lisette said, staring down at her coin.

"Also remember the verse on the other side of your coin. This is God's message to each of you. In it there is a promise."

"I don't see a promise," Willi said.

"Not all promises are immediately evident. Every time you look at your coin, think about what's written on it, and in God's time, the promise will become clear to you."

They were all gazing at their coins now. Josef looked over them like a farmer observing his spring planting. The seed was in the ground. He wondered what kind of harvest it would produce, and when. All of a sudden, the effort seemed so meager, so futile. What was he really hoping to achieve? How could this effort possibly stand up against Hitler's juggernaut of banners and songs and rallies?

"I still don't get it," Willi said, his eyes still fixed on the coin in his hand.

Konrad grabbed the coin from him. "Look, runt. It says, 'Let no man—' "

Josef interrupted him. "Thanks for wanting to help, Konrad, but it's something each person has to discover for himself."

"I don't understand why you're giving these to us," Lisette said.

"It's because he doesn't have kids of his own," Gael replied.

Josef smiled. He had an idea. He should probably talk it over with Mady first, but there wasn't time. "Actually, that's not true, Gael," he said.

There was a moment of confusion among them. Lisette was the first to catch on. She whirled toward Mady. "What wonderful news, Frau Schumacher!" she cried. "When did you make the announcement?"

Surprised herself, Mady smiled sheepishly. "About five seconds ago."

Suddenly, sitting there in the chair, she appeared very maternal with one hand resting on her abdomen.

Lisette was up and standing next to Mady before anyone could say anything else. Her eyes were brimming with excitement.

"We'd appreciate it if you would all keep the news a secret until Sunday," Josef said, "when we'll tell the whole congregation."

The announcement was a gambit that seemed to be paying off. Lisette's excitement alone lit up the room and changed the mood that had prevailed since the incident with the radio. While Mady kept shooting him questioning glances, Josef was pleased to think that at least the evening would end on a positive note.

"My medal's missing!" Willi screamed. He rushed to the tree, searching the branches frantically for the swastika medallion.

"It probably fell off when the tree was knocked over," Gael suggested. She began searching the floor under the tree.

"The way the tree tipped over, it's probably near Frau Schumacher's chair, possibly under it," Ernst said. He then joined in on the search. Neff looked around the doorway, thinking it might have hit the floor and skidded.

Even Konrad helped his brother. "It's his first *Jungvolk* award," he explained.

The only one of the youth who wasn't helping to find the medallion was Lisette.

Willi was close to tears. Even Mady had begun to look. She was on her knees and feeling underneath her chair.

Josef considered palming the medallion and then pretending to find it himself. But Lisette was looking at him.

"I have it," he finally said with a sigh.

"You found it!" Willi cried.

The boy was so relieved the medallion had been located, he didn't think to ask any questions.

Gael was a different story. "Where did you find it?" she asked.

"Yeah, where was it?" Konrad wanted to know.

While Willi busied himself with placing the medallion back on the tree, the attention focused to Josef.

There was nothing for him to do but confess. "I picked it up and put it in my pocket when the tree fell over."

"Sort of an absentminded thing," Lisette offered. She was trying to help out.

"No. It was deliberate," Josef said.

There was an uneasy silence.

"Poor Kaiser?" Neff suggested.

Willi took a step back from the tree. The swastika hung triumphantly again on the glittering Christmas tree.

To Josef's relief, there was a knock at the door. He went to answer it.

Everyone was expecting a parent. Instead, standing on the doorstep was a small elderly man with a package wrapped in newspaper tucked under his arm. A prominent yellow star had been sewn onto his coat.

Printed on the yellow star was a single word.

Jude.

Chapter 4

What do you want, Jew?" Konrad sneered. He had followed Josef to the door.

The hostile greeting forced a mask of bewilderment and fear to the old man's face. He stood trembling on the porch step, his eyes transfixed on Konrad's blue Hitler Youth shirt.

"Herr Meyerhof!" Josef said, stepping forward. "What a pleasant surprise! Come in! Come in! The youth were just leaving."

Konrad turned to Josef. "You invite vermin into your house?"

"Konrad . . . you remember Herr Meyerhof . . . he's a member of our church."

"He's a filthy Jew!" Konrad spat. Grabbing his coat, he shoved past the old man, knocking him backward a couple of steps so that he nearly lost his balance and fell down. Meyerhof stood to one side with his eyes downcast as all the youth filed past him. Willi was the last in line.

"Dirty *Jew*!" Willi said when he passed.

"Willi, that's enough!" Josef scolded.

Gael's father was waiting in the motorcar for her. She and Neff climbed into the backseat, which made sense since Neff's house was close by the Wissings'. Gael's father looked back over his shoulder as they drove away.

Ernst and Lisette walked together into the darkness, silently moving through an inch of freshly fallen snow.

"You'll see that Lisette gets home safely?" Josef called after them.

Ernst turned, waved in affirmation, stumbled, regained his footing, and then continued on his way.

Josef turned his attention to Herr Meyerhof. "Please come in, Herr Meyerhof. Come in and get warm!" Josef said, lending a hand to assist him. Josef could feel the elderly man trembling beneath his coat.

One last motorcar had yet to drive away. Herr Reichmann sat behind the wheel of his black sedan. Konrad sat in the front seat beside his father. Behind the windshield two pair of eyes were locked on Josef's unexpected guest.

Josef waved at the Reichmanns and then turned his back to help Professor Meyerhof into the house. Mady stood inside the open door, her arms folded against the chill. She didn't appear to be pleased to see the professor.

"I was thinking I had the wrong house when that young man appeared," Meyerhof said. "It wouldn't have surprised me. Lately this head of mine serves little purpose other than to provide a place to hang my hat."

"I apologize for his behavior," Josef said. "We had the church youth over for a Christmas party. I'm hoping to—"

Meyerhof stopped abruptly with both feet just shy of the threshold. His face close to Josef, he said, "What's to apologize? You don't think I get the same treatment—and worse—wherever I go?"

"Not in my house," Josef replied.

This brought a smile to the old man. He patted Josef's cheek. "You're a good boy. A poor Hebrew student, but a good boy."

Josef laughed. "I've been meaning to return to my studies, but with Christmas and all . . ."

Meyerhof extended his teaching finger. " 'Poverty and shame shall be to him that refuseth instruction: but he that regardeth reproof shall be honoured.' "

"After Christmas. I promise!" Josef said.

Once inside, Josef closed the door. He attempted to take Herr Meyerhof's coat and hat. The elderly man waved him off.

"It is much too late for guests," he insisted. "I merely wanted you to have this. A gift from me to you and your lovely wife. Merry Christmas." He held out a package that was wrapped in newspaper.

"Bless you, Professor. This is certainly unexpected."

The folds of Meyerhof's cheeks deepened into a smile. "I don't have much," he said, "but God is faithful and occasionally a blessing comes my way. In this case, the blessing came in the form of beef tongue. A dear butcher friend of mine saves a tongue for me every Christmas. And now that my Eva is gone, I don't have anyone to share it with. It is a blessing for me to share it with you."

"How kind," Mady said. "Thank you." She leaned forward and pressed a kiss onto his cheek.

Flustered, Herr Meyerhof looked heavenward and said, "You didn't see that, Eva." Taking Mady by the hand, he said to her, "Had I known this would be my reward, I would have brought you the whole cow!"

BAM! BAM! BAM!

The door shuddered with each blow. Josef opened it.

Reichmann towered in the doorway, a pillar of rage. Shocks of gray hair protruded from beneath his woolen cap. Had Konrad and Willi already told him about the radio?

"What's the meaning of this, Schumacher?" He pointed at Professor Meyerhof without looking at him.

"Rupert, don't you recognize the professor?"

"All I see is a Jew."

His hands shaking, Meyerhof donned his hat. "It's best that I go now," he said quietly.

"Do you think I would have allowed my boys to come to your

house if I knew you'd be harboring a Jew here?" Reichmann shouted.

Josef did his best to remain calm. There was no reasoning with men like Rupert Reichmann. Still, he felt obligated to try. "Professor Meyerhof just stopped by with a Christmas gift for Mady and me," he explained. "There's no cause to—"

"You haven't heard the last of this, Preacher!" This time the finger was pointed squarely at Josef's chest.

Reichmann pivoted and with long strides returned to his sedan. The engine roared to life, and Herr Reichmann steered his motorcar toward home. In the backseat, Willi dangled a string noose against the rear window.

Turning to his guest, Josef said, "Are you sure you won't stay a while?"

Meyerhof shook his head sadly. "I meant to bring a gift to your house, and instead I bring trouble. Besides, it's not healthy for an old Jew to be out late at night. If a gang doesn't get me, a cold germ will!"

He meant this as a joke.

"Let me get my coat," Josef said. "I'll walk you home."

Meyerhof waved his hand and clucked his tongue. "No need. No need," he said. "God has given each of us only so many nights, and you shouldn't waste yours with an old man, not when you have such a beautiful wife."

Josef insisted, but Meyerhof stood his ground.

From the doorway Josef watched as the old man navigated the steps and tottered into the darkness.

While Mady took the beef tongue to the kitchen, Josef plopped wearily into the upholstered chair. When Mady returned, she went straight to the tree and began rearranging ornaments.

"Come here, you." Josef grabbed her wrist and pulled her onto his lap. Her feet dangled over the arm of the chair.

She giggled girlishly. "We must've left the front door open too long," she said.

"Why is that?"

"A wolf sneaked in and ate my husband, and now he's after me!"

His arms around her waist, Josef buried his face against Mady's neck. Her warmth, the scent of her perfume, the sensation of his cheek against her skin reduced the universe to just the two of them. With his nose Josef traced the line of her jaw to her chin. Their breathing synchronized. She turned her face toward him so that they were eye to eye, nose to nose, lip to lip. Josef brushed her lips lightly with his own. Mady closed her eyes.

"It's Saturday," she whispered. "You have a big day tomorrow. Besides, after a day like today, I'd think you'd be exhausted."

"Must be the residual of all those youth hormones here tonight," he said.

Retracing his way along her jaw, he nuzzled her neck.

"Now don't start something you can't finish."

"I don't recall that ever being a problem."

Mady laughed and gave him a playful shove. "I mean it! You have to preach tomorrow."

"Tomorrow doesn't exist," he whispered. "Only tonight. Only this moment."

"Oh!" Startled, Mady jumped and pulled away.

Before Josef could ask her what was wrong, he saw. Kaiser had finally found the courage to come out from his hiding place and had jumped up on her. With his head lowered, he wormed his way between them.

"There you are!" Mady cooed. She freed her arms and stroked the cat's head and ears. "I was worried about you!"

"Can't say I care for his timing."

"Wait until we have children."

"I suppose it won't be long before I'll have to stand in line with ration cards in hand just for a little of my wife's attention."

Mady smiled, still stroking the cat.

Kaiser rubbed the top of his head against Mady's chin, purring loudly, clenching and unclenching his claws. He maneuvered between them until his tail was batting Josef's face.

Josef fidgeted. "Excuse me," he said.

"Where are you going?"

"It's getting a little crowded."

He was hoping she'd put down the cat. But once he was up, Mady flopped back down into the chair with Kaiser stretched out across her stomach.

Josef locked the front door, beginning his nightly ritual before going to bed. Mady nuzzled the kitten with her nose. He started to say something, then thought better of it, choosing instead a more neutral topic. "How do you think it went tonight?" he asked.

"I'm still angry at you for leaving me to face Fräulein Baeck alone."

So that's what this is all about. "I mean after that. Once the party started."

Mady chuckled. "It wasn't dull."

"I think it went pretty well, everything considered."

Mady looked up at him. "Really? They knocked down the tree, scared the life out of Kaiser—poor baby—broke the law by tuning in a foreign broadcast, Konrad is convinced you hate Der Führer, and Herr Reichmann thinks we're harboring Jews. Did I miss anything?"

"Willi's medallion."

"You stole a little boy's medal."

"I didn't want it on my Christmas tree!" Josef defended himself. "Besides, did you see where he placed it? Right in front of where you are sitting. I tell you, the boy's sweet on you."

"He is not!"

"Oh, yes he is! Take it from one who had his share of boyhood infatuations."

"You're telling me you pocketed Willi's medallion because you're jealous of him?"

"Not funny."

Mady grinned. "So it bothers you when other men show an interest in me."

"Not as long as they're under fifteen or over sixty-five years of age."

"You cad!"

Josef stretched, hoping Mady would get the hint. "Well, I think things went pretty well tonight. There were some tense moments, but overall we planted a few seeds and that's what's important."

Mady stroked the cat.

"I'm going to bed," Josef said.

Mady said nothing.

He bent over and gave his wife a peck on the forehead. Kaiser took a swing at him.

"Will you be up long?" Josef asked, glaring at the cat.

"I'll be in as soon as I rearrange the ornaments."

That reminded him. Turning to the tree, he snatched the swastika medallion from the limb.

"Josef!"

"I don't want this thing on my tree!"

Chapter 5

Sunday, April 14, 1940

The ending never changes.

No matter how hard he struggles, how fast he runs, how loud he yells, the result is always the same.

He's too late.

He can't reach them in time to save them.

The nightmare begins as a dream within a dream. He awakens to sounds, indistinguishable at first, hushed and ringing with secrecy. The sounds become words spoken in conspiratorial tones, charged with a sense of urgency, and then as their meaning solidifies, they alarm him, jolt him awake.

Covers are thrown off. The race begins.

One version of the dream has his bare feet slapping the cold cobblestone streets of Berlin. In other scenarios he charges up a stream, the current's fluid grip restraining his legs. Or sometimes he's running up stairs, stairs that stretch into forever, long after his legs have melted and his lungs have burned up.

He never reaches them in time. He's close, but never close enough. Close enough to see their tortured eyes, but not close enough to ease their pain. Close enough to witness their deaths, but not close enough to stop them from dying.

Tonight the dream was no different. The sounds, the words, the alarm, the running, the weariness, the failure at the end.

Awake, he threw off the bedcovers, his heart hammering, his throat gasping. His bedclothes were pasted to his flesh with cold sweat.

"Josef! What's wrong?" Mady sat up next to him. She reached toward him, then recoiled when her hand made contact with his shivering, wet arm. "Are you ill?"

Josef swung his legs over the side of the bed, steadying himself with both arms. Deep breaths slowed his heart and restored a measure of his senses. The pain of his failure—even though it was a dream—would be the last sensation to fade. While it would remain dark for another three hours, for him the night was over. There would be no more sleep. "Go back to sleep," he told her. His voice came raspy, deep.

"Do you want me to call the doctor?"

He chuckled inwardly. Is there a scalpel sharp enough to remove the source of his recurring nightmares?

His feet hit the cold hardwood floor and immediately began inching around for his slippers, like moles seeking a hovel.

"Would it help to talk about it?"

Josef pulled his robe around him, grimacing as it pressed the wet bedclothes against his skin. "I'll be in the den," he said, then closed the bedroom door behind him.

Switching on a light, he picked up his Bible from the end table and removed his notes for the morning's sermon. He fumbled for his reading glasses on the lampstand. The lingering effects of the nightmare clouded his mind. He had to make a concentrated effort to pull the markings on the page into focus. While they formed words, they still held no meaning for him.

He returned the notes to the Bible and the Bible to the end table and then glanced at the basket of embroidery beside the chair. Needle and thread were his secret refuge, an activity that helped him shut out the horror and focus on colors and scenes of beauty. But not tonight. Horror's chill ran too deep, touching his soul.

His eyeglasses clattered on the table when he tossed them aside. Slumping to his knees, Josef used the chair as a kneeling bench.

Faces filled his mind. Konrad. Willi. Lisette. Gael. Neff. Ernst.

His clasped hands began to tremble. Sobs mingled with the sounds of their names. "God in heaven, I pray I'm not too late for them, too."

———

"You're late."

"It's good to see you, too, Poppa," Mady said.

The front door opened wide as Dr. Wilhelm Olbricht removed the ever-present cigar from his mouth just long enough to hug his pregnant daughter. It was at times like this when Josef was re-minded that Mady was a good inch taller than her father. An op-tical illusion, surely. In Josef's eyes the man was a giant.

"Darling!" Edda Olbricht appeared from behind her husband. She wore a white apron over a fashionable forest-green dress. The moment her husband's arms released Mady, she was there to take his place. Of the three, Edda was the tallest. A thin woman with every black hair meticulously in place, she moved and spoke with elegance. Gracious to a fault, she was the perfect pastor's wife.

"Sorry we're late, Mama. A young couple wanted to talk with Josef after the service."

Dr. Olbricht chomped down on his cigar. "Trouble?"

"On the contrary," Josef said, following his wife into the house. "Fritzi Koch and Warren Mienert. They want to get married."

"Fritzi Koch?" Olbricht cried. "Emil's youngest? But she's too young to get married! Why, she's only—"

"Twenty years old, dear," Edda finished.

"Twenty? No . . . she couldn't be more than . . ."

"Poppa, Fritzi's only a year younger than me," Mady said.

For as long as Josef had known the man, he had depended

upon his wife and daughter to remember the ages and birthdays and anniversaries of the members of his congregation.

"If you ask me," Olbricht continued, "both Fritzi and you are too young to be married." Then he glanced at his daughter's swollen belly. "And certainly too young to bear children!"

Edda pushed her husband aside playfully. "I was exactly Mady's age when I gave birth to her," she said. To Mady she said, "How are you feeling, dear? There's certainly no hiding the fact that you're with child now, is there?"

"You were much older when you had Mady," Olbricht contested.

"I was twenty-one!"

Olbricht scratched his head. "Well, maybe so," he groused, "but twenty-one was a lot older in those days."

All it took was one step across the threshold to realize that the Olbrichts' house was different from most others in the city. It didn't have the typical Berlin room, a one-windowed gloomy frontage that led to other rooms set off at right angles. Instead, its entryway was round and spacious, with a skylight that kept it brightly lit and inviting.

"Dinner will be ready in about thirty minutes," Edda announced. "Mady, are you feeling up to giving me a hand in the kitchen?"

"Of course, Mama." She gave her mother a quizzical look.

"Don't even get me started about how unreliable staff is these days," Edda said.

"Preach a good sermon today?" Olbricht asked Josef.

While the women stepped into the kitchen, Josef followed his father-in-law through the parlor to the elder clergyman's study. Nowhere else did Josef feel such a strong sense of old Germany than when at the Olbrichts' house. The household operated under the caste system; everyone had his or her domain. To think of crossing into another's domain was vulgar, as though the universe itself would forever be altered should anyone be found where they didn't belong.

Wilhelm Olbricht's domain consisted of his study, his bedroom, and the parlor when they were entertaining guests. In all the years Josef had known the man, never once had he seen or heard of him frequenting any other than these three rooms.

Likewise, Edda moved and had her being supervising the household staff, sitting in the drawing room, or overseeing the cook. As a child, Mady was confined to her bedroom and the upstairs playroom. But when she grew older she was eventually invited to enter the parlor and socialize with the family's guests. To enter her father's study without his invitation was unthinkable.

"Josef?" Mady intercepted the two men just as they were about to enter the study. "Excuse me, Father," she said. "Josef, could you help me for a moment? The stove needs to be lit."

"That's Cook's job," Olbricht huffed.

"Cook is ill."

Olbricht harrumphed and continued on into his study, leaving Josef to deal with his wife.

"It'll only take a minute," Mady insisted, pulling on his arm.

———

When Josef returned to the study, Olbricht said nothing about the stove lighting. He did, however, have an amused smirk on his face. "How's the church treating you?" he boomed.

In Josef's absence Olbricht had lit a fresh cigar and was now reclining in his chair behind a massive, dark wood desk, his small hands behind his head. He had a bulldog face, round and pudgy, with sharp, intelligent eyes.

Set as a backdrop behind him was tier after tier of theological books. The allure of their titles had at times distracted Josef from his conversation with the elder minister.

To Josef's right, four stately cathedral windows stretched twelve feet high, floor to ceiling. Beyond the windows lay a well-manicured garden with fountains, walkways, and Edda's prized white rosebushes.

Josef settled into one of two familiar padded leather chairs opposite Olbricht. As he did, something caught his eye. There was a new addition to the room since he'd been there last. An oil painting of Adolf Hitler. Its size and brightness dominated the wall opposite the windows, and its presence in his mentor's study disturbed Josef more than he cared to admit.

Clearing his throat, Josef answered Olbricht's question. "The church is doing well," he said.

The standard ministerial response rolled off his tongue without so much as a thought of what he was saying. There was an unwritten code among clergy: No matter how much trouble a pastor's church was giving him, never should that pastor admit to another pastor that anything was wrong. An experienced man like Olbricht knew this.

"They're a good people," Olbricht proclaimed, utilizing a codicil to the unwritten code: Always speak well of the church that one formerly pastored, no matter the trouble that congregation had been. Just be glad they're someone else's problem. "They treated Edda and me well enough for thirty years. Be their pastor in season and out of season, and they'll forgive you most anything. Care for a cigar?"

Josef waved off the offer.

"How about the worship service?" Olbricht asked. "Anything unusual happen?"

"Why do you ask?"

Olbricht puffed and stared at him.

"Did someone call you?"

Olbricht's posture and expression remained unchanged.

"I was in the middle of my pastoral prayer when, out of the blue, drums began pounding outside the church," Josef said. He paused for a reaction. A hint of a smile tugged at the corners of Olbricht's mouth. Josef went on. "Not knowing what else to do, I kept praying, thinking that surely the drums would eventually quit. They didn't! The next thing I knew there were trumpets and shouts. My first thought was that the walls would soon come tumbling down."

Olbricht chuckled.

"Then they started singing. It got so loud that I could hardly hear the words of my own prayer!"

"The Hitler Youth," Olbricht said.

Josef nodded.

"They came to my church, too. Rallying the troops for Hitler's birthday celebration."

"And did your boys get up and leave in the middle of the service?" The pitch of Josef's voice rose. The anger he felt earlier was returning.

On the opposite side of the desk Olbricht puffed away on his cigar. His eyes were a pair of scales weighing the younger minister.

It felt strange to Mady to be treated as an adult in the house of her childhood. She couldn't begin to count the number of times she'd been shooed out of this very kitchen.

"This is no place for a little girl."

"The ingredients and the bowl are all there," Mother said, nodding in the direction of the cutting board. "The aprons are in the bottom drawer."

Edda smiled when she saw the way Mady's apron bulged.

One item at a time, Mady placed lettuce, cucumbers, radishes, and tomatoes on the cutting board, then quickly sliced and tossed them into a large crystal salad bowl.

Her mother checked the veal cutlets.

When Mady was growing up, her parents often served veal cutlets to their dinner guests. She could remember lying in her bedroom upstairs with the door half open and smelling the veal as she eavesdropped on the conversation of the guests downstairs. Now she was the dinner guest.

Picking up the thread of conversation she'd started earlier, Edda said, "The boys at church filed out of the worship service so proud and tall and straight. I have to admit when I first heard that drum banging, I thought your father would fly into one of his holy rages because they were interrupting his service. But he could see how proud the parents were of their boys."

"Father wasn't upset?"

Edda wiped her hands on her apron. "On the contrary, as soon as the boys had all gone, he offered a prayer on their behalf. A number of parents came up to him afterward and thanked him."

Mady turned her attention to the vegetables, hoping her mother wouldn't ask how Josef handled the same situation in their church.

"It was clearly designed to be a political statement," Josef said. "Just one more reminder that Hitler's agenda supercedes everything else, including the worship of God."

Olbricht chewed the end of his cigar thoughtfully.

"They could have waited until the services were concluded," Josef added.

Turning his head, Olbricht spit a piece of tobacco from the tip of his tongue. "Have you noticed my new painting?" he asked.

Josef glanced at the portrait of Hitler.

"A gift from a member of your church."

"Reichmann."

Olbricht let loose a booming laugh. "He's not the demon you believe him to be. He's a proud German. As for the picture . . . well, I haven't joined the Nazi Party, if that's what you're wondering. I use it as a talisman of sorts . . . to keep the evil spirits away . . . in this case, the SS and Gestapo."

"Aren't you afraid it will send the wrong message?"

"What message? We're Germans; he's our chancellor. It's as simple as that."

Josef wished it were that simple.

Olbricht puffed on his cigar. He leaned forward, his elbows resting on his desk. "I know it's difficult for you because of your father and mother and brother," he said. "But look at the way the German people have responded to him. Let's face it, Germans are not cut out to be a republic or a democracy . . . the Weimar Republic fiasco proved that once and for all. Germans have always honored strong leaders—father figures, if you will. Adolf Hitler, like him or not, is such a leader. If it weren't for the Jewish thing, he wouldn't be such a bad sort at all."

"The Jewish thing," Josef mused. "Not an easy thing to ignore."

"You're fortunate to have escaped Turnip Winter."

The statement hung in midair. Mady glanced at her mother. Edda was paused in thought, the wooden spoon in her hand dripping gravy. The memory that played in her head turned her face ashen.

"It started in the fall of 1917," she said, almost in a trance. "It was the coldest, most bitter winter I can recall. Entire families froze or starved to death, and the soup lines stretched on forever. Bread was made with turnips. The meat that was available in stores was half bone and half gristle, or it was crow, squirrel, sparrow, or woodpecker. Coal was more valuable than gold at the time. And shop owners lost their businesses, while wave after wave of young men straggled home from the front, defeated and depressed and looking for work. But there were no jobs.

"What did they find? Living conditions that were just as bad if not worse than what they'd just experienced in the trenches! Then, just when it seemed things couldn't get any worse, an influenza epidemic swept the nation. I lost two sisters and an aunt to the flu."

The kitchen fell silent for a time. The only sound was the *thunk-thunk-thunk* of knife against cutting board.

"The twenties weren't much better," Edda continued. "The banks closed in '23 when inflation made the mark worthless for anything except starting fires in kitchen stoves. I remember reading it would take four trillion German marks to equal a single American dollar."

Mady let out a low whistle.

"Do you remember Frau Faber?"

Mady shook her head.

"She used to make you little dolls out of string and newspapers that she had pulled from trash heaps. The newspapers were stained with food or oil, or who knows what. She'd give you the dolls at church, and as soon as she was out of sight, I'd take the filthy things away from you."

Mady laughed. "I don't remember that."

"Frau Faber had a good heart, and she was a well-educated woman. She meant well. Anyway, at one of our missionary circle meetings, she prayed for a leader who would combat unemployment, and hunger, and need. She prayed that God would send us a 'steel-hardened man' to lead us out of our dark national abyss."

Edda stirred her gravy.

"There are a growing number of people in our congregation," she said, "who believe Adolf Hitler is Frau Faber's steel-hardened man."

"Look at what he's done," Olbricht said. "He's made us proud to be Germans again! Let me tell you something, son"—Olbricht laid aside his cigar—"something inside a man dies when he hasn't worked for months, when he can't feed his wife and children and is forced to watch them deteriorate every day, all the while knowing there's not a blessed thing he can do to save them. I've looked into the eyes of hundreds of men who have done just that, and I tell you there's a hollowness there that's unnatural. Their eyes become tunnels stretching down into empty souls."

He picked up his cigar and leaned back in his chair.

"You don't forget something like that. And it's unreasonable to despise utterly any leader who has put bread on that man's table."

"Dear, if you'll carry the salad and bread to the table, I'll get the potatoes," Edda said. "Then, while I'm dishing the veal, you can call the men."

Cradling the crystal salad bowl with both hands, Mady backed into the swinging door that separated the kitchen from the dining room. When she returned for the bread platter, her mother's back was to the door. She was transferring the potatoes into a serving bowl, and, to Mady's amusement, she was conversing as though Mady hadn't left the room. Either that, or she was talking to the potatoes.

" . . . the Protestant Ladies Aid joyfully recognizes that God has established both Church and state. And while we wish to participate in the rebuilding of Germany, we believe that the Nazi leaders are socially inferior, confused, and inexperienced. At the same time, though, we applaud their emphasis on the German values of community and motherhood. Therefore, we have decided to offer our conditional loyalty to the state."

"That's where Niemoeller was wrong!"

Josef sat back and absorbed the verbal onslaught. It was characteristic Olbricht.

"He and that whole Pastor's Emergency League crowd," Olbricht continued, "but Niemoeller in particular. He was a U-boat commander during the war. A man like that knows better than to challenge the orders of a superior officer. That's why I split from him." Olbricht's eyes searched the ceiling for his next thought. When he'd found it, he said, "Think back a few years ago. You used to hear Hitler speak of God and Providence in his speeches. He even offered an occasional prayer, saying that it's God's grace we are once again proud to be Germans. It was only after Niemoeller challenged him publicly that he came down hard, like a father disciplining an openly rebellious son."

Josef was entering the fray late. While attending the university, he had followed with interest the actions of Martin Niemoeller and the Confessing Church. He admired their courage, but he questioned their effectiveness and the biblical basis of their tactics. He agreed with them that it's the church's duty to resist evil in the world; however, he disagreed when they chose to use the world's weapons to fight that evil. For Josef, the choice was an open admission that the church no longer believed in the power of the Spirit, and of prayer, to effect change in the world.

"And what of Niemoeller's effectiveness now?" Olbricht pressed. "What can he and the other pastors who have followed his lead do from a concentration camp at Dachau? What good are they to their congregations, or to Germany for that matter? How can a shepherd lead his flock from behind barbed wire fences?"

Mady surveyed the dining table as she passed by it on her way to the study. It was set with Mother's best silver and gold-plated china, Grandmother's lace tablecloth, and twin silver candelabras. This was the kind of life she dreamed about. A large house with a table set for influential guests, a pastor-husband, like Father, who was revered by the community, and for the women of the church to seek her counsel like they did her mother's.

Someday.

Then a new thought struck her. She imagined what it would be like for her daughter to come home for Sunday dinner with her husband. The mental image brought with it a shiver of excitement.

Beyond the swinging kitchen door, Mady could hear her mother going on about the Protestant Ladies Aid society. With a grin she wondered if someday her child would be as amused as she was to catch her mother talking to herself.

Josef pulled himself forward in his chair to make his point. "I grant you that Germany has made tremendous strides under the National Socialists. But at what price?"

Olbricht emptied his lungs of smoke hurriedly to answer. "For loyal Germans it's a reasonable price," he replied. "Hitler is predictable. I've studied his tactics. He moves quickly and presses beyond the bounds of public acceptance, then he waits to see who will react. If he deems the reaction manageable, he presses forward some more. All it will take to stop him is for a significant number of Germans to say, 'This far and no farther.' Then he'll back off. At that point a more reasonable agreement will be forged with the National Socialists."

"And who do you suppose will rally this significant number of

Germans that will confront him?" Josef asked.

Olbricht puffed his cigar. "God alone knows the answer to your question," he said.

"And in the meantime, what of native Germans like Professor Meyerhof? Is the price that's paid for this new Germany reasonable for them, too?"

At the mention of Meyerhof's name, Olbricht's face darkened, as if overshadowed by a summer squall. Then, as quickly as it appeared, it cleared. When he spoke next, his words were carefully measured. "While I can't say I approve of this administration's removal of the Jews, neither can I condemn it."

Josef couldn't believe what he was hearing. "How can you possibly . . ."

"The Jews are a detriment to our society. Relocating them to a land where they can live according to the dictates of their own customs is the humane thing to do. Better for them, better for us."

"And if they don't want to leave Germany?"

"When people are confused, sometimes as men of God we have to assist them to do what's best for all concerned. You being a pastor should know that. There's no longer a place for them here. It's our job to help them move on to a better place."

There was a finality in his voice, as definite as the sound of a lid closing on a casket.

"Besides," he continued, "throughout history the Jews have always been a resilient and resourceful people. I'm sure they'll reacquire all they've lost, and more. Just give them a few years."

Josef hadn't felt this uncomfortable in Olbricht's study since the day he broached the subject of marriage to Mady. It was a new sensation, and very distasteful.

The man sitting on the other side of the desk had been Josef's pastor when his father was murdered. Olbricht became like a father to him then and a spiritual mentor when Josef felt God's call to ministry. Later, he proved himself a supportive father-in-law, and now a grandfather to Josef's unborn child. There wasn't a man in Germany Josef respected more than Wilhelm Olbricht.

So if Olbricht had changed his thinking regarding the National Socialists, Josef knew the change hadn't come without careful thought. This realization alone gave him pause.

Olbricht broke the silence. "You're not thinking about doing anything foolish, are you?" he asked.

"What makes you say that?"

From the way Olbricht studied Josef, one would have thought there was playing cards and poker chips between them. Two quick puffs on the cigar and Olbricht anted up. "A phone call from a member of your congregation. Apparently there's growing concern among some of your church members over statements you've been making from the pulpit."

It had to be Reichmann. The man had been a thorn in Josef's side ever since he saw Meyerhof at the youth Christmas party. And it was no secret Reichmann still considered Olbricht to be his pastor.

Josef decided to up the ante. Reaching into his pocket, he pulled out a wrinkled slip of paper and tossed it onto the desk.

Olbricht unfolded the paper and read it aloud. " 'If you are indeed a friend of Luther, use the word *Bulwark* in a sermon and you will be contacted.' Who gave this to you?"

"Someone slipped it into my Bible when I wasn't looking."

"What does it mean, 'friend of Luther'?"

"I used Martin Luther in a sermon several weeks ago as an example of a man who stood up for what he believed regardless of who stood against him."

Olbricht cringed. "Does Mady know about this?"

"No."

"Good. Don't tell her." Olbricht thought a moment. "What have you done about it?"

"To this point, nothing."

"You're playing with fire," Olbricht said, tossing the slip of paper back to Josef.

However, Josef wasn't ready to fold. In truth, his sermon on Martin Luther had probably done more to strengthen his resolve than anyone's in his congregation. He decided to call Olbricht's hand. He said, "I'm not going to let men like Reichmann dictate to me what I will or won't do."

Olbricht studied him for several moments. "It wasn't Reichmann who called me," he finally said. He leaned forward and played his cards. "It was Mady."

Mady crossed the familiar parlor that held so many memories for her, mostly fond ones. Family and church gatherings. Opening presents at Christmas on the Oriental rug. Sitting alone with Josef on the sofa during their courting days. She could hear her father's voice through the open door at the far end of the room.

"Our politics is Germany! Our religion is Christ," he was saying. "Two separate realms, each with its own authority."

Mady reached the doorway. Her father was punctuating his point with characteristic jabs of his cigar.

Her father saw her. He beamed.

"Ah! And what message has this vision of motherhood been sent to deliver?"

Josef turned in his seat.

"Time for dinner, gentlemen."

Both men rose from their seats. As her father rounded the desk, he said to Josef, "Here's how I would advise you. Instead of viewing the Hitler Youth movement as a threat to your church, why not look for ways to incorporate their program into your church program? It will do you no good to oppose the movement. You'll only alienate your boys and their families."

Josef made a noncommittal sound.

"Have you ever attended one of their rallies?"

Josef shook his head.

"Start there! See for yourself what they are teaching your boys. You may be pleasantly surprised."

Another noncommittal grunt.

Placing his arm around Josef's shoulders, Olbricht pulled Josef close to him and spoke softly into his ear. "Remember. You're not just a pastor now. You're a husband and father, too. The things you do will have a direct effect on your wife and children."

Olbricht pulled away and slapped Josef three times heartily on the back. To Mady he gave a wink and said, "I'll just slip into the kitchen and see if your mother needs a helping hand."

As he left the study Mady and Josef stood for a moment in stunned silence. Wilhelm Olbricht in the kitchen! What was this world coming to!

Chapter 6

Monday, April 15, 1940

I t was one of those endless nights, the kind that seems to stretch on forever without giving so much as a nod to the existence of time. Josef had no idea how long he lay awake in bed. All he knew was that it felt like two nights had passed without the normal interruption of daylight.

A soft persistent moon cast a diamond pattern on the window curtains that rippled in a slight breeze, giving them an eerie resemblance to the surface of the sea.

Moonlight split the curtain panels and fell on the sleeping form of his wife, outlining her with a fluorescent silver-and-blue line that emphasized the bulge in her midriff where their unborn child was housed.

Mady lay on her back, her head turned slightly toward him. She hated sleeping on her back. Every night for the past two months as she twisted and turned from hip to hip, yanking the covers and manhandling her pillow, she told him how much she was looking forward to the day when she could sleep on her stomach again.

Josef preferred that she sleep on her back, though he was wise enough to keep this preference to himself. When she slept on her stomach, Mady had a tendency to bury her face in her pillow, and all he could see of her then was the back of her head and maybe an ear protruding from beneath her hair. When she slept on her back, he could gaze at her face for hours, which made eternal nights like this one bearable.

Mady wouldn't let him stare at her when she was awake. It made her self-conscious. In her words, men stared at women for one of two reasons: They found them attractive, or they thought them odd. And since Mady had long before convinced herself she was unattractive, despite Josef's persistent assurances to the contrary, his stares made her feel like a circus oddity.

Even after they were married, if she caught his eyes lingering on her, she became angry and depressed, and there was nothing he could do about it except ride out the resulting storm of moodiness that typically lasted two or three days.

So on nights like this one, as Mady lay asleep on her back, Josef indulged himself by allowing his gaze to rise and fall leisurely over her features. Tonight the sky's lesser light brushed her cheeks with an iridescent glaze. They were rounder than usual, a result of her pregnancy—one more reason for her to feel unattractive. Josef, however, adored her pregnant appearance. To him it was an expression of their intimacy, and he loved her for it.

Because he knew he didn't deserve her.

Had it not been for Olbricht taking him under his wing following his family's tragedy, Josef was convinced Mady never would have entertained the thought of him as a suitor. She fell in love with him only because her father loved him first.

Josef was the heir apparent, the one chosen to be molded into her father's image. She, on the other hand, was her father's only child, the little girl who wanted to grow up and marry a man just like Poppa. Sometimes Josef got the impression he'd been adopted rather than married.

There were times he wondered if Mady loved him at all. It wasn't that she treated him badly, she didn't. And it wasn't that they weren't close, they were. But theirs was a family closeness, not a romantic one. There was no passion in her eyes when she looked at him, no hunger—the kind of passion that drives couples mad while they're apart, that compels them to do reckless things just to be near each other; the kind of passion that keeps a person awake all night just so he can gaze upon the object of his heart's desire.

With the back of his fingers Josef gently caressed Mady's cheek.

It wasn't as though they had nothing in common. They both loved her father, didn't they?

Mady moaned, and Josef was afraid he'd awakened her. He withdrew his hand.

She threw off a blanket.

Once again Mady's breathing fell into a steady rhythm. Josef resettled himself. He sighed, still fully awake.

His tired eyes wandered back to Mady, to the bulge under which she labored. It was a curious mound, one that fascinated him. The thought that a living being was sleeping under that canopy of skin was almost too much to believe. Harder still was it to imagine what the boy—assuming it was a boy, of course—would look like when he grew up. Which of his parents would he resemble?

Josef hoped the boy would have his mother's eyes, though he wondered if they might be too feminine for a boy. Of course, there was the possibility he could look like his father. Hopefully without his Adam's apple. Josef hated his profile. It looked to him as if a hard-boiled egg had lodged itself in his throat.

There was also the chance the boy might resemble Edda, or . . .

Josef choked back a laugh. What if the boy looked like his grandfather? He envisioned a pink, plump infant with the face of a bulldog and a fat cigar protruding from a toothless mouth.

Please, Lord, if the boy gets anything from his grandfather, let it be his intellect.

The thought of Olbricht turned his mind to their conversation in the study and the portrait of Adolf Hitler. Of all locations, that was one of the last places he'd expected to see a portrait of Hitler! Seeing the portrait there had been about as disconcerting as . . .

well, as Wilhelm Olbricht strolling into the kitchen.

"Can't sleep?"

Mady's voice startled him. She blinked her eyes and stretched. "I can go to the study if I'm keeping you awake."

"Are you ill?" Her speech was slurred from sleep.

"Just thinking. Can't seem to convince my mind to shut down."

"About what?"

"Your father in the kitchen."

Though she was still shrouded in sleep, Mady grinned an impish grin. For every male there's an expression his lover can make that will melt him and turn him into her willing slave. For Josef, it was this grin.

"Father in the kitchen," Mady mused. "Never thought I'd see the day. But then, I never thought I'd see the day when I talked politics with my mother in the kitchen."

"Politics?"

Still not completely awake, Mady spoke in a flat monotone. "The Protestant Ladies Aid . . . conditional loyalty to the state . . . references to Hitler being the answer to Frau Faber's vision of a steel-hardened man . . . that's all she could talk about."

"Not *the Prophet* Frau Faber?"

"Don't make fun. It's not nice."

She stretched again, this time longer and with an accompanying groan.

Josef could smell the warmth of his wife's body, that familiar cuddling odor he loved when he'd spoon up against her and bury his nose against the nape of her neck.

"Did my father tell you he supported the Hitler Youth when they marched out of the worship service?" Mady asked.

"Supported them?"

"Prayed for them after they left. Mother said it made the parents proud."

Josef stared at the ceiling in thought. "Do you think I mishandled the situation in our church?" he asked.

Mady didn't respond immediately.

He looked over at her.

She lowered her eyes.

"You think I mishandled it."

"That's not for me to say."

"But your father handled it differently."

Mady stared down at the bed sheets.

"And you think his method was wiser than mine."

Her eyes raised. "Yes," she said softly.

That didn't surprise him. In fact, he wasn't sure he disagreed with her.

Mady edged closer to him. She placed a hand on his chest. It was warm. Comforting. "He's had more years of experience," she said. "It's not that what you did was wrong. It was . . . well, it was . . ." Her eyes moved side to side as she searched for the right word. "It was . . . confrontational."

"Confrontational?"

"Whereas my father found a way to make the most of an irritating situation, you drew a line in the sand that forced the congregation to take sides. Church member against church member. Neighbor against neighbor."

"Church against state."

"You've been doing that a lot lately. . . ." Her voice trailed off. It was evident she was uncertain about the new territory upon which she was now treading. "Like the coins at Christmas," she said.

"What about the coins?"

"They pitted child against parent. Herr Reichmann took them away from Konrad and Willi."

Josef rubbed his eyes. "It was never my intention . . ."

"But that's what ended up happening. Do you really think—" She stopped abruptly.

"Go ahead. Say it."

She debated silently with herself, then said, "You can't change the way things are with a handful of youth, Josef. All you're going to do is get them hurt, and not only them . . . but you, me, and our child, also." Tears came to Mady's eyes.

"Why haven't you told me all this before?"

"I was afraid."

"Afraid? Afraid of me?"

Mady began to weep now. Her words dissolved before they could form.

Josef pulled his wife against his chest and held her with only the bulge of their baby between them.

After a time, he said, "Your father thinks I should attend the Führer's birthday rally to see for myself what the boys are being taught in this Hitler Youth movement."

"It would mean a lot to the boys," Mady managed to say.

"In other words, you think I should compromise."

"Think of it as bridge building. Earn Herr Reichmann's trust and he'll back you like he backs my father."

Josef chuckled. "Maybe then he'll give me a portrait of Der Führer for my study."

"Josef!"

"I was joking!"

"See? You're not taking anything I say seriously!"

Josef could feel her resistance in his arms. "I'll go to the rally," he promised.

She remained stiff.

With his lips close to her ear, he repeated in a whisper, "I'll go to the rally."

Gradually, Mady relaxed.

The two of them lay cuddled in the dark long enough for Josef to think Mady had drifted back to sleep.

"Josef?"

"Huh?"

"One more thing?"

"Yes?"

"I really don't feel comfortable with Professor Meyerhof coming to our house to tutor you."

Chapter 7

Saturday, April 20, 1940

Dusk descended on Berlin like a celestial veil, muting the city's colors but not her spirits. A beehive of a crowd lined Unter den Linden, ten and twelve people deep, to get a glimpse of an endless procession of exhaust-belching tanks, transport trucks, and artillery field pieces as Germany flexed her military muscles for Der Führer's birthday.

Josef walked alone. It seemed he was the only person in the city not swept up by the patriotic fervor. Maybe it was all the hardware. He found roaring engines and clanking machines to be less than soul stirring.

Or maybe it was the changes. This wasn't his Berlin, not the one that had enchanted him since childhood. Unter den Linden, for instance, the grand old boulevard. For two and a half centuries, since the days of the Great Elector, Berlin's main street had been lined with Grimms' fairy-tale shade trees. Now they were gone. Uprooted to make tunneling easier for a new subway. Dignified patriarchs replaced with a quadruple row of upstart saplings.

Hands in pockets, Josef ambled down the boulevard, east toward the river. He passed the Switzerland House, a café for the fashionable, established by an Austrian court confectioner more than a century earlier. Shop windows displayed photos of Der Führer adorned with twig and flower garlands.

When he reached the Opernplatz, he slowed to a stop. The open square was situated between the Royal Library—or Kommode, as Berliners dubbed it for its resemblance to a chest of drawers—and the Opera House. It was here, seven years earlier, that Joseph Goebbels orchestrated the burning of 20,000 books deemed offensive to the Nazis. Students—some Josef grew up with—had danced like dervishes around the bonfire, shouting, "Burn Heinrich Mann! Burn Stefan Zweig! Burn Sigmund Freud! Burn Erich Kastner!"

To him the book burning seemed to typify the Nazi way. Attack and destroy everything with which you don't agree. He was beginning to regret that he'd come. But a promise was a promise.

Behind him the crowd lining the parade route erupted into cheers as music could be heard coming down the boulevard.

An amplified voice cut through the din. "Just as Jesus liberated mankind from sin and hell, so Hitler saves the German *Volk* from decay!"

Josef turned to see a familiar face. Standing in an open-air motorcar was Ludwig Muller, the National Bishop of Protestants, appointed to the post by Hitler himself. A former army pastor and devoted Nazi, the man had no theological credentials to qualify him for the position. He was appointed because of his early declaration that Hitler had been sent by God to save the nation in a time of peril.

"Jesus and Hitler were both persecuted," Muller shouted over the loudspeaker. "But whereas Jesus was killed on the cross, Hitler was elevated to the chancellorship. And while young Jesus renounced his teachers and was abandoned by his apostles, sixteen of Hitler's disciples died for their Führer. The apostles completed their crucified master's work. We hope that Hitler will be allowed to bring his own work to fruition. Jesus built for heaven; Hitler for the German earth!"

The crowd applauded. There was a spattering of *Heil Hitler*'s.

Muller ran one hand over his close-cropped hair, while the other pulled the microphone closer to his mouth. "A powerful nationalist movement has gripped and elevated our *Volk*," he cried. "We shout our thankful 'Yes!' to this historical turning point. God has sent it to us. Praise the Lord!"

Following Muller's motorcar were two hundred pastors sporting brown uniforms, riding boots, body and shoulder straps, swastikas, and medals of honor as well as Christian crosses. Josef recognized many of them. They promoted themselves as Germans with a swastika on their breasts and a cross on their hearts.

They sang a rousing hymn, an impressive male chorus as the parade continued.

No sooner had the pastors' chorus faded than the sound of another male chorus arose behind it, different from the first. These voices were higher in pitch and louder with enthusiasm. It was the sound of the Hitler Youth. Every meeting began and ended with a song. Folk songs. Patriotic songs. Marching songs. Traditional carols during Christmas.

The first of the Hitler Youth units appeared, marching down Unter den Linden on their way to the rally at the Lustgarten. With their right arms raised, they sang the Banner Song:

> Our banner flutters before us.
> Our banner represents the new era.
> And our banner leads us to eternity!
> Yes, our banner means more to us than death!

They were an impressive sight. Identical uniforms. Marching as one. Voices raised in chorus. Josef felt an involuntary shiver of patriotism.

Konrad Reichmann led the third unit. Strong and confident, he looked striking. Ernst and Neff marched side by side in the front row. Willi marched in a section of younger boys.

How different they looked. Josef was used to seeing them fidgeting in the church pews, engaged in horseplay outside the church, flirting with girls, and toppling the Christmas tree in his parlor.

Here they looked disciplined, proud, bold, German.

Josef's chest swelled for them. Tears, the kind a proud father gets, welled up in his eyes.

———

Every seat in the Lustgarten was taken. As darkness settled over the parade grounds, Josef felt himself fortunate to find a place to stand. It turned out that he had a good view of the parade. On his left, he stood shoulder to shoulder with a stout woman with a black hat, and on his right, a clean-shaven SA brownshirt. There was barely enough room for him, and his initial maneuvering into the spot had earned him hostile glances from both sides.

"I have four boys in the rally," he said, nodding toward the illuminated parade grounds.

The woman gave him a half smile; the man pretended not to hear him.

Stretched out before them was an expanse that once was the private gardens of the Great Elector. Like most Renaissance gardens, there had been both a kitchen garden and an ornamental garden. After acquiring numerous exotic species of plants over the years, Lustgarten had become Berlin's first botanical gardens, thus living up to its name, "pleasure garden."

But, like Unter den Linden, this Berlin jewel was later denuded by the National Socialists. As Josef looked over the open expanse, he realized there wasn't a tree or a bush to be seen now. The garden had been reduced to a parade area, which made him wonder what this said about the Nazi's definition of pleasure.

Sky-high vertical red banners loomed over both sides of the grounds, eighty of them in all, hanging in groups of five. In the center of each banner was a circle of white overlaid with a black swastika.

The colonnade of the old museum at the far end of the wide grounds rose majestically from side to side. Stone steps that spanned the length of the building served as the foundation for a speaker's platform upon which rested a podium with at least two dozen microphones sprouting from its top.

Abruptly the lights were switched off, turning the parade grounds into a large black patch. The columns of the old museum caught just a hint of the city's light. In the distance, the horizon had become a thin luminescent line. Unintelligible murmuring sounds rippled in anticipation around the edges of the Lustgarten.

The sound system came alive with a series of simple ascending trills. Wagner. "The Ride of the Valkyries."

With the sound of the first trumpet a spotlight hit a solitary figure on the edge of the blackness, a boy carrying a Nazi flag. The spotlight followed the boy as he marched onto the parade grounds.

With the second phrase of music came a second spotlight, this time to Josef's left. Another boy. Another flag.

A third musical phrase and a third spotlight. And on and on it went until a dozen spotlights followed a dozen boys and a dozen flags.

The music increased in volume. The boys now formed a single line the length of the grounds. Then darkness again, and a pause. Suddenly, the entire area was flooded with light and there, almost magically, filling the expanse stood row after row of Hitler Youth in perfect formation.

The throng of people went wild with applause.

As the music rose to a crescendo, the spotlights appeared once more, rising in perfect unison, like Valkyrie spirits ascending heavenward, until they met at a central point high over the Lustgarten and formed a gleaming dome of protection over the boys.

Josef's skin turned to gooseflesh.

The music stopped. There was a silent beat. Then, as one voice, hundreds of youth shouted, "HEIL HITLER!"

The crowd erupted with shouts and applause.

Not waiting for the applause to die down, the boys launched into a song—"*Es zittern die morschen Knochen*." Their unified voices rang with the clarity of a church bell.

> Today Germany listens to us;
> Tomorrow the whole world.

Today Germany is ours;
Tomorrow the whole world.

Bedlam.

Mothers. Fathers. Sweethearts. Grandparents. Friends. Clapping. Shouting. Jumping. Whistling. Waving. Smiling so hard they looked like they'd burst. Wiping tears from their eyes.

For those at the Lustgarten the memory of the bleak postwar days of suffering and defeat and hunger and privation was expunged. The heart of the German nation beat with pride again. It felt good to be German.

The lights went out.

A single spotlight fell on a small boy on the stone steps of the museum. He wore the same uniform as all the other boys standing in ranks. In his hand was a white piece of paper.

The force of the spotlight disoriented the boy for a moment. He shielded his eyes, then, listening to an unseen voice from offstage, he lowered his hand and made his way toward the podium. Stepping behind it, he disappeared completely.

The crowd chuckled.

For a long moment the boy remained hidden, while the spotlight featured what appeared to be an empty podium. Then his small face peered around the side of the podium.

Laughter rippled over the large gathering.

A brownshirt appeared from the darkness, hurrying down the steps to the podium, carrying a small stool. He lifted the boy onto it and then disappeared into the blackness.

The boy's blond head could barely be seen over the bank of microphones. The spotlight made his hair shimmer brightly, giving him the appearance of a woodland sprite.

A rustle of paper could be heard over the loudspeakers. Then a voice. High-pitched and young. "Thoughts on Der Führer," he said. "A poem."

Often you must feel alone, all by yourself,
When you think of the mission you must fulfill.

82

Your deeds are far beyond what others do.
Yet you seek still greater goals.
We can never reach your heights.
All we can do is follow down your way.
And our banner with its symbol of the sun
Is under your leadership, under your guidance.
Each word that you have given us,
Each look that you have sent our way,
Has cleansed us, led us,
Given new light to our lives' paths.

The rustle of paper signaled the end of the reading. The boy stepped down and started back the way he came.

The roar of the crowd, combined with shouts and whistles from the youth themselves, startled the boy. Then, realizing the reaction to his poem was favorable, he faced the crowd and bowed. And bowed again. And again. He didn't stop bowing until someone came to lead him offstage.

Josef laughed and clapped with the rest of the crowd. He wished Mady could have been here to see the boy's performance. She would have enjoyed it. To his surprise, he realized that his smile wasn't going away. He was having a good time. What's more, he was glad he came.

Next to the platform came a barrel-chested man dressed in the same uniform as the Hitler Youth, striding purposefully to the podium on stocky legs. His close-cropped hair framed his head like a helmet and complemented a boxlike jaw. He spoke in clipped sentences with authority, announcing the presentation of awards to the superior units of the Berlin area.

Awards were given to units from Spandau, Kreuzberg, and Treptow. The unit from Kreuzberg also won a citation in the older youth division, followed by Lichtenberg. That left only one presentation—the highest award.

Box-jaw said, "The final citation this evening goes to the unit that has proved itself outstanding over all other units in Berlin. This unit has been rated superior in all unit competitions including sporting events, the quality of their singing during marches, and Winter Aid collections. Both individually and as a unit they have shown exemplary conduct and achievement. Other Hitler Youth units would do well to emulate them." He looked down at the paper from which he'd read all the other winners. "The award for the outstanding Hitler Youth unit for 1939–40 goes to"—he paused—"Pankow Unit!"

The crowd rose as one with applause.

"Those are my boys!" Josef shouted to the man on his right. "Those are my boys!"

The man who'd been indifferent to him up until now suddenly came alive with praise and congratulations. Grinning, he pounded Josef repeatedly on the back.

Two hands grabbed Josef's arms and spun him around. He came face to face with the lady with the black hat. Her eyes sparkled with joy, her cheeks were red with hilarity. Joining in on the celebration, she bubbled over with congratulations.

On the parade grounds the Pankow unit became animated. Boys were jumping, shouting, laughing, slapping their knees and each other's backs. Josef could see Neff and Ernst doing a little dance. Willi came running up from the back ranks to join them, while Konrad marched proudly toward the podium to accept the award on behalf of the unit.

From the podium, Box-jaw said, "Earlier this week, Konrad Reichmann, who will receive the award for the Pankow unit, was awarded first place in his boxing weight division!"

This was the first Josef had heard of Konrad's achievement.

When Konrad reached the podium, the man with the box-jaw greeted him and shook his hand enthusiastically. A medal was placed around Konrad's neck, and he was handed a banner that identified Pankow as the outstanding Hitler Youth unit of the year.

A line of buglers appeared on the museum steps. Draped on their instruments were flags bearing the ancient Germanic Sig-Rune ⚡, symbolic of victory. The sound of the bugles split the air like lightning.

Across the parade grounds, a sea of brown shirts tossed like waves in a tempest. Everyone in the stands was shouting and cheering and clapping as Konrad marched back to his unit. When he reached them, he was engulfed by the other boys in the Pankow unit.

Josef felt more than proud. His heart beat with excitement for their achievement. Glancing around, he charted a route whereby he could meet up with them following the rally. He couldn't wait to tell them how proud he was of them.

As the celebration continued, the man on his right and the woman on his left chatted exultantly as though the three of them had been friends all their lives.

Suddenly the lights went out.

Josef looked anxiously around him, urging his eyes to adjust to the darkness. Sensing his anxiety, the man next to him whispered, "Der Führer."

A lone spotlight hit the podium. Standing behind it was a tall man, thin to the point of being gaunt, his cheeks hollow, his eyes sunken, possibly exaggerated by the stark lighting. This was not Der Führer.

"Baldur von Schirach," the man on Josef's right whispered. "He's the head of the Hitler Youth. He'll introduce Der Führer."

Schirach's voice boomed over the loudspeakers. "At your command, my Führer, stand here a youth—a youth that does not know class and caste. Because you are the greatest example of unselfishness in this nation, this young generation wants to be unselfish, too. Because you embody the concept of fidelity for us, we want to be faithful, too. Adolf Hitler—the leader of the German youth and people!"

Everyone was on their feet, cheering wildly.

Once again, everything went black. In the darkness the "*Badenweiler Marsch*" played. It was the regimental march of Hitler's war unit and was now used for the official arrival of the chancellor.

A tightly focused beam of light hit the left side of the museum steps. An open motorcar appeared, driving slowly. Seated in the backseat was Der Führer.

As the motorcar pulled to a stop, Der Führer exited and strode up the steps to the podium and took his place a few feet behind it, facing the crowd.

The noise in the Lustgarten jumped many decibels, to a louder sound than Josef had ever heard before. Der Führer stood stoically behind the podium, his hands folded in front of him.

The woman next to Josef grabbed his arm to steady herself.

The man on Josef's right leaned toward him and shouted over the applause, "I hear he leads a Spartan life. Vegetarian. Teetotaler. Doesn't smoke. Celibate." The man gave a nod and a wink, giving approving emphasis to this last characteristic.

Josef had heard as much.

Adolf Hitler stepped to the podium. The light upon him was a dazzling nimbus, shimmering as if he'd been touched by the radiance of heaven. He loomed over the crowd. The podium became the bow of his ship of state, a magical prow that launched him into the human tide below.

The crowd quieted.

He began in a low, almost indistinguishable voice that at first made him seem unsure of himself. Josef leaned forward to hear.

As a physical presence, Der Führer appeared unimpressive. He looked smaller than Josef had imagined him to be—Josef estimated a little more than five and a half feet—with wide hips and thin, short legs. Clearly he couldn't have met the entrance requirements for his own elite guard.

While it was difficult to see them clearly from where Josef stood, the man's pale blue eyes were legendary. Party lore was rife with testimony to his riveting gaze. One tale told of an anti-Nazi police officer assigned to control the crowd at an early Hitler rally. The man was so affected by a single transfixing look from Der Führer that he promptly joined the party. In fact, the German dramatist, Gerhart Hauptmann, described his first gaze into Der Führer's eyes as the greatest moment of his life.

Josef was drawn back to Der Führer's words as he began to speak with more intensity.

"Long ago you heard the voice of a man and it struck your hearts, it awakened you, and you followed that voice. You followed it for years, without so much as having seen him whose voice it was; you heard only a voice and you followed. I feel you, and you feel me! It is faith in our nation that has made us, a small *Volk*, great; that has made us, a poor *Volk*, rich; that has made us, a vacillating, dispirited and anxious *Volk*, once again brave and courageous. A voice that has made us, who had gone astray, able to see—able to join together."

The crowd clapped enthusiastically.

Josef was taken aback by the man behind the podium. He looked like he could be someone's uncle. His tunic was austere. He wore no shoulder boards or collar tabs. His appearance was that of a simple soldier.

"It is our wish and will that this State and this Reich shall endure in the millenniums to come. We can be happy in the knowledge that this future belongs to us completely."

Applause.

"While the older generation could still waver, the younger generation has pledged itself to us and is ours, body and soul!"

The parade grounds erupted. "Heil! Heil! Heil! Heil!"

"We do not want this nation to become soft. Instead, it should be hard and you will have to harden yourselves while you are young. You must learn to accept deprivations without ever collapsing. Regardless of whatever we create and do, we shall pass away, but not you. Germany will live on, and when nothing is left of us you will have to hold up the banner which some time ago we lifted out of nothingness."

Sustained applause, louder on the parade grounds.

"You cannot be but united with us. And when the great columns of our movement march victoriously through Germany today, I know that you will join these columns. And we know that Germany is before us, within us, and behind us!"

"Heil! Heil! Heil! Heil!"

"In our eyes, the German boy of the future must be slim and slender, as fast as a greyhound, tough as leather, and hard as Krupp steel."

Hitler was warming to his theme now and becoming more fluent.

"I promise you a new Reich on earth!" he shouted.

Cheers.

"The German form of life is definitely determined for the next thousand years! For us, the nervous nineteenth century has finally ended. There will be no revolution in Germany for the next one thousand years."

Cheers. Louder and longer.

Hitler lifted his face and fist heavenward.

"Lord, let us never be weak or cowardly. Let us never forget the duty that we have taken upon ourselves! We are proud that God's grace has enabled us once again to become genuine Germans!"

"Amen," Josef said.

The man beside him clapped hysterically; the woman held a hand to her breast and looked up at the speaker, her face transformed as though she were seeing a vision of the Messiah.

The transformation that gripped her had now gripped the entire crowd. As Hitler swayed side to side, his audience swayed side to side. The crowd surged beneath him like a gigantic wave.

"Ultimately, the individual man is weak in all his nature and actions when he acts contrary to almighty Providence and its will. But he becomes immeasurably strong the moment he acts in harmony with Providence! Then there pours down upon him that force which has distinguished all the great men in the world."

"Yes!" Josef shouted. "Yes!" His enthusiasm felt buoyant, carried along by the rising tide of the crowd's emotions.

Hitler's voice grew steadily louder as the tempo increased. Perspiration streamed down the Führer's face. His gestures became sharp and emphatic.

"A writer has summed up the impressions made on him by this time in a book which he entitled *The Decline of the West*. Is it then really to be the end of our history and of our peoples?"

"NO!" the crowd shouted in reply.

"No! We cannot believe it. This age must be called, not the decline of the West, but the resurrection of the peoples of this West of ours! Only that which was old, decayed, and evil perishes; and let it die! But new life will spring up. Faith can be found, if the will is there. Our leadership has the will, and faith is with the people."

"Heil Hitler! Heil Hitler!"

"When I came to power, my fellow citizens, Germany was divided and impotent internally, and outwardly the sport of foreign designs. Today we are in order domestically. Our business is flourishing. Abroad perhaps we are not loved, but respected. Yet we receive attention! That is the decisive factor! Above all we have given the greatest possible good fortune to millions of our fellow citizens—the return into our Greater German Reich."

"Heil Hitler! Heil Hitler! Heil Hitler! Heil Hitler!"

Josef's German spirit stirred. He could not keep still.

"If in the future you continue to stand behind me as one man, in loyalty and obedience, no power in the world will be able to destroy this movement. It will continue its victorious course. If you preserve the same discipline, the same obedience, the same comradeship, and the same unbounded loyalty in the future—then nothing will ever extinguish this movement in Germany. This is the request I make of you, for myself and in the name of all the comrades who are no longer among us."

"Yes . . . yes!" Josef said, his eyes fixed solely on the speaker. At that moment there was no one else in the Lustgarten, just two patriots of equal passion, connecting, sharing a vision of what their country might be.

"There are those who would attempt to thwart our plans for a greater Germany. Shall we permit this?"

"NO!"

Josef added his voice to the thunderous response of the crowd.

"There are those who would deny us our birthright, our home-land, our destiny. Shall we let them?"

"NO!" Josef shouted with the crowd.

"Ein *Volk!*" Hitler shouted.

"EIN *VOLK!*"

"Ein Reich!"

"EIN REICH!"

"Ein Führer."

"EIN FÜHRER!"

The Lustgarten came alive with people shouting jubilantly, thrusting forth their arms in salute to their leader.

Hitler repeated the trilogy. "One people. One country. One leader."

There were no individuals in the Lustgarten. They were a united people. There was no longer a woman at Josef's left and a man at his right; there were three Germans and their leader, swept away by their devotion to their country.

"Sieg Heil! Sieg Heil! Sieg Heil!"

Josef's arm was raised with the rest of them.

"Sieg Heil! Sieg Heil! Sieg Heil!"

Tears coursed down his cheeks.

"Sieg Heil! Sieg Heil!"

His voice grew hoarse, yet he couldn't stop shouting.

"Sieg Heil! Sieg Heil! Sieg Heil!"

Never before had he felt more alive, more full of purpose, more proud to be German.

"Sieg Heil! Sieg Heil! Sieg Heil! Sieg Heil!"

Chapter 8

Friday, April 26, 1940

Is he a Nazi now?"

"If you're asking if I have to salute and say 'Sieg Heil!' before I can kiss him, the answer is no."

Lisette laughed at Mady's remark.

The two of them stood in a line that snaked around a downtown corner. They held meat ration coupons in their hands. Even though it was spring, the mornings were still brisk in the shadow of the multistory brick building. Both women wore heavy wool coats and coverings on their heads. Mady couldn't understand why ration lines couldn't be formed in the sunlight.

"To hear Pastor Schumacher preach Sunday," Lisette said, "you'd think he'd just been promoted minister of Nazi propaganda."

Mady smiled. "My husband never does anything halfheartedly," she said.

"It's his passion that attracts me to him," Lisette said. When she realized what she'd said, her cheeks, already pink from the chill, turned flaming red. "I mean as a minister," she sputtered. "His *religious* passion attracts me to him . . . as a Christian. You know how many ministers become disillusioned. . . ."

Mady placed a hand on Lisette's arms, which she'd folded defensively across her bosom. "I understand what you meant."

With a weak smile, Lisette relaxed, although the color still lingered in her cheeks.

Mady liked this girl. Though she was barely four years older than Lisette, she felt motherly toward the girl. In return, Lisette gave Mady the respect due a minister's wife, one of the few women in the church who did.

Mady shifted from one swollen foot to the other. Her back ached horribly. The weight she'd gained over these last couple of months made ration lines less endurable.

"I wish you'd let me stand in line for you," Lisette said.

"The other people in line would never permit it."

"At least let me get you a chair."

"I'll be all right."

But Lisette had already left the line and disappeared around the corner. She returned minutes later, carrying a white patio chair. "Here," she said as she set it down in line.

The women in line looked at the chair, then at Mady's condition. Approval was given by looking away; scowls registered disapproval.

Two women behind them muttered. "When I was in her condition, I didn't get to sit all day," one said.

"In lines twice this long," said the other.

Mady felt conspicuous. "Maybe you should return the chair."

"It's from a café around the corner. I got permission," Lisette said.

A stocky man with a heavy mustache poked his head around the corner of the building and searched the line. Lisette waved to him. He looked at Mady, smiled, and waved back.

"Herr Freisler!" Lisette called. To Mady, she said, "His daughter is expecting a child. She lives in Munich."

"You know him?"

"I do now."

As the line moved, Lisette would help Mady up, move the chair for her, then assist her into it again. Mady felt like a beached whale flopping toward the ocean inch by inch.

They rounded the corner. Only a half block more and they would be at the butcher's shop.

"Konrad and the others were surprised that Pastor Schumacher attended the rally," Lisette said.

"Were they?"

"So was I. I thought Pastor Schumacher didn't approve of the Hitler Youth."

Mady smiled. "You'd think so from his outburst two Sundays ago."

"Then why did he go?"

"After talking to my father, he had a change of heart."

"Dr. Olbricht talked him into going?"

"Father convinced him there was room for compromise."

"Dr. Olbricht thinks we should compromise with the Nazis?"

Mady felt the barb in the question. "While Pastor Schumacher is still not fond of the Nazis," Mady explained, "he developed an admiration for Der Führer at the rally."

A troubled expression darkened Lisette's face.

"My father has a wisdom that comes from years of experience in these things," Mady said.

Lisette nodded and looked away.

"You don't agree," Mady said.

"It's not my place to agree or disagree."

"But something's bothering you. Tell me."

The young girl glanced at the women who were standing in line immediately behind them. When she spoke, her voice was no more than a whisper. "I like the way Pastor Schumacher was before," she said.

Mady didn't reply right away. Her silence drew an explanation.

"The things he said Sunday. I'm afraid he's given in to them. For me, he's always been a rock in the storm."

"Sometimes it's better to be a reed," Mady said.

"Is it?"

Mady felt her face beginning to flush.

"It's just that, to me, Pastor Schumacher has always been Germany's Apostle Paul. And by giving in like he has . . . well, it seems like he's abandoning his faith."

Her words stung. Anger worked its way through Mady's system. She tried salving the wound with reason. The girl was young, idealistic. Life seems so much clearer at age eighteen. Wait until she has a husband and child on the way and see if she still feels the same way.

What could a young girl know of the agony she went through every time Josef was late coming home? Dealing with mental images of his arrest and torture? Knowing that all it took was a little boy's accusation and Josef might never come home at all? Lisette saw only the figure behind the pulpit. To her Josef was some kind of storybook hero. Well, Mady had to deal with the reality. And she would do whatever it took to see that her family and child were safe.

Without being aware of it, Mady began chewing the ends of her hair.

"Are you angry with me?" Lisette asked. Her eyes were wide and threatening tears. "Did I say something wrong?"

"All of a sudden I'm feeling tired," Mady said, placing a hand on her stomach. "Someday, you'll understand."

"I didn't mean to offend you or Pastor Schumacher," Lisette said. "If I did, please forgive—"

"The line's moving," Mady said.

Lisette started to help Mady up.

"I'm all right," Mady said. "You go on ahead."

It took two efforts for Mady to get to her feet. She dragged the chair behind her. With the gap in the line closed, she leaned on the back of the chair.

"Would you like me to help you sit down?"

"I think I'll stand for a while," Mady said.

Fifteen minutes later the line in front of them began to dissipate to the sound of moans and curses. The supply of meat had run out for the day.

———

How could a man who spoke so eloquently of God and country be the leader of a party with a reputation for hatred and naked aggression?

Josef sauntered down Klaustaler Strasse alone, his hands in his pockets, pondering this riddle. Night was well established over Pankow. The sky was clear, the stars shimmered, and the air was clean and fresh and crisp. Moonlight glistened on the rounded cobblestones that paved his way with hundreds of luminous crescents.

While the enchanting effects of the Hitler rally were beginning to fade now, the repercussions of his attendance and his comments afterward were snowballing. You would have thought Der Führer had presented him with an award.

Mady was happier than he'd seen her since the day of their wedding. She had listened eagerly as he described the rally to her, smiling the entire time, obviously pleased with his reassessment of Adolf Hitler. She was flirtatious, cuddly, and amorous, despite her expectant condition.

Response from other quarters was no less surprising. Dr. Olbricht had slapped him on the back and called him a true church statesman. Rupert Reichmann, Konrad and Willi's father, shook his hand warmly following Sunday morning services, something he hadn't done in months. And the boys themselves—Konrad, Willi, Ernst, and Neff—had approached him *en masse* and told him how much his being at the rally meant to them.

So why did he feel so miserable?

Of course, during the morning worship service he made a big fuss over the boys, their award, and Konrad's individual achievement. The congregation, for the most part, couldn't have been prouder of the boys, and the fellowship that day seemed sweeter than any other day of his ministerial career.

In the past week he'd made greater progress with the church than he had in the entire year preceding it. It appeared that at long last the foundation he sought to lay between pastor and people was solidifying.

So then why did he feel like a modern-day Judas?

He turned the corner to Galenusstrasse. In the distance three silhouetted figures were rolling a large bag of some sort out of the street with their feet. Whatever was in the bag was heavy. It rolled reluctantly. The men who rolled it were exerting themselves. Josef could hear them grunting.

The three men were inching their load toward the Panke River. A wisp of a breeze rose off the river, carrying with it the damp odor of moss and dirt.

Josef quickened his pace. It looked like the three men could use some help. Maybe playing the Good Samaritan would improve his mood.

As he drew closer, he saw that the three men wore Hitler Youth uniforms. A patrol force. And there was something else. Something about the bag. Something was falling out of it. A ball or melon of some sort. Shiny. Its smooth surface caught the moonlight.

Josef's next breath caught in his throat. It wasn't a melon. It was a man's head! What Josef thought was a bag was the man's coat and baggy trousers. Between the thud of each kick, Josef could now hear whimpering sounds. The man was pleading with the Hitler Youth to stop kicking him.

The Good Samaritan within Josef wavered. If he interceded, the jackals would most surely turn on him. Up to this point they were so preoccupied with kicking the man on the ground, they weren't yet aware of Josef's presence. He could easily retrace his steps, slip back around the corner onto Klaustaler Strasse, and take another route home.

That would be the smart thing to do.

The best thing to do.

"Stop that!" he yelled at the attackers. He never was one to do the smart thing.

The jackals turned their attention toward him. Was it his imagination, or did their eyes glow in the dark?

He closed the distance between them, knowing that he was striding toward a beating. He hoped that this act of bravado might give them pause.

It didn't.

One of them came toward him.

Josef was close enough now to piece things together. The man on the ground was elderly. Visible between the folds of his coat was a single point of the yellow Star of David. Josef was close enough to see something else. One of the members of the patrol force was Konrad Reichmann.

The attacker who had separated from the others never stopped but ran right into Josef, giving him a stiff shove, nearly bowling him over.

Josef smelled cheese and onions. What was it about Nazi bullies and their breath? Were they trained to use onion or garlic or liver breath as a form of intimidation?

Josef braced for another assault. He didn't brace hard enough. A blow doubled him over, taking his breath away. Then a forearm straightened him back up and lifted him off his feet. He landed with a heavy thump on his tailbone, which jarred his entire skeletal structure and snapped his jaw shut. Josef tasted blood. He fought for breath. Two kicks to his ribs thwarted his effort. Josef felt himself rolling on the street just as the other man had done when Josef came upon them.

A shout stopped the attack.

The voice was Konrad's.

He stood beside his buddy and looked down at Josef. It took Josef several attempts before he could corral enough breath to talk.

"Good evening, Konrad," he wheezed.

"You know him?"

"He's the pastor of my church."

From the distasteful look on the attacker's face, Josef's occupation failed to register any sympathy.

He stretched out his hand to Konrad.

"What are you doing here?" Konrad asked, ignoring Josef's hand.

"Exercising my rights as a German citizen," Josef replied. He glanced across the cobblestones at the other prone figure who was, at the moment, disturbingly still. The third member of the patrol force stood over his victim like a predator would a carcass. "Is this how you use your prize-winning boxing skills?" Josef asked. "To beat up old men?"

"Shut your mouth!" Konrad's buddy yelled. He cocked his foot, but Konrad pulled him back before it went off.

"Let's go," Konrad said.

From the look on his buddy's face, there were still some pent-up kicks left in him that he was aching to unload. But he yielded to Konrad and backed off. The two of them turned their backs on Josef and walked away.

Josef struggled to his feet. He tried to straighten himself but couldn't. It hurt too much. So he stood bent over. "Konrad!" he shouted.

Konrad stopped and faced him.

Their eyes locked. Every inch of Konrad's stance remained that of a fighter, his face was stone.

Josef looked past the posturing. "You're better than this," he said.

"Let's get out of here," Konrad growled.

Josef stumbled over to the other victim, who was so disheveled it was difficult to see the man among the pile of rags. Wincing back his own pain, Josef knelt beside him and turned him over so that the man was face up. "Professor Meyerhof!" he cried.

The professor's breathing was shallow and his body as limp as his clothing. His eyes fluttered and attempted to focus but then closed again.

"Professor Meyerhof!"

The old man's lips moved without purpose, as though they'd forgotten how to form words.

"Rest easy," Josef said. "I'll get you to your house."

He didn't waste his energy or Meyerhof's by asking why the patrol force had beaten him. The yellow Star of David was a standing invitation to be punched, kicked, or otherwise abused.

Meyerhof's eyes blinked and stayed open this time. His pupils darted with fright. Beneath the pile of clothes his body tensed.

"Easy, Professor, easy . . . it's me," Josef said.

The professor's eyes focused on Josef's face.

Josef didn't rush him. After a time they registered recognition.

Meyerhof spoke. His voice sounded like it had been dragged up from an abandoned well.

"Rumor has it," he said, "you've become a Nazi."

Chapter 9

Meyerhof slipped in and out of consciousness as Josef half-carried, half-dragged the professor to his house three blocks distant. Stumbling up the pair of steps leading to the front door, Josef balanced the elderly man against his hip and reached for the door latch. The door was locked.

"Key," Josef said to Meyerhof. "Where's the key?"

The professor's eyes were closed. He gave no indication of having heard the question.

With his free hand Josef rummaged around in the professor's clothing, looking first for a pocket and then a key.

The door to the residence flew open.

"What do you want?" a bare-chested man shouted. "Get away from my door, or I'll call the police!"

Confusion clouded Josef's mind as he struggled to take in the man blocking the doorway—short, balding, flabby chest carpeted with salt-and-pepper hair, pants, no shoes, eyes bulging with a mixture of fear and anger.

This was Meyerhof's house. Josef was certain of it. Well, almost certain. It was one of those moments when he knew he was right, but now after having been challenged, he doubted himself despite his certainty.

"Are you deaf?" the man shouted. "Move along!" He took a step forward. His belly hung over the waistline of his pants, a pair of suspenders dangled limply against his leg. He turned slightly, and Josef saw that he held a hefty piece of wood in his hand like a club.

"This is the Meyerhof residence, isn't it?" Josef asked.

The man squinted to take a better look at Josef's burden. He seemed to recognize the professor. "In the back!" the man growled, motioning with a jerk of his thumb. The door slammed shut.

Josef fought back the urge to knock on the door again and ask if the man wouldn't mind helping carry the professor around to the back of the house. It was the same urge that prompted him to shout at the Hitler Youth, a dangerously sarcastic urge that he knew would one day be his undoing.

Repositioning his human bundle, Josef stumbled down the steps and dragged the professor around to the back of the house. He found a back door unlocked. It led to a room off the enclosed porch that Eva Meyerhof had used as her canning pantry. Now, instead of canned preserves stacked in neat rows on the shelves, the shelves were crammed with bundles of clothes and papers and books and postcards and shoes and cans and tools and toilet articles. Food sacks hung on ropes from open beams.

Josef recognized some of the items. The anniversary clock from the fireplace mantel. Meyerhof's pipe tree that used to sit on the edge of the professor's desk was now wedged sideways between folded sweaters and a stack of newspapers. The professor's library that once lined his personal study was now stacked high in corners and was situated to form a makeshift desk atop which lay an open Hebrew Bible, some writing paper, and a pen.

On one side of the pantry there was a bed fashioned out of boxes—some of them looking like they'd been opened with an ax—with two blankets, one for the bedding and another for the covers.

A bundled-up pair of pants served as a pillow.

Josef lowered the owner of all these things onto the bed of boxes, laying his head on the folded pants and covering his feet with the top blanket. He looked around for some water or drink of some kind, but all he could find was a basin of old shaving water with whiskers floating in it. A razor, brush, and bar of shaving soap lay next to it.

Meyerhof moaned.

Josef turned toward the professor and, in doing so, knocked down a stack of books and newspapers, so close were the quarters.

"Welcome to my estate," Meyerhof said weakly.

"Rest easy, Professor. You're safe now," Josef said.

"Do you remember the children's game, Kick the Can?" the professor asked. His voice was raspy. "Now I know how the can feels."

"Is anything broken?"

"Nothing that eternity can't heal."

Josef looked around for medical supplies. He was afraid to touch anything lest the stacks topple down on both of them.

Meyerhof spoke to him in Hebrew.

Josef grinned. "Not as much as I should be," he answered. "I've been rather busy."

"Not too busy to become a Nazi."

Josef flinched. "I'm not a Nazi."

"That's not what the goose-stepping crowd is saying."

"They're wrong."

"Imagine that."

Josef shuffled his feet. "Professor, this isn't the time."

"Succumbing to rhetoric, are we? The little man with the mustache is a good speaker; I'll give him that. Have you noticed that he always speaks at night, when people are more susceptible to suggestion? Uses plenty of patriotic music and children and awards to soften resistance. Plans the lighting for dramatic effect. Speaks passionately of eternal values. Sprinkles in a few references to Providence. Gives the people what they want to hear, then calls them to sacrifice to achieve the dream of peace while he makes war."

Josef stared at the professor. It was an astute perspective for one lying on a makeshift bed in a pantry.

"Reminds me of my first motorcar," Meyerhof said. "Bought it at night. Listened to the owner talk about all the good times he'd had in the motorcar. Watched him run a loving hand over the fenders. Listened as he told me how much he was going to miss it. Of course, I fell in love with it, too. Imagine my surprise the next morning. The motorcar didn't look nearly as attractive in the light of day. And when I tried to start it, I thought it would never turn over. When it finally did, it clunked and shuddered and belched smoke and backfired horribly." Meyerhof winced as he repositioned himself. "It was then that I realized I'd been seduced into buying a rattletrap."

Josef didn't know which affected him the most, the point of the professor's story or the theater in which it was performed.

"They took away your house," Josef said.

"I am no longer allowed to own property," the professor said. "My name is on a housing list at the Jewish Community Center. Until something becomes available, I have been granted this pantry." He shrugged painfully. "It's a place to sleep. What hurts is that they took away my occupation. What is a teacher without pupils?"

Meyerhof's eyes closed. He drew in a ragged breath. His eyes opened again, with effort.

"This isn't so bad," he said, waving his hand at the clutter in which he was entombed. "I still have my books. It just takes a while to unearth the ones I'm looking for."

Josef's eyes skittered up and down the stacks of books, recognizing the titles that had once inhabited the professor's study.

"Worst of all is the loneliness," he said. "I miss my Eva."

Josef nodded in sympathy.

"Three years without her . . ."

"She was a godly and wise woman."

There is a soberness that can drain a man's face of hope and joy and life itself, a soberness of expression that is so stark, it's painful to look at. Josef hurt to see the professor's anguish.

The professor leaned forward to reach a framed picture that was propped on top of a stack of books. He handed it to Josef.

Josef handled the picture with the same care as the professor. The photograph was comprised of four faces. Josef recognized them all. The professor's Eva and Edda Olbricht were in the center. They were leaning against each other, their heads touching. On either side of them, like gargoyle bookends, were the professor and Olbricht, as usual with a cigar protruding from his mouth.

"They were schoolgirl friends," the professor said of the women in the picture.

"Really? I thought you became acquainted with the Olbrichts through the church."

Pointing at the picture, the professor said, "Those two were practically raised together, their families were so close."

For several moments the professor sat in silent memory. Josef gave him all the time he needed, by keeping his eyes fixed on the photograph. They all looked so young. And just by the way Edda and Eva held each other it was easy to see that they'd had a close relationship.

"Did you know that Eva loved the cinema?" the professor said.

"No, I didn't."

"There was one movie in particular . . . a circus film . . ." He thought for a moment. "*Wandering Folk!*" he recalled, "and another . . . *The Four Journeymen*. Those were two of her favorites. They were good movies from both a literary and an acting aspect. Do you get to the cinema often?"

"Can't say that we do."

"Pity. We found that the theater was a good diversion from reality. But then I imagine that's why you attend Herr Hitler's rallies."

Josef wanted to say something. To defend himself.

" 'Ye shall know them by their fruits,' " the professor said.

"Matthew, chapter seven, verses fifteen and sixteen. 'Beware of false prophets, which come to you in sheep's clothing, but inwardly they are ravening wolves. Ye shall know them by their fruits.' If I were you, dear boy, I'd stop listening to what is said and pay more attention to what is being produced."

"Will you be all right?" Josef asked. "Is there anything I can get you before I leave?"

"I haven't dismissed class yet," the professor said brusquely. "Over there," he motioned to the stacks that served as his desk. "On the far side of the Bible. That sack. Bring it to me."

Josef found a brown sack and handed it to the professor.

"It's a matter of perspective."

The professor held the bag in Josef's face.

"Perspective," he said again.

He reached inside and pulled out a small booklet with a picture of a kitten on the cover. A red circle with a swastika was positioned prominently in the upper right corner. The title of the booklet was *The Care of the German Cat.*

The professor's eyes lit up. "Impressive, no?" He thumbed the pages. "The Reich director has an essay in this booklet written in grand political style. He explains that cat clubs are now a Reich association and that only Aryans are allowed to join."

Tossing the booklet aside, he reached into the bag again. This time he pulled out a red rubber ball with a swastika on it.

"An official Nazi children's ball," he said. "No doubt of superior design and of higher purpose than an ordinary red rubber ball."

Setting the ball aside, he reached into the bag a third time and pulled out a tube. It, too, bore a swastika.

"Official Nazi toothpaste!" he laughed. "Just like Adolf Hitler uses. What do you think of my collection?"

Josef was speechless.

The professor's face sobered. The teaching moment was at hand.

"When you think you've lost it all. When the oppression becomes more than you can bear. Think of this tube of Nazi toothpaste. The absurdity of it all will put everything into perspective. There is nothing man can take from us that God will not replace a thousandfold."

Chapter 10

Wednesday, May 1, 1940

Josef put it off as long as he could.

He thought of little else all weekend—except for the countless times Mady called him to light the stove. He considered addressing the extremist measures of the Third Reich from the pulpit, but went instead with his planned sermon on the post-Resurrection appearances of Jesus. He wanted to say something every time he saw Konrad—sitting in the pew, at the opposite end of a hallway, with Neff and Ernst out by the motorcars—but the opportunity never presented itself.

He'd have to create an opportunity.

A two-foot-high stone fence separated the small church grave-yard from a dirt road that continued around a bend and passed in front of the church. Mature acacia trees stretched their late afternoon shadows at right angles across the thoroughfare.

While the road appeared smooth, the way Josef's Opel rattled and shook it seemed the victim of a vicious winter. A plume of dust kicked up behind the motorcar.

As the Opel rounded the corner, the purpose of Josef's late afternoon return to the church came into view. Konrad Reichmann stood with the others at the base of the church steps. Ernst was bent over in laughter, alternately slapping his knee and pointing at Neff. When it came to humor, Ernst and Neff were on the same wavelength, with Neff being the transmitter and Ernst the receiver. If Neff ever had any inclination of becoming a vaudeville comedian, he would be wise to take Ernst with him. He found everything Neff said to be humorous. His infectious laughter could prime any audience.

Lisette stood on one side of Konrad, Gael on the other. They, too, were laughing—Lisette genuinely and Gael halfheartedly. Gael seemed more intent on stealing glances at Konrad. As she laughed she risked placing her hand on his arm.

Willi, as usual, was nearby but at a distance. He had a tree branch in his hand that he used to whack anything he happened upon, whether a tree, a rock, a flower, or the side of the church building.

Josef had come at the right time. From all appearances the Hitler Youth meeting had dismissed.

A Mercedes sedan rumbled toward him, its horn blaring. Hands and arms extended from the windows, waving at Josef's cluster of youth. Swastikas were on every shirt sleeve.

Continuing on, the sedan roared past Josef with a couple of short beeps of the horn and more waves. Josef recognized most of the young people inside, as well as the driver, Herman Haeften, a local grocer and member of the church who had been offended at Josef's remarks from the pulpit the Sunday preceding the Hitler Youth rally.

"See you Sunday!" Haeften shouted to him in passing.

All was forgiven now that Josef had seen the light following the rally. Josef nodded and returned the wave.

That's the way it had been for the last two weeks. Everyone was pleasant, friendly, cheerful. The tension of the former days was gone. Worship services were well attended, and everyone was complimentary. Never before had Josef felt accepted by the members of the church like he did now. One elderly couple, charter members of the church, went so far as to comment that they saw in him the same promise they'd seen in one of their other young pastors—Wilhelm Olbricht.

All this made Josef question the wisdom of his present mission. What was he hoping to accomplish? And at what price? He was risking everything he'd gained in the last two weeks. And for what?

One man.

A Jew.

He wasn't overstating the case.

The professor's wife herself had provided a case in point. A schoolteacher at Meissen, Eva once related an incident that had occurred at her school. The way she told it, everyone on staff at the school had been bowing down to the swastika, trembling for their jobs, watching and distrusting one another. One day a young man with a swastika armband came into the school on some official errand or other. A class of fourteen-year-olds saw him and immediately began singing the Horst Wessel song. Singing in the corridor wasn't allowed. Another teacher, Fräulein Wiechmann, was on corridor duty at the time. Her colleagues urged her to forbid the singing.

"You do it!" she'd shot back at them. "If I forbid this singing, it'll be said I've taken action against a national song, and I'll be out on my ear!" So the children in the corridor kept singing, many of them directly taunting their teachers.

"Pastor Schumacher!"

The Opel shuddered, then fell silent. Lisette came running up to the motorcar. As Josef climbed out, she took his arm and walked with him.

"What are you doing here?" she asked.

"Thought I'd come this way and say hello."

"You just caught us. Everyone is headed home."

The others stopped what they were doing, even Willi, and watched as Josef and Lisette approached. Ernst and Neff waved.

"Greetings, boys . . . Gael. Have a good meeting?"

An assortment of nods and grunts and shrugs were his answer, followed by silence and ground staring.

"Ernst, I understand you've been accepted at university. Congratulations."

The straw-haired boy mumbled his thanks.

"Konrad and Neff . . . I assume you'll be headed into the army when school is over."

"Infantry," Konrad said proudly.

"And you, Neff? Infantry, too?"

"They won't let Neff have a gun," Ernst said. "Too dangerous for his own unit."

The way everyone laughed and poked at Neff, Josef figured the comment had a history behind it.

Taking the ribbing in stride, Neff said, "I'm hoping to shoot film instead of bullets."

"Film, huh? And Gael . . . ?"

"School." She spoke the word like it was a prison sentence.

"She's a year behind us," Lisette said.

"The baby of the group," Neff added.

His comment earned him a slap on the arm from Gael.

"I'm the baby!" Willi cried, then he whacked Neff on the shin with his branch.

"Ow! That hurt, you little . . ." Neff yelled. He took a swipe at Willi but missed.

"Actually, I'd like to talk to Konrad for a minute," Josef said. "If you have time."

Konrad took a long, questioning look at Josef.

"Walk with me," Josef said.

The other youth exchanged sly glances and grins.

"Konrad's in trouble," Willi said in singsong fashion.

Neff took another swipe at him. This time he connected.

"Ow!" Willi screamed.

"Serves you right," Neff said.

Josef started down the road. Konrad fell in step with him.

After they'd walked far enough so the others couldn't hear them, Josef said, "I want to talk with you about the other night."

Konrad's jaw clenched. "I was just doing my job."

"Knocking down old men and kicking them in the ribs is your job?"

"He's a Jew."

"He's a believer. A member of our church."

"He's still a Jew." Konrad stopped. "There's nothing more to say. I don't think you want to have this discussion."

There was no mistaking what he meant. It was both warning and threat. Josef could walk away without any repercussions.

"Tell me, Konrad, what has Professor Meyerhof done wrong? What threat is he to Germany?"

Josef had crossed the line. Konrad's eyes narrowed.

"The Jews as a race are the threat. He's one of them."

"He deserves to be beaten simply because he was born of Jewish parents?"

"A poisonous mushroom doesn't choose to be poisonous," Konrad said. "It just is. While it had no choice either way, would you still want it in your house?"

He was drawing from a child's storybook. The tale was about a mother who teaches her child that just as a single poisonous mushroom can kill a whole family, so a solitary Jew can destroy a whole village, a whole city, even an entire *Volk*.

In the story, the child asks the question, "Tell me, Mother, do all non-Jews know that the Jew is as dangerous as a poisonous mushroom?"

The mother shakes her head and says, "Unfortunately not, my child. There are millions of non-Jews who do not yet know about the Jews. So we have to enlighten people and warn them against the Jews. Our young people, too, must be warned. Our boys and girls must learn to know the Jew. They must learn that the Jew is the most dangerous poison mushroom in existence. Just as poisonous mushrooms spring up everywhere, so the Jew is found in every country in the world. Just as poisonous mushrooms often lead to the most dreadful calamity, so the Jew is the cause of misery and distress, illness and death."

"A children's story?" Josef asked.

"An approved teaching of the Third Reich," Konrad replied. "Are you contesting this position?"

A sadness weighed on Josef's shoulders. Konrad held such promise. He was young. Virile. While not brilliant, he had a good mind. A model German youth. To take such a promising young life and imprint hatred and bigotry upon it was criminal.

You shall know them by their fruits.

"All I'm saying is that I know the man, Professor Meyerhof. He's a scholar. He's a Christian brother. He's—"

"A Jew," Konrad interrupted. "Which makes him dangerous to the Fatherland."

Josef couldn't seem to crack the propaganda shell. "Let me ask you this," he said. "Do you think God sees Professor Meyerhof as a poisonous mushroom?"

Konrad's response was quick and fluent. In other words, memorized. "In Germany, our god is the wonderful law of creation, whose amazing unity of all things shows itself in wonderful flowers, in growing trees, in newborn children, in the secrets of a mother, in the growth of our people, in work and accomplishment and creation, in life itself."

"That's it? Is there nothing more for you than creation?" Josef asked. "What about heaven? Eternity?"

His question prompted another quote: "A day in National Socialist Germany is better for me than heaven. This life is where we build the eternity of the nation. When I die I will return to the earth and belong again to the wonderful Mother Earth. If only a blade of grass or a flower grows from my grave, that is enough for me."

It was like talking to a propaganda machine. Plug in the code word and get an automated response.

"Konrad, I know what the Third Reich believes. I want to know what you believe."

"I believe what I'm told to believe. The men who write this stuff are a lot smarter than me." Then Konrad pulled a pamphlet from his back pocket and said, "You want to argue with someone? Argue with them!"

He shoved the pamphlet at Josef. The cover read, "*Why the Aryan Law? A Contribution to the Jewish Question* by Dr. E. H. Schulz and Dr. R. Frercks."

"Look at this . . ." Konrad pointed to paragraphs he'd circled with a pencil. "These are quotes from Jews themselves!" Although his reading skills were poor, his tone was passionate. " ' "We are the chosen ones," says Dr. Berhard Cohn. "We may carry our head high and demand particular respect. We must not only be treated equally, but better. We deserve the particular respect of other peoples." '

"And here's another one. 'The Jewish attorney Maurthner' "— Konrad struggled with the pronunciation, and Josef didn't offer any assistance—" 'in Vienna said back in the 1880s: "It is not just a matter of fighting anti-Semitism. We want to oppose it with Jewish domination!" ' "

Konrad straightened. "World domination! And this one . . . you talk a lot about Martin Luther, the Protestant Reformer, right?"

"Yes . . ." Josef answered reluctantly. He knew where Konrad was headed.

"Look at this!" Konrad pointed to a third paragraph in the pamphlet. "Martin Luther wrote this of the Jews in his book *The Jews and Their Lies.*" Then he read aloud, " 'They hold we Christians captive in our own land. They have seized our goods by their cursed usury, they mock and insult us because we work. They are our lords, and we and our goods belong to them.' " Konrad lowered the pamphlet. "Luther advocated the burning of synagogues, didn't he?"

Josef cleared his throat. "Just because a great man is right about some things, doesn't mean he's right about everything. When it came to the Jews, Luther was—"

A motorcar pulled up beside them.

"Konrad. Pastor." Herr Reichmann leaned out the driver's side window and greeted them. "It's unusual to see you at the church this time of day."

Josef opened his mouth, but it was Konrad who spoke.

"Um . . . I was just showing the pastor some quotes I've been memorizing," Konrad said, displaying the pamphlet.

Reichmann looked at the book, then up at Josef and nodded approvingly. "Climb in the motorcar, son."

Konrad did as he was told.

"See you Sunday, Preacher."

Herr Reichmann's motorcar traveled a short distance before stopping a second time to pick up Willi. By this time the other youth had gone home.

Sunday, May 5, 1940

Had he planned it, he probably wouldn't have had the nerve to carry it out. Had he thought about it, he probably would have talked himself out of it. It was an act of frustration, pure and simple.

The day of worship began well enough. The sky was a shocking blue. The morning chill gave way early to a bold sun with a warm touch. It was one of those German days when everywhere Josef looked creation glistened with color.

Then Frau Wuhlisch spoke. "Good morning, Pastor . . . Mady."

Josef paused from helping his very pregnant wife from their battered Opel just long enough to return the elderly woman's greeting.

"Looks like Führer's weather today, wouldn't you say?"

Führer's weather.

Two words.

The proverbial straw. It drained the color from the sky, turned the sun to ice, and worked its way under Josef's skin like an annoying insect.

Führer's weather.

The saying wasn't even original. As a boy Josef could remember his mother speaking of the Kaiser's weather. The Third Reich had re-dubbed the phrase.

"Josef! You're hurting me!" Mady cried.

He relaxed his grip on her arm. "Sorry," he said.

"Is something wrong?"

"No. I was just . . . everything's fine. Let's just get into church."

The euphoria he'd felt at the Hitler rally was completely gone now, leaving behind a bitter residue. Certainly Konrad was partially responsible for Josef's change of heart—he being both aggressor, in attacking the professor, and victim of the Nazi racist propaganda. Then there was the professor's living conditions and the government's refusal to allow him to practice his life's work of teaching, for which he'd displayed an extraordinary talent over the years.

As badly as Josef wanted to be a good German and work within the system to redirect the course of the nation back to God, it was like trying to stop an avalanche. Furthermore, he felt betrayed by Der Führer. Despite the assurances he'd heard in the grand speech, the professor had been right. It was increasingly impossible for him to reconcile the rhetoric with reality.

You shall know them by their fruits.

Yet, how does one stop an avalanche?

Josef was feeling desperate. Had he been too slow to respond? Was he too late? Was there a way to stop the madness?

Der Führer's weather.

It wasn't just a phrase. It was a reminder that the Nazis would not be content until they had infiltrated every aspect of German life.

Der Führer's weather, indeed. The Third Reich was claiming credit for an act of God.

Blasphemy!

Josef had changed the sermon topic at the eleventh hour. He'd planned to preach on Matthew 7:20, the professor's fruit passage.

Then, in response to radio reports that German forces were poised along the Belgium border, he changed it to Matthew 5:9— "Blessed are the peacemakers: for they shall be called the children of God."

Considering an impending invasion, he thought the sermon had teeth. But from the congregation's response, one would have thought his topic was "Let's all get along together, shall we?"

Dumbfounded by the display of any visible reaction to his sermon, Josef stood in dismay as person after person filed out the front doors.

"Heil Hitler! Good sermon, Preacher," Herr Reichmann said, greeting him with the proper salute. "Boys! Into the motorcar!"

Had the man heard a single word he'd said this morning?

"Heil Hitler! Wonderful sermon. Just what we needed," Frau Gruber said as she shook his hand.

And on it went.

"Heil Hitler! Another good one, Pastor."

"Heil Hitler! You're sounding more and more like Pastor Olbricht every week."

"Heil Hitler! Looks like Führer's weather today, don't you think?"

"No, I don't," Josef replied.

"I beg your pardon?" The poor woman in front of him didn't know how to react.

"This is *not* Der Führer's weather!" Josef said, his voice loud enough to stop all conversation around him. "This is a day the Lord has made."

The woman smiled weakly. "Of course, Pastor," she said. "I didn't mean to imply otherwise. It's only a saying."

"But it's not just a saying," Josef insisted. "It's blasphemy to imply that Der Führer had anything to do with today's beautiful weather."

Everyone stared at him, openmouthed.

Had Josef stopped then, it would have been just a minor incident, easily correctable. But he didn't. The emotions he'd been stockpiling all week were a tinderbox and a fuse had just been lit.

He stepped outside, raised his hands heavenward, and shouted, "This is a day the Lord has made! We will rejoice and be glad in it!"

Like any explosion, once started, there was no stopping it.

"And as long as I'm pastor of this church, not only will we honor God for the things He has done, but we will greet one another as befitting a fellowship of Christians, not like some Nazis in a beer hall!"

There were audible gasps.

"Do you realize how comical you all look?" Josef cried. "Do you know how hard it is to keep from laughing when Frau Wuhl- isch comes by all wrinkled and sweet and thrusts forward a white- gloved hand and says 'Heil Hitler'?"

There were a few guarded titters.

"Can't you remember how we used to laugh at that salute back in Hitler's beer-hall days? It was comical then, and it's comical now! You should see yourselves marching by with your arms flap- ping up and down! You look like a bunch of rusty gates!"

Those who remained in the church began looking for alterna- tive avenues of departure.

"This is God's house!" Josef shouted. "And when we are in God's house we will greet one another in Jesus' name, not Hit- ler's!"

Chapter 11

The SA didn't come for him that afternoon. Josef was expecting them. Der Führer's weather outburst wasn't enough to get anyone's attention. The salute comment was. Up to now he'd been treading on thin ice by not returning the salute to departing worshipers. Publicly ridiculing the official greeting was a serious offense.

He did, however, get a phone call from his father-in-law. The mood of the conversation was light. Olbricht was understanding. Fatherly. His conclusion on the matter was that no lasting damage had been done, as long as Josef apologized from the pulpit the next Sunday. He suggested Josef cite the stress of impending fatherhood by way of explanation. While the telephone conversation ended on a note of good humor, Josef detected an edge to his father-in-law's voice.

Mady wasn't as understanding. The ride home from church was endured in frigid silence, after which she gathered up Kaiser, went straight to the bedroom, and slammed the door. Josef knew better than to go after her. Given her current state of mind, he could stand at the door for a month of Sundays and still not get in. His only chance of sleeping in his own bed that night was to leave her alone until she was ready to come out.

Josef made himself a lunch of a few slices of cheese, bread, and a warmed-up cup of ersatz coffee and spent the remainder of the afternoon listening to radio reports of troops mobilizing along the Belgium border, reading the newspaper, and taking a fitful nap in the armchair, expecting at any moment to be awakened by the SA pounding on his front door.

When he awoke it was late afternoon, with shadows crossing the hardwood floor. Josef got up and walked to the bedroom door and listened. He heard nothing.

Deciding to stick to his Sunday routine, he changed his shoes and went outside for a walk. The outdoors worked on him like an elixir. The breeze refreshed him. The expansiveness of the blue celestial canopy lifted the weight that had been pressing down on his heart all afternoon. The leaves in the trees, like two-dimensional hands, waved in praise to their Creator. Cast shadows became cool oasis islands, beckoning him to tarry and reflect within them. Several times Josef took them up on their offer.

He walked and prayed until the shadows merged into a unified twilight shade. Thrusting his hands in his Sunday pants pockets, he felt a worn piece of paper.

If you are indeed a friend of Luther, use the word Bulwark *in a sermon and you will be contacted.*

He thought he'd thrown the note away. Carefully folding the paper in half, he slipped it back into his pocket.

His afternoon walk had strengthened his resolve. There was something he had to do, and there was no reason to put it off. His steps took on a purpose, leading him on a systematic pattern up and down the neighboring streets.

Within an hour he found what he was looking for. In the distance, Konrad's patrol was walking away from him, looking for someone to bully or abuse, for they had no other real reason to be where they were.

Josef chose to parallel their course on an adjacent street. His paced quickened to just short of a run. At one side street he saw that he had almost overtaken them. After going two more blocks, he cut over. When the patrol had reached the corner of the next street, he was there waiting for them.

Konrad approached him with an amused grin. "I hear you went a little cuckoo after church this morning."

His two comrades laughed.

"I need to speak with you."

"Go ahead."

"Alone."

Konrad signaled his partners to stay where they were. He accompanied Josef a short distance away. "What do you want?"

"I want you to come with me."

"Where?"

"Just come. You'll see."

Konrad shifted uneasily.

"It's nothing nefarious," Josef assured him.

Konrad looked puzzled but said nothing.

"I want you to see something. You have nothing to fear. All I'm asking for is thirty minutes of your time."

"I don't fear you," Konrad said.

"Good. You have no reason to."

The boy bit his lower lip in thought. He turned to his partners. "Take the watch up to Ossietzkystrasse," he said. "I'll meet you there in about a half hour."

"Where are you—"

"You have your orders!" Konrad barked.

He had a bearing about him that could not be ignored. In him Josef saw the embodiment of Germany—its glory, as well as its greatest shortcoming. Neither Konrad nor Germany gave thought to having a soul. They were spiritually destitute. They had no compassion. No mercy. No love for anyone or anything that didn't serve their Aryan purposes. And while they viewed the absence of these things as evidence of their strength, Josef knew them to be a weakness. Worse, an Achilles' heel.

"Well? What are we waiting for?" Konrad said.

"This way."

They walked the streets in silence. Konrad lagged a half step back. Guarded. After several blocks, Josef left the cobblestone streets and turned down a dirt alley. Two ruts marked the passage of vehicles; a strip of green growth separated them.

Several times Josef checked over his shoulder, and each time Konrad regarded him with silent suspicion. Josef offered the boy no assurances or explanations. Better to keep him guessing. If he knew where Josef was leading him, he'd probably bolt.

The night air turned chilly.

At the end of the alley they came upon a large yard with half a dozen fruit trees. A darkened house lay just beyond the trees. Ducking under branches that smelled of citrus, Josef led Konrad to the back door of the enclosed porch.

Konrad's brow furrowed. He studied the house as though something about it was vaguely familiar. He walked to the side and looked toward the street to get his bearings.

His jaw clenched. "This is that Jew's house," he said.

"His name is Professor Meyerhof. And he no longer owns the house."

"So that's your game. I suppose now I'm to pity him and feel sorry for what we did the other night."

"I didn't bring you here to dump a bucket of guilt on your head."

"Whatever your plan, you're wasting your time."

"Talk to him."

"You said he no longer lives here."

"I said he no longer owns the house."

Konrad motioned toward the back porch with the flip of an index finger. "He lives in there?"

Josef nodded.

"It's better than he deserves. He's a stinkin' Jew."

"Talk to him."

"I don't have anything to say to a Jew."

"Then listen."

Konrad stepped back. He turned to leave. "There's nothing for me here," he said.

"I think there is."

"What?"

"A lesson in manhood."

Mady awakened to a dark room, at first confused and frightened by the lack of recognizable features. A warm ball of fur nestled against her legs.

Kaiser.

It came back to her. The silent argument on the way home from church. Her flight into the bedroom.

Kaiser stretched, yawned, and then settled back to sleep.

Mady sat up. The crack beneath the door was dark. Josef had yet to switch on the lights. How late was it? As she moved her legs over the side of the bed, her stomach noisily reminded her she hadn't eaten anything since breakfast.

A twist of the light switch flooded the room with more light than her eyes could handle. It took several blinks for them to adjust.

The clock on the dresser read a few minutes before nine.

Mady shuffled to the door and opened it. The interior of the house was completely dark.

"Josef?"

Moving cautiously in the darkness, she felt her way into the parlor and switched on a light.

"Josef?"

All the other rooms were dark. Stepping from room to room, she turned on lights and searched counters and doors and walls for a note. By the time she was finished, all the lights in the house were on, and she still had no explanation for her husband's absence. She remembered his habit of a Sunday afternoon walk, but he was always back before sundown.

Mady's stomach complained again. She ignored it and slumped into a parlor chair. A seed of worry took root in the pit of her abdomen and germinated with amazing speed.

She began to shake, fearing that the authorities had taken Josef while he was on his walk. Her hands turned icy, then her legs. Although it was difficult given the roundness of her stomach, she curled up into a ball and rocked herself. Tears came from behind closed eyes. Unwanted images followed. The SA manhandling Josef. Pummeling him with their fists. She saw rude, angry hands throwing him into the back of a truck and hauling him away.

The only way to stop the images was to open her eyes. But that didn't stop the questions from assaulting her mind. Did the SA have him, or the Gestapo? Had they taken him from the house while she was sleeping? Doubtful. Nazis were noisy. They never did anything quietly.

How could she find out? Call Father. No, not yet. He would only get angry. But how long should she wait?

Another image came to mind. This one involved flesh and blood, not speculation but memory. Two Gestapo agents pounding on the front door, asking for Father, who greeted them warmly and led them into his study.

She was fifteen years old. At that time Father had aligned himself with the Pastor's Emergency League. Together with Martin Niemoeller, he had been an outspoken critic of Hitler and the National Socialists.

As Father was shutting the study doors, he saw she was afraid and gave her a reassuring wink. Whenever Father shut the doors a battle was about to take place. Sometimes it was with men from the church. Sometimes it was between married couples. Most times it was loud.

But the study was Father's playing field, and Father always won the battles that took place there. Men who marched into his study with solemn expressions emerged relieved and friendly. Those who went in angry came out smiling, slapping Father's back, shaking his hand. The transformation always amazed Mady and made her proud.

This time was different.

While Mady couldn't make out the words that were spoken, the intensity of the voices was unnerving. More unnerving still were the periods of silence. It was unnatural. Men were shouters. Nazis especially. It was eerie for them to be this silent for any length of time.

When the study doors opened, the Gestapo agents came out alone. They walked in step, showing themselves to the door. One of them looked at her. He smiled and winked. A wicked Nazi wink.

For the longest time Mady sat waiting for her father to appear. When she could endure the wait no longer, she walked uncertainly toward the doors, listening for the slightest sound that might indicate activity—the turning of a page, the scribble of a pen, the squeak of a chair. There was nothing, save cold, graveyard silence.

Reaching the door, she hesitated for a moment. She was afraid of what she might see.

Finally, she steeled her courage and peeked inside. Father sat in his chair, his arms on the rests, his face expressionless and deathly white.

She spoke to him.

He gave no response, no sound or gesture, not even the batting of an eyelid.

She spoke again and could hear the fear in her own voice.

A marble statue looked more human.

Defying the rules of the house, she made her way around the desk. She spoke to him again.

He made no reply.

Trembling, she reached out and touched his hand. Never had she felt flesh so cold.

Father's hand moved. It began to shake. Then the other hand shook in concert with the first. This seemed to revive him somewhat. His head moved. He blinked, and his eyes appeared to focus.

What had those men done to him?

Slowly Father turned his face to her. His eyes glistened with recognition, then filled with tears and overflowed. Once the stream started, there was no stopping it. Never once had she seen her father shed a tear. Now there was a torrent of them.

He began sobbing. His icy hand gripped her arm and pulled her toward him with a force that frightened her. He pulled her against him and squeezed her so tightly it forced the breath from her lungs. He buried his face in her hair and sobbed and sobbed and sobbed.

Neither of them ever spoke of the day the Nazis visited. But from that time on, Father publicly distanced himself from Niemoeller and the Pastor's Emergency League.

Even now the remembrance of that day scared her. Mady hugged her legs tightly. She would involve her father in Josef's disappearance only as a last resort. But how much longer could she wait?

"Josef!"

The way she said it, one would have thought it were a curse. Pulling the ends of her hair into her mouth, Mady began to chew on them nervously.

"I'm leaving," Konrad said.

"You're running," Josef replied.

That angered the boy. He spun around, his index finger at the ready. "I told you. I'm not afraid of anything!"

"You're afraid to look an old man in the eyes, afraid you might see something that doesn't support the lies you've been swallowing."

Konrad drew closer to Josef, like a hunter stalking his prey. "I could have you arrested."

"Is that what they teach you? Blindly eliminate anything that threatens you? Don't challenge it. Don't test it to see if there's any truth there. Just get rid of it?"

Konrad raised an accusing finger. "He's a Jew!"

"Talk to him!"

The boy's features were losing their stonelike qualities. His posture slumped slightly.

"If after a few minutes you still see nothing but a Jew, what harm will be done? It will only serve to confirm everything you've been taught. What have you got to lose?"

Konrad pondered this. "Five minutes," he said. "No more."

Josef smiled.

He led the way through the back door. Approaching the pantry door, he knocked lightly. When there was no immediate answer, he knocked louder.

"Professor?"

He knocked again.

When he still got no response he rested his hand on the door latch. It was cold and moist. It clicked open.

Slowly, he pushed open the door a crack. "Professor?"

A sliver of interior yellow light escaped and streaked across his shoes. Following close behind it was the musty odor of the professor's hundreds of books and stacks of papers.

"Professor? It's me. Josef."

He pressed open the door.

"Dear God, no. . . !"

What he saw knocked the breath out of him. An SA fist to the solar plexus couldn't have done a better job. Josef fell back against the doorjamb.

"What?" Konrad asked. He stepped next to Josef and peered inside.

Josef heard a sharp intake of breath.

In Meyerhof's pantry, dangling from the rafters as lifeless as a sack of potatoes, was the professor.

On the makeshift bed of boxes and blankets was a picture of Eva, the Nazi cat booklet, the Nazi red ball, and the Nazi tube of toothpaste.

There was nothing absurd about them now.

With them was another item that Josef recognized immediately. A gold coin. One that Josef had given to the youth the previous Christmas.

There was a shuffle of feet as Konrad backed away. He burst through the back door. Ducking under the branches of the citrus trees, he disappeared down the alley.

Chapter 12

Monday, May 6, 1940

A band of pale violet sky edged the eastern horizon. Josef approached his house weary of heart and limb. He entered quietly, so as not to awaken Mady, and collapsed into an armchair.

His whole body felt numb. There was gravel under his eyelids and cotton stuffing in his head. Though hungry, his stomach revolted at the thought of food. Though tired, his mind told him it was morning, time to wake up. Even if he went to bed, he doubted he could sleep.

Despite the lethargy of his body, his mind was racing.

The professor was dead.

Made to look like a suicide, Josef suspected murder.

The coin.

Planted? Left behind by accident? Or was it a message?

There was no mistaking whose coin it was. The Scripture inscription left no doubt. *The Lord is my rock, and my fortress, my God and my strength.* This was Konrad's coin.

Josef had pocketed it.

The coin wasn't evidence of a crime because, according to the officials, no crime had been committed. Clearly a suicide. And even if they suspected murder, there would be no investigation.

It was one less Jew to remove from Berlin.

But what to do about Konrad?

Josef rubbed tired eyes. He had to think.

Without thinking, he reached for the basket beside the chair and pulled it onto his lap. He removed an unfinished piece of embroidery, his glasses, and replaced the basket.

Skilled fingers worked the needle in a threaded backstitch. His stitching fell into a pattern that was matched by his breathing. Since the days of his youth, when he'd spend long hours in the attic with his brother, he discovered that the rhythm and colors and threads and fabric somehow brought order to a chaotic world. It still did, only his weakening eyes restricted him to an hour, an hour and a half at best.

He was able to lose himself in his canvas creations, to find a sense of completion in the finished project and a sense of confident purpose in the process. There was a tranquility about—

BAM! BAM! BAM!

The front door shuddered from the force of the blows.

Josef bolted to an upright position.

BAM! BAM!

The door exploded off its hinges.

Black-shirted men poured through the opening. Before Josef could utter a sound, two of them had him by the arms and were dragging him out the front door. The next thing he knew he was tumbling headlong down the steps and onto the gravel driveway. He came to rest with his cheek against the ground, his glasses out of reach, his hands and knees skinned, and his temple gashed. He struggled to get up.

"What—?"

A blow to the side of his face knocked the rest of the words from his mouth.

He was hauled up by his arms into a kneeling position. He felt cold metal against the back of his head. His guess, a handgun.

"One word and I'll scramble your brains!"

Mady.

Keeping his head still, Josef strained his eyes in a sidelong look toward the front door.

What would they do to Mady?

He imagined her exit similar to his own. Thrown down the steps. Tumbling onto the ground.

The baby!

More anxious than ever, he strained to see the front door, not knowing what he would do, but certain he would do something if they manhandled his wife.

Several moments passed. The only sounds that came from the house were the sounds of wood splintering and glass shattering.

Josef's breathing labored. It hurt to keep his eyes plastered to the side like they were, but he couldn't look away. Not now.

Scenarios played out in his mind. Possible courses of action that would keep him alive long enough to save Mady. Roll forward and hope to kick the gun out of his captor's hand? Jump up and back, hoping to knock him off balance? No matter what course of action he thought of, they failed at one point. There were too many of them and only one of him. He might buy himself and Mady a few seconds, but the ending was always the same. He'd be shot, and Mady would be left defenseless.

Still, he had to do something.

Just then two of the black-shirted men came through the doorway. Their hands were empty. They were alone.

"There's no one else here," one of them reported.

Were they playing some sort of game? Mady had to be there! He was certain of it . . . or was he? He'd never checked the bedroom. He'd just assumed she was home asleep. But if she wasn't there, where had she gone?

The blackshirts didn't share his dilemma nor did they give him time to worry about his wife's unexplained absence. They yanked him to his feet, handcuffed his hands behind his back, and launched him into the backseat of a black motorcar.

Landing on his shoulder, he attempted to scoot into a sitting position but not fast enough for the blackshirt holding a revolver on him. The man stomped him with his boot like he would stomp trash into a sack, then got in after him.

Soon the motorcar was in motion, throwing gravel behind it before Josef was able to work himself into a sitting position. The man beside him and the two men in the front seat sat stone-faced, their eyes looking forward. They all had on black shirts and carried daggers. Both the shirts and the daggers bore the insignia ⚡⚡.

SS.

The black motorcar barreled through the streets of Berlin, oblivious to traffic, road rules, or pedestrians. Down Unter den Linden, left at Wilhelmstrasse in front of the Brandenburg Gate, right on Prinz-Albrecht-Strasse. It came to a squealing halt at 8 Prinz-Albrecht-Strasse, the most feared address of the Third Reich.

Gestapo Headquarters.

The room in which Josef found himself was a box, each side matching the others in dimensions. The room's only source of light was a lone bulb hanging overhead, insufficient to illumine the room adequately. There were no windows or openings of any kind on the walls or ceiling save the door through which he'd entered, and it was closed.

From the center of the room, where he stood, the walls were muddy brown in color and stained with dark streaks. It gave him the impression that it had been stripped of wallpaper, leaving ugly scars.

The floor upon which he stood was hardwood. There were no furnishings, not even a ball of dust to vary the standing surface. He'd been shoved into the center and told to stand there and not move so much as a hairsbreadth. That was hours ago. How many he couldn't tell. There was nothing by which he could mark the passage of time other than the sound of his own breathing.

His feet and back ached from standing. His shoulders were stiff from being pulled back in an unnatural position, which also made his breathing difficult. He could feel the rawness of his wrists where the handcuffs were chafing them.

Worse was thinking about the ordeal to come. He didn't handle pain well, had spent most of his life avoiding it. Anticipating pain was the worst. He could break into a full sweat at the mere thought of pain. His knees grew weak, his limbs shook, and his breathing came in rapid gulps. At times he would grow light-headed, sometimes even giddy.

It had been that way all of his life. As a boy he would break into tears at the sight of a bee or a needle. He'd hoped he would outgrow the fear when he became a man. He hadn't.

His only weapon against his skyrocketing fear, and it had a spotty record at best, was his mind. If he could manage to focus on something else, he could to some extent control the shaking. So he turned his thoughts to Mady.

He could only hope she was at her parents' house. If only he knew for certain. And then there was the question of why she wasn't home in the first place. Anger over his actions at church played a part, to be sure, but was it sufficient for her to run to her parents? And, if so, was it Mady's idea or had they suggested it?

There was also his unexplained absence to consider. How late was it before she realized he was gone? Had she gone out looking for him?

Like burrowing beetles, these thoughts crawled around in his gut. The thought that troubled him most was the possibility that Mady had gone out looking for him on her own. Something could have happened to her. Someone could have taken advantage of her. If she did go looking for him, the combination of exertion and worry could've been too much for her this late in her pregnancy. She could be lying somewhere, bleeding and hurt. He should have told her where he was going. But there wasn't a blessed thing he could do about it now.

The room's sole portal burst open with a thunderclap. Josef started, yanked from his thoughts by more immediate concerns.

Two men in SS uniforms approached him, the clicking of their boots on the hardwood floor echoed ominously against the walls. The older of the two reached him first. He was small in stature, but beefy. His close-cropped hair was cut so short he appeared to be bald. His eyes were steel balls set in folds of sagging flesh. It wasn't that he was heavy; he just seemed to have too much flesh on his face. So to keep from sagging at his jaw, the flesh found ways to fold itself under his eyes. He walked with short, clipped steps, his eyes fixed on Josef from the moment the door burst open. The insignia on his uniform indicated he was a Sturmbannführer.

Following behind him, a younger, taller man with black hair carried a wooden chair. His hair, loose and straight, fell over his forehead and into his eyes. A Rottenführer by rank, there was a youthfulness about his face. There was also a hint of the sadistic, which revealed itself in a half grin. He set down the chair to face Josef. The senior of the two men sat in it without once removing his gaze from Josef.

With the Rottenführer's hands free of the chair, Josef could now see that he was carrying something else—a wooden ax handle. He placed the handle under his arm while he pulled on a pair of black gloves. Likewise, the man in the chair produced a pair of black gloves that he donned with the meticulous care of a surgeon.

Josef could feel the sweat running down his chest in rivers. His breathing was so rapid he was growing light-headed.

"Welcome to my classroom," the Sturmbannführer said. The folds of his jowls pulled back in an amused smile.

The younger agent finished pulling on his gloves and flexed his fingers to loosen them up. When they were sufficiently limber, he tested them by gripping the ax handle. Then he walked behind Josef, disappearing from view.

Josef was familiar with the Reich's intimidation tactics, but only by rumor and thrice-removed stories. Having experienced the SA brand of intimidation the day Klaus Brettschneider was arrested, he was by no means comfortable in this situation, yet neither was he unduly concerned. He expected there would be a lot of shouting and posturing, but no real violence. After all, his crime—if you could call it a crime—was a minor one. Of greater concern was Mady's whereabouts. He just wanted to get this little exercise over so he could go find her.

"Name."

It was a command, not a question, as stiff as the Sturmbannführer's back in the chair.

"Schumacher, Josef."

"Occupation."

"Minister."

"Minister . . ." The Sturmbannführer made a face as if the word were distasteful to him.

Josef heard a chuckle behind him.

"As such, are you a leader?" his inquisitor asked.

"I prefer to think of myself as a shepherd."

Josef didn't think it was possible, but the man's steely eyes hardened even more. Apparently, the unspoken rules allowed for assent or denial only, not clarification.

The Sturmbannführer jumped up and moved within an inch of Josef's nose. The intimidation had begun. He shouted, "Answer my question! Do you hold influence over other Germans?"

"Yes," Josef said contritely.

He knew the game. They shouted. He acquiesced. To do otherwise was unwise.

Josef's inquisitor backed away, seemingly satisfied with Josef's answer. He sat down on the edge of the chair. "I understand you're having trouble with your arm."

"My arm?"

WHACK!

The blow came unexpectedly, slamming into his right forearm, knocking him off his feet. The force was so great, Josef skidded across the floor.

He barely had time to wince before a face was bending over him, black hair dangling, shouting, "Get up! Get up! Who gave you permission to leave your position?"

The shouting, mere inches from his ear, continued until Josef managed, with his hands still handcuffed behind him, to get to his feet and back to his designated spot. His forearm throbbed with pain.

His inquisitor looked peeved, as though Josef had somehow slighted him by falling down.

"We were talking about your arm."

"There's nothing wrong with my—"

WHACK!

The second blow landed right on top of the first. The pain blinded him for an instant. The force of the blow knocked him from his spot again, but not to the ground. Josef managed to regain his position before his attacker could get in a healthy string of verbal blows.

The Lord is my strength, my shield . . .

His entire body was in shock from the blows. He flinched involuntarily at nothing, expecting a third blow at any moment.

"Release him," said the inquisitor.

Josef's hopes rose. Was that it? Without a doubt, it was more than he'd anticipated, but given the chance he'd gladly walk out the door now and count himself lucky. He winced as the Rottenführer pulled his arms back roughly. Two clicks and his hands were free.

The man in the chair watched him as Josef tested his shoulders and rubbed his sore wrists and the bruise on his forearm.

Like lightning, the inquisitor was on his feet. His arm shot forward in salute. "Heil Hitler!"

Josef hesitated. It cost him.

WHACK!

A third blow in the same place, this one harder than the first two. Josef stumbled sideways and crumpled to his knees, catching himself with his good arm.

"Who gave you permission to leave your place? Get back! Back! Back! Back!"

His head swimming in pain, Josef stumbled back to the designated position.

"It seems we have yet to learn our lesson," said the inquisitor. "Shall we try it again?" He then clicked his heels and thrust out his arm. "Heil Hitler!" he shouted.

This time there was no hesitation, only pain. Josef lifted his bruised arm. "Heil Hitler!" he said and then winced, expecting a blow that didn't come.

The folds on the inquisitor's face stretched into a wide grin. It was the look of a master who had just taught his dog a new trick. "Heil Hitler!" he shouted again.

Josef was ready. "Heil Hitler!" he responded.

His inquisitor nodded. "So, ministers can be taught." Then he approached Josef and said, "You seem to have learned your lesson. But how do I know you will remember it once you leave this room?"

"I give you my word," Josef said.

The man laughed in his face. "The word of a minister? Not good enough. Not nearly good enough." Reaching behind him, the man grabbed the chair and placed it in front of Josef. "Stand on this," he ordered.

Josef did as he was told.

His inquisitor circled behind him and reappeared in front. He snapped to attention. "Heil Hitler!" he shouted.

Josef responded instantly, his feet together, his back straight, and his arm raised in salute.

"Now hold that position," the inquisitor ordered.

Though his right shoulder objected, Josef held the position. The younger Gestapo agent appeared, and the two men looked up at him like he was a statue in Tiergarten Park.

The inquisitor spoke to his subordinate, "Remind Herr Minister of the rules for a proper German greeting," he said.

"Yes, Sturmbannführer!"

The younger man stood ramrod straight as he spoke in clipped sentences. "If people belong to the same social group, it is customary to raise the right arm at an angle so that the palm of the hand becomes visible. The appropriate phrase is 'Heil Hitler' or simply

'Heil'. If one espies an acquaintance in the distance, it suffices merely to raise the right hand in the manner described. If one encounters a person socially inferior to oneself, then the right arm is to be fully stretched out, raised to eye-level, and at the same time, one is to say 'Heil Hitler'. The greeting should always be carried out with the left arm if one's right arm is engaged by a lady."

The inquisitor addressed Josef, who remained in a saluting position. "Do you understand this?"

"Yes, Sturmbannführer," Josef replied.

"Would you like him to repeat it for you?"

"That won't be necessary, Sturmbannführer."

The superior officer then addressed his ward, "I'm in a quandary," he said. "Is there anything socially inferior to a minister?"

His black hair dangling gleefully, the Rottenführer shouted, "No, sir!"

"I didn't think so." The Sturmbannführer chuckled at his own joke. Swiveling on his heel, he turned toward Josef and shouted, "Suppose we find such a low creature. You see it approaching you. Heil Hitler!"

Josef's arm extended in the proper salute. "Heil Hitler!" he shouted.

"Hold that position."

The inquisitor and his assistant circled him again. This time only the Sturmbannführer emerged in front.

The disappearance from sight of the man with the ax handle was unnerving. Josef began to tremble, and not because his bruised arm was tiring, which it was.

"I want you to contemplate on what you've learned here today," he said. "In your current position, of course. And should at any time you lower your arm . . ."

WHACK!

The blow landed just above the back of his knees, buckling them. Josef teetered but somehow managed to right himself without falling off the chair. His arm faltered, though remained in an outstretched position.

"A sample," the inquisitor said. "You'll receive a similar blow every time you lower your arm. Is that understood?"

"Yes, Sturmbannführer."

His inquisitor turned on his heel and marched out of the room, closely followed by the Rottenführer.

Josef stood alone in the room as before, only this time on top of the chair and with his right arm extended. He didn't dare lower his arm. For all he knew he was being watched through some peephole. While gravity worked on his arm, the thought of another blow to the back of his legs worked on his nerves. He grit his teeth.

The Lord is my strength, my shield . . .

He tried to divert his mind from the pain and fear. It did him little good, for all he could think of was Mady and all the same questions came flooding back to torture him. Was she safe? Was she hurt? How could he find out? And when? How long would they keep him here? It wasn't unusual for the authorities to hold people for days before releasing them.

Josef's arm began to waver. It dropped slightly. He raised it again.

The Lord is my strength, my shield . . .

The weight of his arm was growing unbearable. He had to focus all of his concentration on it to keep it from failing.

He strained to hear any sound coming from beyond the door, for sound would indicate someone was coming. He never thought he'd want to see the two SS agents again, but now he was praying for their return just so he could salute them, anything to move his arm.

His arm began to fail.

With renewed effort he told himself he could hold this position indefinitely. But this was an outright lie and he knew it. He prayed for strength, for relief from the pain now pulsing in his shoulder, and for Mady's safety. When he could bear it no longer, he rolled his head, shifted his feet, groaned and winced, anything to keep his arm from dropping.

Yet his arm began to lower involuntarily. His strength was

gone. Already he could feel the slap and sting of another blow to the back of his legs. He fought to raise his arm, but he just couldn't do it anymore.

The Lord is my strength, my shield . . .
The Lord is my strength, my shield . . .
The Lord is my strength, my shield . . .

Sweat poured down his temples, and his limbs quivered from exertion. He couldn't hold this position any longer. What's more, he no longer cared. Let them do what they would to him, he just couldn't keep his arm extended a second longer. And no blow to the back of his legs could be any worse than the pain he was feeling in his arm.

With one final, trembling effort, Josef let out a yell to summon the last remnant of strength. When it arrived, it lasted for thirty seconds, maybe forty. But gravity was going to be the inevitable winner of this battle, and there was nothing he could do to overcome it.

His right arm dropped to his side.

Just then, the door clicked and opened.

Josef didn't care any longer. Let them beat him.

"Josef?"

Into the room walked Pastor Olbricht.

"Son, what are you doing standing on that chair?"

Chapter 13

Mady . . ." Josef said as the Essex Super Six pulled away from 8 Prinz-Albrecht-Strasse. "Do you know where she is?"

Olbricht scowled. Ashes from his ever-present cigar fell onto the steering wheel, then tumbled onto his pant leg. He brushed them away curtly.

Because of wartime rationing, fewer and fewer people could afford motorcars or the petrol to run them, let alone a monstrously big American motorcar like the Essex Super Six. It purred the length of Wilhelmstrasse and turned right onto Unter den Linden.

It was dusk. Josef had spent the entire day at Gestapo Headquarters.

"She's at home."

At home. Whose home? The Olbrichts' or his? Josef wanted to ask, but Olbricht was obviously angry. Josef knew better than to press for more information. When Olbricht was like this it was best to be patient. He would reveal Mady's location soon enough. The important thing was knowing she was safe.

"Thank God," Josef said.

"Thank God, indeed," Olbricht muttered.

The man had a death grip on the steering wheel. He'd bit down so hard on his cigar that he bit the end off and had to throw it away. The Essex rumbled on contentedly, oblivious to its master's mood.

As expected, the dam finally burst.

"What in God's good name has gotten into you?" he thundered.

Josef didn't respond. Truth was, he didn't know what Olbricht was referring to—the Führer's weather comments, the saluting outburst, leaving Mady alone at the house, talking to Konrad, his continued association with the professor—God rest his soul—the fact that he'd been picked up by the SS, or all of them together.

"Well? What do you have to say for yourself?" Olbricht jabbed a pudgy finger at Josef. The jabbing made him realize his hand was devoid of a cigar, a rare occurrence. He fumbled in his coat pocket for a replacement. Finding one, he lit it and took several puffs before returning his attention to Josef. "That stunt you pulled at the church," he said. "What was that all about?"

"We talked about that on the phone. You said no real harm was done."

"That's before I heard from Reichmann and three other families from your church who called me."

Josef's emotions flared. It was a sore point with him. He resented the fact that several families in the church still thought of Olbricht as their pastor. "I said some things in anger," Josef said, "things that needed to be said but, in retrospect, should have been addressed in a different way."

Olbricht chomped his cigar.

The Essex rose and fell smoothly as it crossed the bridge spanning the River Spree.

"And your all-night escapade?" Olbricht asked. "Mady woke us at four o'clock in the morning. She was frantic. She had no idea where you were."

Josef repositioned himself in an attempt to place his shoulder where it didn't hurt. "I was with Professor Meyerhof," he said.

"Meyerhof?"

"He's dead."

Olbricht glanced over at him.

"Hanged."

The cigar chomping stopped as Olbricht reflected on the news. Meyerhof had become a Christian during Olbricht's ministry at the church. Olbricht had baptized him and Eva and was the presiding pastor at Eva's funeral. While the two men hadn't shared the same closeness as Josef and Meyerhof had enjoyed, there still had been a connection between them.

"He never adjusted to life without Eva," Olbricht said.

"Or to a Germany that could no longer accept one of its native born," Josef added.

"You found him?"

Josef nodded.

"And that's where you were all night?"

"Yes."

Olbricht pondered this. He began to ask something else, then stopped himself and said, "I suppose there was no way to let Mady know where you were."

"She was in the bedroom when I left for my Sunday walk. Meyerhof doesn't have a phone."

Olbricht's fierce chewing eased. News of Meyerhof's death must have affected him. Josef wanted to tell him about Konrad's coin and his belief that Meyerhof had been murdered, but now wasn't the time.

"We were worried," Olbricht said.

"Understandably. How did you find me?"

"The house. The door. The interior where no stone was left unturned. Vandals wouldn't have done as thorough a job. It had to be the SS. I made a few calls."

I made a few calls.

The sentence intrigued him. Josef knew enough about SS procedure to know they were not accustomed to giving out information about the people they arrested, not to spouses, not to family members, not to clergy. A person would have to have connections of some kind to obtain that kind of information.

"You arranged my release?" Josef asked.

The poking finger reappeared, this time hooked around a cigar. "These boys don't play around!" he warned. "You don't want to be messing with them!"

Josef heard a note of fear in the elder minister's voice.

It was getting darker. Olbricht pulled a switch, and the Essex Super Six's headlights burst to life.

"They were just toying with you today. You don't want them to get serious!"

Olbricht was right. Josef knew it. Today was nothing more than a cat-and-mouse game.

"When they're serious, they won't come only for you, or your house, or your church. They'll come for Mady and your child. They'll get to you through them. Do you understand what I'm saying?"

The cigar was shaking.

Olbricht's unanswered question hung between them for several miles.

"This is not a seminary quiz!" Olbricht continued, his voice more earnest than ever. "It's real life! With real-life consequences! This is no time to be cocky! Things are different now that you're about to be a father. You have responsibilities. Leave the windmill tilting to the young, unmarried ministers."

The Essex crunched the gravel of Josef's driveway. They pulled up in front of the house. Someone had already re-hung the front door. Lights were on inside.

"Will you come in for a while?" Josef asked.

Olbricht shook his head. "Mother is expecting me for dinner." He jabbed his cigar at Josef. "Think about what I said. Of all people—considering what happened to your family—I would think you'd understand the kind of people we're dealing with."

Josef nodded. "Thanks for tracking me down."

The Essex Super Six door closed behind him with a solid thud. The engine rumbled deeply as it made its way back to the main road.

———

From the coolness of her kiss, Josef could tell there was more between them than the baby in her womb. Adding pain to injury, she squeezed his right shoulder.

"Wash your hands. Dinner will be ready shortly," she said, then disappeared into the kitchen without another word.

Josef had to step over books and papers and clothing and collectibles that still lay strewn about the floor. The furniture had all been righted. The armchair suffered a huge gash across the back.

"Barbarians," Josef muttered.

He went into the bedroom and, with his left hand dominant, changed his shirt. It took him three times longer than usual and every move caused him pain. His arm had already turned a deep purple. By morning it would be black. He walked gingerly, the backs of his legs complaining with each step. He concluded that the SS were experts in knowing where to hit a man where it would hurt the most.

When he emerged from the bedroom, dinner was on the table. Broken plates and cups littering the floor were shoved to the sides and corners to make a pathway. As usual, there were two settings at the small table in the kitchen. Only now, instead of sharing a corner like they usually did, the place settings were set opposite each other.

The silence in the room was so pronounced that every sound was exaggerated—the clanking of a serving spoon, the scraping of a chair, the closing of the oven door.

Josef winced at his first attempt to sit down, catching himself on the edge of the table before his full weight was lowered. Scooting the chair out a little more, he found he could perch on the end of it with minimal pain.

Mady gave no indication she noticed his predicament as she placed a basket with two black-bread rolls on the table, filled the cups with ersatz coffee, and spooned the Knochensuppe into bowls. A vegetable soup enriched by stock and marrow, Knochensuppe was the most nourishing soup that could be made for just pennies.

Josef offered a prayer of thanksgiving for the food.

Without looking up at him, Mady busied herself spreading ersatz butter on her roll as though it were the most important task she would perform all day.

"Can we talk about this?" Josef asked.

Sitting board-straight, her demeanor pure business, Mady took a bite of roll and chewed judiciously.

"I apologize for being out so late," Josef said. "It couldn't be helped."

If Mady's response was any indication, Josef's words had done little more than tumble from his lips and spill into his soup.

"I went to see Professor Meyerhof," he said.

Mady took another bite and concentrated on chewing it.

"He's dead."

She stopped chewing. She looked up at him and swallowed.

"There was no way to get word to you."

Mady's demeanor softened, but only slightly. "I was frightened," she said, staring down at her soup. Her words were barely audible. "I thought something bad had happened to you when you didn't come home."

"Your father told me. You did the right thing going to your parents' house."

The edges of Mady's demeanor softened even more.

For the next several minutes they ate in silence. It was difficult for Josef to use his right hand, for every time he lifted his arm it pulsed a hot complaint. But he didn't want to switch to his left hand for fear of Mady interpreting this as a play for mercy. By the time his bowl was half empty, his hand was shaking, and he was nearly exhausted from the effort it took to lift his spoon.

"You know, it cost Father a lot of money to get you out of there."

"He didn't mention that," Josef said. But it made sense. That was the way the Reich police worked. Sometimes the only recourse families had if they ever wanted to see their loved ones again was to offer a bribe. Josef hadn't thought his offense was as serious as all that.

"There's no excuse for what you did!" she cried. "It was irresponsible and foolish." Mady laid aside what was left of her roll and leaned forward for emphasis. Her eyes flashed in earnest. The dam showed the signs of crumbling. "You were a child throwing a tantrum! And right in front of the entire church! It was inexcusable behavior that had no real chance of changing anything!"

Her words hit him like stones. She was right. While his point was legitimate, his actions had no chance of effecting change. It was a wasted effort with painful consequences.

"Are you listening to me?"

"You're right," Josef said. "It was a foolish thing to do."

It was Mady's turn to be taken aback. Apparently, she had an arsenal of arguments and was ready to fire again, only the target had disappeared. "You agree?"

Josef nodded distractedly, still in thought regarding his oversight. After a moment, he stretched an open hand across the table. His left one. "Forgive me," he said.

Mady looked at his hand, appearing surprised at her quick victory. Almost reluctantly she placed her hand in his.

"It was foolish of me to take a course of action that had no chance of changing anything," he said.

"Then you'll stop trying to change the world?"

The look in her eyes indicated this was more than a clarification of terms. It was a test.

Josef wasn't ready to go that far. "Mady, I have to speak out against wrong . . . against unrighteousness. I wouldn't be doing my job as a minister of the Gospel if I didn't."

Mady's eyes squinted in evaluation. "By unrighteousness you mean ungodliness, lies, adultery . . . moral and ethical issues. Not politics, right?"

Josef could feel his progress slipping away. "If you're asking me to cordon off a segment of society and say it's above the scrutiny of Christian examination, I can't do that."

The lines on Mady's face hardened again. "This isn't a theological examination," she said.

Almost the exact phrase her father used, Josef observed.

"I'll put this as clearly as I can," she said. "Are you going to continue to speak out against the Nazis?"

There it was, out on the table. Josef had been avoiding taking this position. The fact that he hadn't acted on the folded piece of paper in his pocket was evidence of this. Until now he'd looked for common ground with Hitler and the Nazis. He'd hoped to lead Germans back to their historic Christian faith from within the current system, though the Nazis were making that increasingly difficult for him to do.

"It's not that simple," he replied.

"I think it is."

"You're leaving out the possibility of compromise."

"The Nazis leave no possibility of compromise."

It was clear Mady had given this matter a great deal of thought. But Josef couldn't help but wonder how much of this line of thought was hers and how much was her father's.

"You're asking me to look upon injustice and do nothing," he objected.

"I'm asking you to think first of the well-being of your family and second to your place in history."

This one stung. Until now he wasn't aware of Mady thinking the motive of his actions was some kind of personal glory. The comment provided him a diversionary argument. He chose not to pursue it. "How can I claim to be a minister of Christ if I don't speak out against the things that lead people away from God?"

"Do you think God expects you to do that when it endangers the life of your unborn child?"

It was a refrain from her father's argument, but, regardless, one of great concern to her. Josef could see the fear in her eyes.

"We have to trust God to protect us," he said.

Had he slapped her, she wouldn't have looked more hurt.

"So you're saying you'll continue to endanger us?"

"Mady . . ." he stretched across the table to her.

She scooted her chair back and stood. With tears she said, "I have no respect for a husband who knowingly places his wife and child in danger."

She ran out of the kitchen. A moment later Josef heard the door to their bedroom slam shut.

———

He wasn't sure how long he sat in front of his cold Knochen-suppe and coffee. An hour. Possibly two.

Pushing himself up with his left arm, he switched off the kitchen light and headed toward the bedroom, not knowing what kind of reception awaited him.

The door was still closed, and no light shined beneath it. He tested the doorknob. It turned. Mady hadn't locked it.

Slipping quietly inside, he went and stood by the window to use what little light there was outside to undress. He'd managed to get his shirt off and was about to undo his pants when he heard a rustle on the bed.

The bedroom light clicked on.

"Josef!" Mady gasped, staring at his bruised forearm.

She rushed over to him, her eyes fastened on the injury. "They did this to you?"

"It looks worse than it is," Josef lied. He worked on his pants button.

Mady moved his hands aside and undid it for him, gently lowering his pants to the floor.

Another gasp.

Josef felt a finger press against the bruise on the backs of his legs.

"Ow!" He tried to hold it in, but couldn't.

"Anyplace else?" she asked as she examined him.

"That's about the extent of it."

She helped him to the bed and pulled down the covers. With nearly a half dozen winces, and with Mady's help, Josef situated himself on the bed in a way that he felt reasonably comfortable.

"Thank you," he said.

Mady switched off the light and climbed into bed next to him, making every effort not to jiggle it too much.

Josef lay in the dark, unable to sleep. The events of the last forty-eight hours played in his head like a bad movie. His tantrum at church. A very silent Sunday afternoon. His encounter with Konrad that culminated in finding Meyerhof's body. The coin. Coming home and not even realizing Mady wasn't there. The Gestapo raid. The inquisition. The ride home with Olbricht. Dinner with Mady.

"I have no respect for a husband who knowingly places his wife and child in danger."

Lying there in the dark, he noticed the absence of rhythmic breathing beside him. Josef turned his head to check on Mady and saw that her face was lit up by the moon's pale light. She was staring at him.

With tears.

––––––––––

Four days later German forces invaded Belgium, France, Luxembourg, and the Netherlands. Easy victories led some newspapers to predict that Hitler would be standing in London by the first of August.

The different accounts insisted that Hitler "only wants what belongs to Germany, and besides, he has always promised to keep the peace." As for Poland, "We're leaving most of it to Russia and are really only taking what was German before, including Warsaw as well."

As it had been in Germany since 1933, so it now was all across Europe. Der Führer was having his way. His halo of invincibility left Josef unsettled.

Chapter 14

Sunday, May 12, 1940

As a youth, Josef was fascinated with chemicals and their interactions. He nearly became a pharmacist, until he realized his interest in chemicals was limited to interactions that produced explosions.

One of his favorite youthful diversions was combining carbide with water to produce acetylene gas. Typically used to make mantel wicks glow brightly, Josef used the combination for visual entertainment. He discovered that if he put the two elements into a glass bottle and closed the snap-lock porcelain top, the gas pressure would build up, and up, and up, until . . . BANG!

Accordingly, he would stage movie-type explosions for the amusement of his neighborhood buddies. He'd dig a hole, pour a little water in a jar, add the carbide, snap the lid closed, and run. It made for a gratifying explosion of sand and an impressive-looking dust cloud.

On the Sunday following his arrest by the Gestapo, for the first time in his young life, Josef experienced personally the forces that took place inside those bottle bombs of his boyhood.

His congregation looked to be feeling particularly German on that Sunday. The success of Hitler's Luftwaffe in France and Belgium had intoxicated the German people. Also, it was the second

Sunday in May, Mothering Sunday, a day when the nation honored prolific mothers at public ceremonies.

Personally, Josef was grateful for the timing of this red-letter day. It provided him the opportunity to ignore the military news by drawing attention to the mothers in his congregation.

The title of his sermon was "Mothers of Great Men." Three biblical mothers served as examples: Jochebed, the mother of Moses, a brave mother; Hannah, the mother of Samuel, a praying mother; and Mary, the mother of Jesus, a devout mother.

In keeping with church tradition, Josef had all the mothers in the congregation stand and be recognized. It didn't escape him that this would be the last year that Mady would remain seated. Each mother was then given a small white cross of honor. Those who had children born the preceding year were also given a wreath called the Rune of Life. A special wreath was presented to the mother of the most children—an award given annually to Frau Schiller, who had seventeen children.

Added to this stable mixture of patriotism and motherhood was a series of carbide-like incidents.

First, there was the matter of his public apology. Josef did this early in the service to get it out of the way. He cited personal frustration and youthful passion as the sources of his outburst. While his desire was to elevate the Lord, he in no way meant to be disrespectful to Der Führer or the Fatherland. Did not the Bible say, "Let every soul be subject unto the higher powers. For there is no power but of God: the powers that be are ordained of God"?

If the faces of the congregation were any indication, his apology had been generally accepted. The prevailing goodwill of Mothering Sunday certainly didn't hurt him.

But if his apology was a good thing, why did his jaw hurt from being set on edge? He kept telling himself it was the expedient thing to do. Yet he felt a sickness in his soul.

To make matters worse, his in-laws were there to witness his humiliation. Their attendance had come as a surprise. Josef didn't know they'd be there until he walked into the sanctuary to begin the service. Well-wishers buzzed around their former pastor and his wife.

Normally Josef would have been glad to see them. And while Edda insisted they were there for Mady, this being Mothering Sunday, Josef suspected that Olbricht had a somewhat different purpose in mind. Josef couldn't shake the feeling that Olbricht was present to use his influence with his former congregation to smooth things over between them and his wayward son-in-law.

Josef did his best not to show his irritation. During the honoring of the mothers, much to the pleasure of the congregation, he personally presented a white cross to Edda and kissed her on the cheek.

Olbricht nodded his approval.

The third irritant that morning was an even greater surprise, if such a word is sufficient to convey the feeling of fear and loathing. There were two additional guests in the service. Both SS agents. The same two men who had given Josef lessons in the etiquette of Nazi saluting.

Following the sermon, there was one item of business that needed addressing—Professor Meyerhof's funeral. Normally, a person is buried within three or four days following the time of death. The professor's funeral was delayed because of his being Jewish. With no surviving relatives to attend to the funeral arrangements, all week long Josef had battled with civil authorities over where and when the burial would take place. He learned then that there were some who enjoyed abusing Jews even after they were dead.

This didn't surprise him. The surprise came when he called for volunteers to bear the professor's casket into the church, then later to the graveyard. Not a single male in the congregation had raised his hand. Josef faced a sea of folded arms and scowls.

When he reminded them that Victor and Eva Meyerhof had been their neighbors and faithful members of the church for over twenty years, one man hesitantly raised his hand only to have his wife pull it back down. At this point the only way for Josef to get beyond the embarrassment of the moment was to continue with the service.

The congregation sang a hymn, and Josef, as was his custom, moved to the back of the church to greet the departing worshipers. The two SS agents positioned themselves so they had a clear view of him.

Although it was still physically painful for him to do so, Josef greeted each person with the obligatory "Heil Hitler!"

The two agents grinned at him like hyenas. After the last of the worshipers had exited the sanctuary, they approached Josef.

"Heil Hitler!" the Sturmbannführer shouted.

Josef responded appropriately.

"Heil Hitler!" snapped the Rottenführer.

Josef flinched involuntarily and then returned the salute.

With a sadistic grin, the younger agent said, "How good it is to see you again, my brother in Christ. Good service. All except that Jew thing, of course." He slapped Josef on his bruised forearm and walked out into the German sunshine, grinning.

Mady stood beside her parents. The three of them had watched the exchange. For the second time that day, Olbricht nodded his approval.

Chapter 15

Josef shut the study door behind him, glad to be home and alone. After church the Olbrichts had insisted he and Mady join them for dinner at their house. In Josef's current state of mind, it would've been no different had the invitation come from the two SS agents. He didn't want to accept. He went for Mady's sake. The afternoon proved to be a test of his patience.

He simmered over the vegetable soup, steamed when the venison was served, and was boiling by the time they finished the strawberries and cream. The source of his heat was Olbricht's and Edda's comments.

"You really can't blame them," Olbricht had said of the lack of volunteers for Meyerhof's funeral. "Especially with two SS agents among the congregation. The man was a Jew."

"Those two agents seemed like such fine men. Don't you agree? The Sturmbannführer said his name was Wolff. I wonder if he's related to Adele Wolff, you remember her, don't you? Her family used to live near Heinersdorf," Edda said. "Do you think they'll attend regularly? Perhaps if you paid them a visit."

"You handled that apology business with dignity," Olbricht observed. "Right on target. As I predicted, a congregation will forgive just about any foolishness if their pastor is man enough to admit his blunders."

"You should have seen the way the two agents were observing you at the end of the service. They looked very pleased," Edda said. "Did I overhear one of them say he was a Christian?"

"Real shame about Meyerhof," Olbricht said. "But the fact that Victor hanged himself doesn't surprise me. There's something different about them, don't you think? You can see it in their eyes. I'm sure you've noticed it, too."

Throughout the afternoon, Mady had smiled sweetly while Josef tried to keep from going off like a firecracker. With the door shut, safe at last in his study, he tried to put the offense of the morning and afternoon behind him.

There was a soft knock at the door.

"Josef?"

A snap response nearly leaped from his lips. He caught it just in time to tame it. "Yes?"

"Father's on the phone. He wishes to speak to you."

"Tell him I'm busy."

Silence.

Then, "Is that really what you want me to tell my father?"

Josef opened the door.

"You never thanked him for getting you out of Gestapo Head-quarters," she whispered as he passed her.

"Hello?"

"Olbricht here. Are you all right, son? You seemed a bit quiet this afternoon. Edda noticed it, too."

Josef hesitated. Too long.

"Son?"

"I'm fine. Just tired from a busy morning, with so much happening and all. You know how it is."

"Listen, about that comment I made regarding the professor . . ."

"Think nothing of it," Josef said. "But now that you bring it up, there is something I wanted to talk with you about regarding the professor." As soon as he'd brought up the topic, he regretted it. While he did want to tell Olbricht his suspicions, he didn't want to do it now.

"Should I come over there?" Olbricht asked. There was concern in his voice.

"No . . . no, it's not important. Just sometime . . . there's something I'd like to talk about . . . but . . . not now . . . no need to come over now."

The conversation fell silent on both ends of the line.

Josef cleared his throat. "I haven't thanked you yet for coming to get me," he said.

Mady was standing nearby, her arms folded and resting atop her swollen stomach. She smiled at him and nodded approvingly.

"No need to thank me, son," Olbricht said.

"I want to pay back any expense."

"Not necessary. That's what family is for. Given the current climate you never know when I might need to have you do the same for me." Olbricht chuckled.

"I wanted you to know I'm grateful."

"Is Mady close by?"

Josef looked at his wife.

"If she's not lying down, let me speak to her."

Josef handed the phone to Mady.

"It's me, Poppa," she said, cradling the phone to her ear. Josef returned to his study.

He shut the door.

Standing inches from the threshold, he closed his eyes and took several deep breaths to fight back the rage that had been building up inside him since the beginning of the worship service. His hands were clenched. His lower lip trembled. He had this incredible urge to hit something, or to take something in hand—anything, it didn't matter what it was—and throw it as hard as he could against the . . .

Tap, tap, tap.

"Josef?"

He clenched his teeth so hard his jaw hurt.

"Josef?"

"Yes?"

"I'm going to lie down for a while."

"Fine."

Silence.

Josef concentrated again on controlling his breathing.

"Josef?"

"Go lie down."

"Are you angry with me?"

"No. Go lie down."

"Would you like some tea?"

"No. Go lie down."

Silence.

"Would you light the stove for me? I'd like some tea before I lie down."

———

For the third time, the study door shut behind him. The stove was lit. Mady had her tea. This time he locked the door. It was a meaningless gesture, he knew, but given the level of his frustration, meaningless gestures for some reason took on great significance.

He crossed the room and sat in an armchair next to the window that overlooked the garden. Taking up needle and thread, he began stitching. After three stitches, he dropped his work in the basket, stood up, and began pacing.

After four trips from desk to window he dropped to his knees. Eyes closed. Head bowed. Hands clasped. But no words of prayer formed on his lips. No prayerful thoughts entered his mind.

He stood up.

A pencil holder sailed across the room and crashed against a bookcase, spewing pencils in every direction.

He felt better.

A marble paperweight followed it.

"Josef? Are you all right?"

Josef's chest was heaving. "I'm fine."

"I heard a crashing noise."

"It's nothing. Go lie down."

"Your door's locked."

"I just need to be alone for a while . . . I'm praying. I'll talk to you after your nap."

"It was an awfully loud prayer," he heard her mutter.

Soft footfalls indicated she was retreating from the doorway.

While throwing things had made him feel better, it didn't resolve anything. His thoughts soon returned to the morning's events, and the emotions once again began to build.

"Not one! Not one of them had the decency to step forward for Professor's Meyerhof's funeral!" he muttered.

They're afraid. He's a Jew.

"He's a Christian. A member of the church. Their neighbor!"

Still, a Jew. And there were unfriendly forces in the congregation.

"It's a matter of common decency. The man has a right to a church burial."

It's a needless risk. If they wouldn't stand up for him in life, why would they risk standing up for him in death? Besides, the professor's dead. The Nazis can't hurt him anymore. The others have their own lives to think about.

"But what good is a life if it's lived in constant fear?"

The kind of fear that made you apologize when you did nothing wrong?

"That was different."

The kind of fear that made you stand in the back of the church and flap your arm like a wounded sparrow while the Sturmbannführer looked on?

Josef was brought up short by the thought.

You're no better than they are.

"I have a wife and child to consider."

Your God isn't big enough to watch over them?

"A matter of faith?"

You're no better than them.

"A matter of faith . . . I'm no better than them."

What are you going to do? Shut yourself and your family in the attic like your mother and brother?

"But Mady . . ."

What if there was a way to live your beliefs without endangering Mady?

"To effect change without endangering Mady?"

Not just noise, but change.

"Change. Without endangering Mady."

Josef walked to his desk. He opened his Bible and pulled out a worn slip of paper he'd placed there earlier that morning.

If you are indeed a friend of Luther, use the word Bulwark *in a sermon and you will be contacted.*

He sat down at his desk.

"In a way that won't endanger Mady," he said softly.

Pulling a sheet of paper from the drawer, he donned his glasses, took a fountain pen and wrote at the top of it, BULWARK.

For the next two hours he thought and wrote, prayed and wrote, planned and wrote. Nothing in haste. Everything carefully thought out. Planning for every contingency. Protect Mady. Effect change. Live faith. No more living in fear.

Tap, tap, tap.

"Josef?"

"Yes?"

"The door's still locked."

Josef got up and unlocked the door. Mady's anxious face was there when he opened it. She looked past him to the desk.

"What are you working on?" she asked.

"Next Sunday's sermon."

"Already?"

"When inspiration strikes . . ."

"Are you hungry?"

"I could probably eat something."

"Me, too."

Josef expected her to turn and go to the kitchen. She didn't.

"The stove needs to be lit again."

Grumbling under his breath, Josef followed his wife to the kitchen. Saving Germany from national socialism would just have to wait while he lit the stove.

Sunday, May 19, 1940

"When I was young, like most of you, my mother read me stories."

Josef's feet were set solidly behind the pulpit. His voice was strong, confident, his stomach tied in knots. The closer he got to using the code word, the more uncertain he felt. He was about to cross a line that promised dire consequences, a line that he'd avoided for years but could avoid no longer. As he approached it, he hid behind a mask of assuredness.

Before him sat the usual Sunday morning crowd. Absent were the Olbrichts and the two SS agents.

Herr Reichmann was in his usual place—second pew, left side aisle—with his Sunday morning expression, which was stoic, his eyes fixed on Josef. Konrad and Willi sat motionless beside him.

Every time Josef looked at Reichmann, he couldn't help but wonder what role the man had played, if any, in Professor Meyerhof's death. He was convinced Konrad had nothing to do with it. But how then did Konrad's coin get into Meyerhof's room?

In the pew immediately behind Reichmann were Lisette, Gael, Ernst, and Neff, fidgeting and secretly poking each other, whispering, drawing, seeking any diversion to help them pass the time. When their shenanigans became too distracting, Reichmann would turn in his seat and glare them into silence.

Mady sat in the second pew on the right side. Her gloved hands, which she normally placed in her lap on Sundays past when she had a lap, restlessly sought a place to lay themselves. The third-row seats behind her were empty. This was where the professor and Eva had sat in better days.

The mood of the congregation was restrained compared to the previous week. Reports from the front indicated a pause in Hitler's lightning advance, saying that the enemy had taken up battle positions between Antwerp and Namure.

"One of my favorite stories," Josef continued with the sermon, "was about the boy who could not shudder. Do you remember it? If not, allow me to refresh your memory. There once was a father who had two sons. The eldest son was clever and sensible. The younger one, slow. Everyone thought him stupid. Whenever a chore had to be done, the father always sent the older son to do it, knowing that by doing so, the chore would get done. Unless the chore required going past the church graveyard at night.

" 'Not there!' the older son would object. 'It makes me shudder!' For he was afraid.

"The younger son, though slow and sometimes unreliable, was never afraid. When they told stories around the fire at night, stories that would make one's flesh creep, the younger son listened unaffected. He said he didn't understand. He'd never heard a story that made him shudder.

"One day his father said to his youngest son, 'It's time you learned something by which you can make a living.'

"The boy replied, 'I should very much like to learn how to shudder, for I know nothing of that.'

"His brother laughed and called him a fool. His father said, 'You will learn easily enough how to shudder, but you won't make your bread by it.'

"Do you remember how the story goes? The sexton, knowing the boy, hired him to ring the bells in the church steeple and then the sexton dressed up as a ghost to frighten him. Only the boy wasn't frightened of the sexton-ghost and threw him down the stairs.

"When his father learned of this, he ordered the boy out of his house for throwing the sexton down the stairs. Then, as the boy was walking down the road, he came upon a man who learned of his dilemma. He showed the boy a gallows upon which seven men were hanging and suggested that if he sat under the gallows at night he would most certainly learn to shudder. The boy did. That night the wind blew the men on the gallows back and forth, but the boy lit a fire and wasn't frightened by them.

"Next, a carter took up the challenge to make the boy shudder. He took the boy to an inn where he was told of an enchanted castle that held great riches, and that if anyone could stay in the castle for three nights—thereby breaking the spell—the king had promised his daughter, the prettiest maiden in the land, as the prize.

"The boy agreed and entered the enchanted castle. In the course of three nights the youth encountered black cats with fiery eyes, dogs that howled horribly, beds that moved about mysteriously, half a man's body that fell down from the chimney, six men carrying a coffin, and a dead man who tried to strangle him. But nothing in the enchanted castle could make the boy shudder.

"At the end of the third night the spell of the enchanted castle was broken, the boy was given all the gold in the castle and the hand of the king's daughter, the prettiest maiden in all the land."

He had their attention. Even that of the youth sitting in the pew behind Reichmann.

"As a boy I remember thinking, 'If only I could be like that younger son and not be frightened by my fears.' "

Josef paused. From the looks on their faces, he'd struck a nerve. And rightly so. Fear had become the national emotion. They knew it and were now wondering—fearing—where he was going to go with this line of thought.

"In God's Word, we read, 'For God hath not given us the spirit of fear; but of power, and of love, and of a sound mind.' "

Josef closed his Bible. Slowly. Deliberately.

"This is a simple teaching. It does not require advanced theological training to understand it. God has given us three things: power, love, and a sound mind. In direct contrast to these three things is a spirit of fear. This does not come from God. The teaching is clear. Those who live their lives in fear are not living by faith in God. For God knows nothing of fear.

"Yet today, like the elder brother in the fairy tale, there are many among us who live their lives being clever and sensible . . . and afraid. Their fears, not their beliefs, govern their actions."

Josef stepped from behind the pulpit. People began reaching for their belongings.

"I'm not finished yet," he said.

The restless noise ceased. Now he had the attention of everyone in the congregation. Even Willi.

"It's no secret that I'm an admirer of Martin Luther. A man of greatness, a flawed man. A German, in every sense of the word.

"He was a man who knew fear. His vow to become a monk came during a storm when a bolt of lightning knocked him to the ground. As for his first mass? It was a nightmare. The vestments had to be correct, the recitation correct, the state of the priest's soul correct. After all, this was the focal point of the Church's means of grace. The whole difference between clergy and laity rested upon it, as well as the superiority of the Church over the state. In Luther's own words, the fear of making a mistake during such an important ritual made him stupefied and terror-stricken.

"Though Luther knew fear, he did not succumb to it. Instead, he was propelled by his passions. At his best, Martin Luther was a white-hot firebrand of righteousness. At his worst, he was a scoundrel. But there's one thing that could never be said of him—that he was ambivalent. There was no mistaking where he stood or what he believed.

"In his own words, 'A theologian is born by living, nay dying and being damned, not by thinking, reading, or speculating.' "

The time had come.

Josef's mouth suddenly went dry.

"Upon what did Luther base his confidence?"

The sentence came out raspy. He swallowed. Then swallowed again.

A theologian is born by living . . .

"To quote from Luther's famous hymn . . .

"A mighty fortress is our God,
A bulwark never failing;
Our helper, He amid the flood
Of mortal ills prevailing."

He'd crossed the line. There was no turning back now.

"Martin Luther faced his greatest test at the Diet of Worms where he was called upon to recant his position which he'd based upon God's Word. Facing the incredible power of the Church, and knowing that his life was being weighed in the balance, he refused to back down to their threats and intimidation. He said, 'Here I stand; I can do no other. God help me. Amen.' "

Josef stood before his congregation.

"God help us all," he said.

———

Mady was taking her afternoon nap. Josef sat in the parlor embroidering, amazed at how calm he felt. The message had been sent, but there was no way for him to know if it would be delivered. The important thing was that he'd sent it according to instructions. Now it was up to them.

Whoever they were.

If the message did indeed go through, he wondered how long it would be before they attempted to contact him, and how. He decided it didn't matter. He would continue working the plan he'd started last Sunday, regardless.

For now, it felt good to be on a stable emotional plane again. Last Sunday had been horrible and Meyerhof's funeral not much better. Only a handful of church members came to pay their respects.

God forgive them.

This morning wasn't easy. No one seemed to suspect that they'd witnessed an intense emotional decision on his part. But then, why should they?

He set aside the embroidery. It had worked its usual magic. He felt relaxed. Focused. He removed his glasses, stretched, and rubbed his eyes, then reached for his shoes. Time for his Sunday afternoon walk.

The phone rang.

He jumped from the chair and answered it after the second ring, not wanting to wake Mady.

"Yes?"

"Bulwark."

That was all that was said. It was a man's voice. Deep. Josef felt his nerves kick into overdrive.

"Yes," Josef replied as calmly as he could.

"We were beginning to think you weren't serious about being a friend of Luther."

"I am now."

Chapter 16

Tuesday, May 28, 1940

Konrad's such a child!"

"Why do you say that?"

"Because he acts like one."

Mady reclined in a chair in the parlor, her eyes closed and her arms draped over the sides. Lisette sat on the floor with Mady's foot in her lap. She was rubbing it.

"All Gael has to do is bat her eyelashes at him, and he does whatever she wants him to do," Lisette said. "How can men be so dense?"

"Have you tried batting your eyes at him?"

"Frau Schumacher!" Lisette squealed, her cheeks reddening.

Mady laughed. It was short-lived, overcome by an expression of pleasure. "Ooohhhhh . . . that feels so good," she said. "I just don't know how much more of this my feet can take."

"You're due in a month?"

Mady moaned. "Thirty more days of backaches, a child sitting on my bladder, sleeping on my back, emotions running rampant, and aching feet. Every day seems like an eternity."

"But you'll be bringing a new life into the world."

There was a cheerfulness and excitement in the girl's voice that

Mady hadn't felt in what seemed like years.

"Any time you want to trade places," she said.

Lisette put down one foot and moved on to the other, prompting a fresh wave of delighted moans.

"I'd like to have a baby," Lisette said.

"I once thought the same thing. Now I'm not so sure. You don't know how blessed you are not to be married."

"You don't mean that, do you?" Lisette asked.

Mady opened her eyes to see a young face marked with concern. "Don't mind me," Mady said. "It's just the aches and pains talking." She looked kindly at the younger woman. "Don't rush things. Your time will come."

"I don't know. I always thought Konrad and I would marry. But if Herr Nazi isn't making eyes at Gael, he's thinking about marches and guns and maneuvers."

"He does look good in his uniform, doesn't he?" Mady said with a smile.

"Frau Schumacher! You're a married woman!"

"All I'm saying is that he's a handsome man. You'll make a handsome couple."

"I don't know . . ." Lisette said. "Just when I think he's becoming a man, he starts acting like a little boy. Take today at lunch. Do you know how he eats his bread and sausage?"

Mady shook her head.

Lisette stopped rubbing to use her hands to explain. "He lays the bread flat, then places the sausage across the end closest to his mouth. Then, he pushes the sausage with his nose and eats the bread beneath it. He does this until the sausage is rolled all the way across the bread. He says this way the smell of the sausage makes the entire slice of bread taste better."

Mady grinned. "It's different. I'll give him that."

"It's disgusting!" Lisette cried. Taking Mady's foot, she began to knead it again.

"You'll find there are a lot of little things you'll have to adjust to once you're married," Mady said.

"I'd wager Pastor Schumacher doesn't roll his sausage across his bread with his nose."

Mady laughed. "He has his share of annoying habits."

"I find that hard to believe," Lisette said. "He's always so noble and dignified."

"You don't live with him."

A silence fell between them. From the impish smile on Lisette's face, Mady could tell she was aching to know something personal about Josef but was too polite to ask.

"For instance," Mady said, "he throws a tantrum every time I ask him to light the stove."

"I don't believe it!" Lisette squealed.

"It's true."

"Why?"

Mady shrugged her shoulders. "He just does."

Lisette's thumbs pressed deep into Mady's instep, eliciting another moan of delight.

"I can't begin to pay you what you're worth," Mady said.

"You can rub my feet someday when I'm with child."

"Then you'll appreciate what this means to me."

Mady let her head fall back. She closed her eyes. "When is Konrad shipping out?" she asked.

"He doesn't have a definite date yet, but it can't be soon enough."

Mady raised her head.

"I shouldn't have said that," Lisette said.

"Are things that bad between you two?"

"Oh no! It's not us . . . it's his . . . his father."

"Konrad's having trouble with his father?"

"I shouldn't say anything."

"The bruises," Mady said.

Lisette looked up at her.

Mady continued. "He tries to hide them. They're not from training and war games, are they?"

Lisette shook her head.

173

"His father beats him?"

"And Willi too."

Mady fell silent as she contemplated the matter. Then she asked, "Should I have Pastor Schumacher speak to Herr Reichmann?"

Lisette grew horrified. "No! That would only make things worse! I shouldn't have told you."

Mady reached out and touched Lisette's head. "You were right to tell me," she said. "A secret like that is an awful burden to bear alone. We'll just keep it between us."

Lisette smiled weakly. "Thank you."

They returned to their previous positions—Mady slumped in the chair while Lisette rubbed her feet.

"Are you planning to wait for him?" Mady asked.

"If he'll have me."

"Give him a few months in the army with nothing but cold food and the company of men. My guess is he'll return with a whole new outlook on life."

"I used to think that, but now I'm not so sure. Maybe I should look for someone like Pastor Schumacher. But I don't think there are any more like him around, at least not that I've seen."

"What do you see in Pastor Schumacher that's so attractive?" Mady asked. It wasn't idle curiosity. Lisette's comment had taken her by surprise. Mady hadn't thought of Josef as being attractive to other women. Her question appeared to make Lisette uncomfortable, yet not enough to keep her from answering.

"Well . . . the way he enjoys being around you," she said.

"What makes you think that?"

"The embroidery basket beside the chair in his study. I think it's sweet that he allows you to sit in his study with him and embroider while he's working."

With the mood of confession in the air, Mady debated whether or not to reveal to Lisette the truth about the embroidery basket. She decided against it. "Well, not everything is as it seems," she said.

Lisette's shoulders slumped. She looked like a balloon deflating. "Don't say things like that!" she cried. "You and Pastor Schumacher are the only hope I have!"

"Only hope?"

"If the two of you can't be happy in a marriage, who can?"

Mady scolded herself. She'd spoken without considering that Lisette's life at home was little better than Konrad's. Naturally, the girl dreamed of something better. Given time, she'd learn the truth about married couples. She didn't need to be disillusioned now.

"All I'm saying," Mady said, "is that there are times when Pastor Schumacher prefers his privacy. Even after a year and a half of marriage, there are still things about him I don't understand."

She kept her tone light, not wanting to reveal to Lisette her current concerns. Josef had been spending greater amounts of time in his study. Arranging his files. Cataloging his books. Writing page after page, much more so than he normally did for his sermons.

There was also the increasing number of trips to Berlin on the tram. Josef never used to volunteer to stand in ration lines. Now he insisted. At first she thought he was being considerate of her condition. But most times he came back empty-handed, saying they'd run out before he reached the front of the line. She didn't think anything of it until Fräulein Baeck and her twin sister stopped by recently and offered her their ration of milk. "Little mothers should drink plenty of milk," Fräulein Baeck had told her. Josef had left before the twin fräuleins on the same errand, yet he'd returned home after them, with nothing more than an excuse.

The wife in her immediately suspected there might be another woman. But then Mady dismissed the idea, for Josef wasn't romantic enough to attract other women.

"How did you and Pastor Schumacher meet?" Lisette asked.

"At church. He and his family were members of the congregation when my father was pastor."

"Are they still around? Pastor Schumacher never speaks of his family. Does he have brothers and sisters?"

"He had one brother. They're all dead now. His father was

killed by the Nazis. A case of mistaken identity."

"How sad."

"I'm not certain how his mother and brother died. Josef never speaks of them. All I know is that it was some kind of tragedy. My father was called out one night, and he brought Josef home with him."

"Josef lived at your parents' house?"

Mady smiled and shook her head. "Only for a night. He was attending the university at the time."

"And were you attracted to him then?"

Mady reflected a moment. "Come to think of it, yes, I think my attraction to him began that night. Before that time I knew who he was, but never paid any attention to him."

"What was it about him that caught your attention?"

"I think it was his vulnerability. He took the death of his mother and brother pretty hard."

"And you don't know how they died?"

Mady shook her head. "Father wouldn't tell me. And Josef still hasn't. I imagine he would if I asked him. I've just never pressed him to tell me."

"Did Pastor Schumacher's brother look anything like him?"

"I never met his brother," Mady said.

"Was his brother younger or older?"

Mady pondered a moment before answering. "Younger, I think."

From the expression on Lisette's face, Mady assumed the girl found her lack of knowledge about her husband's family odd.

"What finally brought the two of you together?" she asked.

Relieved that she knew the answer to this question, Mady said, "That's easy. My father."

"Your father played matchmaker?"

"I hadn't thought of it in those terms," Mady said. "But, yes, I think he did. Josef was coming to the house regularly by then, discussing theology with my father. They'd spend hour upon hour in Father's study, shouting at each other."

"Shouting?"

"It's amazing how men can get worked up over theology. I used to sit in the parlor and wait for Father's door to open. Then I'd pretend I was reading a book or sewing."

"And then Pastor Schumacher started courting you."

"He never would've begun courting me had not Father put the idea in his mind. Josef . . . Pastor Schumacher is amazingly single-minded about things. At that point in his life he was focused totally on his studies, books and theology."

Lisette shook her head. "Just like Konrad with his guns and the military. So what did you do?"

"I batted my eyes at him. You know . . . flirted."

Mady said it in all seriousness, but she could hold back her laughter only so long.

Lisette was wide-eyed, appearing aghast until Mady laughed. She then asked, "Was he romantic when he courted you?"

The smile on Mady's face faded. Their courtship had little to do with romance. Rarely were they alone as a couple. Mostly it was the four of them together—she and Josef and her mother and father—playing parlor games, talking over coffee, strolling on a Sunday afternoon.

She couldn't even remember the first time Josef had kissed her, if indeed he did before they were married. After a time it was just assumed they would get married, and Josef went along with it. Mady did too, because it was the practical thing to do. Her family liked Josef. She liked him as well. He was following in her father's footsteps. Becoming so much like her father.

"Well? Was he romantic?" Lisette asked again.

"Yes," Mady replied with a smile, hoping it was real enough to convince the girl.

"Maybe I should ask Pastor Schumacher to give Konrad a few lessons," Lisette said lightheartedly. "He knows nothing of romance or what a girl wants. To him, I'm just another one of the boys."

"That'll change," Mady assured her. "You wait until he comes home after his first tour with the army. You'll be surprised at how amorous he'll be."

Lisette blushed. "A girl can hope, at least," she said. With a sigh, she stood. "It's getting late. I must be on my way."

With both arms straining, Mady managed to push herself up to a standing position. She walked Lisette to the door. "Thank you," she said to the younger girl. "You are a treasure."

Lisette smiled. "I enjoy coming over here. You and the pastor have been so sweet to me. To all of us, really. I know there are some people in the church who say some bad things about him, but they'd complain if the Apostle Paul himself were their pastor. Even Konrad is impressed with him."

"Really?" There was no feigning surprise. The news that anyone in the Reichmann household thought kindly of Josef was surprising. She'd have to tell Josef.

"Oh yes! Just yesterday, Neff was making fun of the pastor over something—he was just being Neff, he didn't mean anything by it—and I thought Konrad was going to slug him."

"I'll have to tell Josef. He'll be pleased to hear this about Konrad. Again, thank you, dear."

Lisette gave Mady a peck on the cheek. Then she was gone.

Mady slumped into the chair. After a short time, her feet began aching again. She rested. It was so easy for her to grow short of breath these days.

She smiled at the thought of Lisette. Such a remarkably sweet girl considering her upbringing. Mady hoped that if she gave birth to a girl, she would grow up to be like Lisette. She relished the idea of having someone like Lisette to talk to every day. To have a close relationship with her daughter was a wonderful thought.

As she rested, her mind replayed portions of their conversation. She was amused by Lisette's yearning for romance. She was like that once. Looking back on it now, they were little-girl thoughts. Lisette would realize this, too, someday. Romance was an illusion, the product of imaginative minds. Life was hardly romantic.

Still, it was a nice dream. She wished life were different. Romantic. She pitied the young people. They'd have to find out for themselves.

For Konrad, the thought of battle and life in the military was a romantic dream. He'd learn otherwise soon enough. And for Lisette, the thought of a relationship between man and woman was but a fanciful dream. Like Konrad, she too would be introduced to reality.

Her thoughts left Mady somber.

Everyone has to grow up sometime.

With the weight of her unborn child pressing down upon her, Mady wondered if she would ever love the father of this child.

Chapter 17

Monday, June 10, 1940

By now Josef knew their route and was waiting for them. Three strapping young men in Hitler Youth uniforms came striding toward him. One was Konrad. Josef recognized one of the other two from his previous encounters; the third face was new to him.

"Well, look who we have here," said the familiar face. To the unknown boy, he said, "Watch this."

He strode up to within a couple of feet of Josef. "Heil Hitler!" he shouted.

Josef returned the greeting, halfheartedly.

His greeter laughed, then saluted again, "Heil Hitler!"

Rather than risk giving them a reason to harass him, again Josef returned the salute.

"Heil Hitler!" the boy shouted a third time.

"Heil Hitler," Josef replied.

"That's enough," Konrad said.

The third member of their party giggled. He ran up to Josef. "Is this the one? Heil Hitler!" he shouted.

Before Josef had a chance to reply, Konrad roughly shoved the new member of the team aside. "I said enough!"

Both boys continued laughing. They also backed off.

Konrad then said to Josef, "I would think you'd have enough sense to stay home at night. You're lucky I'm here. I was nearly assigned to another patrol."

Konrad's comment was not lost on Josef. While events of the days since the Bulwark sermon had bolstered his boldness, he wasn't devoid of fear. He came close to returning home twice while waiting for the patrol to arrive.

"I need to talk to you," Josef said.

"Again? Are you going to take me to another dead Jew's house?"

His two buddies grinned like hyenas at this.

Josef didn't dignify the comment with a response. He knew Konrad had said it for the benefit of his buddies.

"Over here," Konrad said. He led Josef around the street corner, out of earshot but not out of sight of his patrol. "What now?"

Josef removed the gold coin from his pocket. He held it toward Konrad on the flat of his hand.

Konrad stared at it.

"Do you recognize it?"

"Of course I do."

"It's your coin."

"So?"

Konrad was no longer looking at the coin. His eyes were obsidian blades leveled at Josef.

"I know you didn't kill Professor Meyerhof," Josef said.

The comment disarmed Konrad. Clearly, he was expecting an accusation.

"You didn't recognize the house when we approached it that night," Josef explained. "Did you see the coin on his bed?"

Konrad gave the slightest of nods. "That's why I ran," he said softly. His ego rallied back. "But I could have killed him," he said.

"Why do you say that?"

"Two reasons. First, he was a Jew. And second, I'm a soldier of the Third Reich."

Josef chose not to comment, for the moment. "How do you

think your coin got into the professor's house?" he asked.

"He probably stole it," Konrad said.

"You don't believe that."

"Jews are notorious thieves."

"I suppose next you're going to tell me Professor Meyerhof overpowered you when he stole it."

Konrad's jaw set. He didn't appreciate Josef's humor.

"It's as easy to believe that scenario as it is to believe he would have sneaked into your house and stole it."

Konrad said nothing.

"When did you see the coin last?" Josef asked.

"The night you gave it to me."

"What happened to it?"

"I never saw it after that night."

"It was in your pocket when you left. Was it there the next morning?"

"Maybe I threw it away and the old Jew found it alongside the road. He was always walking the streets at night after curfew. Even that night at your house. The Christmas party."

"You're telling me you threw it away?"

"I could have."

"Did you?"

Silence.

"When did you see the coin last?" Josef asked again.

From the way Konrad's eyes moved side to side, it was evident there was a debate raging in the boy's mind. Josef could only pray that the truth would win.

"My father took the coin from me," he said at last. "Mine and Willi's."

Reichmann. So, what Mady had told him was true. Should he leave it at that, or press forward?

"Go ahead. Say it," Konrad prompted him.

"Say what?"

Wrong response. It only angered Konrad.

"Say it!" he shouted loud enough to draw the attention of his buddies. "Say it!" This time he punctuated his words with a shove to Josef's shoulder. "You think my father killed that Jew, don't you?"

"I didn't say that."

"You didn't have to!"

"Konrad . . ."

"And what if he did? He's a hero. Decorated by the Kaiser himself. That professor of yours was nothing more than an infestation, a cockroach to stomp on."

Josef's heart failed within him. He'd hoped he had made a little progress with Konrad. Apparently not.

Konrad turned the tables. "You know my father is suspicious of you," he said. "A single word from him, or me, could earn you another visit from the SS. Is that what you want?"

The threat achieved an internal victory. The reminder of his first visit to Gestapo Headquarters was sufficient to start Josef's stomach to churning.

"Is that how you see me, Konrad? Am I a cockroach to be stepped on, too?"

Konrad glared at him. "Just stay out of my way," he said. Turning smartly on his heel, Konrad marched back toward his buddies.

They continued their patrol and within minutes were out of sight. Josef walked home.

Tuesday, June 11, 1940

This is crazy. Ministers are supposed to preach and perform weddings and funerals and give spiritual counsel. I must have missed the lecture at university on pastoral espionage.

The voice on the phone had instructed him to go to a pub in Stralau, which turned out to be a dimly lit, filthy place. He was to order a Bulwark beer, something that had sent the pub's owner, a hairy, overweight man who looked like a pile of unwashed laundry, into a cursing frenzy.

A mug of draft was slammed down in front of him, half the contents sloshing over its sides. Still speaking in curses, the owner told Josef that he had but one tap and Josef would drink from it like everyone else or get out.

Convinced he had the wrong pub, Josef was about to leave when he saw a paper corner protruding from beneath the mug. He stared at it a long minute before making any move. Then, slipping his hand as casually as he could to the base of the mug, he retrieved the paper, paid for the drink, and left the pub on shaky legs.

He had to pull out his glasses to make sense of the blurred markings on the paper. It was a Kreuzberg address. Josef sighed heavily. He didn't know if he could continue.

For the past several weeks the voice on the phone had sent him on one errand after another, such as picking up a sealed envelope beneath a bench at the Tiergarten and leaving it on his tram seat at the Barn District; or picking up a small package from a Spandau tailor and delivering it to a clothing store owner on the Unter den Linden; or relaying a phrase from a cemetery mourner in Neukolln to a tuxedoed gentleman at the Opera House.

He'd expected to be tested. What he hadn't anticipated was the damage the tests were doing to his nerves. It was all becoming too much for him. He developed the feeling that everyone he passed was scrutinizing him—at church, walking down the street, on the tram. Hardly a moment went by when he didn't feel someone was watching him. Then there was Mady. His excuses were growing thin, and she was becoming increasingly irritable.

He looked at the paper in his hand. Kreuzberg.

Shoving it in his pocket, he set off on foot, wishing now that he'd brought the motorcar despite the fact that by doing so he would be using fuel rations needed for pastoral duties. If he didn't make it out of this neighborhood alive, the fuel rations would do him little good.

The streets through which he walked had a tradition of violence. Secret societies protected their territories with knives, guns, and clubs. These gangs of racketeers had taken over the places of entertainment, had furnished alibis for its members, and offered bribes to lawyers while pressuring any witnesses. The last Josef heard, there were eighty-five such societies in this area.

This was also the former haunt of mass murderer Karl Grossman. Before he was caught, twenty-three mutilated bodies were found either slumped over on park benches, lying in wastebins, or floating in the canals. In some respects, the residents here made the Third Reich seem almost friendly.

The air was saturated from the river that ran parallel to the street he walked, the moisture causing Josef's shirt and pants to stick to his limbs as he hurried along. He tried to stay clear of buildings, quickly moving from light to light. Occasionally, he'd catch sight of a figure or two in the shadows. Keeping his eyes straight ahead, he picked up the pace of his walking.

He reached the river crossing at Markgrafendamm. Old Treptow Park could be seen on the far bank. Josef crossed the bridge, relieved to get Stralau behind him.

Just as he was about to make it to the other side, a figure stepped out from the opposite riverbank and blocked his way. A glint of steel extended from his hand.

"Empty your pockets."

The voice was raspy. A grating cough followed the demand.

"I don't want any trouble," Josef said.

"You're in luck. The price for a trouble-free crossing is your money."

Josef reached into his pockets. "I don't have much," he said. As he pulled his pockets inside out to show the thief, the piece of paper with the Kreuzberg address fell to the ground. Josef reached for it.

"Stop!" the thief shouted.

Josef froze mid-reach.

"What's that?"

"Just an address. It's not worth anything to anyone but me."

"Hand it to me."

"No." The word popped out of his mouth before Josef realized what he'd said.

"You want to get stuck, don't you?" the thief shouted, brandishing the blade.

His eyes fixed on the blade, sweat coursing down his temples, Josef insisted, "It's not valuable to anyone but me." He began to reach for it again.

"Back away! Back away!" the thief yelled. He advanced on Josef with jabbing motions.

Remaining crouched, Josef backed up, trying to remember the address on the paper. He couldn't. All he could remember was Kreuzberg.

"It's nothing valuable!" But the more Josef insisted, the greater value the man placed on the paper. He looked down at it as if it were a bar of gold.

At that moment everything was reduced to the tiny slip of paper lying on the bridge. For the thief, it was a treasure of some kind. For Josef, it was the culmination of everything that he'd done in the past few weeks. Lose the Kreuzberg address and everything would be lost.

The thief bent down to get the paper. The tip of his blade lowered.

Without thinking about what he was doing, Josef launched himself forward, screaming at the top of his lungs and startling the thief. His swift action brought the man upright and caused him to take a step back so that he was caught off balance. Josef lowered a shoulder and plunged into the man's chest, sending him reeling backward, arms flailing like windmills. Pushing forward, Josef's momentum backed the thief up against the bridge railing. He then continued shoving him up and over the railing, falling and wailing, until the river enveloped the man and swallowed the sound of his cry.

Josef stood transfixed, staring down at the agitated water, barely able to comprehend what had just taken place. Urging his shaking limbs onward, he retrieved the piece of paper from the ground and ran toward the park.

He stumbled toward a lamppost and leaned against it, his heart doing flip-flops in his chest. Several deep breaths later, he rushed on to his destination.

In Kreuzberg there were buildings with factories on five floors and a lift that connected the different levels. This was the Kreuzberg mix—buildings combining offices, workshops, small-scale factories, and flats. The address on the paper Josef had been given at the pub indicated the location of one of these abandoned buildings.

It had a stark façade, a naked hideousness. The courtyard was nothing more than a hole through which a patch of stars could be seen. Josef entered a narrow stairwell, its cement stairs and walls coated with grime and filth. He made his way to the third floor.

From all appearances, the building was deserted, though Josef figured some of the rooms were still occupied. But it was too dark to see any evidence to confirm his suspicion. It was just a feeling. The same feeling told him he was being watched.

At the top of the stairs he found a door with a number matching the one on the paper. A hole in the wall let in enough light for him to read the number. Had the room been farther down the hallway, Josef wouldn't have been able to see the numbers in the darkness. And he hadn't thought to bring matches with him.

He stood at the doorway. One more crossroad in his journey. Enter, knock, or walk away? Common sense argued for him to walk—no, run—and not turn back. Return to his study and shut the door and forget this nonsense. What difference could he really make? Better to spend his days embroidering, keeping his mouth shut, muttering his opinions to himself, and quietly raise his soon-to-be-born child.

But what kind of world would his child enter? What kind of Germany would he or she inherit from a father who hid while the Nazis shaped it into their image?

Josef knocked on the door.

He waited. There was no answer.

He knocked again.

There was a sudden rustling down the hallway. Something scrambling through the papers and trash that caused his heart to start. He couldn't see anything in the blackness, but whatever it was—a cat or some kind of rodent—it ran away from him.

The door latch sounded. But the door didn't open.

"Yes?"

It was a whisper. Josef couldn't tell if the person on the other side of the door was male or female, adult or child.

He answered as he'd been instructed. With a single word. "Bulwark."

There was a pause.

Then, "Adolf."

Josef found it humorous that the countersign he'd been given was the Führer's first name. Who said espionage agents didn't have a sense of humor?

The door opened a crack. A forehead appeared, then a pair of eyes much lower than Josef expected. They stared at him.

"Bulwark," Josef said again.

"I heard you the first time."

The door swung open. A wiry man, barely a hundred and sixty centimeters tall, backed away.

"Don't just stand there. Come in."

Josef crossed the threshold.

"Close the door! Quit dawdling!"

Closing the door behind him, Josef stepped into the small flat. It appeared to have only three small rooms. A single candle in a wooden spiral holder burned atop a tiny table. The light illuminated scarred walls and a littered floor. He saw no evidence that anyone lived here.

"Where are the others?" Josef asked.

"What others?"

"I was led to believe this would be my first meeting."

"It is," said the tiny man.

"Well?"

"It's a meeting between you and me."

Josef felt his ire rise. "I've come all this way for this?"

"Disappointed?"

"Well, yes. Haven't I been tested enough?"

"Life is full of disappointments." The man stood on the other side of the table with his arms folded. Squinting eyes looked Josef up and down. "We had to see if you could follow directions."

"I think I've proven myself in that regard," Josef said. "You've sent me all over Berlin."

"And now you can go home."

"That's it? I walk in here and you tell me to go home?"

"You were expecting the lights and music and fanfare of the Lustgarten? We don't do that sort of thing."

"When will I meet the others?"

"In good time."

"Are you going to test me some more? What do I have to do to convince you?"

"That's not for me to say."

"So I just go home?"

"Do you still have the piece of paper you were given at the pub?"

"With this address on it?"

"That's the one."

"I still have it."

"Let me see."

Josef reached into his pocket and produced the paper.

The man snatched the paper from his hand. Furious, he shouted, "This paper can get both of us killed! Why do you still have it?"

"So that I could find . . ."

"You don't have a brain? You can't remember a simple address?" His voice rose with each sentence.

Josef thought of the man on the bridge.

"Never leave anything in writing! Memorize it, then destroy it!"

The man was nearly hysterical. And rightly so. Had Josef been stopped by police or SS, the paper would have revealed their place of meeting.

"I wasn't thinking," Josef said.

"And that will get us all killed every time!"

"It won't happen again."

"Well? What are you waiting for? Destroy it!"

Josef looked at the paper.

"Destroy it!" the man shouted again.

Josef held the paper toward the candle flame.

"Not that way."

Josef stopped. "Then how?"

"Eat it."

"Eat it?"

"That's what I said. Eat it. There will be times you don't have a flame."

"But there's one here now."

"This way you'll remember the lesson longer."

Josef grinned. "I'll remember." He held the paper to the flame.

"I said EAT IT!" the man barked.

Josef paused, looked the man in the eye, crumpled the paper, and placed it in his mouth. It took several chews to make the paper soft enough to choke down.

"Three nights from now, at ten P.M., 22 Brüderstrasse. You'll meet the others."

"Understood," Josef said.

"Repeat it."

"Ten P.M., 22 Brüderstrasse, three nights from now."

The man called Adolf nodded. "I'll leave first. Count to thirty, then you leave." Without another word, he strode past Josef and out the door.

Alone in the room, Josef took a deep breath and allowed his shoulders the luxury of slumping. This entire night flashed through his mind—deceiving Mady, slipping out of the house, the pub in Stralau, the thief on the bridge, dining on crumpled paper in an abandoned flat—this was going to make a better Germany?

He waited for what he considered to be an adequate count to thirty without actually counting, blew out the candle, and exited the flat.

Letting his weight carry him down the three flights of stairs, his thoughts turned to the trip back home. If he hurried he might be able to catch the tram to Unter den Linden and from there . . .

As soon as his foot descended from the last step he was hit by three spotlights. He froze, the bright lights blinding him.

"Halt! If you value your life, don't move!"

All he could make out were forms, but there were a lot of them. The lights were mounted on motorcars. Several blinks and Josef's eyes adjusted somewhat to the light, enough to see Adolf, his hands raised, with two men in uniform on each side of him, their side arms pointed at him.

A figure passed in front of one of the lights.

"Well, well, if it isn't the Reverend Schumacher."

The voice was familiar.

"I suppose you'll tell me you're simply out visiting a member of the flock." The form drew nearer. Josef could just barely make out a Gestapo uniform. With the click of his heels, the man in the uniform saluted and shouted, "Heil Hitler!"

Josef raised his arm and offered a weak but appropriate response.

"Good! You haven't forgotten me."

With another step forward, the fleshy folds of skin under the man's eyes became prominent in the harsh light. Sturmbannführer Wolff grinned at him.

Chapter 18

Wednesday, June 12, 1940

The pains woke her.

"Josef?"

Mady felt the bed beside her. Josef wasn't there.

"Josef!" she shouted into the darkness.

Her cry went unanswered.

She plunged her head against the pillow, clenching her teeth as the pain grew. She lay stiff and immobile, taking desperate gulps of air. Beads of sweat formed on her forehead. Finally, the pain began to subside. She lay there for a while, panting, then wiped her brow with the bed sheets and threw them off.

With a moan she maneuvered her legs over the edge of the bed and pushed herself up into a sitting position. She rested.

"Josef!" Her voice was weaker.

Still no answer.

Where are you?

She fought a panic rising within her. The baby was coming, and she was alone. Her feet set down on the cool wooden floor. Her hand guiding her, she felt her way around the edge of the bed to the light switch.

There was a sudden onslaught of light.

The clock indicated it was a few minutes past 2:00 A.M.

Her gaze fell on the empty bed. She fought back a new pain, this one caused by anxiety.

"Josef?"

Maybe he'd fallen asleep in his study. Lately, he'd been given to working well into the night. Whatever it was he was doing.

She made her way to the study, switching on lights as she went. The study was as empty as her bed.

A fresh pain started. Mady braced herself against the doorjamb with one hand; with the other she held her stomach. As the pain escalated, she stumbled toward the chair in Josef's study and managed to collapse in it. Everything in her world ceased to exist; her only thought was the feeling of lightning shooting through her abdomen. Throwing her head against the back of the chair, she cried out.

As in bed, the pain reached a peak, and then subsided, leaving her weak and sweaty. Her eyes closed, her breathing coming in short gasps, she sat there, helpless.

She began to cry.

Get to the phone. Call Father.

She doubted he could get to her in time. And where was Josef?

Adolf, for this was the only name by which Josef knew the short man, stood nervously, his hands behind his head, his feet shifting his weight from one to the other.

"You led them here!" he screamed at Josef.

Before Josef could defend himself, one of the agents guarding the short man shouted for silence.

The Sturmbannführer, a smug smile on his face, took out a pair of gloves and made a show of putting them on. Josef had seen this show before. Gestapo Headquarters. An empty room lit by a single light bulb. Two men. Two pair of gloves. One ax handle.

"Seems you have graduated to a far more serious offense," the Sturmbannführer said, flexing his hands. "I must confess I was mistaken about you. I took you for an intelligent man, one who could learn a lesson."

"Don't tell them anything!" the short man shouted at Josef.

His outburst earned him a blow that knocked him to the ground. When he stayed down too long, the two guards kicked him until he got back on his feet.

Josef stood there, his thoughts divided between his present predicament and Mady. He wasn't surprised at being captured. He knew it was a possibility from the outset. Only he didn't think it would come this quickly, before he had a chance to do anything significant. His risk was for nothing. Mady would never forgive him.

A streak of activity caught the corner of his eye. Adolf bolted and slipped past the cover of light into the darkness of the open courtyard. He was a quick little man. He'd taken his guards, who now shielded their eyes against the glaring light, by surprise.

"After him!" bellowed the Sturmbannführer.

Just as Adolf had done, the guards crossed the sharp line that separated the light and the darkness.

Shouts came from the dark, ordering Adolf to halt. Then rifle fire. Two shots immediately followed by a sickening thump, like a sack of turnips falling off the back of a truck.

Everyone in the light listened to indiscriminate sounds coming from the darkness until one of the two guards stepped back into the light.

"Report!"

"Dead, Sturmbannführer."

The report was acknowledged with a nod. And that was it. A soul had passed from life to eternity that quickly, followed only by a simple nod. The Sturmbannführer turned his attention back to Josef.

The stark reality of it all struck Josef with force. Adolf's killers gave him no more thought than an accountant gave one of his entries when he moved it from one column to another. To them killing was a transaction. They'd removed a man from the *live* column and placed him in the *dead* column. He was no longer a concern.

Suddenly the role of the Nazis in Germany became as clear to Josef as an accountant's column of numbers. He saw beyond the rhetoric, beyond the public works improvements, beyond the emphasis on building a stronger youth and a vibrant Germany, beyond the increased number of jobs. What he saw now was a single overriding principle: Remove anyone who gets in the way. Move them from one column to the other. The Jews to Poland. The Communists to Russia. The dissidents to work camps. And those who dare to speak out—move them from the live column to the dead column.

Tonight the Sturmbannführer was the accountant, and Josef was a cipher.

"As you can see, we're efficient," the Sturmbannführer said. "And now, you will tell us who sent you here and for what purpose."

Josef stood alone. All the lights were trained on him. All eyes were focused on him. All guns were pointed at him. The threat of pain was imminent. This was the moment he'd feared. He wasn't sure how much he could take before telling them what they wanted to know.

You're not alone.

The words came to him unbidden, as clearly as if someone had spoken them. In them he found a measure of strength, and the words to speak.

"I am the Lord's servant," Josef said.

The Sturmbannführer was taken aback by his answer. When he recovered, he laughed. "You're telling me that God sent you here?"

"Yes."

Turning to the armed shadows standing behind the lights, he said, "He says God sent him here!"

Male laughter echoed in the courtyard.

The back of the Sturmbannführer's hand was lightning quick, snapping Josef's head to one side.

"Since it would be difficult for us to verify that God sent you," he said, "I'm afraid we'll need another answer."

Josef tasted blood. "Then you'll need to ask another question," he said.

A second blow snapped his head in the opposite direction.

"I'm a minister," Josef explained, "not a political operative. I seek to follow God, not the will of any man or group of men."

"And if that will conflicts with the will of the Führer?"

Josef knew his answer would get him another blow to the face, or worse. But he'd come this far. "Then the will of the Führer must give way to the will of the Father."

The anticipated blow never came.

"Your next contact. Where, when, and with whom?"

Three nights from now, ten o'clock, 22 Brüderstrasse. The information popped into his head as if on cue. Rather than risk saying too much, Josef decided to say nothing at all.

The backhand to his jaw, while expected, hurt badly, nonetheless.

"Your next contact," the Sturmbannführer prompted.

Josef said nothing.

A hand motion by the Sturmbannführer caused Josef to flinch. It summoned an armed agent to Josef's side, who then raised a handgun to Josef's temple.

"Reverend Schumacher, I'm not a patient man. Don't test me. You will give me names, locations, and times."

"And if I do?"

The Sturmbannführer's head lifted like a hound dog finding a scent. "If you do, and if the information proves valuable, you will return to your beautiful wife and . . . has she given birth yet?"

"No."

"You will return to your beautiful wife and your unborn child and your pulpit to carry on your work."

It was a big carrot the Sturmbannführer dangled in his face, too big for Josef to believe. But the stronger persuasion was in the form of a gun barrel that hovered inches from the side of his head. He thought of the nameless, faceless people who would be arrested by the SS and Gestapo if he revealed the location of the meeting. He found it difficult to consider giving his life for people he'd never met. Who would know the information came from him? What if they were led to believe that Adolf leaked the information before he was killed?

No. How could he live with himself knowing he'd sullied a dead man's reputation just to save his own neck? Maybe he should make it easy on himself and do what Adolf had done. If he could make it across the courtyard and into the abandoned building, he could possibly lose them in the maze of black corridors.

"Well?" the Sturmbannführer shouted.

It wasn't a grand gesture, but Josef managed to hold out with a stubborn shake of his head. Out of the corner of his eye, Josef saw the guard look to the Sturmbannführer for instructions.

"Not here," the Sturmbannführer said. "Put him in the motor-car."

The guard grabbed him by the arm. Another guard grabbed the other arm, and Josef was dragged to a waiting motorcar. He managed to gain his feet and took a step toward the open back door.

The guard on his right laughed. "Traitors don't ride in motor-cars like normal people," he said.

The trunk of the motorcar was opened, and Josef was thrown inside. Before he could adequately fold himself, the trunk lid was slammed shut, banging against his knees.

Curled up in the tight black quarters, he heard the doors slam shut and the engine start. A second later the rear tires spun in the dirt before taking hold. He bounced around like an insect in a jar. Exhaust fumes filled the small compartment and nauseated him.

By the time Olbricht arrived, Mady's pains had subsided. She sat in the parlor, balancing a cup of hot tea on her stomach.

It was nearly 3:00 A.M.

The door burst open and a harried Olbricht flew in, a cigar

protruding from his mouth. Edda was close behind. Through the open doorway Mady could hear the rumble of the Essex Super Six, its motor still running.

"Mady!"

The sight of his daughter, calm and holding a cup of tea, wasn't what he'd expected to find. It temporarily dumbfounded him, causing him to stop in his tracks and stare at her. Edda nearly ran into him. She was quicker to size up the situation.

"The labor pains have stopped," Edda said.

Mady gave an embarrassed shrug. "I tried calling you again, but you'd already left."

"Are you all right now, dear?" Edda asked.

"Where's Josef? Hasn't he come home yet?" Olbricht growled. His hands flexed like they wanted to tear into something.

"He's not here," Mady said. "I'm sorry to bring you all the way over here in the middle of the night."

Edda knelt by her side and stroked her forehead. "You did the right thing, dear," she said.

"Get your things," Olbricht ordered.

"It's all right, Father. The pains have stopped and—"

"I said get your things!" he snapped.

There was no arguing with him when he was in one of his moods.

Mady handed her mother the teacup so that she could push herself up. Edda handed it right back.

"You stay there," she said. "I'll pack your things."

While Edda went into the bedroom, Olbricht stormed out of the house, leaving the door open. Seconds later the motorcar's engine stopped running.

Never before had Mady heard her father curse. She did tonight.

Josef was sick and light-headed from the exhaust fumes when the motorcar finally pulled to a stop. While it was difficult to tell, he guessed they'd been traveling for nearly twenty minutes. The motorcar had started and stopped often and rarely picked up any speed to speak of.

He felt the motorcar shake as doors were slammed shut. Moments later the trunk opened. He was greeted by two flashlight beams in his face.

"Get out!"

His knees were stiff as he climbed out of the trunk without assistance.

"Over there."

A beam from one of the lights directed him to walk around the driver's side of the motorcar. Josef did as he was told.

The size of the party had diminished. Although there were still three motorcars, from what Josef could see, there were only five men. They were all armed.

Standing on the edge of a large patch of woods, he found he didn't recognize the location. The ground beneath his feet was soft and moist. The air was cooler, fresher than it had been under the lights in the cramped courtyard.

"Keep walking."

Josef was led into the woods. He thought of escape. If he lowered his shoulder, he might be able to knock over at least two of the three men who were directly behind him. The problem was the flanking guards, one on each side. What were the chances of his escaping into the woods under cover of darkness without being shot?

Not good. Not good at all.

He was a pastor, not a soldier. They were trained in handling prisoners and situations like this.

"This is far enough."

They were out of sight of the motorcar and the road now. One of the guards produced a shovel, which he threw against Josef's chest.

"How tall are you?" asked the Sturmbannführer.

"One hundred and eighty-eight centimeters," Josef said.

The Sturmbannführer looked him up and down and said,

"Start digging. We need a hole ninety centimeters wide, one hundred and eighty-eight centimeters long."

A chill shook Josef's body. This was the Gestapo's way of eliminating opposition without having to do a lot of paper work. He was about to become one of a growing number of Germans who simply disappeared.

Mady would never know what happened to him. His child would never know a father, only stories of how he left home one night and never returned. Olbricht, of course, would make inquiries, but he'd never learn anything. There would be no uproar. Disappearances like this were far too frequent, and Josef was far too unimportant to prompt an investigation.

The blade of the shovel sliced into the soft earth. Josef tossed a shovelful of dark earth to one side. Then another, and another. His captors made themselves comfortable, leaning against trees, lighting up cigarettes.

When the hole was mid-calf deep, Josef's breathing became labored. Sweat ran down the sides of his face and dripped off his chin. His back and arms ached.

"His wife is an attractive woman," the Sturmbannführer said to a guard standing next to him, "for a woman about to give birth, that is."

The guard grunted like an animal.

"Precisely," the Sturmbannführer said with a laugh. "Give her a few months. She comes from good stock."

"Worth a visit?"

"You won't be disappointed."

Josef knew what they were doing, and it was working. The shovel blade cut deeper now. Two forces swelled his chest as exertion was joined by anger. His eyes darted with each toss of dirt. There were simply too many of them, and they were placed too far apart.

Still, he had to try. Better to die from a bullet in the back while attempting to escape than from one in the back of the head while bending over a self-dug grave.

"Get him out of there," the Sturmbannführer commanded.

Had the Sturmbannführer detected what he was thinking? Four guards closed in on Josef before he had a chance to react. One ripped the shovel from his hands, and two hauled him out of the hole by his arms. The fourth aimed a rifle at his chest.

They lifted and turned and tossed him to the ground at the foot of the hole. Josef found himself on his knees, hands bound, head bowed, staring into his grave before he could muster any kind of resistance. Mercy and grace dangled from his neck over the pit.

The Sturmbannführer took a last draw on his cigarette, dropped it to the ground, and snuffed it out with the toe of his boot. Pulling his pistol, he walked behind Josef.

The next thing Josef felt was the cold barrel pressed against the base of his skull.

"Where and when are you to meet your contact?" the Sturmbannführer asked.

The strangest thing happened next. Josef's breathing eased, his heart calmed, his mind cleared. It was as if liquid assurance were being poured, and his body was the receptacle. His fear vanished.

Years of theological study, all theory up until this day, suddenly became real to him. The life that he'd experienced paled to insignificance compared to the life that awaited him. At that moment he realized no amount of suffering, or hardship, or pain, or heartache in this life would be remembered one second after a person first tasted the glory of heaven.

"Where and when?" the Sturmbannführer shouted.

Josef smiled. He began to sing:

"And though this world, with devils filled,
Should threaten to undo us,
We will not fear, for God hath willed
His truth to triumph through us."

The crack of a Gestapo pistol echoed through the woods.

Chapter 19

Mady bolted upright, suddenly awake. She thought she'd heard something. A cracking or popping sound of some sort. She strained to hear it again, but heard nothing except her own breathing.

Probably just the house settling. It was old, and she'd been away from her parents' home long enough to forget the noises it made.

She lay back down and stared at the ceiling. It felt so strange to be in her old room and pregnant. Her earliest memories were of this room. Would it provide her child's earliest memories, too?

She glanced at the curtained window. It was getting light outside. There would be no more sleeping tonight.

Why hasn't Josef called?

Surely if he came home and found she was not there he'd come for her, or at least call to make certain she was safe . . . wouldn't he? And if he wasn't home yet, where was he? Being late was one thing; staying out all night was completely unlike him.

As she'd been doing with greater frequency, she began to worry. For some reason, she worried better standing or sitting up, and with a cup of tea.

Pulling on a housecoat, she made her way downstairs and to the kitchen. The stove needed to be lit.

Mady began to cry.

"Now, now, what's this?" Father entered the kitchen.

Mady swiped at her tears. "I was about to fix myself a cup of tea."

Olbricht saw the stove's condition and set about lighting it, little realizing that the task was the cause of his daughter's tears.

Placing the teakettle on the flame, he turned his attention to his daughter. "I thought I heard a little mouse down here," he said, his eyes wrinkling with his smile. "Couldn't sleep?"

"Has Josef called?"

Olbricht's face clouded. He shook his head.

"This isn't like him," she said.

"He isn't the man we thought him to be, is he?" Olbricht replied.

The comment took Mady by surprise. While she expected sympathy, her father's statement indicated thoughts of which she'd not been aware.

Reading the surprise on his daughter's face, Olbricht said, "It's no secret his actions have been erratic of late, and frankly, I'm disappointed in the boy."

"He's been spending a lot of time in his study at home," Mady offered.

"Doing what?"

"I don't know exactly."

"Alone?"

"For hours at a time. Then he gets a phone call and he's gone."

"Suspicious. Where does he go?"

"He says it's church business or ministry, this or that, and while he's out, does he want me to have him stand in a ration line. Only he never comes home with anything."

"He's lying to you." It was a statement, not a question.

"I don't know," Mady answered anyway.

"For how long has this been going on?"

"About a month."

Suddenly Olbricht realized he didn't have a cigar between his teeth or in his hand. His hands fumbled in the air, then felt in his housecoat pocket and came up empty. With a look of chagrin he resigned himself to his cigarless state.

The teakettle began to steam. Father and daughter each fixed themselves a cup of tea and moved to the parlor to drink it. Through the windows Mady could see a pink sky, the promise of a clear spring day. She wished her future was as clear and rosy.

"I shouldn't tell you this," Father said, setting his tea on a small table and himself at the end of the sofa. Mady sat on the other end.

"Shouldn't tell me what?"

Her father's face screwed up, indicating that what he was about to say would be distasteful. "Your mother has never liked Josef," he said. "She didn't approve when he was courting you, or when you married."

Mady was stunned.

"She feels you married beneath yourself, and—while I was supportive of the marriage at first—now I'm afraid I must agree with her."

"Mother has never said anything. . . ."

Olbricht reached for his teacup and took a sip and shook his head as he swallowed. "Of course not. She was hoping she was wrong. Sadly, it now seems she was the insightful one."

"I . . . I don't know what to say," Mady stammered.

"The boy has bad blood in him," Olbricht explained.

"Bad blood?"

"You never knew his parents, did you? Odd sort. His father, Karl, was a brakeman on the railroad. A fanatical man. A Nazi. No common sense about him at all. He was a man of unbridled passions and almost no education. A dangerous combination. Do you remember how he died?"

Mady nodded. "Shot by the Nazis. A mistake, the way I remember it."

Olbricht took another sip of tea. "Had he lived, who knows

what kind of influence he would have had on Josef"—he motioned with a free hand toward her stomach—"and his grandchild."

A sip of tea.

"Has Josef ever told you how his mother and brother died?" he asked.

Mady shook her head.

"Not surprised, not surprised at all."

There was a long pause as her father stared off into the distance. Mady held her breath. Was he going to tell her, or was he waiting for her to ask?

"What has he told you about his brother?"

"Only that he was younger."

Olbricht nodded. His next swallow of tea drained the cup, which he then set aside. "The boy wasn't right in the head," he said. "His mother came down with the measles when she was carrying him. After he was born, when it became clear that something wasn't right with him, his father concocted a story, which he circulated at church and around town, that the boy caught fever and died."

"But he didn't," Mady surmised.

"They buried an empty coffin and hid the boy in the attic. Couldn't bring themselves to do away with him, but they couldn't allow anybody to see him, especially as Karl began to progress within the Nazi party."

"Aryan purity."

Her father nodded. "Then, after his father's death, Josef helped his mother secretly care for his brother as much as he could while still attending university. He offered to discontinue his university studies, but his mother forbade him to do that. The strain on her grew steadily worse.

"Then late one night, when Josef was home—who knows why she chose to do it then, rather than when he was away—he awoke and heard some kind of commotion in the attic. When he went upstairs to check on his brother, he found both his mother and brother dead by her hand."

"How awful!" Mady cried.

"When you think of it, though, there was a blessing in it," Olbricht mused. "Absent from the body, present with the Lord. There was no longer a place for them here, so God made a place for them in the hereafter."

Mady began pulling at her hair and absentmindedly chewing the ends.

"Like I said," Olbricht concluded, "bad blood."

"I knew their deaths were tragic, but I always thought it was some sort of accident," Mady said.

"Now you know why your mother had reservations. I was blinded by Josef's academic acumen. I only saw the things I wanted to see. And now Josef's unstable side is coming to light."

Olbricht took Mady's teacup from her and set it on the small table. Then he took her by the hands. To Mady's recollection, never in his life had he held her by the hands like this. He caught her gaze and held it. His eyes glistened.

"I don't tell you this often enough . . ." he began. His emotions choked off the rest of the sentence.

"I know, Poppa," Mady said softly.

With a determined shake of his head, Olbricht regained control of himself. "No, I have to say this." He blinked back tears, and then reestablished eye contact. "When your mother was carrying you, I didn't know if I wanted children. I was so determined to make something of myself in those days, and I thought children would only be a nuisance. And then you came along. . . ."

He smiled. His emotions rose again, and again he fought them back.

"I wasn't prepared for the impact you would have on me," he said. "The first time I saw you . . . you won me over. And there's nothing I wouldn't do for you. You know that, don't you?"

Mady was engaged in a struggle of her own. Her face was composed of tears and smiles.

"And I swore a long time ago that I would do anything . . .

anything to keep you from harm. It's a vow I intend to keep to my dying breath."

Images of the day the Nazis visited her father in his study flashed in her mind. Mady squeezed her father's hands. "I know, Poppa," she said.

"Sometimes it may seem like I'm meddling. . . ."

"I know you only want the best for me, Poppa."

"As God is my witness . . ."

"I love you, Poppa."

"And that vow goes for the little one on the way, too." He nodded toward Mady's midriff.

Edda appeared in the doorway. "There you are! Both of you!" she cried.

Olbricht took her entrance as his cue to get up and go to his study in search of a cigar.

Edda took his seat on the couch close to Mady. "How are you feeling this morning, dear?" She reached over and felt the ends of Mady's hair. Finding them wet, she shook her head.

"I'm all right, Momma," Mady said.

"Still no word from Josef?" She patted Mady's hand and stood. "We'll have your father make some calls after breakfast. Meanwhile, you go upstairs and get dressed."

"Yes, Momma," Mady said.

———

The only sound around the table was the clicking of breakfast dishes. Mady spread strawberry jam on a biscuit and took a bite. She had to admit, it felt good being waited on. Her food had been prepared for her. Everyone in the house insisted she stay off her feet; they brought her everything she wanted. All she had to do was ask.

Olbricht cleared his throat and shoved aside his plate, which still had a few untouched scraps of ham and eggs. He wiped his mouth with a napkin and, breaking the silence, said, "I've been talking with your mother and she agrees with me."

Mady looked at her mother, who nodded her agreement.

"We'll drive you back to the house where you'll gather together the things you need to move back here."

Edda reached over and patted Mady's hand. "It's for the best," she said.

"If you like," her father continued, "we can tell the church it's just until the baby comes. That'll give us sufficient time to figure out what should be done next."

"It will be better for both you and the baby," Edda said. "It frightens me to think of you all alone in that house. What would have happened had you given birth last night?"

Mady didn't want to move home. But she was scared. Having birth pangs without anyone around to help her had scared her. Josef's mysterious disappearance scared her, too. She was beginning to fear the worst, and the thought of being afraid and being alone was too much for her.

Her father pushed away from the table. "I'll bring the motorcar around," he said.

Edda stood. "While you're gone, I'll get your room better situated for you and the baby."

Mady made no attempt to stop them.

Chapter 20

Gunfire echoed through the woods.

Josef's right ear rang from the single shot. The next thing he knew, a pistol dropped to the ground next to him. Someone was clawing at the rope that bound his hands.

To the man, the SS guards were staring. Nodding. Their expressions no longer hardened.

His hands free, Josef was lifted to his feet and spun around. His face was inches from that of the Sturmbannführer.

"My brother!" The SS agent hugged Josef with such ferocity it took his breath away. There were tears in the man's eyes. To the others, he said, "Didn't I tell you? Are there any doubts now?"

Each man in turn came by and shook Josef's hand. Some of them wished him God's blessings. Then, exchanging good-byes, they made their way to the motorcars as though they'd been out all night on a hunting party.

"I knew you were our man," the Sturmbannführer said.

Josef was still shaken, his mouth unable to form words.

"Forgive me for the blows. We have to be careful. But I knew you were our man."

Josef didn't know which was more unsettling for him, facing a scowling Sturmbannführer, or a grinning one. He managed two words: "A test."

The Sturmbannführer nodded. "Had you given us the location of the contact . . ."

The implication was clear.

He didn't say it! Josef thought. *He alluded to it. Called it the location. A trick?*

The Sturmbannführer read his expression. He let loose a booming laugh. "Good. Good!" he said. "You have the mind of an operative. But if you are to survive, you will need to develop a poker face." Then, with a smile, he said, "Ten P.M., 22 Brüderstrasse, in three nights."

"And Adolf?"

"One of our best."

"He's not dead?"

"No. Again, I apologize for the ruse. The lights. Shots in the air. Ever concerned with detail, Adolf insisted on falling to the ground. Did you hear that? Was it effective?"

"It was effective."

The Sturmbannführer slapped him on the back. "Come, I'll take you home. Mady must be worried about you."

Not until they walked back to the motorcar did Josef, still in a daze, realize that the day had dawned.

Mady found it harder to leave than she'd expected. While her father wandered aimlessly from room to room with his hands in his pockets, puffing his cigar, she packed a travel case.

Secretly, she'd hoped to find Josef home when they arrived and that he'd have an explanation of some tragedy in the church family that required his presence all night, a home that had no telephone.

When she stepped into an empty house and Josef wasn't there, she didn't know if she was more angry or upset or embarrassed. She took his unexplained absence personally. What kind of wife was she not to know where her husband was? And what kind of marriage did they have when her husband was continuously sneaking out of the house?

By the time she'd finished throwing the last of her things in the travel case, she had decided. She was more angry than anything else. For Josef's sake, she hoped something bad had happened to him; otherwise she'd never forgive him.

The SS staff motorcar traveled north, leaving Berlin's skyline behind it. This time Josef sat in the front seat.

"Yes, I *am* SS," the Sturmbannführer said. "What better way to know the Reich's plans and investigate possible operatives like yourself?"

"The Rottenführer, the one with the ax handle, is he . . ."

"No. He's a brute of a man, as you can attest."

Josef was still in shock. The voice and uniform were that of his interrogator, while the demeanor and conversation were that of a colleague. He still hadn't adjusted to looking over at the Sturmbannführer and seeing a smiling face, or to calling the Sturmbannführer by his given name, Martin Wolff.

"Several times you've made reference to a larger organization," Josef said. "When am I going to be apprised of its purpose and goals?"

Wolff's smile faded. "Now," he said. "It's my task to brief you regarding your mission."

Josef resettled himself in the seat and blinked his eyes in an attempt to clear his head. He was weary and sore and sleepy. But this was hardly the time to relax.

"Aktion T4," Wolff said. "Heard of it?"

"No."

"Not surprised."

Wolff gripped and regripped the steering wheel. He had no difficulty controlling the motorcar, but his emotions were a different matter. Watching a disciplined SS Sturmbannführer struggle to maintain his composure was disturbing to Josef. What was so horrible it would have this effect on the man?

Wolff gave no apology for the momentary pause. "It is an internal message," he said, "typed on Hitler's personal stationery. The *T4* is the designation of the headquarters for this operation, Tiergartenstrasse 4."

A mental picture of the area formed in Josef's mind. He was familiar with the street and surrounding area. Stately two-story buildings. A park with trees, grand expanses of green, ponds, walkways. Yet, behind the doors of Tiergartenstrasse 4, there apparently was a horror of sufficient magnitude to unnerve a Gestapo agent.

"Aktion T4 was instituted last October, retroactive to the first of September. It requires midwives and physicians to register children age three and below, who show symptoms of deformity—physical or mental—with the Reich Health Ministry."

"Will it hurt?"

"No, baby, you won't feel anything."

"Will the angels have wings? Can I touch them?"

"You can touch them."

"I'm scared, Momma. Please don't leave me."

"I won't, baby. When you get to heaven, turn around, I'll be right behind you."

"Register them," Josef said, shaking off the memory.

"A questionnaire is completed which is then reviewed by three physicians. Each physician places one of two marks on it—a plus sign with a red pencil or a negative sign with a blue pencil. If the evaluation results in three red plus signs, a warrant is issued, and the child is picked up and delivered to the Children's Specialty Department where . . ."

Wolff clamped his mouth shut to stifle his emotions again. His eyes turned glassy.

" . . . where they're either given a deadly injection or they're starved to death."

"Dear God in heaven . . . has it come to this?"

"They call it 'life unworthy of life.' "

"And if a child receives less than three red plus signs?"

214

"Then they're kept under observation, and after a while, another attempt is made to get a unanimous decision. Mind you, this decision is made based on a questionnaire. The physicians never examine the child or consult his medical records."

Josef sat back in his seat. How much more could he endure? Nothing was as it seemed. A führer who looked and spoke like a savior but who generated division and hatred. The professor's suicide that may in reality have been a murder, perhaps committed by a member of his own congregation. An SS agent with a heart. A park residence being used as the headquarters for infanticide.

He wanted to run home, gather up Mady in his arms, and flee into his study. Then he'd barricade the door and pretend he knew none of this was happening, to spend his days reading of a nobler Germany, of decent men who espoused lofty ideals.

Suddenly, he despised the world in which he found himself. A world of duplicity, deception, hatred, and brute force, a world that murdered its own children.

"The program has expanded since its inception," Wolff added.

O God, it gets worse.

"Questionnaires have been sent to hospitals and other institutions that care for the sick. Patients are to be reported if they suffer from schizophrenia, epilepsy, senile disorders, therapy resistant paralysis, syphilitic diseases, retardation, encephalitis, or any neurological disorder. These are transferred to Hadamar, one of six killing centers. The program is headed by an SS man named Christian Wirth."

Josef closed his eyes. He struggled to assimilate it all.

The two men rode on in silence, each with his own thoughts. When Wolff spoke again, his tone was distant.

" 'In Ramah was there a voice heard, lamentation, and weeping, and great mourning, Rachel weeping for her children, and would not be comforted, because they are not.' "

Josef looked over at him. "King Herod. The murder of the innocents when Jesus was born."

"Operation Ramah. Your mission."

"Rescue the children?"

"As many as we can."

Clearly this was not what Josef had in mind when he'd contacted the underground, how could he? It was taking him a while to make the transition. The memory of his brother in the attic was a great persuader.

"I've been praying for God to send us a man," Wolff said. "I believe you're the answer to my prayer."

Just when Josef thought he could no longer be surprised, along comes a Scripture-quoting, prayer-believing SS agent. Then, as he stared at the man behind the steering wheel, a realization hit him. "This mission," he said. "It's special to you."

Wolff looked at him. "They took my two-year-old son."

Olbricht was coming down the steps with a travel case in his hand when Josef and Wolff pulled up. Mady was two steps behind her father, Kaiser in her arms. She was pulling the door closed. When they noticed the motorcar approaching, Olbricht threw the case into the trunk of his Essex and slammed it shut, while Mady stood frozen in the doorway, unsure of what to do.

Josef was out of the motorcar before it came to a complete stop. He ran past Olbricht to Mady. "Is the baby coming?" he asked.

Mady didn't answer him. She looked to her father.

Before Olbricht could speak, Wolff stepped forward. Every inch of him was a Sturmbannführer. "Heil Hitler," he said to Olbricht.

Josef's father-in-law returned the greeting.

With clipped steps Wolff strode over to Mady. "Frau Schumacher," he said, "I trust you're feeling well."

"I am," Mady replied with a quick glance at Josef.

Both she and her father wore matching expressions of puzzlement. The SS's transportation was normally limited to one-way traffic, ending at 8 Prinz-Albrecht-Strasse.

Taking Mady's hand, Wolff said, "Please forgive your husband's absence, which I'm sure has been a hardship on you. Be-

216

lieve me when I say it was unavoidable."

Mady looked to Josef, then to her father before stammering, "I was concerned."

"Of course you were," Wolff said. "Again, I apologize for the inconvenience. It is entirely my fault. Pastor Schumacher, at my request, assisted me in a matter of utmost importance to the Fatherland."

Olbricht's eyebrows raised.

"Had there been any way to inform you in advance or during the mission, we would have done so. Security demanded otherwise. I want to tell you how impressed I am with your husband, Frau Schumacher. You married a man of remarkable courage, a true German. You should be proud. And with your permission, I may need to call upon him again for the good of the Fatherland. Hopefully, it will not inconvenience you as it has this time."

Mady looked at Josef as if she'd never seen him before. "I'm glad my husband could be of service."

"And please understand that for security reasons, he's unable to discuss anything that transpired last night." Wolff glanced at Olbricht as he said this.

Olbricht nodded.

Mady said, "I understand."

"Now I must return to my duties," Wolff said. His eyes dropped to take in Mady's swollen form. "And may God bless you with a healthy child, Frau Schumacher."

There was a slight catch in the Sturmbannführer's voice. Josef noticed it. The others gave no indication they did.

The three of them watched as the Sturmbannführer drove away.

Josef looked at Olbricht, who was still standing by the trunk of the Essex.

Mady said to Josef, "When you didn't come home last night, we thought it best that, being this close to delivery, I should have someone close by. But now that you're home . . ."

Olbricht opened the trunk and retrieved the travel case. He

carried it toward the house. Josef offered to take the case from him, but his father-in-law insisted on carrying it inside himself.

"Assisting the SS," Olbricht said as he passed by. "You surprise me, son. You really surprise me."

Chapter 21

Thursday, June 27, 1940

A sheep in Wolff's clothing, that's how Josef came to think of his new comrade. It was difficult to believe he was the same man who had interrogated him at Gestapo Headquarters.

"What was your son's name?" Josef asked.

"Edel."

The two of them sat at a scarred table in a dimly lit, cavernous warehouse on Reuchlinstrasse in the Moabit district, waiting for the arrival of Adolf.

Josef knew the area for its September strikes back in 1910, when workers demanded higher salaries for heavy work—what they called "bone work." Strikebreakers were brought in, and riots ensued. By April of the next year the workers were finally granted their pay raises, but not until hundreds were wounded or killed, including 104 policemen. Josef remembered this as he thought of the police in the area again; this time they would arrest him and Wolff if they discovered what the two were planning.

He fidgeted. It wouldn't go over well with the church if he were caught. Or with Olbricht and Edda.

"Edel," Josef said. "Good name. You said he's two years old?"

"Three this November," Wolff said.

"Any other children?"

Wolff shook his head. He was pensive, which was understandable. If tonight's mission went as expected, he'd learn of the location and status of his son. Direct requests for information, despite his SS rank, garnered little more than bureaucratic doublespeak.

"I married late in life," Wolff said. "She was worth waiting for."

Josef grinned. The thought of an amorous SS agent seemed a contradiction in terms. But there was no mistaking Wolff's love for his wife. Josef had counseled enough couples to recognize the look in the man's eyes, a look only a woman could put there.

"Berdine died in childbirth," Wolff said.

"Oh . . . I'm sorry."

"You didn't know."

Rarely was there a time when Josef didn't know what to say. After all, he had been trained to minister to people during their times of loss, and in the short time he'd spent with Martin Wolff, he'd come to know him to be a man capable of deep emotion. So a blow like losing his wife must have left a deep wound.

"Complications in childbirth," Wolff explained. "Only one could be saved, mother or child. Berdine insisted the baby be given every chance at life. For a time I thought I'd lose them both. During the delivery the baby stopped breathing. The midwife was able to get him breathing again, but the damage was already done. My son is retarded."

Josef nodded. Tonight's mission had suddenly taken on names and faces.

Wolff looked over his shoulder into the dark reaches of the warehouse. Adolf was late.

"I hope you don't mind me asking this," Josef hedged.

Wolff turned to him.

"But since I've gotten to know you personally . . . I find myself drawn to you . . ."

"We're brothers in the Lord," Wolff said.

"Yes, I've come to realize that. Which, again forgive me, begs the question . . . why the SS?"

Wolff grinned and said, "Is it so hard for you to believe that a Sturmbannführer can be a follower of Christ?"

"Well . . . frankly . . . yes."

The grin widened. Even sitting here with Martin Wolff wearing a long-sleeved work shirt, the cuffs rolled up to his forearms, it was difficult to think of him as the same man whom Josef had come to despise in an official capacity.

"Sibling rivalry," Wolff said. "Two older brothers. One is a Generalmajor in the Wehrmacht and the other is a Generalleutnant in the Luftwaffe. As you might've surmised, I come from a military family; my father was a Generaloberst in the war. He's a hard man to please. Being more city-oriented in my tastes, the SS seemed a way to impress him and my brothers without having to live in a dirt trench to do it."

"Did you? Impress them, I mean."

"My brothers? No. With Father it's hard to tell."

"But don't you find it—"

"Difficult to be SS and Christian?" Wolff finished his sentence for him. "Not at first. There's a noble veneer to the Nazi Party that's attractive."

Josef nodded. "But it wears away quickly," he added.

"Which explains my presence here. I know my days with the SS are numbered. But until that day I'll use the resources that are available to me."

"And your father?"

"He's a Nazi to the core. Once I'm forced to go underground, he'll never forgive me."

The scuff of a shoe snapped their attention toward the back of the warehouse. Adolf emerged from the darkness. It was the first time Josef had seen him since Kreuzberg. Without apologizing for his tardiness and with no greeting, the short man took a seat at their table.

"We go," he said.

"Good," Wolff replied.

Josef's stomach formed a knot.

Adolf sized Josef up. He turned to Wolff and said, "I can do this without the preacher."

"He goes," Wolff said.

"I don't trust him."

"I do," Wolff said.

Adolf shook his head. "He's untempered steel. He'll break."

"I think he'll surprise you," Wolff said.

"We don't need surprises." He turned to Josef. "Pull out your pants pockets."

Josef looked to Wolff. When he didn't object, Josef pulled his pants pockets inside out. To do so, he had to empty one pocket of a coin.

"What's this?" Adolf cried, snatching the coin.

"It's just a pocket piece," Josef said.

Adolf read the words on the coin. " 'Rooted in the soil. Reaching for the sky.' " He turned it over and continued reading aloud, " 'The Lord is my rock, and my fortress, my God and my strength. Psalm 18:2.' " Then glaring at Josef, he shouted, "I ought to make you swallow this!"

"This is different," Wolff interjected.

While it surprised Josef at first that Wolff knew about the paper-eating incident in Kreuzberg, he quickly realized that Adolf had undoubtedly given Wolff a full briefing on what took place in the flat.

"It's just a Scripture coin," Wolff said. "Hand it back to him."

"It's needless trouble," Adolf insisted.

"Hand it back."

Adolf tossed the coin on the table. "It'll land us in the work camps," he said.

The set of Wolff's jaw indicated he considered the matter closed.

Adolf got up and stalked back into the darkness.

"He's a good man," Wolff said. "His caution keeps us alive."

Josef pocketed the coin.

Tiergartenstrasse 4 was a two-story facility. A pair of stairs in the front stretched out like wings leading to a central entrance. The corners of the building's flat roof supported a series of short ornamented spires, which took on the appearance of horns against the night sky. The building had no characteristics that would identify it as a processing center for death.

As planned, Wolff took up a position in the shadows across the street. Far too valuable to risk getting caught in a simple burglary, he served as lookout. Josef and Adolf—whom Josef learned was a former Gestapo agent who had been forced underground—would make the actual insertion, Josef because it was his project, and Adolf because he was experienced.

As they approached the building, Josef noticed there was no shortage of curtained windows. He assumed they would make their entrance through one of them. Adolf had other plans.

At the foot of the stairs the ground gave way to a basement entrance. Adolf pointed to the subterranean doorway. "Stay low and wait for me there," he whispered.

"Where are you . . . ?"

"Tst! Tst!" Adolf accompanied the sound with a hand signal, a double slash across his throat, and an angry look.

With a shove, he started Josef in the direction of the basement door, then disappeared around the corner of the building.

Crouching, Josef made his way down the slope. From his position by the door he could no longer see the street or Wolff. He didn't like this. It was his responsibility to keep an eye in Wolff's direction. Two quick flashes from a flashlight with a red handkerchief covering the lens signaled trouble. How could he watch for a signal if he couldn't see?

But Adolf told him to wait by the door, and that's what he was going to do. After all, Adolf was the expert.

So Josef waited. Blind to the signal. And worse, he was trapped should anyone approach the building. He had a locked door to his back and stone walls on either side of him. There was only one way out—up the slope, retracing the way he'd come. If a motorcar showed up, or a guard, especially without warning, he had no way to escape. And how could he be warned if he couldn't see Wolff?

Still, he waited.

Adolf was the expert; he was only a preacher.

Josef was convinced Adolf didn't like him, and he didn't want to do anything that would make the short man angry. He reached into his pocket and felt the coin. He wondered if Adolf would have really made him swallow it had Wolff not interceded.

Josef leaned against the stone wall. It was cool to the touch. The vulnerability of his position weighed heavily on him. He checked the basement door again. Locked. He looked up the ascending pathway. All he could see were the tops of trees and stars.

What was taking Adolf so long? And why had he insisted on going alone? The plan was for them both to enter the building. He was beginning to think that Adolf had placed him here with orders to stay, the same way a mother might tell a child to wait for her while she did her business.

But Adolf told him to wait, so that's what he continued to do. Adolf was the expert.

However, if he returned with the documents in hand . . .

The sound of an approaching motorcar caught Josef's attention. Distant at first, it grew louder. The top edge of the pathway became more visible from the headlights getting closer. Josef crouched low as the light breached the ridge and hit the top of the basement door. The sound of the motorcar's engine grew even louder. His heart hammering, Josef found himself perspiring and chilled at the same time. Like a little boy playing a game of hide-and-seek, he held his breath, his eyes riveted on the cement horizon.

The motorcar passed by. The light disappeared. The sound of the engine grew steadily fainter till all was quiet again.

Josef exhaled.

Then he became angry. What if the motorcar had turned into

Tiergartenstrasse 4? And what if Wolff had tried to warn him?

Adolf was taking far too long. Expert or no, Josef could no longer stay out of sight when it was his responsibility to watch for Wolff's signal.

Clinging to the shadows, he inched his way up the incline until his line of sight was sufficient to see across the street. While it was too dark to find Wolff, he at least had put himself in a position to view Wolff's general direction.

"Tst! Tst!"

The sound came from behind him. Josef swung around to see Adolf's eyes glaring at him through a crack in the open basement door. He slipped back down the walkway and through the door into a musty room. The door clicked behind him.

"What were you doing? I told you to wait by the door!" Adolf shouted at him in a whisper. "By the door! By the door! Is that too hard for you to understand?"

Josef took the reproach in silence. Every part of his being wanted to defend himself, to remind Adolf that it was his responsibility to watch for a signal, and to ask him what had taken him so long getting inside. Instead, he simply absorbed Adolf's verbal blows and followed him into the depths of Tiergartenstrasse 4.

———

Her eyes closed, Mady slouched in the parlor chair as she listened to the radio. It had taken her nearly fifteen minutes to find a German station that played orchestral music. Nowadays the airwaves were crammed with speeches and news reports and martial music. Which all depressed her. Almost as much as the bowling ball of a child that now sat on her bladder.

She prayed the child would come soon. Her feet were swollen and sore. Her back ached horribly. Half the time she felt like crying, the other half she wanted to hit someone or throw something. Motherhood was not the sentimental experience she'd always imagined it would be.

Josef's frequent absences and the lack of good radio at night didn't help. The strife was escalating. Two weeks ago the announcers broke in with what they described as "momentous news." Soon after a new voice commenced ranting for hours on end, beginning with Italy's the Duce, who had just announced his country's entrance into the war. Everyone seemed excited about it. Everyone except Mady. She wanted her music.

The radio commentators had explained that, following the English withdrawal from Narvik and the capitulation of Norway, Italy's air force would provide the *coup de grâce* to England and France. The predictions were proving accurate. The French government had fled Paris. According to the reports, German troops were now hunting down the guilty men who had resisted. Synagogues were set on fire. Atrocity stories and accusations were rampant. There were reports of brutalized Negroes, of stomachs slit open, and corpses mutilated.

Then, when the Nazis brought to Berlin Foch's Pullman car, Napoleon's traveling coach and the symbol of the German surrender in 1918, there was no end to the news coverage. That night Mady gave up in her quest to find a music station.

She was sick of it all. Sick of the news reports. Sick of being left alone. Sick of being pregnant. Sick of being married. Sick of her life.

She hated the daily trips downtown to shop. The long lines. The shortages. The coupons. How she longed for one quiet evening in Berlin where she could dine at a hotel without having to wonder if she had enough rationing coupons, followed by a night at the Opera House, then coffee—real coffee, not ersatz—at a sidewalk café under the stars, preferably with a flat stomach.

An announcer broke into the music. More atrocities in France. With a frustrated grunt, Mady got up and switched off the receiver.

The incursion into Tiergartenstrasse 4 had gone without incident. Adolf and Josef found the files they wanted. They recorded the information on microfilm and quickly got out.

"There was less security than I expected," Josef said.

"Security draws attention to itself," Adolf replied.

"Why would other nations care that Germans are killing their own?" Wolff added. "Besides, T4 is an internal matter that few people even know about."

The site of the debriefing was the warehouse on Reuchlinstrasse. Josef nervously fingered the scars on the wooden table.

Adolf removed the film from the camera and handed it to Wolff.

"Any surprises?" Wolff asked.

Adolf and Josef exchanged glances.

"Everything went as planned," Adolf said flatly.

If Josef was going to complain about being stranded at the basement door, he recognized this was the time to do it. "As planned," he said.

"Good," Wolff replied. He held up the film cartridge. "What will I find on this?"

Adolf gave a nod to Josef. "It's your project," he said.

"A schedule of deaths," Josef answered.

"Where?"

"Hadamar."

"When?"

"Thirteen children were transported there yesterday. From all indications they won't last a couple of weeks."

Wolff nodded solemnly. "We'll have to act quickly."

Considering they had just completed a mission successfully, the mood around the table was dirge-like. The black emptiness of the warehouse matched what Josef felt inside.

A chair scraped the floor. Adolf stood and dismissed himself. As he had come, so he left, the darkness swallowing him.

Wolff lowered his head. When he spoke, it appeared as though he were addressing the film in his hand. "You don't have to tell me," he said. "I already know."

Josef ached for his friend. "I'm sorry."

"It's confirmed then."

"We found a record of death."

"When did he die?"

"Two days ago."

Wolff could no longer hold back the tears. "How?" he asked.

"Martin, there's no need to—"

"HOW?" Wolff shouted. His voice echoed in the warehouse. "We're talking about my son!"

Josef's voice was soft, clouded by his own emotion. "Edel . . . was starved to death," he said.

Chapter 22

Saturday, June 29, 1940

N o. We have to think of another way."

Wolff was emphatic. His Sturmbannführer uniform gave his answer added weight and made Josef question his plan. Adolf wasn't as easily swayed.

"It's a valid plan," the short man said. "Might work."

"Too risky," Wolff insisted.

"I've given it a lot of thought," Josef said.

"No."

"It's biblical," he argued.

Wolff stared at him in disbelief. "You're just saying that hoping to convince me."

"It's biblical," Josef repeated.

Both Wolff and Adolf looked at him like he was crazy. Josef had an ally in Adolf, but the short man was obviously not impressed with this line of argument.

They stood on a dirt road north of Berlin. It was a remote area to which they'd arrived in three separate motorcars at three different times—Josef first, Wolff last. A stand of trees lined both sides of the road, cooling half the road with their shade. A virgin sky stretched overhead.

"There are plenty of strategic lessons to be learned from the Bible," Josef went on.

This time Wolff didn't argue with him, but he wasn't agreeing either.

Adolf jumped in. "It doesn't matter where the idea came from, it's a good—"

"Prove it," Wolff said to Josef.

Josef was ready for him. "David," he said. "When Saul was king of Israel."

Adolf rolled his eyes. "This doesn't have anything to do with giants and slings, does it?"

"There's more than one story about David in the Bible," Josef replied. "This one has to do with him fleeing from Saul, who was seeking to kill him. David went to Gath, hostile territory. He was recognized. As his enemies closed in on him, David feigned madness."

"You're making this up," Wolff said.

"First Samuel, chapter twenty-one, verses ten through fifteen. David feigned madness by clawing at the gate like a wild animal and drooling spittle into his beard."

Wolff and Adolf just stood there.

"I'm not making this up," Josef insisted. "First Samuel, chapter twenty-one."

Wolff was still skeptical.

"Regardless, the plan makes sense," Adolf said. "We can provide him with the necessary papers."

"And time is short," Josef added.

"The house isn't ready yet," Wolff said.

"It'll have to be," said Josef. "Thirteen lives depend on it."

The impact of his statement registered on Wolff's face, and Josef knew he'd won. "Once inside, I can find out where the children are located and the best time to move them. You provide the bus, and we can be in and out within two days."

"How will you relay the information to us?"

"You can arrive to interrogate me."

Adolf nodded.

Wolff mulled over the proposal. "So many things could go wrong," he said. "They'll medicate you."

"We can put it in his paper work that he's already medicated and isn't to receive any more medication for forty-eight hours," Adolf suggested. "That will give us the time we need."

"I don't know . . ." Wolff said. "If something went wrong, I'd hate to have to face Mady."

This angered Adolf. "It's a necessary risk," he said, his voice rising, "and the kind all of us take every day! You're letting your feelings cloud your judgment. The plan is a good one. Let's do it."

Finally, Wolff gave his consent with a nod.

"When do we go?" Josef asked.

"It's best you don't know beforehand," Adolf replied. "You could be walking down the street or asleep in bed, and the next thing you know, you could be in a motorcar heading to Hadamar."

"But Mady . . ." Josef objected. "She'll give birth any day now."

"Make the necessary arrangements," Adolf said. "But don't tell her anything."

"I can't just leave her without an explanation."

Adolf's fuse was as short as his stature. "I thought you wanted to do this!" he shouted.

"An hour," Wolff interjected. "We can give you an hour's notice. No more."

Adolf huffed. "This is the second time you've made a special concession for this man. It's a weakness. Leave enough loose ends and one is bound to hang you."

The accusation made no impact on Wolff. "If you had a wife or child, Adolf, you'd realize they sometimes require special concessions. One hour will not impede our plans."

Adolf wasn't appeased, but he knew better than to argue the point.

"You'll receive a phone call," Wolff said to Josef. "The message will contain a single word: *Bulwark*. After that you can expect visitors within the hour."

"Agreed," Josef said.

Their meeting concluded, Wolff said, "Josef, you leave first. Adolf and I will follow in twenty-minute intervals."

"If it's all the same to you," said Josef, "would it be possible for Adolf to leave first? I have something I want to discuss with you."

Wolff and Adolf exchanged glances. Adolf shrugged his shoulders. "Suits me," he said.

Adolf climbed into his motorcar, which was as dented and rusty as Josef's aged Opel. A cloud of dust followed him down the road.

"I have a request," Josef said.

"I'm listening."

"Should anything happen to me . . ."

Wolff harrumphed. "That's the first thing you've said this afternoon that's remotely realistic. Good. At least you're aware of the precarious nature of this plan."

"It isn't my plan," Josef said.

"Not your plan?"

"God gave it to me."

"God."

"I believe He did," Josef said, "after prayer and much thought. At first I resisted it. But I couldn't stop thinking of those children."

Wolff nodded. "Your request?"

"Should anything happen to me, will you deliver a message to Mady for me?"

"A written message?"

"No, verbal."

"And the content?"

"Tell her that it's important that she continue her embroidery."

Wolff waited for more.

"That's it," Josef said.

"It's important she continue her embroidery," Wolff repeated.

"Yes."

A sly grin spread across Wolff's face. "A code."

"Of sorts."

"Incriminating documents?"

"More a husband-and-wife thing."

Wolff took a long look at Josef.

"Oh, one more thing," Josef said. "Tell her especially the one depicting the California redwoods in my office."

"She's making an embroidery of *American* trees?" Wolff asked.

"An interest of mine. They're the tallest living trees in the world. They often exceed ninety meters in height, and their trunks can be three to five meters in diameter. Guess how long it takes them to reach maturity."

Wolff stifled a laugh. "I must have missed that day in my SS training."

Josef answered his own question. "Four hundred to five hundred years. Some of them are known to be more than fifteen hundred years old."

"Fascinating," Wolff said, though from his tone he was far from being fascinated.

Josef laughed. "I *do* have a point to make."

"I certainly hope so."

"How long have the Nazis been in power?" Josef asked.

"Since 1933. Seven years."

"And how would you characterize the pace of change in Germany since then?"

"Everything has happened quickly, of course."

"Exactly. Even now, *blitzkrieg*, lightning war. We want changes and we want them now, but at what price? We're not thinking of the long-term effects of the changes or our methods in achieving them."

"Hitler speaks of a thousand-year reich."

"But can a thousand-year reich be built on a foundation that focuses only on immediate results?"

"What's your point?"

Josef rubbed his hands together. "Allow me one more question. What is our goal?" Wolff wasn't sure how to answer, so Josef clarified. "As Christians," he said, "what is our goal?"

"To lead Germany back to a Christian foundation."

"Exactly. And, like the National Socialists, we want immediate results. But how can we expect eternal results when we use Nazi-blitz techniques?"

Wolff's eyebrows raised.

"Don't you see? If we act like Hitler, no matter what our motives, we're no different. We're simply dressing the same methodology in a sanctified set of clothes. We might just as well straighten the swastikas on the armbands and turn them into crosses."

"There are some who believe that for us to succeed, Hitler must die," Wolff said.

Josef had heard rumors of Christians talking seriously of assassination. Wolff merely confirmed it.

"Hitler must die," Josef agreed.

"But haven't you just argued . . . ?"

"He must die to himself, that he might live in Christ."

Wolff was taken by the concept. Adolf Hitler becoming a follower of Jesus Christ.

"The Apostle Paul was once a persecutor of Christians," Josef said. "He called himself the worst sinner of all. And consider Constantine, the Roman emperor. After three hundred years of Christian persecution by the Roman government, there arose an emperor who followed Christ, and a new era of Christianity dawned."

"Intriguing," Wolff said.

"But whether this happens or not, I believe our hope is in the growth of the redwood, not the lightning bolt. It took Christianity three hundred years, but Rome eventually was converted. This is our hope for Germany. To remain true to what we believe, knowing that Christianity will outlive national socialism. Our task is to plant spiritual seeds that will grow for the next fifteen hundred years."

"That's what you've learned from the redwoods," Wolff said.

"Exactly. And one of those seeds is a busload of retarded children."

————————

Monday, July 1, 1940

The waiting was intolerable. Knowing it could happen at any moment, that at any time during the day his life would suddenly undergo a dramatic transformation after which he'd never be the same. He tried to prepare himself for the moment but never knew if he had prepared enough, if he were ready or not. What did it matter? These things don't ask if a person's ready. They just happen. Ready or not.

"What are you stewing about?" Mady asked.

"Nothing," Josef replied.

He glanced furtively at the telephone. Would it ring tonight? Two days from now? The waiting was killing him.

"I'm going to bed," Mady announced.

She swayed from side to side as she walked now, just to keep from toppling over. One hand rested on her abdomen where it seemed to have found a permanent roost.

Josef was too anxious to sleep. It was his own fault. He'd worked himself up into a frenzy—and for no reason. He'd been given no indication the call would come today. In fact, he hadn't heard from Wolff or Adolf or anyone else since their meeting on the dirt road.

How long does it take to forge papers? he wondered.

"Are you coming to bed?" Mady asked him.

"I think I'll stay up a while longer."

She gave him a half smile and then moved slowly toward the bedroom. She looked tired, and not because it was the end of the day. The child within her seemed to be draining more and more of her energy. She slept a lot.

"On second thought," said Josef, "I think I will come to bed now." He knew he wouldn't sleep for several more hours, but was feeling guilty for leaving her alone.

"Suit yourself," she said.

While Mady changed to get ready for bed, Josef started his nightly routine of turning off the lights and securing the door.

Tap. Tap. Tap.

The sound startled him. He was certain he'd heard something but couldn't determine the sound's source. His heart jumped in his chest.

Is this the signal? It was supposed to be a phone call!

He cocked his head. Listening.

Tap. Tap. Tap. Tap.

It was louder this time. The parlor window.

Josef half-ran to the window and drew back the blackout curtains. A face stared back at him. The light of a flashlight shone in his eyes.

Fräulein Baeck. Her seventy-year-old duplicate, minus the air-raid-warden armband, stood behind her.

"I see light coming from your window!" the wrinkled old lady shouted. "This side." With a slicing motion, she indicated the side of the window to Josef's left.

His mouth twisted in chagrin, Josef nodded. Then he stood back and pulled the curtains closed, giving the left side a tug. "How's that?" he said in a loud voice.

"Now there's light coming through from the other side!" Fräulein Baeck yelled back.

Josef tugged the other side of the curtain. "Now?"

"The left side again!"

Josef didn't feel like playing this game tonight. He stood back and placed his hands on his hips. "What about now?"

"I can still see some light!"

He counted to five. "Is that better?"

There was a pause. Josef heard some rather loud whispering. Then, "I guess that'll do!"

"Thank you, fräulein!" he shouted.

"Be more careful!" she shouted back. "There's a war on, you know!"

Mady was grinning at him when he walked into the bedroom. She lay on her back, the covers pulled over her. "Girlfriend trouble?"

"Not funny," Josef replied, though he, too, was grinning now.

He put out the light, dressed for bed in the dark, and climbed in. He was more awake than ever.

"Josef! Wake up! Wake up!"

His head moved side to side as Mady shook him.

"What? The baby?"

The words came out of his mouth, but they sounded distant to him, as if someone else had spoken them. And his head felt heavy, like a full-sized blanket had been stuffed into his skull. Mady kept shaking him.

"The phone!" she cried. "The phone's ringing."

He heard it now, a discordant ring. He propped himself up on one elbow. His head swam in murky waters.

Mady had stopped shaking him. Now she was pushing him out of bed. "The phone! The phone!" she kept prompting him.

"I'm . . . I'm going." His feet hit the floor, then he stumbled to the doorway and steadied himself against the doorjamb.

The ringing seemed to get louder, insistent, even angry that it was taking him so long to reach it.

"Yes . . . um, yes." It wasn't poetry, but it did stop the ringing. "Bulwark."

A click and a buzzing sound followed.

Josef was fully awake now.

Mady lay waiting for him in the dark of their bedroom. "Someone from the church?" she asked.

He climbed into bed next to her and said, "Within the hour someone will be coming for me." His voice was low, solemn.

"Coming . . . for you?" she asked fearfully.

"Not to arrest me. It's something I have to do."

"The Sturmbannführer?"

"It's better that you don't know," he said.

"How long will you be gone?"

"Two days. Possibly three," he said, just to be safe.

Mady ran a hand over her prominent middle.

Josef placed his hand on top of hers. "That's my concern, too. How are you feeling? Do you have any indication that you're going to give birth soon? Because if you are, I'll stay."

"Any indication," she repeated. "You mean besides this balloon that looks ready to pop?"

Josef caressed her cheek with the back of his hand. "Tell me to stay, and I'll stay," he said.

Mady shook her head wearily. "The way I feel, this child isn't going to make an appearance for at least a week, if ever."

"Are you sure?"

She gave him a wide-eyed look that told him how ridiculous his question was.

"In the morning, call your father. Stay with them until I return. It'll put my mind at ease."

"Father's gone on a trip. Besides, I'd rather stay here."

"Mady, no. What if . . ."

"I'll have Lisette come and stay with me. If anything happens, she can call Mother and the midwife."

That was acceptable to Josef. "I want you to know that if there was any other way—"

BAM! BAM! BAM! BAM!

A heavy fist pounded on the front door.

"They said an hour!" Josef complained.

He threw back the bedcovers, thrust his feet into his pants legs and shoes with a single motion, grabbed a shirt, and started buttoning everything as fast as he could while Mady watched from the bed.

BAM! BAM! BAM! BAM!

Josef's blood was racing. His hands were cold and shaky, making it that much harder to finish dressing. His eyebrows framed his eyes with frustration as he glanced at his wife. "They said an hour!" he apologized.

An anguished expression looked back at him. Josef wished he had the time to soothe away her worry lines. But he didn't.

He rushed to her side of the bed. "Call Lisette," he said.

He bent over to kiss her. She turned her head, and his lips found only cheek.

"Mady?"

"Go," she said.

BAM! BAM! BAM! BAM!

The banging came louder now.

"Go!" she insisted.

The words *I love you* perched on his lips. He recalled them. But from the distant look in his wife's eyes, he figured it was the worst thing he could say at the moment. So he said nothing.

The coolness of the night air greeted him when he stepped outside, nothing more. His Opel was parked off to the side, a silent hulk, cold, tinged with the blue of night, looking like it had given up the ghost. Everything lay still.

Josef stood frozen for a moment. He watched for some sign of life, possibly a signal. There was none.

He began walking fast, his footsteps crunching the gravel. With his senses on full alert, he made his way out to the road.

A pair of headlights came to life.

An engine roared.

In its haste the black sedan squealed its tires, lurched toward him, and stopped just before it passed.

A door flew open.

"Get in."

Chapter 23

Tuesday, July 2, 1940

In a rare display of wit, it was Adolf who chose the patient name by which Josef would be admitted to the Hadamar facility: David King.

The trip to Hadamar from Berlin was a long one, which gave Josef plenty of time to be briefed on his assignment. He was to locate the children's ward, determine a route of evacuation, and assess the best time to perform the rescue. He had approximately thirty-six hours to do this before Wolff would return to interrogate him, at which time final arrangements would be made for the rescue to be undertaken the next day. Josef would remain inside and be rescued along with the children.

According to his admission papers, Herr David King was a schizophrenic, subject to severe bouts of depression. The papers indicated he'd been heavily medicated for the journey and was not to receive any additional medications until after Sturmbannführer Wolff interrogated him the following day; the SS wanted him lucid for the interrogation. The only other information on his record was that he'd been a former assistant to Heinrich Himmler and therefore had been privy to top-secret information. Hadamar staff were instructed not to talk to him.

The institution was about eight kilometers from Limburg, on a hill overlooking the town of Hadamar. It had served a variety of purposes, most recently as a nursing home before being renovated and furnished as a facility where mercy killings could be performed.

Adolf had visited the town and gathered as much information as he was able in the short time allotted him. Most disturbing were the things he heard coming from the mouths of the village's schoolchildren. Several times a week, buses arrived with a load of victims. The children of the area knew this vehicle and would often say to one another, "There comes the murder-box again." And when calling each other names, they'd say, "You're crazy! You'll be sent to the baking oven on the hill!"

Likewise, adults of the village were fully aware of what was going on at the facility nearby. They watched as the smoke billowed out from the chimney. When the direction of the wind was just right, they complained that the sickening sweet odor that accompanied the smoke annoyed them.

Getting inside the Hadamar facility was easy enough. No one questioned the arrival of a Sturmbannführer or the papers he presented with his patient. Josef himself was unnerved by the transformation in the man he'd befriended. Wolff once again became the interrogator who had instructed him in the art of saluting.

For Josef's part, he went limp, letting his head loll from side to side as though he had no neck muscles. He stared vacantly at nonexistent objects, mumbled incoherently, and, adding something only Wolff and Adolf would appreciate, he drooled.

Within thirty minutes of his arrival at Hadamar, Josef was whisked down a long green-tiled hallway in a wheelchair, stripped of his clothes, placed in a gown, then locked away in a room that had a bed with a plastic covering over the mattress. A single window, high and out of reach, was covered with wire mesh.

For the most part, everything went as expected. There was only one moment when Josef felt tempted to act out of character and object to what was happening, but he had the good sense to hold his tongue. When they removed his clothing, they searched his pockets and found Konrad's coin. Josef didn't want to lose it, but neither did he want to call attention to it. He chastised himself for not thinking ahead. Naturally they would confiscate his personal possessions. It was an oversight he now regretted. But if that was the greatest sacrifice that was made to rescue thirteen children, it was worth it.

"He's a quiet one."

Josef heard the two male staff members talking behind his back about him. He stood in some sort of community room, a long room with square pillars. Like that of the hallways, the flooring was green tile. Inmates sat at tables or in chairs or just wandered about aimlessly. Josef had positioned himself in front of a large window. He did so with a twofold purpose: to spy out the land in anticipation of an escape and to keep from having to look at the faces of the walking dead.

Gaunt and sallow was the fashion at Hadamar. There was an incessant shuffling of feet, though it was difficult to tell what animated most of the inmates. While their eyes were open, they held no spark of intelligence. There were a few, like him, who still had meat on their bones. Josef assumed that these were the recent arrivals.

While the green-tile floor shone like glass, the patients' gowns were soiled with food and feces, their hair was matted, their teeth yellow or rotten or missing altogether. Hadamar was an animated graveyard.

A shift change was taking place. The staff member who came on duty was being brought up-to-date on the day's activities. Josef noted the time.

"His name's King. He's been staring out that window for the better part of an hour. Don't know what he sees out there that's so fascinating."

"Medication?"

"None until tomorrow. The SS wants to have a chat with him."

"SS? What do they want with him?"

"From what I heard he was some kind of high-level secretary for Himmler."

"Himmler?" There was a shiver in the man's voice when he spoke the name. "I'd be willing to bet there's some scary data locked up inside that man's head."

"And if you know what's good for you, you'll see that it stays there. The SS boys want to tap it. Or erase it. We have orders not to engage King in conversation, that is unless you want to be included on the SS's guest list."

"I have better things to do with my time, thank you."

Keeping his back to the two men, Josef smiled to himself. Everything was going as planned. The cover story was working to perfection. The window, despite the security mesh, gave him an unobstructed view of the north side of the building, which he had now committed to memory. Of course, he wouldn't know if the information would be useful until he located the children's ward.

The entire night he lay awake due to a combination of duty and unfamiliar surroundings. He lay on a cot that crinkled every time he moved, and listened, trying to identify and locate each strange sound.

Throughout the night he heard bouts of shouting and screaming and whimpering, mostly adult voices. Twice he thought he heard children's screams. Distant. Probably on the far side of the building. Somehow he was going to get over there. The problem was that when inmates were taken from location to location, they were either taken separately or herded in small groups. And all the doors were locked on the inside of the rooms.

Somehow he was going to have to find a way to break free long enough to locate the children's ward before Wolff arrived.

Wednesday, July 3, 1940

Breakfast provided no opportunity for him to slip away. The staff was practiced and efficient. Doors opened and closed in orchestrated fashion. Patients were led by the arm. As the morning hours slipped by, Josef grew more and more anxious. He feared Wolff would come and he'd have insufficient information for them to formulate a workable plan. His inability to do the job would cost thirteen children their lives. He prayed.

Lunch came and went and still no opportunity presented itself. He chastised himself for his lack of preparation. He should have planned for this contingency, arrived with an idea of how to create a diversion that would give him a chance to slip away.

By early afternoon he once again found himself in the community room with its square pillars and green tile. He expected to be summoned to meet Wolff at any moment.

Josef resigned himself to failure. He began formulating an argument to convince Wolff to allow him to remain an extra day. Wolff could tell the directors that pressing business prevented him from completing the interrogation and that he would return tomorrow. That would give Josef an additional twenty-four hours.

Just then a deep-throated scream came from the far corner of the room. As Josef turned toward the commotion, a woman of ample bulk landed on top of a thin man with a surprising shock of white hair. There was gouging, biting, and hair pulling as the nurses rushed toward the ruckus.

Josef's prayer was answered. He'd been standing near a door where he expected to be ushered to Wolff when the incident occurred. A nurse had just opened the door when the woman shrieked. The nurse's attention was drawn immediately to the disturbance in the corner. When he ran to help, Josef caught the door before it closed and slipped into the hallway.

His time was short, and he knew he had only one chance, so he moved quickly. If someone caught him before he located the children, it would all be over. His eyes were wide to catch movement, his ears keen to the slightest sound. While his body felt taut with nervousness, he prepared himself to go limp and sleepy-eyed should anyone appear.

His suspicions led him toward the south end of the building, but then the sound of a child's cry took over. Reaching a corner, he pressed himself against the wall and listened for conversation or footsteps. Josef heard nothing but the persistent wail of the child. He held his breath and peered around the corner.

A woman with an armload of linens was unlocking a door not more than ten meters away. He pulled back. Just as he did, he thought he caught a glimpse of her head turning his direction. Had his movement caught her eye? He pressed against the wall.

No, that looks suspicious. What then? Go limp and sleepy-eyed? Walk toward her or away from her?

It was then he realized how unsuited he was for this work. His indecision could prove fatal.

He was fortunate. The woman never came.

There was the clicking of a door lock. Then the door shut. He listened, but still no footsteps. For the second time he slowly peered around the corner. The hallway was clear. Nothing but green tile.

Stepping gingerly, he glided down the hallway. The crying had stopped, the passageway became hushed. Josef was left to his own devices.

There were a half-dozen doors to choose from. He could stick his head into each one, but he didn't like his chances. What if one of them happened to be a nurses' break room? Or a security office? The wrong door would end his search abruptly.

So Josef went to each door and, pressing his ear close to it, listened. Surely in a ward full of children there were bound to be noises. The first two doors yielded only the sound of his breathing being reflected back at him.

Noises filtered through the third door, the one at the end of the hall, yet the sounds were indistinguishable. Definitely not the sound of any children Josef had ever been around.

A voice, definitely male, definitely urgent, echoed down the hallway and around the corner.

"You take the south corridor; I'll take the west corridor."

The sound of hurried footsteps followed this.

Josef's time had run out.

He tested the doorknob. It turned freely. With no other options available to him, he swung open the door, stepped inside, and closed it behind him.

Josef's heart nearly failed him.

He'd found the children's ward.

Sturmbannführer Wolff was waiting for them.

The male nurse dragged a listless Josef into the room. He pulled out a chair, one of ten at a large conference table, and sat Josef in it opposite the SS agent.

"Again, my apologies, Herr Sturmbannführer," the nurse said. "We found him in the children's ward. He was curled up on the floor in a fetal position."

"Is it your practice to let the inmates wander from room to room as they please?" Wolff asked.

"No, Herr Sturmbannführer. I've worked here more than a year, and this is the first time something like this has happened. Believe me, the person responsible for this will be identified and disciplined."

"See that he is!" Wolff snapped.

The nurse stepped back and took up a position by the door.

"Your presence is no longer required," Wolff said.

"But it's our policy to—"

Wolff simultaneously pounded the table and stood, causing his chair to do a somersault behind him. He cursed the institution's policy, then said, "If you prefer, you can explain your policy to Herr Himmler himself!"

The nurse's complexion paled. "No, Herr Sturmbannführer. That . . . won't be necessary."

Wolff had scared the nurse silly. Fumbling for the doorknob, he couldn't get out of the room fast enough.

Staying in the Sturmbannführer character, Wolff righted the chair and sat back down. He folded his hands on the table and stared at Josef. Only after several seconds had passed did he allow the corners of his mouth to tug his lips into a grin. "Wander off and get lost, did we?" he said.

Josef straightened himself in his chair. "I found them," he said. His voice sounded heavy with grief. Josef felt the weight of his own words.

They had a similar effect on Wolff.

Lack of sleep, nerves, and the scene Josef had just witnessed combined together to make it difficult for him to control his emotions. He had to pause to compose himself before he could continue speaking.

"There was so little sound coming from the room," he explained. "That's what perplexed me. I expected to hear the sound of children acting like children. It . . . was ghastly. Half of them look like miniature cadavers. They'll have to be carried out. That's why there's no sound. Most of them don't have the strength to talk, or even to cry."

Wolff seemed to be fighting back tears, no doubt thinking about his son, Edel.

"They're not feeding them," Josef went on. "They're not caring for them at all. The children are lying in their own feces. The ward is little more than a canning closet, where children are shelved until they can be taken out and buried."

"We'll get them out," Wolff whispered.

"One more thing."

"What's that?"

"There are over two dozen of them."

———

Josef had insisted Wolff slap him. A few marks on the face for realism. Just hard enough to show red.

When Wolff left the room, the plan was in place. The rescue would take place just before the morning shift when it was still dark. Wolff would come for Josef, while Adolf positioned the bus on the south side of the building. It was Wolff who provided the logistic details for this exposure. A single door led outside to five steps set at a right angle to the building. There was an iron railing.

After taking Josef outside—presumably to a waiting motorcar—Wolff would then return to the administration desk and create a disturbance to draw attention away from the neglected south corridor. At that time Adolf and Josef would carry the children down the steps and into the bus, taking as many as they could. The moment they were discovered, they were to get in the bus and drive away. Feigning assistance, Wolff would do what he could to hinder any pursuit.

It was a simple plan. One that needed more manpower than they had, but it was too late to enlist additional help now.

Josef remained in the room for five minutes after Wolff departed before someone came for him. When the door opened, he was slouched in his chair with his head cocked at an odd angle, his cheeks burning red.

The nurse called for assistance. Soon after, flanked by two nurses, Josef was lifted to his feet. He hung limp between them, letting them earn their pay.

Despite his stinging cheeks, Josef felt encouraged. All that remained for him to do that day was to wait in his room till morning dawned.

"Well, well. What have we here?"

The sound of the familiar voice nearly brought Josef upright and back to his sane self.

"Herr David King," a nurse answered. "Just had a visit by the SS." Apparently the nurse felt the need to explain the marks on Josef's face.

"Herr King, is it?"

To the surprise of the nurses, Josef placed his feet on the green-tile floor and stood without their assistance. There was no use pretending any longer.

Standing in front of him was his father-in-law.

Chapter 24

The brief encounter in the hallway with Olbricht had generated a thousand questions in Josef's mind for which he could imagine no answers. All he knew was the sound of crunching plastic when he sat on the edge of his bed, the soft padding of his steps when he paced, the thoughts that chased each other in his head, and the feeling, for the first time since he'd arrived, that he was a prisoner.

With the sudden appearance of his father-in-law everything had changed. The click of the lock on his door had a finality to it. Somewhere in the Hadamar facility Olbricht and the authorities, who at present had no faces, positions, or ranks, were discussing his presence in their facility, and also his fate.

One unresolved thought that surfaced more frequently than all the others was how this would affect Mady. What would be her reaction when told her husband had been found in a psychiatric center under an assumed name? How would he explain this to her? For that matter, how would he explain to his congregation should his actions leak out? He dreaded the thought of having to make another apology.

The lock clicked, and the door to his room opened.

Olbricht entered carrying a wooden chair. The familiar odor of his cigar followed him in.

Without looking at Josef, Olbricht placed the chair so as to face the bed and then sat. Josef took a seat in front of him. He leaned forward, his forearms resting on his legs, his hands folded. He waited. He'd given no forethought to strategy. This was Pastor Olbricht, his mentor and father-in-law. They both assumed their respective positions that had been honed by years of conversation. Olbricht would speak. Josef would listen.

Olbricht seemed in no hurry. He sat back in his chair and appraised his son-in-law, while wreaths of smoke swirled around his head. After what seemed an interminably long time to Josef, Olbricht rendered his first judgment, a slow shake of the head.

"I don't know if I can get you out of this one," he said.

Josef said nothing. Nothing was expected. Olbricht frequently began conversations with an opening gambit.

He poked his cigar toward the door. "They're asking a lot of questions out there," he said. "They're wondering what a Berlin minister is doing inside their facility, using an assumed name. I sure don't have any answers for them."

"This is more than just a psychiatric facility," Josef said.

"Is it?"

There was something about the way Olbricht spoke the words that urged caution. The question itself was the appropriate one, yet there was no surprise, no hint of moral concern in the elder minister's voice.

"Mercy killings," Josef said.

"And that's why you're here."

He was probing now. Josef needed more before he could confide in him. "Isn't that enough?" he asked.

Olbricht took a long draw on his cigar. He exhaled an equally long, if not exasperated, stream of smoke. "I'm disappointed in you, son," he said. "Thought you had more sense than this."

"It doesn't trouble you that they're killing innocent people here?"

"I'll tell you what troubles me," Olbricht said. "It troubles me that you haven't been leveling with me."

"What do you mean?"

"Sturmbannführer Martin Wolff."

How much did Olbricht know? Josef suddenly felt threatened. Which bothered him, for he'd felt intimidated by his father-in-law before, but never threatened. Not until now.

"Well?" Olbricht thundered.

"He's SS," Josef replied. "The man who interrogated me."

Olbricht scowled. "He's involved with this somehow, isn't he?"

So he didn't know for sure.

"I came here expecting to find him, but instead I stumble into you. Don't you think that odd?"

Josef offered no response.

"When he brought you home that day, I became suspicious. Later I made some inquiries, enough to prompt an internal investigation." Olbricht took a few self-important puffs of the cigar. "Care to guess what they found in his desk drawer?"

He loved showing off his knowledge, whether of theology or parenting or gardening. Josef decided to let him talk.

"No guesses. . . ? They found a death certificate for his infant son. Official. From the Consolation Letter Department of the Registry Office. Cause of death was acute fever. There was another paper with it. An official record stolen from the T4 offices, also with his son's name on it. It's that paper that led us here to Hadamar."

"Us? What's your involvement in this?" Josef wanted to know.

Olbricht's eyebrows raised. "You're not the only one who works in conjunction with the authorities," he said. "I'm here in a ministerial capacity, training chaplains to minister to the patients of this facility. And also to see if the Sturmbannführer showed up. His superiors thought that, given the fact that he knew of me through you, I might be able to get him to reveal his motives."

"Instead, you found me."

"And here we are."

Josef awaited a ruling, or perhaps a lecture or disclosure of some sort. He could do little else. He had no options. At the moment he was at the mercy of his father-in-law.

He got a lecture.

"You still don't understand, do you?" Olbricht started. "How can you not see the writing on the wall? The National Socialists are in control. Think, man! What are our options?"

"Compliance, collaboration, or resistance," Josef said.

Olbricht's face wizened. "There's another option," he said. "Think, boy! Think!"

Josef repeated the three choices to himself in search of a fourth. "Give into them, work with them, work against them . . . another option would be to leave."

"Escape!" Olbricht pronounced the word like a pleased teacher.

Josef shook his head. "I'm a German," he said. "I could never leave my country."

"But you will," Olbricht said.

Josef stared in disbelief at his father-in-law. "Deported? I'm to be deported?"

"Not deported. Think of it theologically."

Theologically?

Olbricht prompted him. "What do you do when you live in a country that no longer has a place for you? You move to a better place."

"The Jewish solution," Josef said, remembering their discussion back in Olbricht's study.

"And what do you do if you live in a *world* that no longer has a place for you? You move to a better world. Or to put it another way: What do you do when life is no longer worth living?"

Josef could hardly believe what his father-in-law was saying. Olbricht had used all the T4 code words—*when life is no longer worth living*. Surely he didn't mean . . .

"As a Christian minister, you of all people should realize that death is not final, but merely a passageway to a better life."

Josef shifted uneasily at the implication. The bed crinkled with his nervousness.

Olbricht waved his cigar hand airily and said, "You're missing the grander purpose behind this place. Yes, the Nazis created it for political purposes, but there's an element of compassion and humanitarianism that you as a theologian should appreciate. Death is deliverance, after all. It's life, just as much as birth."

"But the timing is a matter for God, not men."

"Nonsense!" Olbricht objected. "God gave us minds to make decisions in this life. You've been in the community room. Tell me, is that any kind of life to live? Who in there wouldn't in a minute trade a life of filth and bedsores for the glory of heaven?"

"It's still not our decision to make," Josef insisted.

"But it's the compassionate thing to do. An act of love and pity. Your mother understood that."

Josef was blindsided by Olbricht's comment. "She was confused . . ."

"Yes, she was confused. But she understood enough to realize that the Nazis had created a world that held no place for your brother."

Then the horror of what Olbricht had implied took root in Josef. "You . . . counseled her," Josef said.

"When people are confused, sometimes as men of God we have to assist them to do what is best. Your mother was distraught. Bone weary. The secrecy and pretense over the course of years became too much for her."

Josef's chest tightened. So intense was the emotion rising in his throat, he could barely force the words out. "You counseled her to kill my brother!"

"To assist him to a better place," Olbricht clarified as evenly and calmly as he would had they been talking about driving Josef's brother across town to stay with relatives. "Pity she took her own life, too. You have to believe me when I say I didn't counsel *that*. Killing herself was her own idea, and was wrong."

Anger and grief mushroomed inside Josef. Hot tears blinded

him. "You killed them both!" he screamed.

Olbricht appeared offended by Josef's angry response. "I opened heaven's doors to them!" he shouted back.

"At your suggestion, my mother killed my brother and herself!" Josef wailed.

Olbricht took pains to calm himself. "I accept your rebuke. As I said, I didn't anticipate her killing herself."

Josef was on his feet before he knew it, powered by a rage he never knew existed within him.

"Guards!" Olbricht called.

The door flew open, and two SS agents—not nurses—flanked Josef, slamming him to the bed and pinning him there; one held his knee to Josef's chest.

Olbricht moved to the bedside and looked down at him. "What has come over you?" he said. "We've had theological differences before and you've never attacked me."

"Our theological differences never killed my mother!"

Olbricht clucked his tongue. When he spoke again, his voice had turned coldly clinical. "She's in a far better place. Are you so blinded by this world that you can't rejoice with her? As for our theology, if it doesn't shape the choices we make in this world, what good is it?"

Josef's rage refused to subside, but he did manage to rein it back somewhat. Though he'd ceased struggling, the guards didn't relax their grip on him.

"I still have business with him," Olbricht told the guards. "Let's give him some time to calm down. I'll return in five minutes." He then turned and left the room.

Josef stared at the ceiling, still reeling from the confessions of his mentor. "You can take your knee off my chest now!" he seethed. "I can't breathe."

The two guards may as well have been deaf. Neither one gave any indication they heard him.

It was difficult for Josef to know how long Olbricht was gone. Seconds tick slowly when breathing is next to impossible.

When he returned, Olbricht strolled casually into the room, as if it were his study and Josef had been waiting for him. Two quick puffs on the cigar and he looked down at Josef. "You can let him up now," he said to the guards.

The guards backed away, though not without the one giving Josef an extra shove in the chest with his knee. Josef sat up, rubbing the spot.

Satisfied that Josef wouldn't attack him again, Olbricht dismissed the guards and then sat in the wooden chair. Reaching into his pocket, he pulled out a coin and tossed it to Josef. "Recognize this?" he asked.

With the coin resting on his open palm, Josef studied it, recalling the image of the bear standing on his back legs and the words, *Rooted in the soil. Reaching for the sky.* He turned the coin over. *"Let no man despise thy youth; but be thou an example." 1 Timothy 4:12.*

This wasn't Konrad's coin! It was Willi's.

"Reichmann brought those over to me shortly after you gave them to his boys. He was concerned that you were forming some sort of secret society with the young people."

Coins. Boys. Plural. A new fear began to gnaw on Josef's insides.

"He gave you both the boys' coins?" Josef asked. He had to be sure.

Olbricht didn't answer him. He leaned back in his chair and studied Josef like he had done hundreds of times before. A glimmer of achievement lit his eyes. Josef's heart sank. In his eagerness to test his mentor, he himself had been tested.

"Good," Olbricht surmised. "You have Konrad's coin."

"I picked it up where you left it," Josef said.

Olbricht nodded. "I had to be sure. I figured either you or the boy had it. It makes it easier knowing it was you."

"Why did you leave it behind?"

"I couldn't be certain there wouldn't be an investigation. If there was, the coin would point to Reichmann." Olbricht shrugged. "As it turned out, it was unnecessary. You know, one less Jew."

Josef was confounded. He didn't know the man sitting across from him. "That's how you thought of Professor Meyerhof? Vermin to be exterminated?"

Olbricht flushed. "Victor was my friend!" he snarled.

"You murdered him!"

"I assisted him to the other side."

"Did he go willingly?"

Olbricht was slow in answering. "Stubborn!" He said it like a curse. "Victor failed to understand that times had changed, that there was no longer a place for him here. He was prevented from teaching, and Eva was gone. He was despondent. Well, he's despondent no longer."

The most bizarre part of this conversation was that Olbricht was sincere in what he was saying. But there was more. Josef sensed it. He remembered the picture the professor had showed him and took a chance.

"Edda."

That's all he said. It was enough.

"So you know," Olbricht said. "I wondered if Victor told you."

In truth, Josef didn't know what Olbricht was talking about. If he was patient, Olbricht would tell him.

"Then you know the threat. To Edda. Me. Mady. Even to my grandchild."

The pieces were coming together. Edda and Eva grew up together. Same neighborhood. Close families. Now it made sense. "How much Jewish blood does Edda have in her?" Josef asked.

"Her grandmother was Jewish," Olbricht said. "But now with everyone gone . . . Victor was the only one left who might leak that unfortunate information."

"So you killed him."

Olbricht brushed off the accusation. "I had to do what was best for my family."

"And what about me?" Josef asked. "Am I family, or am I a threat?"

"That hurts," Olbricht said. "I love you like a son."

The way he said the words chilled Josef's flesh.

Olbricht continued. "However, you've made it clear you can't live in peace in the new Germany."

"You're sending me to a better place?"

Tears came to Olbricht's eyes. He said in a fatherly tone, "I won't allow you to endanger my daughter and grandchild. Once you're gone, you'll be better off, and they'll be better off."

Josef didn't even try to assure Olbricht that he would remain silent and learn to embrace the Third Reich. He could never speak the words convincingly.

"Your records here will be destroyed," Olbricht explained. "You'll be readmitted under a different name with a different diagnosis."

"One that marks me for death."

Olbricht ignored the comment. He stood.

"What will you tell Mady?"

"Your disappearance will remain one of the many mysteries of war. Now stand up, my boy."

At this point Josef was reluctant to do anything Olbricht told him to do, but he could think of no good reason to disobey such a simple command, so he stood.

"May I hug you?" Olbricht asked. Without waiting for an answer, the elder minister placed his arms around Josef's neck and drew him close. He whispered in Josef's ear, "If I understand my theology of eternity correctly, as soon as you reach heaven the rest of us will be right behind you. However, if there *is* an interim, spend it preparing a place for Mady and your child." With that, Olbricht released Josef and, with a proud smile, patted him on the shoulder. Then he ordered the door open and was about to leave, when he suddenly turned back and asked Josef, "Why David King?"

"King David," Josef replied.

Olbricht grinned. "Ah! Gath. Clever, but inaccurate. David wasn't king yet when he was in Gath. Can't say I was as clever in choosing your new name, Leo Speidel. A store clerk. Edda was going to marry him before I came along. After the wedding we lost touch with him. Oh, the coin." He held out his hand.

Josef tossed Willi's coin to him.

The cell door clanked shut, and the bed in Hadamar's psychiatric facility crunched as Leo Speidel sat on it.

Chapter 25

Friday, July 5, 1940

Mady wasn't prepared for childbirth. She thought she was, but she wasn't. For the last couple of months she'd been saying this day couldn't come soon enough. Now, given the severity of her contractions, she was willing to entertain the idea of carrying the child inside her forever, if only the pain would stop.

Her knees gave out. She sank to the kitchen floor.

Josef, I need you!

With her cheek pressed against the hardwood floor, she fought the pain. Her eyelids were clenched, and her breathing came shallow and labored. Mady knew for certain she was going to die in her own kitchen.

Then the pain began to recede a little, enough for her to take a deep breath. It eased until there was only a lingering sense of tightness across her abdomen. She rolled over onto her back and stared at the ceiling, drained of energy, panting, and perspiring heavily.

Josef hit the floor, the side of his face skidding against the green tile, propelled by the weight of his own body. The Rottenführer with the ax handle could learn a thing or two about inflicting pain from these two thugs. Josef spent more time sprawled on the floor than he did in the straight-backed chair in which they kept sitting him. Each time he came around after having blacked out, he awakened to a blurry green hue before being hauled back into the chair.

He began to loathe the color green. Seeing it meant the pain would start up again.

"Lisette!"

Mady's voice was weak. It barely carried to the next room. How could Lisette possibly hear her outside the house? Still, she had to try.

She called again, then listened for the door latch. But all she heard was the raspy sound of her own breathing. She tried to sit up. She couldn't. She tried again, this time rolling onto her side. She didn't have the strength.

Rolling onto her back again, she managed a chuckle. One of life's little revelations. After today she'd have more sympathy for turtles.

Kaiser wandered into the room and cocked his head in puzzled fashion at seeing Mady lying on the floor. The cat jumped up onto the kitchen counter—something he knew he was forbidden to do—and stared down at her. Mady told him to get down. He looked at her brazenly. She shouted at him, but he casually glanced away. Mady began to cry. She felt so helpless.

Josef's voice was little more than a broken croak. "Mady . . ." He slumped in the chair from the effort. His arms hung limp at his sides, and he could barely hold up his head.

"Mady! Mady!" His interrogator mocked him. A blurry face entered Josef's field of vision. "Be willing to bet she's a sweet one," he taunted. "Ooh . . . we have plans for Mady. We're going to go see her right after we're finished with you, aren't we, Fritz? Oh yes, we're going to have a good time with Mady."

Josef knew he was no match for them one at a time, let alone two against one. He could barely lift his arms. He doubted his knees would support him even if he managed to stand. But none of these realities prevented him from taking a swing at his interrogator's face.

Surprisingly, he made contact.

He heard laughter. Apparently Fritz found the blow humorous. The interrogator without a name didn't.

The next thing Josef knew, he was lying against the blurry field of green again.

Mady heard the thud of the front door.

"Lisette!"

Steps. Going away from her.

"Frau Schumacher?" The girl's voice grew fainter.

"Lisette! In the kitchen."

The footsteps grew louder.

"Frau Schumacher!" Lisette cried. The girl dropped the basket of dried laundry she was carrying and rushed to Mady's side. "Frau Schumacher! Are you hurt? Did you fall?"

"Help me get to the bed," Mady said. She reached up. Lisette took her hand, positioning herself to assist Mady to her feet.

Mady let out a wail. The pain was returning, building. "Put me down! Put me down!" she screamed.

A frightened Lisette lowered her back down to the floor.

"Birth pang," Mady said with a grimace. She laid her head back as the contraction escalated. When that wasn't enough, she closed her eyes and tried to tell herself she could withstand it. She didn't believe herself. The pain continued to build. She whimpered. Then she moaned. Then she cried out.

This one was worse than the last one. Mady was frantic. If they got any worse than this she didn't think she could endure it. Finally, the pain began to ease.

When she opened her eyes, she saw a tearful Lisette looking down at her. The girl was holding her hand. Mady wasn't even aware her hand was being held until she saw the clasp.

"Call Mother," Mady said. "Tell her to bring the midwife."

"Do you want me to help you to the bed first?"

Perspiration dripped freely down Mady's temples. "I'll rest up for the journey while you call."

Josef began praying for unconsciousness, or death. He didn't know how much longer he could hold out.

"Tell us Wolff's role in this operation!"

"Is he the mastermind?"

"Who else is involved?"

"Tell us and we'll take you back to your room and leave you alone."

He didn't believe their promises. But he hurt so badly, any promise that the pain would stop had to be considered. Both eyes were nearly swollen shut. His lower lip was twice its normal size. He tasted blood with every swallow. He was certain his left arm was broken. And they'd beaten his feet so badly that the pain was nearly unbearable just from touching the floor.

"Tell us what we want to know and you can rest!"

He felt someone grab him by the hair. His head was yanked back.

"Sturmbannführer Martin Wolff . . . where is he?"

If his lip wasn't so swollen, Josef would have smiled. Wolff had eluded them. The news was encouraging.

"Tell us what you know about Sturmbannführer Wolff!"

" 'The Lord is my . . . shepherd; I shall not want,' " Josef murmured.

"What did he say?" the interrogator asked.

"I couldn't make it out. Something about the law."

" 'He . . . maketh me to lie down in green pastures . . .' "

They bent over closer to hear him.

" '. . . he leadeth me beside still waters.' "

"Stillwater! I heard him say 'stillwater'!"

"That's an English name, isn't it? Do you think the Brits are involved in this? Have you heard anything about an operative named Stillwater?"

" 'He restoreth . . . my soul . . .' "

"I can't make it out. He's incoherent."

"I told you not to hit him in the mouth! How do you expect him to tell us anything if he can't talk?"

Josef eased into unconsciousness like he would ease into a quiet black pool, victorious in the thought that he had told them nothing.

Mady strained to hear what Lisette was saying. It was taking far longer than she'd expected for Lisette to return. And while Mady couldn't make out the words of the telephone conversation, the tone of Lisette's voice was troubling. The girl appeared seconds after the talking stopped.

"Frau Schumacher, are you ready to move now?"

"Is my mother coming?"

Worry lines formed on the girl's forehead. "I think so."

"You think so? What did she say?"

Lisette's hands wrestled with each other. "It feels awkward to talk to you while you're lying on the floor like this," she said. "Why don't we get you into your bed first."

"What did my mother say?" Mady shouted.

Lisette jumped. Tears glazed her eyes. "She was really upset. Your father is on a trip and isn't due back until tomorrow. She said she didn't know how she was going to get over here."

"What about the midwife?"

"She said she'd call her."

The phone jangled. Lisette looked in its direction, then back at Mady.

"I'm all right for now. Answer the phone."

Lisette ran out of the room. This time Mady was able to make out two words in the conversation. *Please hurry.* When Lisette returned, her tears had spilled over onto her cheeks. Others were quick to follow.

"Oh, Frau Schumacher . . . that was your mother. The midwife . . ."

"What about the midwife?"

"She's downtown. Your mother said she's not expected back for a couple of hours."

Mady could feel the panic rising within her. Her back and the back of her head were beginning to ache from lying on the floor. "Help me up," she said, raising a hand.

"What are we going to do?"

"Right now we're going to the bedroom."

"I mean about the baby."

"I know what you mean. Help me up."

Lisette sprang to her side. Between the both of them—with Mady steadying herself against the kitchen counter—they managed to get her on her feet. Mady felt light-headed. Lisette at her side, the two inched their way in the direction of the bedroom.

Halfway through the parlor the next pain began.

"Ohhhhh . . . God have mercy!"

"What's wrong?" Lisette cried.

"I'm not going to make it!"

Mady stopped.

"What do you want me to do?" Lisette asked in a frantic tone.

Stopping was the wrong thing to do. Just like before, the pain was building, and Mady knew she had no chance of coping with it while standing up. "Help me over to that chair," she said, pointing.

It became a race to get to the chair before passing out. With each half step, the pain increased. Mady began reaching for the chair before it was within reach, as if willing the chair to meet her halfway. She closed her eyes, trusting Lisette to see for her.

One step. Then another. And another. Each one more difficult than the last; each one threatening to buckle her knees.

"Almost there," Lisette said. "Almost . . ."

Mady fell into the chair just as the pain peaked. She let out a cry.

Josef felt the brush of smooth tile against the tops of his feet. With a nurse supporting each arm, he was dragged down a long corridor. The SS was finished with him. He was taken to another room with another chair. The green floor was the same.

He was thrust into the chair and ordered to stay there. The order was unnecessary. He couldn't have walked out under his own power no matter how hard he tried. He couldn't even stay seated in the chair.

Slipping in and out of consciousness, twice he awoke to curses and manhandling as he was hauled up off the floor and shoved back into the chair. After the second time they found long leather belts and strapped him in.

Gradually, the times of consciousness became longer than the times of unconsciousness. Whereas the room in which he was interrogated had only a few wooden boxes stacked in one corner, this room had shelves of medical supplies and equipment.

A bespectacled man wearing a white lab coat entered. With little more than a glance at Josef, he walked to the counter, pulled out a metal tray, and began selecting items from the shelves. His body shielded Josef from seeing what he was doing. Twice Josef heard the cold sound of metal clanking against metal.

"I need a stand," the man in the lab coat said.

One of the two nurses rolled a stand to him. He placed the metal tray on it and rolled it next to Josef. There were a couple of hand instruments Josef didn't recognize. Two syringes, each loaded with clear liquid, were easily identifiable.

The man with the eyeglasses stood a few feet away in front of him. He was of average height, his build difficult to assess because of the lab coat, which concealed so much of the man. He had a strong chin that thrust forward as he looked at Josef down a narrow nose. As he did so, he pulled on a pair of rubber gloves.

The man's eyes traced his features the way Josef had seen other men examine horseflesh.

"Hold him," the lab coat said.

Although Josef was already strapped to the chair, he felt four heavy hands fall on his shoulders.

"His head, too."

Hands pressed against Josef's temples like a vice.

Without so much as a word of explanation or warning, the bespectacled man thrust a gloved hand in Josef's mouth and ran his fingers over Josef's gums, teeth, and tongue. "You bite me and I'll have them break your jaw," the man said. He uttered the words in such a mechanical tone, the only reason Josef could be certain the man was speaking to him was because he happened to be the only person in the room with another man's fingers in his mouth.

The hand came out. The man stepped closer and, without wiping off his hand, began to inspect Josef's swollen eyes, none too gently. Josef could feel his own spittle on the glove.

"Barbarians," said the lab coat to no one in particular.

Josef could smell the sourness of the man's stomach on his breath.

"Bare his arm."

One of the nurses pulled up the sleeve on Josef's smock as the man reached for one of the syringes.

Death at Hadamar comes in two forms. Starvation and injection. Wasn't that what Wolff had said?

Between contractions, with Lisette's help, Mady finally made it to her bedroom.

"Do you want me to get someone?" Lisette asked.

"Don't leave me."

Mady clung to the girl's hand. The pains came more frequently now. They frightened her. For the last six months every mother she met felt compelled to relate horror stories regarding childbirth, stories that, at present, played out in her mind.

"What do you want me to do?" Lisette asked nervously.

Mady's jaw tensed. She felt a contraction coming. The pattern began to feel familiar, but this didn't make it any easier. She squeezed Lisette's hand so hard that both their hands shook. Her hair and clothing were soaked with sweat. Then, from the depths of her being, a scream formed. She tried holding it back but couldn't. And like a volcano it erupted, and with it came an incredible urge to push the baby out of her womb.

"It's coming!" Mady cried. "The baby's coming!"

"It'll be all right," Lisette said with a quivering voice. She covered Mady's hand with both her hands, and prayed, "Dear God in heaven, you've been attending births since Eve. Please attend this one. Help Frau Schumacher to deliver this baby."

A weak smile spread across Mady's lips.

"It's going to be all right, Frau Schumacher. It's going to be all right."

Without an interval, another contraction started.

Josef was awash in sensation. Seconds after the needle pierced his arm he began to feel a warm wave covering him. His head felt as if it were inflating, then floating. At first it was liberating. There was no more pain, and he felt almost giddy.

Then something gripped his insides. A huge iron fist closed around his stomach, squeezing tighter and tighter. His feet lifted off the floor as he doubled up, but the leather straps held him to the chair. The grip kept twisting his internal organs. Josef hollered. His own voice sounded distant to him, like it was originating from across a mile-wide ravine and growing fainter.

Mady was exhausted.

Lisette had positioned herself at the foot of the bed. "I see the head!" she cried.

Raised in modesty, Mady thought she'd be humiliated during childbirth. However, modesty was the last thing on her mind. She panted so heavily she had to work up a breath to speak. "Cradle . . . the head when it comes out!" she said.

Her eyes transfixed by the birthing process, Lisette moved in closer. She extended her arms.

Mady plunged her head back against the pillow. She stared vacantly at the ceiling, gathering what little strength she had for another push. This one would have to do it. She didn't have enough strength for another one.

"Aaaaahhhhhhhhhhhhhhhh!"

Josef's voice was back and in full volume.

He closed his eyes, because if he didn't he was sure his eyes would eject from their swollen sockets. His head jerked violently from side to side.

"Aaaaahhhhhhhhhhhhhhhh!"

His eyes flew open. He looked down at his hands to see his fingers curling backward, full circle, touching the backs of his hands.

A blur of white caught his eye. The bespectacled man in the lab coat. Injecting him with something else.

"No . . . no . . . no . . . no . . . !" Josef pleaded.

Ice filled his veins. And with it a sense of foreboding. Of sinking. His breathing became restricted. His throat swelled shut. He gasped for air, or at least tried to. All he could manage was a choking sound. He became light-headed, then amazingly he was very calm, serene; his eyes opened, and he could see everything with crystal clarity; he knew he was dying, but it didn't matter; nothing mattered anymore; he felt at peace; his eyelids became sleepy, heavy. He closed them. There was no pain. He felt content.

"She's beautiful!" Lisette cried.

The girl cradled the newborn in her arms, cleaning the infant's face and chest with the corner of the sheet in which she was wrapped.

Mady, limp from the ordeal, couldn't stop smiling—because she'd survived the birth, because there was a new sound in the room—a baby infant's first cry—and because Lisette looked so sweet holding her.

Lisette carried the baby to her, and Mady saw her daughter for the first time. The infant, red as a strawberry, blinked against the brightness of the room. Her lower lip quivered.

"Have you chosen a name for her?" asked Lisette.

"Elyse," Mady answered. Then to the baby, "Your name is Elyse."

Lisette bent over the bed to get a better look. "Hello, Elyse," she said. "I can't wait to see the look on your poppa's face when he comes home."

Chapter 26

Sunday, July 7, 1940

A few of the guests came to see Josef and Mady's daughter, though the majority of them came to see Edda's granddaughter. Comprised mostly of older members of the congregation, they were those who had been active workers during the tenure of Edda and Wilhelm Olbricht. They shuffled in and out of rooms and took turns hovering over and holding baby Elyse.

The reception was all Edda's doing. The date was of her choosing. Mady wanted to wait a week, but Edda insisted on the Sunday afternoon following Elyse's birth. Edda coordinated the guest list, supervised the refreshments, greeted everyone at the door, graciously thanked them for the gifts, and kept a careful record of everything in a ledger. Vintage Edda.

In the months prior to the birth, Mady had wondered what role her mother would play with this child. Despite Edda's repeated insistence that she wished to be present at the birth, Mady never could picture her mother in the room. When Mady was a child, Edda had been quick to enlist and delegate the messy tasks of motherhood to others, and birthing was anything but neat and tidy. Of course, that's what midwives were for. Still, Mady had found it difficult to imagine her mother involved in the whole process. She still couldn't. Edda had arrived a good three hours after the baby was delivered. The reception was her way of redeeming herself.

Regardless of Edda's persistent efforts to the contrary, the absence of the baby's father hung uneasily over the celebration. At church earlier that morning Mady's father filled the pulpit on Josef's behalf. The explanation as to Josef's whereabouts was deliberately kept vague. The reassuring presence of the elder minister had checked most of the tongue wagging. But later at the reception, the mystery of the father's absence was felt much more keenly.

No matter how bright Mady's smile, or how much she beamed at the praises heaped upon her baby, there was a tangible radiance to her anger. She kept telling herself she should have seen it coming. Hadn't Josef established a pattern of disappearing when it came to this baby?

Fräulein Baeck held Elyse in her aged arms, while Mady sat in a chair nearby. The baby's head rested against the woman's air-raid-warden armband. Her mirror image of a sister cooed and waggled a wrinkled finger while awaiting her turn to hold the baby.

Bending her head close to the baby's left ear, Fräulein Baeck made a clucking sound. She lifted her head, then made the same sound in the baby's right ear. A concerned expression covered her face. "You were alone when you gave birth?" she asked, looking down at Mady.

"Lisette was with me."

"Lisette? She's but a child herself!"

"She handled the situation beautifully."

"Where was the midwife? And your mother?"

"They arrived afterward."

"And your husband?"

"Away."

All afternoon Mady had confined her answer to the single word. Josef was *away*. No explanation. Just away. She thought that by answering like this she could conceal her anger.

She couldn't.

"Your poppa should be more responsible, shouldn't he?" Fräulein Baeck said to Elyse. "What could possibly be more important than you?"

Mady agreed, but held her tongue, choosing instead to seethe inwardly. Josef had said he'd be gone two days, three at the most. On the fourth day, Mady worried. On the fifth day, she was furious. While worry was attempting a comeback, it fought a futile battle, her anger being firmly entrenched now.

Father, as he had done before, promised to make a few phone calls. Mady could tell he had news by the way he glanced at her frequently from across the room. During a lull in the reception, she went over to him and inquired. Then the Baeck sisters arrived, and he whispered that he'd tell her after the reception.

Mady slipped the ends of her hair into her mouth, realized what she was doing, and pulled them out again before her mother saw. Her patience with Josef had run out. She married him, thinking he was like her father. But Josef was nothing like her father, and she feared he never would be.

Rupert Reichmann, his back as straight as a Prussian general, walked over to Mady while making every effort to disguise his limp. Konrad and Willi flanked him on either side. As usual all three were decked out in their uniforms, which shared more than a dozen Nazi swastikas between them.

Willi rushed up and hung on Fräulein Baeck's arm to get a better look at the baby, nearly pulling the elderly woman over. There were more than a few shrieks and gasps as the elderly woman teetered, then caught her balance. Konrad moved instinctively to save the woman and the child.

Herr Reichmann seized his younger son by the back of the neck and tossed him aside. He snarled, "You don't have the sense of a dirt clod, do you?" He ordered Willi outside.

The boy began to protest, but his father's upraised hand quickly silenced him. Willi glanced over at Mady, and his face flushed a bright red. Turning, he left the house.

"My apologies, Frau Schumacher," Reichmann said.

"He was just anxious to see the baby," Mady said.

"That's no excuse. He's as dumb as a stump and getting dumber every day." Reichmann leaned over and glanced at the baby with only polite interest. "Nice son," he said.

"It's a girl!" Fräulein Baeck protested, taking his remark as a personal affront.

Reichmann wasn't intimidated. "Too bad," he said.

Fräulein Baeck bristled.

"So, Konrad," Mady interjected, "have you received your orders yet?"

"Soon," Konrad replied. "I'm looking forward to walking the streets of London."

Reichmann laughed heartily and clapped his son on the back. "The boy's every inch a soldier. They don't come any finer."

Konrad beamed.

There was a commotion at the door as Lisette, Gael, Ernst, and Neff tumbled in. They all gravitated toward Konrad.

"Make way for Germany's newest midwife!" Neff announced. "Babies delivered, no waiting."

His remark got a laugh from everyone.

Lisette blushed.

"She should be given a medal," Mady said, "for courage under fire."

Reichmann wasn't one for levity. "It's time to leave, Konrad," he said.

"Yes, sir."

With his son in tow, Reichmann paid his respects to Olbricht and Edda and then was gone. Fräulein Baeck and her sister were right behind them. Lisette was handed the baby.

"Do you want to hold her?" Lisette asked Gael.

Gael backed away, clearly uncomfortable with the idea.

"Here, let me show you." To the surprise of everyone, especially the younger guests, Olbricht moved in and took the baby. He did it with ease and confidence.

"Support the head and back," he said by way of demonstration, "and don't be nervous. If you're tense, the baby will be tense." He began speaking to the baby. "Isn't that right, little Elyse? My, but you are a pretty little thing!"

It was a side of the churchman most people never saw. Their open mouths registered their surprise. Her father's actions didn't surprise Mady, though. She'd been the recipient of his love and protection her entire life. She knew what it was like to be the center of his universe. As she watched him hold his granddaughter, his recent vow came to mind. *I would do anything, anything to keep you from harm. And that goes for the little one, too.*

The way he cradled and cuddled Elyse was a physical reaffirmation of that vow.

Olbricht looked up. "Who wants to hold my granddaughter next?"

"I do!" Neff said eagerly.

"Have you ever held an infant before?" Olbricht asked.

"No, sir."

Olbricht grinned a grandfatherly grin, "Then this will be a unique privilege for you."

Neff extended his arms. Olbricht moved cautiously toward him and showed him how to support the head. The transfer was made.

To everyone's delight, little Elyse seemed to be taken by Neff. Ernst couldn't get over the fascination the baby had with his friend. He laughed and slapped his knee as Elyse's tiny fists batted against Neff's nose.

A loud banging at the door startled everyone. Elyse included. The infant shuddered, then began to cry.

Father opened the door, and four SS agents pushed past him into the room.

"Frau Schumacher?" an Untersturmführer shouted. He scanned the room looking for someone to respond.

Mady stood. "I'm Frau Schumacher," she said.

Father stepped forward. "I'm Dr. Wilhelm Olbricht," he said.

"The girl's father. I was assured this would not take place until later tonight."

The Untersturmführer sneered, "The SS is not run by personal convenience."

"This is a social gathering," Father insisted. "A reception for my new granddaughter. Surely you can return at a later—"

The agent ignored him. Stepping over to Mady, he asked, "Where are your husband's personal papers?"

"I must protest!" Father shouted. "What is your name?"

The Untersturmführer pulled out his weapon. "One more word and I'll arrest you for interfering with an official police investigation."

Father sputtered and fumed, but then backed off.

While the SS agents were shown to Josef's study, the remaining guests quickly gathered their belongings to leave. A flustered Edda did her best to thank everyone for coming as they stampeded toward the door.

"They said they'd come later," Father apologized to Mady.

Neff handed Mady her baby. The four youth followed the others out of the house, leaving Olbricht, Edda, and Mady standing in silence with the baby in the parlor as Josef's study was being ransacked.

Fifteen minutes later three of the men carried boxes of confiscated items outside. The Untersturmführer approached Mady. "Where is your husband?" he asked.

"I haven't seen my husband in five days."

"Where did you see him last?"

"In the bedroom. It was late."

"Where did he go?"

"I don't know."

"Were you awake when he left?"

"What difference does it—"

"Were you awake?" the Untersturmführer shouted.

The baby started crying again.

"Yes, I was awake."

"I find it hard to believe a man would leave his house late at night, as you have described, and not tell his wife where he was going."

"He said he'd be gone for two days."

"That's not what I asked!"

"I'm telling you all I know!"

The Untersturmführer glared at her.

Mady's father made a move as if to intercede, then suddenly held his position.

"Your husband, was he acting alone?" the Untersturmführer asked.

"No."

"Name his conspirators."

"The SS."

The Untersturmführer's face registered shock, followed by anger.

"I'm sorry if you don't like my answer," Mady said, "but that's what I was led to believe . . . that he was working in cooperation with the SS."

"That's true, Herr Untersturmführer," Father said, finding the courage to speak. "A report has been filed at headquarters."

The Untersturmführer stared at Olbricht. Turning his attention back to Mady, he said, "He told you he was working under the direction of the SS?"

"Yes."

"And you believed him?"

"I had no reason not to believe him."

The Untersturmführer mulled this over and then turned toward the door.

"Do you know where my husband is?" Mady called after him.

The Untersturmführer walked out the door without answering her.

While Edda tidied up the parlor, Father pulled up a chair.

Mady sat cradling a squirming Elyse.

"I called my contacts," her father began. "The news isn't good." He started to relight his cigar but looked at the child and thought better of it. He satisfied himself with chewing the tip.

"Do you know where Josef is?" Mady asked.

Edda busied herself in close proximity to the discussion, hanging on every word.

"I don't know where he is," Olbricht said. "And neither do the SS."

"How is that possible? This is *their* mission!"

Father looked at her sadly. "No, it isn't."

"But the Sturmbannführer . . ." Mady wrestled with Elyse. Finding it difficult to handle a baby and carry on a conversation at the same time, she turned to her mother. "Could you take Elyse?" she asked.

"I'm sorry, dear, my hands are full," Edda said, holding up some teacups. She disappeared quickly into the kitchen.

It was then that Mady realized her mother had yet to hold the baby. She pressed Elyse to her shoulder and rocked back and forth in an attempt to get the infant to settle down. Truth be told, her emotions were more restless than the baby, if that was possible. She was on the verge of tears. "What are you telling me, Father?"

He lowered his gaze to speak the next words. "You were speaking of Sturmbannführer Wolff," he said.

Mady recognized the name and nodded.

"Wolff's a renegade agent."

"A renegade agent," she repeated.

"There was no SS mission. Wolff was acting on his own."

Mady was stunned. If the SS wasn't the SS, then what was she to believe about any of this? "Acting on his own to do what?" she asked.

"It's still unclear. All we know is that he's involved with some kind of plot to undermine the Third Reich."

"He? Wolff or Josef?"

Father withdrew the cigar from his mouth. He pursed his lips. "Both, I'm afraid."

Mady sat back in the chair. This wasn't making any sense. At least Elyse was settling down. She'd found her fist and was sucking on it. Now if only Mady's anxiety could find something to soothe it.

"You're telling me Josef is involved in some kind of plot . . . against the Third Reich," Mady said. She said the words aloud, hoping they'd make more sense that way.

Her father studied her face.

"Sturmbannführer Wolff has implicated Josef in this plot?"

"Wolff is missing, too. The Gestapo found evidence in his desk, implicating him and Josef."

Mady was stunned by the news. "I . . . I don't know what to say."

Father patted her knee. "It's my fault," he said. "I should have seen this coming a long time ago."

"I *did* see it coming a long time ago!" Edda chimed in from the kitchen. "But nobody would listen to me."

Mady gazed down at Elyse. Slumber covered the infant like a warm blanket. Her lips encircled the knuckles of her white fist, though she no longer sucked on it. She had a cherubic countenance, completely unaware of the troubles that engulfed her family.

"What should I do?" Mady asked.

"You'll come home with us, of course," her father said.

Edda appeared again.

Mady glanced at the baby. "No, I'm staying here. This is our home."

"Nonsense," her father said. "Think about this. There's a good chance you'll never see Josef again."

The thought hadn't occurred to her. It struck her hard enough to produce tears.

"And even if you do see him," Father continued, "what then?

He's an outlaw. The Gestapo is looking for him. Who knows what he'll do?"

A stubbornness arose within Mady. She didn't know its origin or its purpose. All she knew was that she wasn't going to be dragged to her parents' home. "I'm staying here," she repeated.

Chapter 27

Thursday, July 18, 1940

Mady had just put Elyse down for her afternoon nap. In keeping with her routine, she gathered up laundry items and left the bedroom, stepping quietly so as not to awaken the baby.

A lone figure standing in the parlor caught her eye. She pulled up and gasped.

Sturmbannführer Wolff. Or was it Herr Wolff? He was dressed in gray work pants and a plaid long-sleeved shirt, its sleeves rolled up to his forearms.

"Frau Schumacher," he said quietly. "Forgive the intrusion." He held a felt hat in his hands. He threaded the brim through his fingers as he nervously rotated the hat.

It took a moment or two before Mady was able to rally her senses. When she did, anger was the chief thing she felt. "What are you doing here?" she snapped. "And where's my husband?"

"May I sit down?"

Wolff looked weary, exhausted. His clothes were wrinkled and soiled. He stood hunched over.

While she didn't offer him a chair, neither did she object when he made his way toward one. He moved like a man twenty years his age. Mady remained standing. She felt more comfortable . . .

safer, that way. For a long moment Wolff said nothing. Leaning forward, his forearms resting on his legs, he worked the hat round and round.

"You need not be frightened of me," he said. "I won't harm you."

"Where's Josef?"

Wolff lifted his head as though a heavy weight were pressing down on it. "I'm here at his request."

"You know where he is! Tell me!"

Wolff's mouth worked but no words came out. He hung his head and gathered strength for another attempt. "I'm not good at this," he said. "I do have information . . . that is to say . . . it's important that you know . . . your husband is dead."

Mady wasn't prepared for this news. Although the thought had crossed her mind, she never granted it an audience. Instead, she listened to her anger rant about how Josef had abandoned her and their child, how he gave greater priority to a hopeless crusade than to his own family, and how his foolhardiness was endangering them all. While it was true she didn't love him, she depended on his love for her. Loving her was his choice and with it came certain responsibilities—responsibilities he couldn't fulfill if he were dead.

"I'm sorry to be the one to bring you this news," Wolff said.

Mady was flustered. Her emotions, primed to discharge, no longer had a target save the one sitting in her parlor. And even though he looked like a transient from the train yard, she still saw SS in him, and it frightened her. When she spoke, her voice had an edge to it. "You're certain he's dead?"

Wolff lowered his head, finding it hard to come up with the right words. "We lost contact with him. So we sent in another operative who found records indicating that he died."

"Contact. Operative. Records. You make it sound like you were on an official mission."

Wolff sat up. He studied her face, presumably to assess how much she knew.

"How did he die?" she asked.

"I can't tell you that."

"Natural causes? An accident? Was he shot?" Her anger made her bold.

The hat in Wolff's hands rotated faster. "All I can tell you is that he died performing a heroic duty."

Mady folded her arms. For reasons unclear to her, she now grew bolder still. "I'm sure you'll understand if I remain skeptical until I receive notification of his death."

"There won't be any notification."

"Why is that?"

"Josef was operating under an assumed name."

"Then I have only your word."

"Yes."

"The word of a renegade SS agent."

Wolff winced at the word *renegade*, but he didn't refute it. "This isn't easy for me," he said. "I admired your husband. He was a man without guile, one of the truest Christian men it has been my good fortune to know."

His words knocked Mady off-center. These weren't the words of one associated with the SS. There was an earnestness in his voice that bordered on veneration.

"He made me promise to tell you something," Wolff said. His gaze returned to the hat. "Your husband requested that if anything happened to him, you would continue with your embroidery work."

Mady's brow furrowed.

"He was particularly anxious about the project depicting the American redwoods. He told me of his fascination with them."

Mady bit her lower lip in thought.

"Does this not make sense to you?"

It didn't. But she didn't want Wolff to know this. "Consider your promise to Josef fulfilled," she said.

A puzzled expression formed on Wolff's face.

Mady was stalling, trying to take it all in. *Josef dead*. The words were there, yet not the reality. Wolff might just as well have told her that Josef would be coming home later than he'd expected. Then there was the embroidery message. It didn't make sense. While it was commonly believed that the embroidery was hers, Josef knew it wasn't. But why would Wolff fabricate such an odd message?

An infant's cry erupted from the bedroom. It brought Wolff to his feet.

"The baby!" he said.

He glanced at Mady's midriff as though he needed confirmation. In his distress, apparently he hadn't noticed that Mady was no longer in the same condition in which he'd seen her the last time they met.

"May I see him?"

"Her," Mady corrected. She took a protective step toward the bedroom door.

Wolff moved more quickly than she'd anticipated. He was past her and heading toward the crib before she could say or do anything. She helplessly trailed after him. Very close after him.

With an experienced scoop, Wolff lifted the child from the crib. He rocked her gently in his arms. His face transformed with a joy that Mady had never seen on a man. It made her skin tingle. SS or not, a man wearing an expression like his was no danger to the baby.

"Her name?" he asked without taking his eyes off her.

"Elyse."

Tears came to his eyes. He was unable to control them. His chin quivered beneath a toothy smile. Elyse, wide-eyed and content to be held, stared up at him.

"She's beautiful," Wolff said.

"The way you handle her," Mady said, "you must have children."

Wolff didn't reply. He began to weep. Then, his voice breaking, he said, "She'll never know her father."

Josef is dead!

The reality of his death began to seep through the cracks of her defenses. Her heart grew heavy until it felt like a lump of lead in her chest. Her knees grew weak. She found it difficult to breathe.

Wolff said, "God in heaven, I pray you let me live long enough to tell this little one what a good man her father was."

Mady's knees became weak. She collapsed onto the edge of the bed awash in despair.

Wolff, struggling with his own emotions and apparently unaware of hers, turned suddenly and thrust the child at her. He headed for the door.

Then suddenly he stopped, steadying himself against the doorjamb. For several moments he stood there, his head bowed. Turning back, he gazed at mother and child. His eyes were preoccupied with a thought. "A midwife attended you?" he asked.

"After the birth."

"Afterward . . ." Wolff said. He lifted his hand to his mouth. "Did the midwife note any concerns . . . any abnormalities?"

Mady's defenses rose. "There's nothing wrong with my child."

Wolff walked back into the room. "That's not what I asked," he said. There was a tinge of the interrogator in his voice that set Mady's nerves on edge. "Did the midwife note any abnormalities?"

Two images flashed in her mind. The midwife, as she snapped her fingers near the baby's ears, and Fräulein Baeck, leaning close to the baby and making clucking sounds. Both women wore the same expression of concern.

"There was something, wasn't there?" Wolff said. "Let me see the child."

But Mady clutched the baby to her chest and turned from him.

"Mady, it's important you tell me. Believe me when I say I'd give my life for the well-being of your baby."

Believe you? The man who took my husband from me . . . took him away to die.

Wolff approached her. He dropped to one knee so that he was no longer looking down at her but faced her eye to eye. "You have to trust me," he said. "In the name of all that is holy, you have to trust me!"

She thought of the way he'd held Elyse. The joy. Hadn't she just concluded this man was no danger to her child? Still, she was reluctant to trust him.

Wolff waited on her in silence. She expected him to plead more. Or possibly threaten. Wasn't that the way of the SS? But he didn't. He pleaded only with his eyes, as though he knew how difficult this must be for her.

"Her hearing," Mady whispered. "The midwife was concerned about her hearing."

Wolff reached a hand toward the baby. Like the midwife had done, he snapped his fingers close to each ear and evaluated the infant's response. He did it a second time. Then he stood.

Mady's heart quickened. Had she made a mistake in telling him?

"Listen to me carefully," Wolff said. "Did the midwife register the birth with the Reich Health Ministry?"

The last few weeks had been a whirlwind of activity. With Josef gone, Mady had to contend with everything on her own—the trauma of the birth, learning to be a mother, receiving relatives, answering the midwife's questions, greeting guests at the reception, beginning her own physical recovery . . .

"I'm not sure . . ." Mady said.

Wolff grabbed her shoulders. His grip frightened her. "This is important!" he cried. "Did she fill out a questionnaire of some kind? Think, Mady!"

Mady tried to remember the events of the day Elyse was born. Her mother was in the room, jabbering about Mady's birth while the midwife asked questions and examined Elyse. She remembered feeling both tired and excited. She'd wanted to close her eyes and rest, to forget the pain, but she also wished to continue to hold her child, at times wanting to be alone and at other times wanting to tell the world that she had a new baby daughter. There were so many conflicting feelings and thoughts. She tried to replay the convoluted scene in her mind.

"I remember the midwife turning from the crib and writing

things down while she was examining the baby."

Wolff nodded solemnly. He looked around for something. Not finding it, he bolted from the room.

Mady looked after him, not sure what to do. When he didn't return immediately, she got up and started for the parlor. Wolff nearly bowled her over in his hasty return. He shoved a scrap of paper at her.

"Listen carefully," he said.

Mady looked at the paper. It had a phone number written on it.

"If anyone contacts you from the Children's Specialty Department, you're to call this number immediately! Do you understand?"

"What is . . ."

"Immediately! Do you understand?"

"The Children's Specialty Department."

"If they show up at your door, stall them. Run from them. Anything, just don't let them take Elyse."

"Take Elyse?"

"Under no circumstances are you to allow them to take your daughter."

"You're frightening me," Mady said.

Wolff nodded sympathetically. "If anyone comes for her, call this number," he repeated. "And when someone answers, say the word *Bulwark*."

"Bulwark?"

"That's all you need to say and help will be on its way."

Wolff turned for the door. "For Elyse's sake, Mady," he said. "In the meantime, I'll do what I can to take care of this."

"Take care of what?" Mady shouted.

But Wolff was gone.

Chapter 28

The only time Mady picked up Josef's embroidery baskets was when she was cleaning. Now that he was dead, moving them felt as if she were disturbing a grave.

Elyse was down for the night, so Mady finally had time to act on the puzzle that had dogged her all afternoon.

Continue your embroidery work.

That's what Wolff had said. *Your* embroidery work. But it wasn't hers. She had only the barest knowledge of embroidery and was inept with her hands. Josef knew this, so why then would he give Herr Wolff such a message to deliver? And if the message hadn't come from Josef, it made even less sense. Why would anyone want her to embroider?

Sitting in the parlor chair, she rummaged through the basket, expecting to find a piece of paper with a note of some kind. She found nothing except an old pair of Josef's reading glasses. She emptied the basket of its contents and studied the inside of the basket itself. Nothing. She turned the basket over. A weaving pattern and signs of wear, nothing more.

She slumped in the chair. Confused. Weary. Angry. Vulnerable. She didn't know what to believe—about anything!

"Continue with your embroidery work."

"It doesn't make sense," she muttered.

Mady made her way to the study, startled at the quietness of the house, particularly at night. It felt eerie. All the little sounds that she never heard during the day were accentuated at night—the sliding of drawers, the soft thud of her own footsteps, the creak of doors and of bedsprings. They seemed determined to remind her she was alone in the house, in the sense of having no adult human companionship. Maybe forever.

She approached the door to Josef's office and hesitated. It had remained closed since the SS ransacked the room during Elyse's reception. Because Mady's days were crowded with motherly duties, she hadn't yet concerned herself with cleaning the mess they had made.

As Mady swung the door open it pushed papers across the hardwood floor. She tried not to step on the mess and nearly tripped over a book in the effort. The lamp on the desk had been knocked over. She righted it and switched it on.

The room like her life was a shambles. Papers everywhere. Books, pulled from the shelves, were strewn about open-faced on the floor. Josef's office chair lay on its side. File cabinets gaped open, emptied of most of their contents. The room had all the earmarks of a Third Reich visitation.

Picking up a few books from the floor, Mady stacked them on top of the desk. Unfamiliar with Josef's library system, she had no idea where they belonged on the shelves, which at the moment resembled a gap-toothed smile.

A part of her wanted to bring a sense of order to the chaos. But at the moment she was driven by a greater desire—that of solving the mystery of Josef's riddle.

She spied the other embroidery basket, the one Josef kept in his office. The upturned basket sat in a corner, the contents scattered around it. She examined it as she had the one in the parlor, only in reverse order—first, the basket itself, and then the contents as she placed the threads and needles back inside the basket. And, like the one in the parlor, she found no note, no explanatory message.

Her fingers took on a new sensitivity as they touched the contents of the basket, knowing they were last touched by Josef, and would never be touched by him again.

Wiping away tears, she saw several pieces of unfinished work thrown up against a wall. One was a still life of an old water can used as a pot for daisies. There was another of a lighthouse, and a third, the largest of the three unfinished pieces, of tall trees.

"He was particularly anxious about the project depicting the American redwoods."

Wolff's words came back to her. Mady set aside the daisies and the lighthouse and concentrated on the scene with the redwoods. It was a tall canvas, one suited to capture the size of the trees. Mady held it at arm's length. Barely a third of it was complete. A single trunk done in browns and some leaves.

She searched the canvas for any unusual marks but found none. She turned the canvas over. It was clean. There was nothing about the work that seemed to separate it from any other. The stitches were precise, as always, and the colors striking. Once completed, it would be breathtaking.

But that would never happen. Despite Josef's message—whatever it was—Mady couldn't see herself completing Josef's work.

Mady draped the canvas over the pile of books on the desk and stepped back. Was it as simple as that? Did Josef merely want to ensure that this particular piece of embroidery be finished? Possibly as a reminder of him? Did he see himself as an American redwood? Or did he want her to think of him as such? Or possibly his hope was that his child would come to think of the father she'd never know as a tall, enduring symbol?

Bewildered, Mady shook her head. Could it be as simple as that? Maybe she was making this entire thing more complicated than it actually was. And while she knew she could never finish the piece, she could get one of the ladies in the church to do it for her, to serve as a memorial of sorts to Josef.

That would be just like him, Mady thought. *He had this tendency to make everything a big deal.*

The lateness of the hour, combined with the weariness that comes from mental exertion, began taking its toll on her. She covered a yawn while taking one final look at the embroidery of the redwood. The workmanship was exquisite. Regardless of her reservations, she felt there was more to this piece than she could see at the moment.

Saturday, July 20, 1940

For two days Mady stared at the redwoods and was no closer to learning its secret than the day she first found the embroidery in the study. She hung it in the kitchen as she fixed her meals and in the bedroom as she nursed Elyse. Then she hung the daisies on one side of it and the lighthouse on the other. Hadn't Wolff told her that Josef was *particularly* interested in the unfinished redwoods? Did this mean in relationship to the other two unfinished pieces?

She wracked her mind comparing the three. Flowers, trees, lighthouse—what did these have in common? All three of them were unfinished, did that mean something? Or maybe it was the degree of incompleteness? Of the three, the redwoods had the least amount of work done to it, followed by the lighthouse, then the daisies. They were three separate scenes with but a single artist completing them—any significance to that?

The whole thing drove Mady to distraction. Putting Elyse to bed for the night, she stood over the child and rubbed the baby's back as she stared at the pictures again. Elyse had been fussy all day, and Mady was tired.

Something touched her foot. Mady jumped. "Kaiser! You startled me!" she whispered, careful not to wake the baby.

With her foot she shoved the cat aside, but he came straight back and rubbed against her leg, demanding attention. He'd been that way ever since Elyse's birth.

The baby was asleep. Mady retrieved the three embroideries, pushed the cat aside once again, and went to the parlor. After collapsing into the chair, she spread the three pieces on the floor in front of her. Kaiser walked on them, threading his way through her outstretched arms. Mady quickly shooed him away.

She sat back in the chair and, with a sigh, gazed down at the pictures. After a few moments she decided the embroidery held no message. Apparently, something had been lost in the transmission. Either Josef had not given Wolff enough accurate information, or Wolff had left something out—a word or two that would have made sense of it all.

Kaiser jumped onto Mady's lap and proceeded to rub his face against Mady's chin and chest. Mady was about to toss him aside again, but then thought better of it. It wasn't as though Kaiser was getting in the way of anything. There was no message.

Mady relaxed and concentrated on rubbing Kaiser's head and ears and face. The cat purred contentedly. His response to affection was somehow satisfying to Mady. Mady closed her eyes and pulled the cat closer to her, warmed by his warmth, soothed by his purring.

When she opened her eyes, her attention fell on the redwood embroidery. It was a brief glance, but in that glance she thought she saw something among the roots of the tree. For a moment, it looked like the letter *G*.

She looked again, and the letter seemed to disappear among the root structure.

Setting the disgruntled Kaiser aside, she reached for the canvas. She studied the tops of the roots. Traced her finger along the lines of thread.

She saw it again.

G

A coincidence? An unplanned pattern of thread?

No! Next to the *G* was a small *e*. And then what looked like an *n* or possibly an *m*!

Gen? Gem?

The letters were encased in a single root. There were no other letters in the root. What about the other roots?

With the eagerness of a gold digger striking a vein of ore, Mady searched for more. On the root to the right of the one containing the letters she found a number—29. Nothing else on that root.

Gem 29. Gen 29. Gen. A preposition. Towards. Towards 29? What did that mean?

On the next root she found another number—10.

How could she have not seen these until now? The letters and numbers were worked into the pattern of the roots, and they were of the same color thread. But now that she saw them, they stood out with embarrassing clarity.

She checked the other roots for hidden letters and numbers. And then the tree trunk. On one root she thought she saw an elongated *E*, but then concluded it was a part of the root pattern and not a letter. There was nothing on the trunk. That left her with 10, 29, and Gem or Gen. Or, from left to right, Gem 29 10 or Gen 29 10.

Gen! *Genesis?*

Genesis 29:10?

Mady leaned back in the chair and laughed out loud. Was that really it? Genesis 29:10?

Kaiser took the appearance of her lap as an invitation to jump onto it again, but no sooner had he landed then he found himself on the floor again as Mady jumped up.

A moment later she returned with her Bible, thumbing through the pages at the beginning of the book.

"Genesis 29:10," she mouthed as she searched. She found the passage.

And it came to pass, when Jacob saw Rachel the daughter of Laban his mother's brother, and the sheep of Laban his mother's brother, that Jacob went near, and rolled the stone from the well's mouth, and watered the flock of Laban his mother's brother.

"That's it?" she said aloud.

Mady slumped in her chair, more confused than ever. This was getting tiresome.

"Josef, if you wanted to tell me something, why couldn't you just write it down on a piece of paper like everyone else?" she muttered.

She read over the verse a second time to see if she'd missed anything. Jacob and Rachel. Daughter of Laban. Sheep of Laban. A mother's brother. Jacob rolled the stone from the well's mouth.

What did any of this have to do with her?

With an abruptness that comes with frustration, Mady snatched up the three canvases from the floor and carried them to Josef's office, where she tossed them onto his desk. The redwood canvas, being longer than the others, didn't find enough of the desk's surface to hold it there. It slid to the floor.

Mady bent down to pick it up.

She paused.

Lying next to the fallen canvas was one of Josef's sermon files, discarded by the SS. What interest were sermon files to them? But it was the tab of the file that caught Mady's attention. Josef filed his sermons by text. This one was "Romans 5:1–5." She picked up the file and its scattered contents. Inside the folder Josef had written the date on which the sermon had been preached: September 11, 1938. Included in the folder were his sermon notes, research notes, pages of random thoughts and quotes.

A thought occurred to her. Maybe the message on the redwoods canvas referred not to the biblical passage itself but to a file folder that contained a sermon based on that passage.

She went to the metal files that Josef used to store all his sermons. The fact that the Romans 5:1–5 folder was found on the floor was no guarantee that the other sermon folders would still be there. In their furor, the SS might have dropped it.

Mady opened the drawer. To her relief, she found it filled with folders, filed according to text. Apparently the SS considered such folders unimportant.

The files themselves were arranged in biblical order, with Genesis in the front and Revelation in the back. She flipped through the first few folders and found the one she was looking for—"Genesis 29:10–30."

She extracted it from the metal cabinet. Taking it to the desk, she switched on the light, sat behind the desk, and opened the folder. On the top of the first page, written in Josef's handwriting, were the words *The way of man and a maid.* Beneath this were three points:

> 1. *Jacob saw Rachel, verse 10 (the look)*
> 2. *Jacob kissed Rachel, verse 11 (the touch)*
> 3. *Jacob loved Rachel, verse 18 (the devotion)*

Underneath the points Josef had written: *Note verse 20. It says Jacob served seven years for Rachel, and it seemed but a few days for the love he had for her. I don't believe women realize the extent of the passion that they inflame in men, that it could reduce seven years to a few days.*

Mady felt strangely warmed as she read these words. A cloak of melancholy covered her. Reading Josef's thoughts made it seem as if he were nearby. Then it struck her. She didn't remember hearing this sermon. When had he preached it?

She checked the folder in the same place where Josef had recorded the date when he'd preached the Romans sermon. It was blank. There was no date. Had he forgotten to record it? Mady went to the metal file again and randomly checked a half-dozen file folders. All of them had dates recorded on them. Yet this one didn't. Perhaps it was a sermon in progress. One that he planned to preach . . .

Cruelly, her mind completed the sentence for her, . . . *and now never would.*

Mady turned to the next page. It was covered with Josef's

handwriting in paragraph form, like the text of a sermon. She began to read.

The central thought of this passage is clear—Jacob loved Rachel. It is stated twice: once as a matter of fact (verse 18), and again comparatively to Leah (verse 30). For seven years he demonstrated his love for her every morning when he got up and went to work. And then again for another seven years after Laban tricked him by giving him Leah first in marriage. Fourteen years of sweat and toil testify to Jacob's love for Rachel.

Notice the quickness with which Jacob fell in love with Rachel. On the same day he first saw her (verse 10), he kissed her (verse 11). Considering the lot of women in that day, this cannot be explained away by the customs of the day. Nor can it be easily dismissed when taking into account the central theme of the passage. It is clearly another indication of how much Jacob loved Rachel.

The word that is used to describe his devotion to her is also worth noting. It is used elsewhere to describe the way Jonathan befriended David in the passage that describes their friendship as two souls knit together (1 Samuel 18:1). It is also used of God's love for the righteous (Psalm 146:8). Clearly this love is a deep, lasting love, a righteous love, one that reaches far beyond infatuation or sexual attraction between a man and a woman. Jacob wanted to knit his soul to Rachel's soul; he loved Rachel with a holy passion.

In order to obtain the object of his heart's desire, Jacob had to go through Laban. This would not be the last time a man would go through a father to win the hand of the woman he loves.

Mady stopped reading. She straightened up, pondered this sentence, and then read it again.

This would not be the last time a man would go through a father to win the hand of the woman he loves.

It was far too familiar to be a general comment.
She continued reading.

There is something about this passage that is disturbing to me. While it is very clear in its portrayal of Jacob's love for Rachel, nowhere are we granted insight into Rachel's feelings for Jacob. While the theme is Jacob's love for Rachel, surely the writer could have included some clue to her feelings. In the passage about Jonathan and David it is clear how both men feel about each other. Why is it not as clear here? Is it possible that Rachel didn't love Jacob with the same intensity with which he loved her? Is it possible she didn't love him at all?

While Jacob's love for Rachel was not dependent on her reciprocation, it is sheer torture to think that a man would love a woman who didn't love him. That he would marry her. That they would have a baby. Could there be any worse purgatory than to be in a marriage where love is one-sided? Yet the love of a man for a maid is such that it can thrive regardless of her response. Jacob loved Rachel. Of that, there is no doubt.

Mady stared blankly at the wall. Tears filled her eyes. She blinked them back.

Chapter 29

Monday, July 22, 1940

By the time she'd discovered the second file folder, Mady realized that all the mysterious hours Josef had spent in his study were spent preparing these messages for her.

On the last page of the Genesis file she had found a scriptural reference with no explanation. Song of Songs 4:9. Mady went to the metal cabinet and found the file with that reference. Like the Genesis folder, this one had no recorded preaching date. She started reading.

> *Many scholars believe that these writings are an allegory of God's love for His people. I will not dispute their claims. Yet neither can it be disputed that the surface reading is a love song, the mutual expression of endearments between a man and a woman.*
>
> *The writer's passion for his maid resounds with every word: "Thou hast ravished my heart, my sister, my spouse; thou hast ravished my heart with one of thine eyes."*
>
> *His passion is surprising when you consider the lover was a man known for his wealth and wisdom. But love is no respecter of rank or privilege. It enthralls the strongest and the weakest among us, the richest and the poorest, the statesman, the soldier, the actor, and the dock worker. Some men will never strive for greatness as this world*

*counts greatness; they will forever live in the shadow of great men.
Yet often it is these men who know great love and who burn with
infinite passion all their lives for a single maid.*

*Heaven help the man whose heart has been ravished by a maid.
He is forever lost to himself. For had his heart not been ravished, he
would have given it to her willingly.*

Like Solomon's song, Josef's writing had two levels. There was
the surface level that resembled preaching notes, but there was also
a deeper level, which, with each new passage, was becoming increasingly clear to the one for whom the message was intended.

Mady felt Josef's presence in the room as she read his words.
They softened a heart that had become stiff from the daily routine
of marriage and life. Not since their courting days had she felt this
way. She found herself dreading the last page of the file, fearing
there would be no more.

But there was.

Again, a single scriptural reference led Mady to a file marked
"Ecclesiastes 4:9–11." Josef had written the entire biblical text in
his own hand:

> *"Two are better than one; because they have a good reward for
> their labour. For if they fall, the one will lift up his fellow: but woe
> to him that is alone when he falleth; for he hath not another to help
> him up. Again, if two lie together, then they have heat: but how can
> one be warm alone?"*
>
> *What a powerful passage about companionship. We were not
> created to be alone. Every human being has an intrinsic need to
> share life with another. We are stronger, better, happier when we
> have someone with whom we can share life's experiences.*
>
> *And while this passage teaches a welcomed truth about the ad-
> vantages of two persons who are mutually committed to each other,
> the benefits of those joined in marriage are far greater.*
>
> *Ephesians 5:31: "For this cause shall a man leave his father
> and mother, and shall be joined unto his wife, and they two shall be
> one flesh."*
>
> *O blessed mystery! Love knows nothing of arithmetic. Love*

transcends such menial concepts. In marriage one plus one equals one. They are no longer two (one man, one woman), but one flesh.

Some couples, to their detriment, never comprehend the bliss of this concept. They struggle against the truth. Attempting to live as though they were still separate beings, they torture and scar themselves as surely as if they had taken a blade to their conjoined bodies. Oh, but those who embrace this essence of marriage, to them is reserved a joy that is unparalleled in this world or the—

The door to the study creaked as it opened. Mady jumped. A blond head of hair poked inside. "Frau Schumacher?"

"Lisette! Thank God, it's you!"

"You didn't answer the front door when I knocked."

Mady closed the file and rested her hand on top of it, though she didn't know why.

"I saw the laundry on the line," Lisette said. "Do you want me to bring it in?"

"Thank you, dear. The basket's in the bedroom. Don't worry about waking Elyse."

Lisette left as quietly as she'd arrived.

Mady sat at the desk, her heart flip-flopping like a schoolgirl who got caught passing a love note in class.

———————

Lisette balanced Elyse on her lap as Mady finished making two butter-and-jam sandwiches. She cut them diagonally, placed them on plates, and set one on the kitchen table in front of Lisette alongside a glass of milk.

Mady was constantly amazed by how comfortable Lisette looked with Elyse. Mady still felt clumsy, at times inept, handling her child.

"Frau Schumacher, may I ask you a question?"

Mady took a bite of sandwich and nodded.

"Is Pastor Schumacher dead?"

With difficulty, Mady swallowed the bite in her mouth. She kept forgetting that few people knew for certain he was dead. To the church, their pastor was still missing and unaccounted for. Naturally, there were rumors and speculation, most of them unkind. One rumor said that he'd been taken to the forest and shot by the Gestapo. Another said he'd defected to England with damaging secrets that would cost the lives of thousands of German soldiers. Where people came up with such ideas was anybody's guess.

And so the church was beginning the process of replacing Josef. Mady's father had encouraged such a move. He said it was best that the church go forward.

"Why do you ask?"

Lisette laid her sandwich back on the plate without taking a bite. "That's what people are saying, that he's dead."

The anguish in the girl's eyes was evident. She was looking to Mady for a word of hope or comfort, and Mady had none to give her. But how much should she reveal? "I'm afraid there isn't much hope."

Tears came to Lisette's eyes. Her voice trembled as she spoke. "I miss him terribly. I feel like I've lost a father."

Her words hit Mady with unexpected force.

"And I'm not the only one who misses him," she continued. "Konrad, Neff, Ernst . . . everyone does. More than they let on. Konrad especially. He's always talking about him."

Lisette began to weep.

The bite in Mady's mouth might have been spread with despair rather than butter and jam, because it went down bitter. The girl's emotions touched off a cascade of pent-up feelings within Mady, chief of which was guilt. Here was a young girl who was crying over Josef, when his own wife hadn't shed a single tear! What kind of woman was she not to weep over the death of her husband, a man who—if the writings in the files were any indication—had loved her deeply?

How many people were hurt by his death? Lisette and Konrad and Neff and Ernst. He had touched their lives. And what about Sturmbannführer Wolff? He too had wept for Josef, saying he never knew a man like him. An SS agent, of all people! What kind of monster was she when an SS agent wept over her husband and she didn't?

Now that it was unleashed, guilt continued its rampage as Mady looked at the infant on Lisette's lap.

Not only had Lisette loved her husband more than she had, the girl was now proving to be a better mother to Elyse. What good was she to anyone? She was a bad wife and mother. She wasn't even a good pastor's wife—nothing like her mother.

Mady pulled at her hair. She stuck the ends in her mouth. A darkness settled over her, making it hard for her to breathe. Sobs bubbled up from deep within, wracking her body. Then she began weeping so hard she found it difficult even to hold up her head.

From the other side of the table, Lisette wailed, "I'm sorry, I'm sorry, I'm sorry!" She came to Mady's side of the table and put an arm around her. "I shouldn't have brought it up. I should have known the pastor's disappearance would still be very painful for you!"

Mady managed to shake her head. "It's . . . not your fault."

Their emotions spilled over onto the baby. Little Elyse began to cry, too.

Lisette sank to her knees. With one arm around the baby and the other around Mady's waist, she laid her head against Mady's leg and continued to cry.

The baby wailed on her lap.

Mady rested her cheek on top of Lisette's head and sobbed.

Kaiser appeared at the kitchen doorway, unsure whether or not to enter. He stared at the commotion for a moment, then cautiously hopped up onto the kitchen counter a safe distance away from the three weeping humans.

———

After feeding the baby, Mady invited Lisette into the study. Going to the desk, she picked up a file folder and said, "This is one of them."

Following lunch—the butter-and-jam sandwiches remaining

uneaten—Mady and Lisette got to talking about Josef. The recent bond that came from their commingled tears caused Mady to be more open with Lisette than she might have been otherwise. She told Lisette about the files.

"If they're too personal . . ." Lisette said.

Mady opened the folder and read, " 'The central thought of this passage is clear—Jacob loved Rachel.' "

The Ecclesiastes file led them to a file marked "Philippians 2:3–4." Mady read it for the first time, aloud to Lisette. Baby Elyse fell asleep to her father's words. " 'I am convinced that these words—though directed to a church fellowship—hold the key to any relationship, be it friendship, business, family, or marital.' "

"That sounds just like him, doesn't it?" Lisette said, smiling. "I can hear his voice in the words."

Mady smiled back at her and said, "I've thought the same thing." Then, turning her attention back to the page, she said, "Here, he quotes the Scripture passage." Clearing her throat, she began to read. " ' "Let nothing be done through strife or vainglory; but in lowliness of mind let each esteem other better than themselves. Look not every man on his own things, but every man also on the things of others."

" 'This then, is the key: If a man and a maid commit themselves to each other in this fashion, I can virtually guarantee them many years of happiness in marriage. And just the opposite is true, too. If a man and maid spend their days thinking only of themselves—their needs, their wants, their desires—I can guarantee a marriage of endless strife and bickering. This is a powerful truth, not to be taken lightly, to be ignored only at one's own peril.

" 'Never once have I had a husband or a wife come to me for counseling and say, "My spouse thinks only of my good, night and day. They're constantly doing the things I want to do, never what they want to do. I can't stand it anymore! I want a divorce!"

" 'Once married, if he is wise, a man soon learns that when he truly loves a maid, nothing makes him happier than to see his wife happy. Nothing.' "

"A man and a maid," Lisette said. "His code words for you and him."

Mady nodded in agreement.

"Pastor Schumacher loved you very much."

"More than I deserved," Mady admitted.

"And he had a romantic streak in him," Lisette said. "Not that I'm surprised. It must be nice though. The only way Konrad would be capable of romance would be if they printed a procedure for it in the infantry manual."

Mady laughed with her. "Hmmm . . . Nazi romance," she said. "Now, there's a thought not worth thinking."

They laughed again.

Mady was beginning to feel good again. Talking to Lisette about Josef had stirred deep-seated emotions. Good emotions. Warm. Loving. But bittersweet, too. She felt herself falling in love with him.

You have only yourself to blame, she thought. *You had your chance, but didn't realize what you had until he was gone. And now you're falling in love with a dead man. Sad. Very sad.*

She fought back tears.

"Is that the last of the folders?" Lisette asked.

Mady turned a page. Her heart smiled. "There's another one," she said. " 'Proverbs 3:1–2.' " She retrieved the file from the cabinet and, as she always did, looked for a preaching date. There was none. Mady smiled and opened the folder expectantly. "The Scripture passage is at the top of the page," she said. Then she read it.

" ' "My son, forget not my law; but let thine heart keep my commandments: For length of days, and long life, and peace, shall they add to thee."

" 'As with Jacob and Rachel, when God blesses a man and a maid, he often does so by giving them a child. As the writer of Proverbs discovered, there is no greater privilege for a man than to sit down with his son and teach him the things of God.

" 'God willing, someday I will know that joy.' "

Mady stopped reading. She looked down at her daughter asleep on a blanket on the floor, and began to weep.

Not a son, but a daughter. Josef had become a father. Before or after he died? Mady would probably never know.

Chapter 30

Thursday, July 25, 1940

What are you doing here?"

With two clicks of the door, Dr. Wilhelm Olbricht entered the white room that had no windows. Josef had aroused only moments before. He found himself propped in a corner on the familiar green-tile floor. The room had no furniture, only a grated drain in a corner, filthy with stains.

"Get out," Josef said.

He spoke softly, yet each word came as a hammer blow to his head. Time and night and day were lost concepts to him. His existence had been reduced to that of a receptacle into which people in white lab coats pumped vial after vial of various solutions into him. His arms and stomach were riddled with needle tracks. His insides were a ball of knotted string. He would fall asleep without warning and awaken retching.

Unconsciousness had become the great escape, for when he was awake his fingers felt as if they were being held backward to his wrists. And any attempt to stand only resulted in a nosedive to the green tile. Drug-induced illusion and reality flip-flopped on him without warning, and his vision was such that everything looked as though he were peering through waves of rising heat.

His emotions cycled from anxious to paranoid to suicidal to exuberant to melancholy. If he wasn't laughing, he was screaming or whimpering or crying. At the moment, he was fighting an extreme case of giddiness.

"I said get out," Josef said. He covered his mouth and giggled, as if he'd delivered the punch line to a joke.

Olbricht kept his distance. An unlit cigar jutted out from his face, which for him was a natural-looking extension. He worked it with his teeth as he looked down on Josef. He examined first the small room, then Josef, and his nose wrinkled in disgust. "You look like a drowned cat," he said.

"*Meow.*" Josef howled at his own humor.

Olbricht chomped his cigar and scowled.

Josef stood on the bank of the river. It was during holiday. The sun warmed his bare chest. Water lapped at his feet, up to his ankles. He felt someone holding his hand. His little brother.

"*Don't let go of his hand, Josef!*"

"*I won't, Momma.*"

Josef's skinny chest swelled with pride. He liked big-brother moments like this one. The two boys giggled at the feel of the cold water between their wiggling toes.

" . . . here because I want us to part on friendly terms," Olbricht was saying.

Josef was back in the Hadamar cell. He wiggled his toes and giggled.

"Are you listening to me?" Olbricht asked.

"Every third word."

Olbricht fumed. "This is impossible. What have they given you?"

"Giggle juice!" Josef replied, laughing. He snapped his fingers. "Garçon! Giggle juice for everyone. Put it on my tab!"

Just then a spasm seized his gut with a cast-iron grip. Josef doubled over, falling to his side. The grip tightened. Then again. His eyes clenched so tightly they squeezed out tears. Then, as abruptly as the pain began, it eased, leaving behind a residual ache that kept him from straightening up completely.

The giggles were gone.

"You brought this on yourself," Olbricht said. "You have no one to blame but yourself."

"What do you want?" Josef asked.

"I thought we might pray."

"A confessional?"

"If you feel you need one."

"I was thinking of you."

"Me? What would I possibly have to confess?" Olbricht said.

"Seems like the sixth commandment has taken quite a beating at your hands."

"Murder? You wound me, son. I've not killed anyone."

"Tell that to my brother and mother. And Professor Meyer-hof."

"You tell them. You'll be seeing them soon enough. However, I think you'll discover that they bear me no ill will."

Olbricht sounded confident to the point of arrogance. In an odd way, it was almost nostalgic.

The whispers woke him.

"Will it hurt?"

"No, baby, you won't feel anything."

"Will the angels have wings? Can I touch them?"

"Yes, you can touch them."

"I'm scared, Momma."

"There's nothing to be scared of. Soon everything will be all right."

"Don't leave me, Momma. Please don't leave me."

"I won't, baby. The moment you get to heaven, turn around. I'll be right behind you. Now close your eyes."

"It's going to hurt!"

"No, baby, you won't feel anything."

Josef blinked. Green tiles came into focus. "Mady," he said.

Olbricht's eyebrows raised. He grinned a familiar grin, the same one Josef had seen on a hundred Sunday afternoons. "Of course! You don't know, do you?"

"Know what?"

A long dirt road stretched before him. Josef felt his hands gripping the handlebars, his leg swung over the middle bar of the bicycle. He was determined that this was the day he would ride. . . .

Josef forced himself back to the present. "Mady . . ." he said again.

"Quit interrupting and I'll tell you," Olbricht said. He removed the cigar from his mouth. "I'm a grandfather!"

"And God blessed them with a child . . ." Josef mused, "a son . . ."

"A daughter."

"A daughter? I have a daughter?"

"Elyse."

Josef stared up at his father-in-law. A wave of emotion sloshed over him, reducing him to trembling and weeping. And with it came a familiar dark melancholy that doused all hope and joy, just as a pail of water douses a fire. His moans echoed off the cavelike walls. Rocking back and forth, he whispered his daughter's name in an attempt to keep his sanity from slipping away completely.

Olbricht was little more than a wavy apparition staring down on him from on high. His voice sounded distant, muted, all vowels and no consonants.

Josef tried to throw off the melancholy, but it was like trying to toss back darkness. He felt his consciousness drifting.

Jacob loved Rachel. But nowhere are we granted insight into Rachel's feelings for him. Surely there must be some clue as to her feelings. Is it possible that Rachel didn't love Jacob with the same intensity with which he loved her? Is it possible she didn't love him at all? It is sheer torture to think that a man would love a woman who didn't love him. That he would marry her. That they would have a baby. Could there be any worse purgatory than to be in a marriage where love is one-sided? But Jacob loved Rachel. Of that, there was no doubt.

The sound of the cell door brought him back. Olbricht was looking over his shoulder, half in, half out of the room.

"Ah! You're conscious again," he said. To the guard in the hallway, "I'll be just a moment longer."

Olbricht stepped back into the room. He shook his head. It was one of those parental headshakes. The kind that indicates disappointment.

"You should see yourself," Olbricht said. "You really are pathetic."

Josef felt his senses returning, at least momentarily. A measure of strength flowed into his limbs. He straightened himself in the corner. Had he thought he could stand, he would have done so. "What do you expect? You dropped in unannounced," he said. "Had I known you were coming, I would have had the servants prepare hors d'oeuvres."

Olbricht jabbed his cigar at Josef. "That's the attitude that landed you in this place," he lectured. "That's always been your weakness. You've allowed your hubris to overrule common sense. The difference between you and me is that I have not lost sight of what has been the sensible thing to do. Common sense has ruled my every action."

"Fear, you mean. You confuse the two."

Olbricht's face reddened. "I'm a survivor!" he shouted. "I do what it takes to survive! In a few days you'll be dead and I'll still be here! Then what good will you be to anyone?"

"And what good will you be when everyone sees you for the coward that you are?"

"Coward?" Olbricht shouted.

"What else do you call it when out of fear you toss aside everything you've believed and taught all your life? There's a reason the Nazis don't trouble you. You've sold your soul to them."

Olbricht took a threatening step toward Josef, then stopped. His eyes glared yellow with rage. Taking his half-chewed cigar from his mouth, he threw it at Josef, hitting him in the chest. Then, turning his back on his son-in-law, he pounded on the door and demanded to be let out.

Chapter 31

Friday, July 26, 1940

Last. Konrad says that's all he can tell me," Lisette said. "Why does everything have to be so secretive? He's such a little boy at times. Sometimes I think the whole army is just a bunch of little boys playing war games."

"According to the radio, everything's heading east. Troops, guns, tanks . . . everything," Mady replied.

They sat in the parlor. Though the late afternoon shadows were creeping across the floor, it remained oppressively hot. Mady made a mental note that the next time she had a baby she must make sure to have it in the wintertime. Holding Elyse felt as though she were cradling a smoldering log from the fireplace.

Every window in the house was wide open. The front door stood open, as well. Mady had done everything she could to coax a breeze into the room.

The baby was fussy, and Mady didn't know what else to do with her. She'd been fed. She was dry. She'd just awakened from a nap. Still, little Elyse balled up her fists, turned red in the face, and wriggled discontentedly. Mady was growing wearier by the moment.

It seemed like taking care of the baby was all she did anymore.

If she wasn't feeding the baby, then she was either changing the baby's diapers, or rocking the baby to sleep, or washing the baby's clothes, or cleaning up the baby's mess. Mady couldn't remember what she did with all her time before Elyse was born.

"I'll hold her for a while," Lisette offered.

Mady didn't object.

The baby calmed as soon as Lisette sat down. When it came to baby Elyse, Lisette had the magic touch.

"Neff's going east, too," Lisette said, continuing the conversation. "He'll report for duty with Konrad. Sad, really. He requested an assignment as a photographer. They handed him a rifle."

"And Ernst?" Mady asked.

"He starts classes at the university in a few weeks."

"It's going to seem odd not having them around." Mady fanned herself. She wished the sun would go down so that it would get cooler.

"Frau Schumacher?"

"Yes?"

"May I ask you something?"

"You know you can ask me anything."

Lisette hesitated. "I'm afraid it's an imposition."

"We'll never know until you ask."

"You'll tell me, won't you?" Lisette said. "I mean, if it's an imposition. You'll tell me, won't you?"

Mady sat back in her chair and fanned herself.

"After all, you did just have a baby . . ."

"Lisette, ask me!"

The girl grinned at her sheepishly. "Do you think it would be possible for us to have . . . I'd do all the work, that's not the problem. But my parents won't let me have . . . do you think it would be all right . . ."

"A farewell party for the boys is a great idea," Mady said. "And, yes, you can have it here."

Lisette brightened. "Yes? It's not too much trouble?"

"I've been thinking the same thing. It's a great idea. You never know when all of you will be together again."

"I can do all the work."

"Between the two of us, I think we can handle it."

"It'll have to be soon. Konrad and Neff are scheduled to report—"

The sound of a motorcar pulling up in front of the house interrupted them. Mady didn't recognize the motorcar or the driver until he climbed out.

"Isn't that one of the SS agents who attended our church services?" Lisette asked.

"Sturmbannführer Wolff."

"I didn't recognize him at first without his uniform."

Wolff approached the open front door. He carried papers in one hand. Like everything else that day, he looked wilted from the summer heat. As he drew closer, he looked bedraggled and more tired than when Mady had last seen him.

Mady met him at the doorstep. Lisette was right behind her with the baby in her arms.

Upon seeing Lisette, Wolff slyly positioned the papers behind one leg.

"Sturmbannführer Wolff," Mady greeted him coolly.

"Frau Schumacher." He glanced at the girl behind her.

"This is Lisette Janssen," Mady said. "She's a member of our church and an ever-present help to me."

"I can see that," Wolff said, his eyes on Elyse.

Lisette shot a quick glance at Mady. Only after receiving an approving nod did she lean forward and allow Wolff a better view of the child.

"Frau Schumacher, may I have a few moments of your time?"

"I can take Elyse to the bedroom," Lisette said.

"It's stifling back there," Mady said. "You stay here in the parlor. Sturmbannführer Wolff and I will talk outside."

Mady followed Wolff down the porch steps.

When she stopped just a few feet away on the gravel, he said, "It's highly confidential."

"Over here," Mady said.

She led him to the woods a short distance from the house, the same woods the boys had disappeared into in search of a Christmas tree six months before.

Had it only been six months? It seemed a lifetime ago.

The sparse woods provided meager shade. Not enough to give them any comfort from the heat.

"How is Elyse?" Wolff asked.

"She has more energy than her mother," Mady said.

Wolff grinned. "As a father I remember days when—"

"You said you wanted to speak to me confidentially," Mady said, directing him back to the business at hand.

Wolff handed her the papers.

The top sheet bore the symbol of the Reich. It was a government form. Printed on it was Elyse's name and pertinent information about her birth—date, weight, length, father's name, mother's maiden name, and so on. The questionnaire the midwife had filled out.

"The next page," Wolff said.

Mady flipped to the second page, which had the heading, REICH HEALTH MINISTRY. Below it was Elyse's name and a case number. Below that were three boxes on the left with three doctors' names next to them. The first two boxes had red plus signs in them with signatures over the doctors' printed names. The third box was blank. There was no accompanying signature.

"We took this from T4 headquarters," Wolff said.

Mady stared at the stolen document. The red plus signs frightened her, though she couldn't remember why they should. Pointing to them, she said, "Refresh my memory."

"Three doctors evaluate the health questionnaire," he said. "Three red plus marks and they come for Elyse."

"Come for her?"

Wolff nodded. "You would never see her again."

Mady's knees became weak. She looked instinctively toward the house. "My baby!"

"Elyse is safe," Wolff said.

Mady looked at the papers again. "Because there are only two red pluses?"

"They no longer have a record of her."

"This is it?" Mady asked.

Wolff nodded.

Despite the heat, Mady threw her arms around Wolff's neck and hugged him. "Thank you. Thank you."

Wolff didn't share her relief.

"You can never take Elyse to a doctor," he said. "And she can't go to school, either."

Mady sobered. "What am I supposed to do, hide her for her entire life?"

Wolff looked at her sadly.

Mady's arms slumped to her side in a gesture of helplessness. The thought of keeping Elyse's condition a secret from everyone was overwhelming. Fräulein Baeck already suspected the truth. What was she going to do about that? And what kind of life could Elyse expect to have shut away in the house? She would be a prisoner all her life!

"There's something else," Wolff said.

Dear God, more? Mady thought. She didn't know if she could take any more right now.

"Your husband may still be alive."

Mady's thoughts were so embroiled concerning Elyse, it took a moment for Wolff's news to register. "Josef . . . ?"

"I don't want you to get your hopes up," Wolff cautioned.

Too late. "Josef? My Josef?" Mady cried.

"When we were searching the T4 facility for Elyse's records," he explained, "this fell out of one of the folders." Wolff then reached into his pocket and produced a coin, which he handed to Mady.

She held it in the palm of her hand. It bore the image of a bear.

The inscription read *Rooted in the soil. Reaching for the sky.*

Her hand began to tremble.

Josef cradled his head in his hands, deep in thought.

Though he had never seen her, he loved her. Though he would never hold her, he believed in her.

He knew her. They'd communicated. Touched. Well, not directly, but through the wall of Mady's womb. While he could have hoped for more, at least he had that much. Someday, when she joined him in heaven, they'd be able to laugh at how they used to touch hands through the wall.

"Elyse."

Josef said his daughter's name aloud. He liked the sound of it. Besides, it gave him an additional point of focus to take his mind off the pain and to fight the hallucinations. He had Mady. And now there was Elyse, his little girl. He felt stronger with the twin focus.

"Mady."

"Elyse."

Josef laughed with joy. This time it was real, not drug-induced.

"Elyse. Come here, Elyse. I have a daughter; her name is Elyse. Allow me to introduce my daughter, Elyse. Children? Yes, one. A girl. Her name is Elyse."

Josef reclined onto his back, his arms spread out at his sides. He stared at the ceiling, which looked exactly like the four walls, with the exception of a bare bulb on a wire sprouting from its center.

He tried to imagine what Elyse would look like, not as a baby, because babies all looked alike to him, but as a schoolgirl, then as a young woman. To his surprise, the image his mind conceived was that of a young Mady. This only made him love both wife and daughter more.

A double click and the door swung open. Two attendants marched in dutifully. They didn't ask him to stand. They didn't greet him or tell him what they wanted with him. They strode in, flanked him, grabbed him under the arms, and lifted him to his feet, which didn't work.

Ducking under his arms, they made of him a human yoke while they played the part of the beasts of burden. With their burden secure, they trod toward the door.

"I have a daughter," Josef said. "Her name is Elyse."

For all their interaction, he might just as well have been a sack of flour or potatoes. They hauled him down the hallway and into a familiar room with silver trays.

"Noooooooooo!" Josef wailed. "Dear God, no! No more injections! Please, no more injections!"

They flopped him into a chair and restrained his arms and legs with heavy leather straps. One of the attendants wheeled a cart beside him. Three syringes were laid out in order.

"No more injections!" Josef cried. He could feel the tears running down his cheeks.

A man with an unfamiliar face and wearing a white lab coat entered the room. He was clean-shaven with a strong jaw. He didn't look at Josef, only at a chart. Nodding his head, he set the chart aside and examined the syringes.

Josef had not seen this man before. "No injections," he pleaded. "I have a daughter. No more injections!"

"Lift his shirt," the man in the lab coat said.

The attendants came upon him from both sides. They exposed his stomach.

The lab-coat man looked at Josef's stomach and frowned. But what he saw apparently wasn't enough to discourage him from his task.

"Her name is Elyse," Josef said again. "Please, I don't want to forget my daughter's name!"

The first needle slid deep into his belly. Josef felt a burning sensation in his gut that quickly spread to his legs. The second and third needles followed in quick succession. The burning moved up his chest, encasing his heart.

Josef felt sick. "Elyse . . . Ely . . . El . . ."

A wave of nausea washed Elyse's name from his mind.

"That's your husband's coin, isn't it?" Wolff asked.

Mady turned the coin over. *"The Lord is my rock, and my fortress, my God and my strength." Psalm 18:2.* She couldn't remember which of the youth this coin belonged to.

"Josef had them made," she said.

"He carried this one with him," said Wolff. "He and another operative had a dispute over it."

Mady weighed the coin in her hand. She put a lid on her rising hope. "What is it about this coin that leads you to believe my husband is somehow resurrected?"

Wolff pulled out a handkerchief and wiped the sweat from his forehead and neck. While the heat could have prompted the action, Mady got the impression he was buying time. He looked as though he hadn't yet decided how to tell her, or how much to tell her.

"Your husband was involved with a mission at a health facility," he began. "Their records are kept in the same place we pulled the papers on Elyse."

Mady was puzzled from the start. "What on earth was Josef doing at a health facility that would have gotten him killed?"

"I can't go into that," Wolff said. "It's enough for you to know—"

"Can't go into it?" Mady hissed. "Herr Wolff, it appears you have known all along exactly where my husband has been, what's happened to him, and what possibly caused his death—if indeed he *is* dead—and I want to know everything!"

Wolff raised a pleading hand. "Frau Schumacher, the information is dangerous. Josef didn't tell you before he left in order to protect you, and I won't tell you now for the same reason."

"But, Herr Wolff, I'm Josef's wife! I demand—"

"Please . . . Mady, for your sake, for the sake of your daughter, it's better that you don't know."

"Let me judge what is—"

Wolff cut her off. "I know this is difficult for you," he said. "It's been difficult for all of us. Let me tell you what I can."

His demeanor more than his words appeased her. He had the eyes of a wounded man.

It took Wolff a moment to remember where he was. "Josef entered the institution with an assumed name. While there, he encountered an unforeseen development that compromised his identity. That's when he disappeared."

"Why didn't you go in and get him out?"

"It wasn't that simple. A nervous attendant tipped me off the last time I tried to make contact with him; otherwise I would've been arrested. My identity was also compromised. I had to leave everything behind. My position. My house. Everything I own. I am now a hunted man."

This accounted for his unkempt appearance. And his weariness.

"So we sent someone into the facility undercover. When he made inquiries with patients, they told him Josef was dead. The records at the institution confirmed it."

"Then you found the coin . . ." Mady prompted.

Wolff smiled. "The coin was the key."

"Josef's still alive?"

"We think so. They've given him another name. But we don't know how often they update the charts at the records center."

"But now you have something to go on. You can go in and get him."

"Possibly."

"Possibly?" Mady hissed at him again.

"Frau Schumacher, other lives are at stake. We're considering our options."

"If there's even a remote possibility . . ."

" . . . then we'll go after Josef."

It was the way he said Josef's name that stopped any further objections. He left no doubt that he cared for Josef.

"Thank you, Herr Wolff," Mady said.

They stood opposite each other among the trees, the lowering sun throwing diagonal shadows across them.

"What name did they give him?"

Wolff squinted his eyes. "Why would you want to know?"

"Curiosity," Mady said.

Wolff pondered her request. Then he said, "Leo Speidel."

The name had a familiar sound to it. It lodged in Mady's mind, working on her like a burr works its way into a sock. She'd heard the name before. Where?

"What is it?" Wolff asked.

"I don't know . . . I think maybe . . . I don't know . . . Leo Speidel." She said the name aloud, hoping it would help, but just the opposite occurred. All of a sudden the recognition was gone, as though by saying the name she'd scared it away.

"Give it time," Wolff said. "It'll come to you. And when it does—"

"Oh no!" Mady cried.

"What is it?"

A hand flew to her mouth. "Good Lord, no!"

"Mady, tell me!"

She slumped to the ground, her legs too weak to hold both her and the emerging truth. The name proved to be a little key to a giant door, one that concealed terrifying truths she didn't want to know.

Wolff knelt beside her and took her hand.

"Josef!" she said. "He's at Hadamar Mental Facility."

A shocked Wolff stared at her. "How did you know that?"

"My father . . . he . . . he . . ."

Wolff's expression went from disbelief to despair. He knew now he'd said too much. He'd given her the key that unlocked the door. "You're not supposed to know," he said. "I was trying to protect you."

But she'd come this far. There was no turning back. "The unforeseen element," she said, "the thing that compromised Josef's identity . . ." Then she swallowed and said, "It was my father, wasn't it?"

Wolff was in pain. It broke Mady's heart just to look at him.

Still, she persisted. "It was my father, wasn't it?"

"You were never meant to know that."

Her hand went to her hair. She pulled it into her mouth.

Wolff stroked her arm. "Hadamar. Your father. How did you know?"

"The name," Mady said. "Leo Speidel. My mother was going to marry a Leo Speidel. And then Father came along."

Chapter 32

Monday, August 5, 1940

Mady sat on the floor of the study, surrounded by file folders and photographs. Elyse lay nearby on a blanket. Having found her fist, the baby had fallen asleep on her stomach to the sound of sucking noises. She looked angelic.

Her skin was perfect. Soft. White. Smooth. Not a mark on her. Nothing to indicate she was unfit to live in Der Führer's Reich.

Mady rubbed the baby's back for a moment, then turned her attention to the items in front of her.

> *I don't believe women realize the extent of the passion that they inflame in men, that it could reduce seven years to a few days.*
>
> *Clearly this love is a deep lasting love, a righteous love, one that reaches far beyond infatuation or sexual attraction between a man and a woman. Jacob wanted to knit his soul to Rachel's soul; he loved Rachel with a holy passion.*
>
> *Heaven help the man whose heart has been ravished by a maid. He is forever lost to himself. For had his heart not been ravished, he would have given it to her willingly.*

She picked up a framed photo. Their wedding day. Josef looking thin and tall and young in his double-breasted suit. She stood close beside him in a white satin gown, the train pulled from behind and fanned out on the floor in front of her. She was looking at the camera, trying her best to look radiant. Josef was looking at her.

Is it possible that Rachel didn't love Jacob with the same intensity with which he loved her? Is it possible she didn't love him at all?

Mady's fingers lightly touched the image of her husband's face. A tear fell on the frame's glass.

———

"Come in, Father."

Mady gave Olbricht a hug as he crossed the threshold.

"Where's that granddaughter of mine?" Olbricht asked. He touched the end of his cigar to make sure it wasn't lit.

"She's sleeping."

"Doesn't that child do anything except sleep and eat?"

Mady grinned. "I thought it best to wait until she's six months old before teaching her how to cook."

Olbricht stepped toward the bedroom.

"She's over here," Mady corrected him.

She led him to the study door and slowly opened it far enough for him to see the baby, but not far enough to go inside.

A huge smile creased his bulldog face as Olbricht admired his granddaughter. "Pretty as a picture," he said.

Mady saw his eyes wander to the files and photos spread out on the floor. He said nothing, and she didn't offer an explanation.

"We can talk in the parlor," she said. She closed the door to within a couple of centimeters, just enough to be able to hear the baby if she woke up.

Olbricht loosened his collar. He cursed the heat. "These August days take their toll on an old man," he complained.

"I've made some lemonade. Would you like some?"

"I'd sell my soul for a glass."

Mady returned a few minutes later with two tall glasses of lemonade. She handed one to her father, who removed his cigar long enough to down half of it. He commented on how good it tasted, then asked, "What did you want to speak with me about, dear? Ready to come home?"

Mady took a casual sip of her drink. "Have you heard anything new about Josef?"

Olbricht shook his head sadly and said, "Latest information is the same as it has always been. Missing. Presumed dead."

"When was the last time you inquired?"

His eyebrows raised. "Have you heard something?"

Mady scolded herself. She was pressing. "Well, as you might imagine, it's been on my mind," she said. "He is—was—my husband."

Olbricht leaned forward. "Come home. It will make your mother happy."

Mady frowned, then said, "I can't. Not until I know for sure that Josef is dead. If I moved home now, it would look like I was giving up hope."

"Hmmmm." Olbricht sat back, weighing her words. He swallowed the last of his lemonade.

He was thinking. Mady could always tell. His eyebrows knit together, and his eyes moved side to side.

"I'll give you the same advice I gave the church," he said. "Move on. Josef's disappearance will forever be a mystery. He's not coming back."

Mady hung her head.

"I know this is hard on you. . . ." Olbricht added.

"I just wish I could be as certain as you. But until I am, I refuse to give up on him. How can I do any less? He's my husband."

"And if you never can know for certain? How long will you wait without hope?"

Mady shrugged her shoulders. "I don't know."

Olbricht set his glass down on the end table beside his chair.

"Would you like more?" she offered.

Cigar in hand, Olbricht waved off the offer.

"When was the last time you saw Josef?" Mady wanted to know.

Olbricht rubbed his chin. "The morning the Sturmbannführer brought him home. I had my suspicions then. I should have acted on them. Had I acted sooner, maybe none of this would have happened."

He was fishing for reassurance. Mady obliged, though grudgingly. "You couldn't have known," she said.

Olbricht sighed heavily. "I guess not."

Silence fell between them. Just as it was about to become uncomfortable, Olbricht slapped his knee. It was his way of announcing a decision.

"Mady, what I'm about to tell you can't leave this room," he said. "It could get me in a lot of trouble."

Mady leaned forward.

Olbricht paused as though he was contemplating changing his mind. He said, "Now, this is serious. I've been ordered not to tell anyone. But, well, you're his wife. You should know." He paused again, then told her, "The Gestapo has proof of Josef's death."

Mady sat back in reaction to the news. "I see," she said softly. "And why haven't I been informed?"

"I wasn't given the details, mind you, but the way it was explained to me, they can't reveal that they know about Josef's death because it would compromise their search for their renegade agent."

"Sturmbannführer Wolff," Mady said.

"He's the one. They believe him to be responsible for Josef's death."

"I see," Mady said.

"Remember, they made me give my word I wouldn't tell anyone."

Mady nodded.

"The only reason I'm telling you now is because . . . well, because you need to know."

"Thank you for telling me, Father."

Olbricht chomped his cigar for a few moments. Mady stared at her lemonade.

Her father reached toward her and touched the back of her hand on her lap. "Will you be all right?"

She smiled at him weakly. "This merely confirms what I've suspected."

After a while, Olbricht cleared his throat and asked his daughter, "You don't think less of me for withholding the information, do you?"

"You gave your word."

"Exactly."

A few more moments passed in silence.

"And you don't think less of me for telling you, do you? For breaking my word?"

"It's not something you'd do lightly."

"Of course not. I've always prided myself on being a man of my word."

"And I've always admired you for that."

"Well . . ." Olbricht picked up his empty glass, looked at it, and then set it back down.

"I can get you some more," Mady said.

"No . . . no, thank you." He slapped his knees and stood.

Mady set her glass of lemonade aside and stood, as well.

"So then," he said, "I can tell your mother you plan to come home soon."

"We can discuss it. Soon."

"Good enough," Olbricht agreed. "She'll be pleased to hear it."

He pulled at his collar to indicate once again that the heat was too much for him. Mady stared at the floor.

"Mady, I want you to know how sad I am that your marriage didn't turn out the way we'd all hoped it would. Like I told you before, I feel I'm to blame, having taken Josef under my wing the way I did. By doing so, I feel you felt some sort of obligation to marry him."

"It was no one's fault," Mady said.

"Good . . . good. Will you be all right here by yourself? I mean, considering the news about Josef and all . . ."

"I think a part of me suspected it all along. I'll be all right."

"You're sure?"

"I'm sure."

She took a step toward her father and kissed him on the cheek. He patted her shoulder in a fatherly way and then walked to the door. He turned back.

"When my granddaughter wakes, give her a kiss for me."

"I will."

The gravel crunched under his feet as he walked to the Essex Super Six. The motorcar door slammed. The engine roared. Mady watched the back of her father's motorcar, which carried him away in a cloud of dust.

She stood in the doorway long after the dust had dissipated. Her heart was as cold as a stone.

Like every child, when she was growing up, Mady had experienced difficult moments of transition from childhood to adulthood. Such as when her parents did or said something that proved they were less than perfect. This was one of those times.

Only this time the impact was greater than mere disillusionment. Mady was devastated.

Never had she imagined her father capable of lying like he had lied to her today. Yet he sat in her parlor with all the self-assurance that she'd always associated with him, and he lied to her. He looked her in the eye, and he lied to her. He drank her lemonade, and he lied to her.

She would never be able to think of him, or look at him, or talk to him the same way again. To think that all these years she had revered this man.

Mady went to the bedroom where she retrieved a piece of scrap paper that had a telephone number written on it. She dialed the number.

After two rings, a male voice answered. "Yes?"

Mady hesitated. She bit her lower lip.

The silence on the open phone line begged for her to speak. But by speaking she knew she would be making a choice, an irreversible one.

She spoke but a single word.

"Bulwark."

Chapter 33

Thursday, August 8, 1940

It was a small party, but everyone who needed to be there was there. Ernst and Neff, the inseparable friends who were soon to be separated, laughed and joked and punched each other in the arms in the center of the parlor. Konrad, every inch of him looking military, stood stiffly next to the radio console with a cup in his hand. Lisette, the instigator of the party, preceded Mady into the room. She was carrying a tray of pastries. Mady followed her with a fresh pitcher of punch.

Gael and Willi had also been invited, but Gael was on holiday with her parents at the river and Willi was somewhere else. That's all Mady was told. Apparently the boy was known to wander off for hours without explanation.

"Pastry?" Lisette held the tray in front of Konrad.

"Over here, wench!" Neff called to her. "We would taste your wares."

Ernst slapped his knee and howled.

Lisette raised a fist. "I'll give you a taste of my wares," she threatened.

Neff and Ernst shook with mock fear.

The parlor was once again alive with the sounds of youth.

Mady liked the sound. Not since Christmas had such gaiety visited her house.

"Remember when Konrad knocked over the Christmas tree?" Ernst cried.

Apparently the youth were all thinking the same thing.

"Yeah?" Konrad said defensively. "Well, just keep Lisette away from the radio or we'll all be listening to that pompous prime minister of England!"

The three boys laughed at Lisette, who pretended to be offended, but Mady knew the look. How many times had she given it herself when she was Lisette's age? The girl was enjoying the male attention.

A wail came from the bedroom.

"Now look what you've done!" Lisette cried. "You've awakened the baby!" She shoved the pastry tray into Konrad's chest, forcing him to take it.

"I'll get her," Mady said.

"That's all right, Frau Schumacher. I don't mind." Lisette disappeared into the bedroom.

Mady had planned on asking her mother to care for Elyse during the party. She was wary of having other women watch her. She couldn't risk them discovering Elyse's hearing impairment. This was a risk with her mother, too, but Mady figured she was going to have to tell her parents the truth about Elyse sometime anyway.

When Lisette learned of Mady's plan for the baby for the evening, she argued that Elyse would be no trouble. She reappeared now from the bedroom, carrying the red-eyed baby.

"Now the odds are even," Lisette said. "Three women, three men."

Neff begged to differ. "I wouldn't classify the baby as a woman," he said.

"Then the odds are still even," Lisette replied. "Because I wouldn't classify you as a man."

Neff's face burned red. Ernst and Konrad laughed at his expense. To Neff's credit, he was enough of a friend to appreciate a good joke. He laughed, too.

The sound of a motorcar coming up the gravel driveway caught Mady's attention.

It was time.

While Lisette tried to get a reluctant Konrad to hold the baby, Mady hurried to the door. Two men climbed out of the motorcar. One of them was a stranger. She welcomed them into the house.

The presence of the men quieted the youth.

Mady stood between the two men and the youth. She offered the men a seat in the parlor. To the youth, she offered an apology. "Forgive me for having a secret agenda for this gathering," she said. "But Pastor Schumacher needs your help."

———

"They're holding him against his will?" Konrad asked.

"That's correct," Wolff replied.

"At a medical facility?"

"Correct."

"Why doesn't the SS just go in and get him?"

"This isn't an SS matter."

"Everything's an SS matter," Konrad countered.

"This isn't."

Wolff and the man he'd introduced as Adolf sat side by side. Wolff did most of the talking. In general terms, he explained to the shocked young people his belief that Josef was alive and in danger.

Mady was flanked by Wolff on one side and Lisette holding Elyse in her lap on the other. Of the youth there, Lisette was the least shocked by the things they were hearing. Mady had confided in her the discussions she'd had with Wolff.

Despite Wolff's pleas, the underground organization had deemed a rescue effort too dangerous and with no significant value to the cause. It was a cold calculation but the kind made every day in a war.

However, there was nothing cold about Wolff's feelings for

Josef. The only thing stopping him from mounting a rescue effort on his own was the lack of manpower. To his surprise, Adolf approached him and suggested they go after Josef themselves. While he welcomed the offer, they still needed more help.

It was Lisette's idea to involve Konrad, Ernst, and Neff. The boys had recognized Wolff the second he stepped through the door, even with his being out of uniform. It wasn't every day a Gestapo Sturmbannführer attended their worship service.

"What was Pastor Schumacher doing at the facility?" Ernst asked.

"That doesn't matter," Wolff replied. "All you need to know is that our time is short. His life is in danger."

"If he isn't dead already," Adolf added.

Konrad was shaking his head. "This doesn't ring true," he said. "You're not telling us everything."

"You're a soldier," Wolff said. "Does your commanding officer explain his orders to you?"

"You're *not* my commanding officer."

With a nod, Wolff seemed to know he'd taken the wrong approach. "Then, as a friend," he said, "when your friend's life is in danger, do you question whether or not he should be saved, or do you save him?"

Neff spoke up, saying, "It's just that this sounds sort of subversive."

"It is," Adolf said.

Wolff shot a disapproving glance at his partner.

"They should know what they're getting into," Adolf said.

Wolff clapped his hands together, rubbing them back and forth. "You're right," he said.

The room fell silent for a moment as Wolff arranged his thoughts. Then he said, "You could be arrested for what we're asking you to do. And if you are arrested, it will reflect on your careers."

"Or terminate them," Adolf added.

Wolff started to object to this but then thought better of it.

Konrad leaned forward, his forearms on his thighs, his hands clasped. Ernst sat back in his chair, eyes wide open. Neff wore a silly grin. He seemed to find amusement in the fact that the pastor of his church was involved in something illegal.

Wolff glanced at Mady. "It was called Operation Ramah."

"The Christmas story," Lisette said, instinctively pulling Elyse closer to her.

"The medical facility is a holding place for infants who are less than whole."

"Retarded . . ." Ernst said, more a clarification than a question.

"They have all kinds of deformities or disabilities," Wolff said.

"Holding them for what?" Lisette asked.

"For elimination. The babies are killed."

Konrad shook his head in disbelief. "I can't believe that the Reich would sanction—"

Wolff cut him off. "My infant son was taken from me and killed at that facility." He paused, then added, "You're young. But not too young to learn that not everything is as it appears in your Reich."

"Elyse!" Lisette said softly with tears.

Mady looked at her. "You know?"

Lisette nodded. To the boys, she said, "She can't hear in one ear and has poor hearing in the other."

"You didn't tell me about his baby," Adolf complained.

Wolff ignored him. "Pastor Schumacher entered the facility in an attempt to rescue the children there. He was discovered."

"Why did they keep him? Why wasn't he arrested?" Ernst asked.

"I don't know why," admitted Wolff.

"They experiment on humans," Adolf said.

"We don't know that they've done any experimenting on Josef," Wolff replied.

"Why else would they keep him?" Adolf said.

"Exactly what are you asking us to do?" Konrad asked.

Adolf answered, "Surveillance. Insertion. Extraction."

"Frau Schumacher has told us about you," Wolff said. "Which one of you is Neff?"

Neff raised his hand.

"You're the photographer."

Neff beamed.

"Soon to be infantry," Konrad added.

"We'll need surveillance photos of the facility. And you're Ernst?"

Ernst nodded.

"We may need your electrical skills to create a diversion."

"I'm a physicist," Ernst said.

Wolff looked to Mady.

"He fixed our Christmas-tree lights," she said.

Wolff asked Ernst, "Are you saying you can't do electrical work?"

"Oh, I can do it. I just don't think of myself as an electrician."

"That's good to know," Adolf said dryly.

"And you're military," Wolff said to Konrad.

"Is it that obvious?" Konrad asked.

"Oh yes!" came a chorus of replies.

"We can use each of you," Wolff concluded.

The moment for a decision had come. The former Sturmbann-führer wasn't one to waste time. "All I want from you is one word: *In* or *Out*. But before you make your choice, hear me out. I am a German. I believe in God and duty to my country. And I believe in good men. Josef Schumacher is such a man. I don't know of another man who has had a more dramatic impact on my life and my faith than Josef. Here is a man who has risked his life to rescue infants from mass slaughter. I admire him. I want to be more like him. And if his life is in danger, I'll do everything I can to rescue him. But I can't tell you what to do. Each of you must decide for yourselves. So . . . are you in or out?"

There was a moment of reflective silence.

"I thought we were here for a party," Neff said.

Nervous laughter eased the tension.

Neff reached into his pocket. When he opened his hand there was a coin in it. Everyone in the room recognized it. It was the coin from the youth Christmas party.

"There have been a lot of things said about Pastor Schumacher these last six months," Neff said. "But all I can say is that I know he believes in me and I believe in him. I'm in."

In similar fashion, Ernst produced his coin. "I'm not one for speechifying," he said. "I'm in."

It was Konrad's turn. He sat up straight in his chair, his hands resting on his knees. He stared at the floor and shook his head. "I can't," he said. "Too much . . . too much to lose."

"Konrad!" Lisette cried. "How can you? All this time you've been telling me how much Pastor Schumacher has meant to you. How you never had to prove anything to him. That he made you feel good just for being you!"

Konrad stood. He was angry now. "The things I told you were just between you and me!" he yelled.

"It's all right," Wolff said to both of them. "Konrad, it's your decision."

"And how do we know that what they're doing at that hospital isn't for the best, anyway?" Konrad cried. "I mean, they are doctors. Doctors! They know what they're talking about!"

Lisette had had enough. "Sit down!" she said to Konrad.

"What?"

"I said, sit down!"

With a glare, Konrad sank into his seat, not knowing what to expect next. The others in the room were looking at him.

Lisette marched over to him, still holding Elyse, and dumped the baby in Konrad's lap. It was the first time he'd held her. Clumsy arms attempted to cradle her and hand her back to Lisette at the same time. Lisette stepped back so he couldn't.

"Look at her!" Lisette said.

Konrad fidgeted. "Lisette, take the baby."

She stood her ground. "Look at her!" she said again. "Take a good look!"

Konrad glanced around the room helplessly. No one came to his aid. He looked down at the baby in his arms.

"Now smother her!" Lisette said.

"What?" Konrad cried.

"Smother her! Choke her. Stab her. I don't care how you do it. But kill her!"

Baby Elyse wriggled in Konrad's arms. He began to tremble. As he looked down on her, tears came to his eyes.

"The men that you're defending want to kill this baby," Lisette said. "Are you going to let them?"

Konrad was struck dumb.

"They also want to kill this baby's father. A man you say you admire. Are you going to let them?"

Konrad couldn't take his eyes off Elyse. Quietly he said, "I'm in."

Mady stood and disappeared into the bedroom. When she returned, she held out an open palm to Konrad.

"My coin!" Konrad said.

Wolff said, "If that's the coin I think it is, Josef carried it with him."

"Yes, he did," Adolf said. "It's how we found him."

Chapter 34

Tuesday, August 13, 1940

The town of Hadamar appeared to be stuck in the Middle Ages. Its age was showing. From the ancient hill upon which it sat, to the simple stone column in the Marketplatz, to the arched stone bridges over the river, to the colorful half-timbered houses that huddled together on its cobblestone streets.

The town had nothing that could compare to the imposing seven-spired cathedral that greeted visitors in nearby Limburg. The edifice seemed to grow directly out of the cliff on which it was situated. The only thing greeting visitors at Hadamar were the rumors surrounding the psychiatric hospital. While other towns had their vineyards or hot springs or wine taverns, Hadamar had its hospital with its reputation of death.

Mady could see the hospital from the second-story hotel room on Schulstrasse. She leaned her forehead against the windowpane, aching in the knowledge that Josef was so close yet was still out of reach. She told herself to be patient. She reasoned that the loving God she worshiped wouldn't allow her to fall in love with her husband and then take him away from her before she could tell him.

" 'The upright love thee,' " she whispered against the glass.

Song of Solomon. Having cherished the quotes in Josef's

messages, she'd taken to reading the book herself. She discovered that it was a dialogue between two lovers. In anticipation of seeing Josef, she'd memorized some of the stanzas.

" 'By night on my bed I sought him whom my soul loveth: I sought him, but I found him not. I will rise now, and go about the city in the streets, and in the broad ways I will seek him whom my soul loveth.' "

"Did you say something?" Wolff had come up behind her.

Self-consciously Mady pulled away from the window without turning around. She tugged at the ends of her hair and attempted to hide the rising blush she felt in her cheeks. "I was just thinking of Josef," she said.

He stood behind her and looked out at the facility. "Every night I pray God will keep him alive long enough for us to get to him."

"As do I," Mady said.

"It's refreshing to see a married couple so evidently in love with each other," Wolff said.

Shame pricked her. She didn't deserve the comment. "We're closer now than we've ever been," she told him.

"Separation has that effect."

"It most definitely has for me."

Wolff gave Mady an update on the progress of their mission. Neff and Ernst were at the moment circling the building, taking photographs of every side. Adolf and Konrad were monitoring the entrance to the building to record the facility's daily schedule. Security was minimal. It didn't take much to keep the elderly and infants from escaping, and who in their right minds would ever think of breaking in? Everyone would report when they returned shortly after dark.

"Have you called Lisette?" he asked her.

"A few minutes ago."

Wolff waited for more.

"The baby's fine. Lisette is remarkable for being so young. And thank you for your concern."

Wolff smiled. "I know how mothers worry." He left her standing at the window.

Mady folded her arms. A thin column of black smoke rose from the facility against a clear blue sky. There was something about it that bothered her.

Wednesday, August 14, 1940

Konrad wore the Sturmbannführer uniform because he was the same size as Wolff. While Adolf was the senior member of the team, he was too short for it. He wore his own uniform of one rank lower, Hauptsturmführer.

The Sturmbannführer uniform made Konrad appear older than he was, but it couldn't hide the age disparity between the two men. There was something odd about the older man being of a lesser rank. Wolff considered this and dismissed it as insignificant. Young ambitious men rose quickly in the SS ranks. Few would openly challenge it. For it was the younger officers who were more than eager to prove their authority.

Wolff would have preferred going in himself. But his previous presence at the facility prevented it. No one at the facility had ever seen Konrad or Adolf.

Their mission was simple. Use the power of their uniforms to walk Josef out the front door. If this were to fail, they were to gather as much information regarding Josef's location and status as they could in preparation for a more formalized rescue plan.

Konrad climbed out of the black motorcar with a mixture of emotions stirring in his gut. First, he loved the uniform. More precisely, he loved the way people looked at him when he wore it. While his experience wearing the uniform had been a brief one—walking from the hotel to the motorcar—the respect, and fear, on the faces of the people on the street was unmistakable.

But the uniform also made him angry. Wolff had waited until they reached Hadamar to inform him he was no longer with the

SS, but a fugitive. A criminal! Konrad patrolled the streets for criminals; he didn't form associations with them. He felt he'd been tricked. And if the mission had been anything other than to rescue Pastor Schumacher, he never would have agreed to be part of it.

In fact, had it been any other man but Pastor Schumacher in the Hadamar facility, Konrad would have argued that the man was there because he deserved to be there.

But Pastor Schumacher was not like other men. Images of the man drove Konrad onward.

The pastor walking to the church and calling him aside from the others just to talk with him.

Blaming the cat for tipping over the Christmas tree.

Defending Lisette for the BBC broadcast.

Waiting for him on dark street corners.

Braving the crowded Lustgarten to congratulate him.

Staying true to his friend the professor in spite of the risk.

Believing him when he said he had no part in the old man's death, despite evidence to the contrary.

Konrad knew no other man like him.

Everyone else lived in fear of what other people said or did or thought. Pastor Schumacher lived what he believed, no matter what others said or did or thought.

He might not always agree with the man, but he respected him nonetheless. And Pastor Schumacher had respected him.

Konrad knew he wasn't alone in his admiration of the man. Lisette loved him. And who else could be the inspiration and bond for such an unlikely rescue attempt? As soon as they heard the pastor was in trouble, Konrad knew Ernst and Neff would volunteer to help. And two SS men! To Konrad's knowledge, there was only one man who could win the devotion of Gestapo types.

The motorcar doors slammed shut. Adolf joined Konrad at his side. They approached the medical facility through a garden garage, designed with an overhang so people could enter without being seen. Adolf sprang forward and opened the entrance door for him. Konrad liked that.

The soles of their shoes clicked in rhythm on the green-tile floor. Removing their hats, they approached the administrator's station, a long counter cluttered with metal charts and hand-printed signs and schedules. The top of a male attendant's head appeared behind the counter. He was busy filling in a record on a clipboard.

Konrad didn't wait for him to look up. "We're here to interrogate one of your patients!" he barked. "Speidel. Leo Speidel."

The male attendant ignored them. He continued writing. Then, when he finally looked up and saw the uniforms, his eyes widened noticeably.

"Speidel," Konrad repeated.

He loved this uniform!

The flustered attendant searched the counter top and shelves beneath it, lifting one metal chart after another in search of one bearing the name Speidel.

"We don't have a patient by that name," he said.

Konrad's heart skipped a beat. They all knew this might be a possibility. They'd simply refused to believe it.

"No . . . no Leon Speidel here," the attendant said, continuing his search.

"*Leo* Speidel," Konrad corrected him.

The attendant searched another pile. "No. We don't have any Speidel." He looked up, certain of his conclusion but fearing the reaction.

"Look again," Adolf interjected.

The attendant lifted his hands in a helpless gesture. "I can look again, but I'm certain there's no patient here by—"

"Look again!" Adolf shouted.

The attendant dove back into the charts. About halfway through his search, he said, "I'll be right back. I think you need to talk to Dr. Gabriel."

He ran down the hallway, looking in open doorways as he went. At the end of the hallway he encountered another attendant. With excited gestures, the counter attendant spoke to his co-worker.

The co-worker pointed down the hall toward Konrad and Adolf.

Half running, half walking, the counter attendant hurried back toward them, then past them, all the while muttering apologies. "He's down here," he said.

A few moments later he reappeared, looking like a puppy dog as he trailed behind a thin man dressed in a white lab coat, who didn't appear at all intimidated by the SS uniforms.

The man walked with one hand in his pocket. With the other, he doffed wire-rimmed glasses. Red, tired eyes examined Konrad up and down with an accompanying glance at Adolf. "You're looking for Leo Speidel?"

"Is there a problem?" Konrad asked.

The man cleaned his glasses with the flap of his lab coat. Putting the glasses back on, he took another look at Konrad. "Let me see your orders."

They had none. Because Wolff was acting on his own, the underground resources hadn't been made available to them. And even if they had, there wouldn't have been enough time to make them up.

"What's your name?" Konrad demanded.

The man shook his head. "Your bullying tactics won't work here," he said.

"Your name!" Konrad said again, this time with more of an edge in his voice.

Hard blue eyes stared back at him. Konrad met the man's gaze and held it.

"Gabriel," the man said. "Dr. Walter Gabriel."

"Dr. Gabriel," Konrad said, "we're not here to bully you. You know as well as we do that Leo Speidel is a . . . shall we say, *unique* patient. Paper work is kept by necessity at a minimum."

A glint of concession registered in Gabriel's eyes, and Konrad knew he'd won the first round.

"Still, I'll need some form of proof," Gabriel said.

This time it was Adolf who spoke. "The matter at hand is of

special interest to the Reverend Wilhelm Olbricht," he told the doctor.

Konrad was puzzled. Reverend Olbricht?

But Gabriel recognized the name. Round two.

"Let's go to my office," Gabriel said.

He led them a short distance down the hallway to a small room with a desk, a chair, and a desk lamp. In contrast to the front counter, the room was immaculately clean and tidy. An array of diplomas and certificates covered the walls. Gabriel shut the door behind him.

"You must understand," the doctor said, "my orders are clear. No visitors."

"The SS doesn't visit hospital patients," Konrad said.

Gabriel nodded at the implication. The glasses came off. Without an attendant watching him, he appeared more amenable. "Even so, this is contrary to my orders. Without confirmation, you must understand my reticence, especially considering the test tomorrow."

"The test is tomorrow?" Konrad asked blindly.

The glasses went on again. "Yes."

Konrad glanced at Adolf, then said, "Good. Very good."

Gabriel appeared pleased.

"Forgive us, Dr. Gabriel," said Adolf, "but we have not been completely honest with you. We are here to ensure the test is done as scheduled with a human subject."

"You think we would use an animal?" Gabriel cried. He was aghast. "That would defeat the purpose of the . . ."

"And it must be Leo Speidel," Adolf added.

"Let me put your fears to rest. Herr Speidel has been prepared to be the subject of this final test as presented in our proposal."

"Will there be any others?" Konrad asked.

Gabriel shot him a suspicious glance.

"SS humor," Adolf said.

The doctor grinned. "Ah!"

Konrad breathed a sigh of relief. For a moment he thought for sure they'd been knocked out in the third round.

"Come," Gabriel said. "Let me show you the test facility."

The mood in the hotel room was somber as Konrad and Adolf gave their report. The good news was that Josef was alive. The bad news was that he wouldn't be for long.

"The test is scheduled for eleven tomorrow morning," Konrad said.

Mady sat hunched in a chair, her hands rubbing each other anxiously. The conspirators formed a circle. Ernst and Neff sat close to each other, cross-legged on the floor. Konrad was on the edge of the bed with Wolff and Adolf sitting in upholstered armchairs to his left.

The midmorning light spilled in through the open window. No one seemed to notice the crispness of air at this elevation.

"Eleven o'clock," Wolff said. "That doesn't give us much time. Neff, can you have the photographs printed by then?"

Holding the negatives he'd developed in the bathroom earlier that morning, he answered, "We still haven't located a studio that has an enlarger."

"Then we'll have to go without them," Wolff concluded.

"I can still make prints," said Neff. "They'll just be smaller."

"How small?"

"The size of the negatives."

"What'll you need?"

"A pane of glass. A light. And three trays. I already have the chemicals and paper."

"And a magnifying glass," Ernst suggested.

"Get to it," Wolff said.

Immediately the boys were on their feet and out the door.

"Tell us exactly what you saw," Wolff said to Konrad.

Mady felt a chill go through her. In response to Wolff's request, Konrad looked at her.

Wolff noticed it, too. "Mady, it's a lovely day. Why don't you take a walk," he suggested.

Mady unclasped her hands and sat up straight. "I'm not going anywhere," she told him.

Wolff stood. "Mady—"

"Konrad, tell us what you saw," she said, ignoring Wolff.

When Wolff saw there was no use trying to persuade her, he sat back down.

Konrad took a deep breath. He glanced over at Adolf, who gave him an encouraging nod. "It's in the basement. They call it 'the showers'," he said. "The room has pipes and shower heads installed in the ceiling. Yellow tile on the walls. But there's no water. It's a gas-chamber room."

Mady's hand rose to her hair. Then, slowly, deliberately, she put it back down to her lap.

Konrad continued. "Gabriel made a big deal of the fact that they could fit sixty persons in the room at a time."

The room was silent for a time.

"Doesn't make sense," said Wolff. "Sixty persons at a time? That's an assembly line! Why would they possibly need a room that large?"

"He also showed us an oven," Adolf said, "designed to burn one body after another. Specially built by Tops & Sohne."

Again there was silence.

Wolff broke it when he said, "I don't know about the rest of you, but I feel the need to pray."

Chapter 35

Wednesday, August 14, 1940

Josef awoke dreaming of Elyse and Mady.

In his dream, Elyse was walking and had a three-word vocabulary—*Poppa, Momma,* and *kitty*. While the setting was unfamiliar to him, it was idyllic, lush with trees and grass and dahlias and zinnias. Mady was swinging lazily in a hammock, her hand combing the grass. He lay next to her on a blanket with an open Greek textbook in his lap. It eluded him why he was parsing verbs on such a glorious day.

Elyse was toddling after Kaiser whose attempts to curl up in the grass were being frustrated. As soon as the cat settled in one place, Elyse would catch up with him and pounce, or more accurately, stumble on top of him.

Mady, her eyes sparkling in the summer sun, was just about to say something when the clanging of a metal bucket in the outer hallway woke him. Josef was once again in the windowless white cubicle with the dingy green-tile floor, the bare bulb high overhead, and the crusty drain in the corner. His shoulders and hips ached.

The double click at the door signaled someone was about to enter. Two male attendants stepped in. One of them, whom Josef hadn't recalled seeing before, wrinkled his nose in disgust. Josef didn't smell anything out of the ordinary.

"Time for your shower," the other one said.

They moved quickly toward him and hauled him to his feet without much effort.

"Can you stand?"

Josef tested his feet. They were curled inward from lack of use. With effort he was able to place them flat on the floor. It'd been a couple of days since his last injections, so his legs felt that they might still have some strength left in them. The attendants let go of his arms. He wobbled slightly, but then stood on his own.

"Can you walk?"

Josef looked down at his feet in making the attempt. He willed his right foot forward. It moved a few centimeters.

"At this rate we'll reach the shower room by mid-century," the new attendant complained.

"What's your hurry?" the other one asked.

"My shift's about to end, and Nixie and I have plans for this afternoon. We're driving down to Frankfurt."

"Frankfurt? How are you getting there?"

"Her father's motorcar."

"You lucky dog! What time do you get off?"

"Nine. We hope to be on the road by ten."

"It's nearly nine now! Let's get this guy to the basement."

Josef's attempt at walking was cut short. With an attendant under each arm, he was whisked down the corridor, then down a flight of stairs to the basement. A tall man with wire-rimmed spectacles stood beside an open door. He took the glasses off, cleaned them with a handkerchief he pulled from the pocket of his lab coat, then put them back on.

"Herr Speidel," he said. "How good of you to join us. It's time for your shower."

He examined Josef's eyes, ears, and mouth and thumped his chest, front and back. "Can you stand?" he asked.

"He can stand," the attendant answered for him. "But he can't walk."

"Good enough. Take him inside."

Josef was carried into a newly refinished room that had yellow tile on the walls. It was the largest shower he'd ever seen. The man in the lab coat followed them in.

"Strip him," the lab coat said to the attendants.

Josef's clothes were taken from him. The man in the lab coat unceremoniously handed him a bar of soap.

They left him standing there.

The attendant who was going to Frankfurt looked at his watch as they left the shower room. He clapped his co-worker on the back. "Don't work too hard," he quipped.

"Yeah? Don't spend all your money on Nixie in Frankfurt," the other attendant replied.

The lab coat took one last look at Josef before shutting the door. The lock sounded.

Josef stood in the middle of the large basement shower holding a bar of soap and surrounded by yellow tile. He couldn't remember the last time he'd had a shower, nor could he believe his good fortune. Turning his face upward, he waited for the cleansing water to pour down on him.

"It won't be long now," Wolff said.

He folded the receipt the desk clerk had just handed him and stuffed it in his shirt pocket. Mady stood nervously next to a pillar in the hotel lobby, clutching her travel bag with both hands.

She hadn't slept all night. And it wasn't Adolf's snoring coming from the bedroom serving as a men's dorm that had kept her awake. She was nervous about seeing Josef again. He must hate her. The way she'd treated him all this time was unforgivable. He deserved better.

"What's with the face?" Wolff asked her.

Mady managed a weak smile.

"Better, but not by much," he said.

"It's the best I can do."

He took her travel bag from her and started for the door. She followed a half step behind him. As they walked out to the street curb, Wolff began humming. Mady recognized the tune but couldn't place it.

Wolff put her bag in the trunk and got into the motorcar on the driver's side. She climbed into the front passenger seat. The engine came to life, and Wolff steered the motorcar down the narrow street. Little shops of all kinds paraded by her side of the motorcar; a small stone wall separated them from the river on his side.

"What was that you were humming?" Mady wanted to know.

"What?"

"Back there. You were humming."

Wolff's brow furrowed in thought.

"As we were leaving the hotel," Mady coaxed.

"Ah! I remember," he said. "A hymn. Written by Martin Luther. The Reformer."

"I know who Martin Luther is."

Both the comment and the tone had an edge to it. Wolff noticed it, but said nothing.

" 'A Mighty Fortress Is Our God.' That's the name of the hymn."

Mady nodded. She remembered now.

Wolff slowed to negotiate around a small crowd of shoppers that had spilled out into the street. They were gathered around a fruit stand.

" 'And though this world, with devils filled, should threaten to undo us,

" 'We will not fear, for God hath willed His truth to triumph through us.' "

Mady looked over at the man who had become such an important part of her family's life.

"The third verse. My favorite," Wolff said. He repeated it for her. "Appropriate for today, don't you think?"

Mady turned her attention to the tight, winding roads of Hadamar.

The water seemed a long time in coming. Gripping the bar of soap, Josef looked to the door, then back up at the shower head. It was dry. It was so dry Josef doubted whether water had ever run through any of the hundred or so holes that punctured it.

His legs were getting tired.

Then, the lights went off.

Josef blinked. He looked around him but could see nothing. Not a sliver of light, not a ray, could be seen anywhere. The room was so dark he couldn't see his hands. He could feel his fingers wiggle, but he couldn't see them. If it weren't for the aching in his knotted stomach muscles, he could almost imagine himself a disembodied spirit floating in a sea of darkness.

He waited, but nothing happened.

"Hey! The lights are off!"

He listened. He could hear banging pipes or doors. It sounded distant. Had they forgotten he was in here? Surely somebody knew they'd left him in the shower—the man in the lab coat. But he probably gave an order to an attendant and then left to more important duties, and that attendant had gotten distracted, forgot he was in here, locked up, and turned off the lights on him. Probably Nixie's boyfriend.

"There's somebody in here!" Josef shouted.

Until now, he'd remained in one place to keep from falling. He turned toward the general area where he'd last seen the door. A mistake. His head began to swim. He stopped and took a couple of deep breaths till his senses returned.

"Is someone out there?" he shouted.

In a way, it was funny. They'd forgotten all about the naked guy in the shower. Turned the lights off and left him standing there clutching his bar of soap for a couple of hours. The attendants would be telling the story for weeks.

There was a rattle of pipes. Josef expected to be hit with a spray of water from above, but it never came. Instead, he heard a couple of thumps on the other side of the door.

"In here!" Josef screamed.

He heard a click. Then the door opened.

A silhouetted figure stood in the doorway. Definitely military.

"Pastor Schumacher?"

That voice! And his name!

"We need a light in here!" the voice shouted.

"Konrad?"

Josef's knees gave way. He sank to the tile floor.

A flashlight bobbed in the hand of its bearer. Then it trained on him. The light hurt. Josef shielded his eyes.

"Pastor Schumacher!"

"Konrad?"

The boy dropped to his knees beside Josef.

"Konrad, have you joined the SS?"

Ernst and Neff crouched low as they made their way along the side of the building to the rendezvous point. Ernst was carrying a pair of heavy wire cutters.

"West side! West side!" Neff whispered, pulling on his friend's shirt.

"That's where I'm going!" Ernst whispered back.

"That's north. West is this way," said Neff, pointing.

"Are you sure?"

"Sure I'm sure," Neff said. "How about you? Are you sure you cut both the power and the phone lines to the entire building?"

Ernst stopped and looked at his friend. "As sure as you are that this way is west."

"We've come to get you out of here," Konrad said.

"My legs," Josef said. "I can stand, but I can't walk."

Konrad shined the light on Josef's legs as though by doing so he would be able to confirm the truth.

"And, if we're not in too much of a hurry, I'd like to pick up some clothing on the way out," Josef said.

Ducking his head under Josef's arm, Konrad lifted him to his feet. The boy was strong. He had little trouble assisting Josef to the door.

"Adolf! Is that you? This is almost like a reunion!"

The former Gestapo agent was holding a gun on three staff members. One of them was the man in the white lab coat, the other two were attendants Josef had never seen before.

Seeing Josef's need, Adolf waved the gun at his prisoners and said, "You two . . . inside the shower room." The attendants glanced at the dark opening. Adolf persuaded them to enter. "And you, Dr. Gabriel. Take off your clothes."

"What?"

"My friend needs them."

"I will not!" Gabriel huffed.

Adolf turned to Josef. "I assume you'll still wear them even if there's a bullet hole in them?"

Gabriel got the message. Starting with his white lab coat, he stripped down to his shorts.

"You can join the others now," said Adolf. He waved the handgun in the direction of the shower room door.

"What are you going to do to us?" Gabriel asked.

"Complete the test, of course," Adolf said.

He then shoved the doctor into the shower room and locked the door. The banging from the other side started immediately.

Adolf and Konrad assisted Josef in getting dressed, complete with the white lab coat.

"You could have at least waited until I had my shower," Josef said.

Konrad looked at him strangely.

While Josef buttoned his shirt, Adolf said to the boy, "You learned a lesson today. Never play by someone else's time schedule. Create your own."

Wolff pulled the motorcar to the side of the road and stopped.

He turned off the ignition and set the brake. "Now we wait," he said. He looked at his watch. "Ten after nine. They should have him by now."

Mady rolled down her window. The fresh summer breeze, finding a new passageway, dove through the opening and out the other side. She tried to concentrate on the scenery—the river, the valley, the quaint houses. But she couldn't.

Something touched her hand. She jumped.

"I didn't mean to startle you," Wolff said.

Mady smiled. She barely felt him patting her hand.

"I'm not leaving without them!" Josef said emphatically. With his arms draped around the necks of his two rescuers, Josef pleaded his case. "I came for the children. I won't leave without them!"

"We don't have time for this!" Adolf argued.

Konrad agreed. "We can come back for them some other time, Pastor Schumacher."

Josef shook his head. "No, I won't leave without them."

"You don't have much choice," Adolf told him.

"Konrad, stop," Josef ordered. "Put me down right now!"

Konrad slowed, looked at Adolf, then stopped. Adolf had no choice but to stop, too. They propped Josef against a wall.

"Be reasonable," Adolf said. "The plan was to get you out of here. We have a motorcar waiting and there are five of us. Not enough room for any children."

"Five?" Josef said.

"Ernst and Neff," Konrad said. "They cut the power."

"We'll just have to secure other transportation," Josef said.

"There's no time!" Adolf argued.

"A bus or a truck," Josef went on. "Enough to carry two dozen small children. Ernst and Neff can help us load them. We can be out of here in no time."

Adolf raised his hands in disgust.

"We're just wasting valuable time debating it," Josef said.

Adolf shook his head. He looked at Konrad. "Do you think you can carry him by yourself?"

Josef didn't let the boy answer. "There are steps on the south side," he instructed Adolf. "Get the boys and the transportation and meet us there."

Mumbling something incomprehensible, Adolf turned and hurried down the corridor.

Josef raised his arm. Konrad ducked under it, and they were under way again.

"I just can't leave them behind," Josef explained.

"I know," Konrad replied.

His head swimming from all the movement, Josef stared through the mind haze. His stomach began to feel sick.

"Are you all right?" Konrad asked.

"Turn right at the end of the hallway," Josef said.

Those they passed in the darkened corridors paid little attention to them. With the electricity off, everybody had something to do.

"This is the south corridor," Josef said.

When they reached the door to the children's ward, Josef reached for the handle and pulled it open.

His heart sank.

"Dear God, no!" he cried.

"This isn't the west side," Ernst said.

"Yes, it is," Neff insisted.

"If this is the west side, where's Konrad? He should have been here by now."

"He'll be here."

"We're going to get left behind."

"Why do you say that?"

"Because this isn't the west side."

"Yes, it is."

Adolf appeared suddenly from around the corner. He was out of breath. "We need a truck or a bus," he said. "Neff, do you remember seeing one in the photographs?"

Neff visualized the tiny prints. "Uhh . . . southeast corner," he said. "There was a loading dock. We might find a truck there."

"Let's go," Adolf said.

The two boys followed on his heels.

"I told you this was the west side," Neff whispered.

Josef was shaking. In his anxiety, he was barely able to hold on to conscious thought. "They're gone! Dear God, they're gone!" he moaned.

"I count six," Konrad said.

"There were two dozen!" Josef said.

The faces of the frail forms in the beds turned toward the commotion. Those that could. Josef, his face drawn like that of a patron saint, looked sadly upon them. His expression became sadder still when he looked at the empty beds.

"I've failed them," he cried.

A low rumble could be heard outside. Leaning Josef against the doorjamb, Konrad opened the exit door. A large green truck with a tarp-covered bed pulled up to the steps. Adolf was behind the wheel. Ernst and Neff sat beside him.

Adolf remained behind the wheel as the three boys quickly carried the children past Josef and loaded them in the back of the truck. Sacks of flour and grain and canned goods were used to fashion makeshift beds.

It took only two trips. The boys weren't even breathing hard. Their burdens, emaciated little bodies, proved not to be burdensome. Josef wished there was time to assure the children that everything was going to be all right, but even if there were time, he doubted they would comprehend. Their faces were expressionless, their eyes vacant.

Konrad came back for Josef. "I'll ride in the back with Ernst and Neff and the kids," he said as he assisted Josef into the passenger seat.

"Only six," Josef said.

Konrad looked up at him, then closed the truck door.

"We fight the battles as best we can," Adolf said.

Josef knew Adolf was right, but this was little solace to him now.

"Ernst! Ernst! Is that you?"

The voice came from the far side of the parking area.

"I think we've got trouble back here!" Konrad shouted from the back of the truck.

"Ernst? Neff?" the voice shouted again. It was gruff sounding, scratchy.

Josef looked in the side mirror. He moaned.

Adolf checked his mirror. "What do we do?"

"Drive," Josef said. "Get us out of here."

Gears ground. The truck jolted forward.

In the side mirror, Josef watched as the image of Wilhelm Olbricht grew smaller and smaller.

Wolff looked at his watch. He said nothing. He didn't have to. Something had gone wrong. Adolf and the others should have been here by now.

"How much longer do we wait?" Mady asked him.

"At this point it's anyone's guess," Wolff replied.

Like he'd done a hundred times already, he craned his neck out the window and checked the road. It was as empty of traffic as it had been for the last thirty minutes.

"I should have gone with them," Wolff said.

"You know that wasn't possible. If someone recognized you . . ." The sentence didn't need finishing.

Mady looked at her watch. She didn't mean to, especially after Wolff had just looked at his. The images of Josef lying on the floor of a showerlike gas chamber and of Adolf and the boys locked up in a cell haunted her mind.

"Would they have gone back to the hotel?" she asked.

"We no longer have a room."

"Still, can you think of a reason why they might—"

Wolff leaned forward and started the engine.

"What are you doing?"

"I can't just sit here."

"Where are we going?"

"To the medical facility."

"He's following us," Josef said.

The front grille of the Essex Super Six displayed prominently in the truck's side mirror.

"We can't outrun him on the open road," Adolf said.

"The town?"

"The streets are a maze. It's our only hope of losing him."

It didn't seem like much of a plan to Josef, but he couldn't think of anything that offered a better chance of success.

"What will he do if he catches us?" Adolf asked. "Does he have a gun?"

"He's a minister," Josef said.

"Ministers can carry guns."

"Not this one."

Adolf felt for his gun. "That gives us an advantage," he said.

The truck rolled into town. It wasn't much of a chase. Fighting the wheel at every turn, Adolf rounded one corner after another. With equal difficulty the bulky Essex followed them. At one sharp turn Adolf had to stop, back up, and make a second attempt. Olbricht waited patiently for them to complete the turn, then continued the pursuit.

"You're a minister, aren't you?" Adolf said.

"You know I am."

"Then why don't you do something?"

"What do you suggest?"

"Pray for a miracle."

"A miracle?"

"I don't know . . . pray for a sudden fog to hide us, or the river to part, or for us to turn invisible or something!"

"You really *are* asking for a miracle."

"God still does that sort of thing, doesn't He?"

"It's possible."

"Well?"

"Well, what?"

"Ask Him!"

Josef knew their situation must be desperate if Adolf was turning to prayer. Still, the request shamed him. He should have been praying all along.

Josef closed his eyes. Almost instantly the swirling started again. Josef could feel his head sway from one side to the other, he couldn't control it. The sensation drained into his belly. The swirling turned to nausea. Try as he might, he couldn't concentrate long enough to form a complete sentence. All he could manage was, "Dear God, Dear God, Dear God, Dear God . . ."

"Now that's what I call an answer to prayer!" Adolf cried.

"What?"

Josef opened his eyes. Buildings moved in front of him. He became disoriented and had to grab the dashboard to steady himself.

"Look!" Adolf exclaimed. He nodded at the side mirror.

Josef checked the mirror on his left. The Essex was gone. "Where did it go?" he asked.

Adolf shrugged. "He was there, then he wasn't. Have to give you credit. When you pray, God listens."

Josef wasn't about to take credit for Olbricht's disappearance. For one thing, he knew the problem hadn't disappeared. There would be a day of reckoning. Maybe not today, but it would come.

Adolf was infused with new life. He wore the biggest grin Josef had ever seen on him. "Let's meet up with Wolff and Mady and then it's north to Berlin," he said.

"Mady's here?"

Adolf turned his silly grin toward Josef.

Josef slumped back in his seat. *Mady!* He blinked several times in an attempt to clear his head. While he ached to see her, he didn't want her to see him like this.

What was she doing here?

Wolff and Mady. He'd said Wolff and Mady. That meant she knew about the mission. But how much? Did she know about the children? And if she knew, Olbricht knew. That explained his presence. What now? She'd never forgive him for this. He couldn't go back to the church. So where did that leave them? He needed time to think. But even if he had the time, he couldn't. His head was heavy with clouds. Thoughts just disappeared.

His attention was jolted back to the truck as it bumped over a curb and onto a three-tiered stone bridge.

Out of nowhere, the black Essex appeared. It blocked the far end of the bridge.

Adolf hit the brakes.

Olbricht stared at them through the windshield. The door opened, and he climbed out of the motorcar. Josef could smell his cigar.

Suddenly, Adolf threw the truck into reverse.

Josef put his hand over Adolf's on the gearshift. "Let's settle this now," he said.

It looked like a hospital.

Mady stared through the windshield at the building. It was unimposing. Modular in shape. An entryway with an overhang. Elongated windows. A drain pipe down the side next to cement steps. A parking area with curbed oases of grass and bushes.

"See anything?" Wolff asked.

"Nothing," she replied.

"Let's circle around."

Wolff turned the wheel, nosing the motorcar into an unexplored section of the parking lot.

"There!" Mady shouted.

"I see it."

The motorcar Adolf had been driving now sat stone-still in a parking stall. Wolff pulled up next to it, got out, walked around and peered through the motorcar's windows.

"The wire cutters are sitting on the backseat," he said, climbing in behind the wheel.

"What does that mean?" Mady asked.

"I don't know."

Together they stared at the building.

"What do we do now?" Mady wondered.

Wolff hunched over the wheel, his eyes fixed forward, though he was no longer looking at the building. His vision turned inward. "Only one thing we *can* do," he said.

Mady waited for him to finish his thought.

"I have to go in there."

"No!" she cried.

He turned to her. "Mady, we have no choice."

"Let me go," she said.

"Out of the question!"

"If anyone's going in there, it's me," she insisted. "They don't know me."

Wolff shook his head. "I won't allow it."

"I've lost one man to that building," Mady argued. "Who knows what has happened to the others? I'm not going to lose you too."

"You're *not* going in there!" Wolff told her.

"Then neither are you!"

"Fine!"

"Fine!"

Olbricht met them more than halfway. He was livid. "What's going on here?" he shouted.

Adolf was already standing in front of the truck by the time Josef managed to swing his legs out the door. Konrad met him and helped him down. Then, as he did in the hospital corridor, the boy served as Josef's legs.

Ernst and Neff stood at the back of the truck.

"Are you out of your mind?" Olbricht shouted at Josef.

"Nearly," Josef replied.

It wasn't far from the truth. All the excitement was catching up with him. Without Konrad holding him up, he would crumple to the ground. And it was only with concentrated effort that he was able to focus on the moment, let alone form coherent sentences.

Olbricht turned to Konrad. "Konrad! Look at you! You could be shot for this! What are you going to do when your father learns of this?"

The boy looked down at the SS uniform he was wearing, then back at Olbricht. To his credit, he said nothing.

"And Neff. Ernst. Do you know what you've gotten yourselves into? You're throwing your lives away! You ought to be ashamed of yourselves!"

Adolf had heard enough. He drew his handgun. "Clear that motorcar off the bridge," he said to Olbricht, "and let us pass."

"No."

It was Konrad who spoke, his remark directed at Adolf. "Put the gun away," he said.

"Shut up, boy. We'll handle this," Adolf said.

"You heard him," Josef said. "This is not a time for guns."

Adolf stared at them as though they were both crazy. The gun remained leveled at Olbricht's chest.

"Move me closer," Josef said to Konrad.

It took a moment, but the boy understood. He carried Josef until they were standing in front of Olbricht, and also in front of the line of fire.

Summoning what little strength he had, Josef lifted his head. He bullied his thoughts to form first words, then sentences. "You're right," he said to Olbricht. "It was foolish for them to involve the boys."

Olbricht chomped hard on his cigar. "Foolish doesn't begin to—"

"Let them go," Josef said.

Olbricht's eyes wizened in thought, as they had hundreds of times before in his study. For the moment it was just the two of them. Mentor and student. On opposite sides of the chessboard.

Josef was making his move. Olbricht, as always, wore the face of the victor.

"Let them go," Josef repeated. "The boys. Adolf. And the children. I'll go with you back to the medical facility."

"Children?" Olbricht said.

"In the back of the truck. Six. From the children's ward."

Olbricht looked heavenward. "Of all the stupid plays!" he shouted.

"That's the deal," Josef said.

Olbricht was beside himself. "What did I ever see in you?" he said. "Edda warned me you were a bad seed. Would to God I had listened to her!"

"Is it a deal?" Josef pressed.

It took a little while, but Olbricht managed to calm himself and focus on the game at hand.

"They're pawns," Josef said. "You don't win by capturing pawns; you win by trapping the king."

"King?" Olbricht scoffed. "You're anything but a king."

Josef took the rebuke without argument. While his analogy may have been faulty, he knew the tactic was sound. The only way for Olbricht to win was for Josef to lose. It had always been that way.

"Checkmate," Olbricht said.

"No!" Konrad objected.

"It's over," Josef said to him. "Go home now."

A motorcar pulled up behind the Essex. The doors flew open, and Wolff and Mady jumped out.

"This is a nightmare!" Olbricht bellowed upon seeing his daughter. "What are you doing here?"

Mady didn't answer him. She ran straight to Josef. Tears rolled down her cheeks as she cradled his face in her hands. Her nose touching his nose, she whispered, "I never would have forgiven myself had I lost you."

"Mady, I'm speaking to you!" Olbricht yelled.

Gently, she kissed his lips, his cheeks, his chin, his nose. Over and over she repeated, "Can you ever forgive me?"

"Mady!"

"I love you," she whispered in Josef's ear. "I do. I love you."

"Step away from him!" Olbricht ordered.

With one last kiss, Mady backed away. Taking Josef's free hand in hers, she held it.

Wolff had Olbricht by the arm now, restraining him.

"Mady, get in the motorcar!"

She gripped Josef's hand tighter.

"Josef, talk to your wife," Olbricht said. "We have a deal."

Mady turned to Josef. "A deal?"

Olbricht answered for him. "He's going back to the medical facility. In exchange, I'm willing to forget that these boys had anything to do with this ridiculous charade."

"Josef, you can't go back!" Mady said.

"It'll be all right. It's the only way."

"No, it won't be all right! I won't let you!" To her father, she pleaded, "Don't do this! Don't make him go back there!"

"It's his choice," said Olbricht.

"Why?" Mady screamed. She let go of Josef's hand and stood in front of her father. "Why are you doing this?"

Olbricht shrugged his arm free from Wolff. "This isn't the place to discuss it," he said.

"Just exactly where is the place you go to discuss killing people?" Mady shouted.

Olbricht glared at her. "You're beside yourself. Get in the motorcar."

He reached for her arm. She recoiled.

"I don't know you," she said. "All these years and I don't know who you are!"

"Mady . . ."

She recoiled further.

"I worshiped you!" she shouted. "Every man I ever met, I measured against you! I married Josef because I thought he could be just like you! To think that all these years, I prayed that he—"

she broke down in tears—"that he . . . would someday be just like you."

Olbricht spoke softly to her. She wasn't listening.

"You know what I discovered?" she cried. "He's nothing like you. He never will be like you. And do you know why? Because he's better than you. You could live the rest of your life trying to be like him, and you would never measure up to him!"

"She's obviously distraught," Olbricht said to no one in particular. "Josef, it's time to fulfill your part of the deal. Come with me, son."

"Don't you touch him!" Mady shouted.

Her anger was a blazing sword. Olbricht stepped back in surprise and fear.

"Go with you for what reason? So you can kill him?" she seethed. "Why stop with him? You'll need to kill Herr Wolff as well. And Herr Adolf!"

A baby's wail split the air.

Mady turned toward the sound. Ernst glanced into the back of the truck, then disappeared from sight.

"Is there a baby in there?" Mady asked.

"Six," Josef replied.

"Pastor Schumacher wouldn't leave without them," Konrad explained.

The infant's cry dominated everyone and everything on the bridge. Mady stared at the truck. Tears glazed her eyes as Ernst reappeared with a baby in his arms. Mady walked to him as though in a daze. Ernst gently handed her the infant. Mady looked down in disbelief at the undersized bundle and then carried it to Josef.

"Babies . . ." Mady said to him softly. "Oh, Josef . . . forgive me. I've been such a fool." Suddenly she spun around and approached her father. "You would kill this baby, too?" she asked. "This one and the others in the truck?"

"Mady, listen to me. There are some things you don't understand. There comes a time when life is not worth living—"

"And Elyse? Would you also kill your own granddaughter?"

Olbricht reacted as if she'd slapped him. "That's uncalled for!" he cried. "How can you say such a thing? You know I worship her."

"And I also know she's deaf!" Mady said.

Olbricht stood there. Mouth agape. Speechless.

"That's right! Deaf. Flawed. Living a life not worth living. And if it wasn't for Herr Wolff, your granddaughter would be in Hadamar right now in the same ward as this little one, waiting to be put to death."

Olbricht staggered back, then steadied himself by leaning on the fender of the Essex. He stared at the baby in Mady's arms, at Mady, at Josef, but mostly he stared at nothing.

"One ear mostly," Mady said. "The other, well, we're not so sure. But the midwife marked her for removal. It was just a matter of time, really . . . until your friends came . . . the ones you're defending . . . and took her—" she began to break down—"and killed her. . . ." Mady buried her face in the bundle of infant. Her shoulders shook with sobs. Then, slowly she lifted her head. Her eyes were ablaze. "But you couldn't see that, could you? You were too busy playing God to know there was something wrong with your own grandchild!"

Each sentence came as a hammer blow, chipping away at Olbricht's statuelike stance, weakening him, leaving him stooped, a sad replica of a self-assured man.

Everything had come down to father and daughter. Olbricht and Mady.

"I was only doing what I thought was best . . ." he whimpered.

"Look at this child!" Mady shouted.

She strode toward him and shoved the baby at him. He refused to take it. Or he couldn't take it. He recoiled at the sight of the emaciated infant in rags.

"I only wanted your happiness," he whispered, "and safety."

"You vowed to do anything to protect me and Elyse," she said. "Did you mean it?"

The remembrance of that moment on the couch seemed to strengthen him. "You know I meant it," he said.

"Then let this truck pass. Let these good men save these babies." She paused, then added, "And give me back my husband."

For several moments Olbricht stared at nothing, on the edge of defeat, yet unwilling to admit it.

With a nod of his head, Wolff signaled Adolf to get into the truck. Adolf placed the handgun in his waistband and climbed into the cab. Konrad began to assist Josef to the truck.

"You'll never make it," Olbricht said.

Everyone froze.

"We have to try," Josef told him.

The two men stood eye to eye like they had so many times before. It was Olbricht's move.

He said, "They'll be looking for a truck traveling north."

Wolff motioned to Neff and Ernst. "Climb in," he said.

"But they won't be looking for a black Essex traveling south."

Josef gazed at his father-in-law, the man who had tried to kill him. He understood and nodded his thanks.

"It'll take longer, but you'll be safer," Olbricht said to his daughter.

Wolff to the boys, "Put them in the Essex. Adolf, you're with me."

In short order the transfer was made. Then, as Konrad was helping Josef into the backseat of the Essex, the truck's engine suddenly started.

"Father?" Mady cried. "Father!"

Olbricht was behind the wheel of the truck. Before anyone could stop him, he jammed the gearshift into reverse. The truck backed across the bridge. Without looking back, Reverend Wilhelm Olbricht steered the truck down the narrow Hadamar street. Heading north.

He never said good-bye to his daughter.

———

For several miles they rode in silence, wondering what would happen to Olbricht when the authorities caught up with him. Then the time of grieving turned to the thrill of victory and, as it was so often between Neff and Ernst, giddiness.

"You can stop giggling now. You sound like a bunch of girls," Josef said.

Ernst looked over his shoulder from the front seat. He sat in the middle. Konrad was in the passenger seat. Neff was driving. The two boys not driving held babies.

"We can't help it," Ernst said. "We never thought we'd get a chance to drive an Essex Super Six."

Mady checked the children beside her. One was on the seat, two shared the floor. Josef was holding one. For the moment they were all content.

"Adolf should be taking care of at least one baby, don't you think?" Josef asked.

The sound of Mady's laughter worked on him like a tonic. "I'll let you suggest it to him at the next stop," she said.

Josef gazed at the child in his arms. "Is our baby as beautiful as this one?"

"You're kidding, right? There has never been a baby born more beautiful than our Elyse."

"That's what I thought. Just checking."

"I can't wait for you to see her. She's going to adore you."

Josef smiled.

"But not nearly as much as her mother does." Mady inched closer to him and kissed him on the cheek. She said, "I've been studying my Bible while you were away." Leaning closer to him, she whispered in his ear, " 'I sleep, but my heart waketh: it is the voice of my beloved. I am my beloved's, and my beloved is mine.' "

Josef kissed his wife. "Maybe I should go away more often," he said.

Epilogue

Wolff slumped in his chair, his feet propped inches from the fire. Three logs burned gloriously in the fireplace. "Have you noticed how people are saying 'Good morning' more frequently and 'Heil Hitler' less?" he said.

Josef, sitting in the chair next to him with Elyse on his lap, gave him a deadpan look. "That's funny, especially coming from you."

Wolff grinned. "I thought you'd like it. Actually, it's the grocer's observation. Just thought I'd pass it along."

Outside it was snowing. It had been a hard, cold winter, and the war shortages made it even harder. Coal was at a premium. Roads were frequently closed. There was no meat. No butter. No fish. But it was Christmas, and the mood in the house was festive.

Ramah Cabin, as it was called, was hidden in the hills north of Berlin. Since the Hadamar incident, three more children had joined the enclave, making a total of nine, ten if you counted Elyse.

Mady and Josef ran the house. Lisette had moved in to help. Wolff stayed with them frequently, Adolf less frequently.

With increasing shortages in the cities and fewer victories in the field, people were growing tired of the war. The September barrage of London had resulted in heavy Luftwaffe losses and no invasion.

Then, in November, the Americans reelected Roosevelt, which promised an increase of goods being shipped to England. America's presence was being felt indirectly now, and there was rumor of direct intervention.

Konrad and Neff had been stationed somewhere in Poland. Ernst was at university in Berlin. And Josef and Mady had pretty much lost touch with Willi and Gael, who were both still in school.

Following Hadamar, Olbricht disappeared. Neither he nor the truck were ever seen again. At least not that anyone reported. Edda suffered an emotional breakdown and moved to Cologne to live with her aged mother.

Mady appeared, an apron tied around her waist.

"Adolf won't be joining us for dinner," Wolff reported. "I think he was afraid he'd be taking food away from the children."

Hands on hips, Mady said, "Now, if this isn't a peaceful picture."

Elyse had fallen asleep on her father's chest.

"Well, gentlemen, enjoy it while you can. Because I don't think I can keep the children away from the tree much longer."

The room in which they sat was the largest room of the house with a cathedral ceiling and a large window overlooking the forest. A small lake was visible during the summer months. In winter it froze over and disappeared beneath all the snow. In the corner of the room stood a large Christmas tree, which, for lack of young bucks to do it for them, the two men had chopped down and hauled inside.

The walls of the gathering room, as they referred to the cozy space, were decorated with many of Josef's embroideries. The redwood scene figured prominently over the fireplace. Its completion proved to be a joint effort. After Hadamar, Josef's hands shook so badly he could no longer hold a needle. The result of the drugs. So he taught Mady his stitches, and she carefully finished it.

Mady lifted Elyse from her father's chest. "Brace yourself," she said. "After I put this one down, I'm releasing the hoard."

"Wait!" Josef said. "Lisette mentioned she had a surprise for us! Shouldn't we have our surprise first?"

"Yes! Good idea. The surprise," Wolff agreed.

"You're stalling . . ." Mady said as she left the room.

Josef and Wolff enjoyed several minutes of peace and quiet in front of the fire. Neither spoke.

"Here we are!" Lisette cried.

Then Mady appeared behind her. She carried a tray. "Who wants hot apple cider?" she asked.

While Mady handed out the cider, Lisette told them her surprise. "I wrote to the boys, and they all wrote back a special Christmas greeting!" She held up three letters.

"The boys can write?" Wolff said.

"You would wonder, as infrequently as they do it," Mady said.

Lisette opened each of the letters and read them aloud, beginning with Konrad's. "This part's just for me," she said, tucking a separate sheet of paper away.

"Read that one, too. I want to hear it," Josef said.

Lisette blushed but couldn't be persuaded to read her private letter.

The boys all reported they were doing fine. Konrad and Neff both said they were freezing where they were. Neff hated the infantry and was continually trying to talk someone into replacing his gun with a camera. Konrad excelled, of course, but there was a less-than-enthusiastic tone about military life in his letter. Ernst was doing well with his studies. He enjoyed the increased level of study. He missed Neff.

"Now the surprise," Lisette said.

"That's not it?" Josef asked.

Lisette only smiled at him. Reaching behind her, she produced three coins that dangled at the ends of pieces of string. "Recognize them?" she asked Josef.

Tears filled his eyes as he stared silently at the gold medallions.

"I attached string to them so we could hang them on the tree," she said.

"What a wonderful idea, Lisette!" Mady exclaimed.

Lisette handed the coins to Josef. With shaky fingers, he examined each one. Then, walking to the tree, he hung them from three different branches.

"One more," Lisette said. "Mine."

She handed a fourth coin to him. After hanging it on the tree—next to Konrad's coin, of course—he gave her a hug.

They stepped back and admired the four coins on the Christmas tree.

"Lisette, you've made this a very memorable Christmas," Josef said.

Lisette smiled, then asked, "Does anyone mind if I search for some Christmas music on the radio?"

Date Due